XANATHAR'S GUIDE
TO EVERYTHING™

CREDITS

Lead Designers: Jeremy Crawford, Mike Mearls
Designer: Robert J. Schwalb
Additional Design: Adam Lee, Christopher Perkins, Matt Sernett
Development: Ben Petrisor

Managing Editor: Jeremy Crawford
Editor: Kim Mohan
Additional Editing: Michele Carter, Scott Fitzgerald Gray

Art Director: Kate Irwin
Additional Art Direction: Shauna Narciso
Graphic Designer: Emi Tanji
Cover Illustrator: Jason Rainville
Cover Illustrator (Alternative Cover): Hydro74
Interior Illustrators: Rob Alexander, Mark Behm, Eric Belisle, Zoltan Boros, Christopher Bradley, Noah Bradley, Sam Burley, Jedd Chevrier, jD, Olga Drebas, Jesper Ejsing, Wayne England, Leesha Hannigan, Jon Hodgson, Ralph Horsley, Lake Hurwitz, Julian Kok, Raphael Lübke, Warren Mahy, Mark Molnar, Scott Murphy, Adam Paquette, Claudio Pozas, Vincent Proce, A.M. Sartor, Chris Seaman, David Sladek, Craig J Spearing, Cory Trego-Erdner, Beth Trott, Jose Vega, Richard Whitters, Ben Wootten, Min Yum

Project Management: Stan!, Heather Fleming
Production Services: Cynda Callaway, Jefferson Dunlap, David Gershman, Kevin Yee

This book includes some subclasses and spells that originally appeared in *Princes of the Apocalypse* (2015) and *Sword Coast Adventurer's Guide* (2015).

Other D&D Team Members: Bart Carroll, Trevor Kidd, Christopher Lindsay, Shelly Mazzanoble, Hilary Ross, Liz Schuh, Nathan Stewart, Greg Tito

Playtesters: Charles Benscoter, Dan Klinestiver, Dave Kovarik, Davena Oaks, Kevin Engling, Teos Abadia, Robert Alaniz, Phil Allison, Robert Allison, Jay Anderson, Paul Aparicio, Paul Van Arcken, Dee Ashe, Andrew Bahls, Chris Balboni, Jason Baxter, Jerry Behrendt, Teddy Benson, Deb Berlin, Stacy Bermes, Jim Berrier, Lauren Bilanko, Jordan Brass, Ken J. Breese, Robert "Bobby" Brown, Matthew Budde, Matt Burton, David Callander, Mik Calow, Richard Chamberlain, Wayne Chang, Emre Cihangir, Bruno Cobbi, Garrett Colón, Mark Craddock, Max Cushner, Brian Dahl, Derek DaSilva, Phil Davidson, Krupal Desai, Scott Deschler, Yorcho Diaz, Mario A. DiGirolamo, Adam Dowdy, Curt Duval, Jay Elmore, Russell Engel, Andrew Epps, David M. Ewalt, Justin Faris, Jared Fegan, Frank Foulis, Max Frutig, Travis Fuller, Kyle Garms, Ben Garton, Louis Gentile, Genesis Emanuale Martinez Gonzalez, Derek A. Gray, Richard Green, Kevin Grigsby, Christopher Hackler, Bryan Harris, Gregory Harris, Randall Harris, Fred Harvey, Ian Hawthorne, Adam Hennebeck, Sterling Hershey, Justin Hicks, Will Hoffman, Scott Holmgren, Paul Hughes, Daniel E. Chapman II, Stanislav Ivanov, Matt Jarmak, James Jorstad, Evan Jorstad, Alex Kammer, Joshua Kaufman, Bill Grishnak Kerney, Jake Kiefer, Chet King, Atis Kleinbergs, Steven Knight, David Krolnik, Yan Lacharité, Jon F. Lamkin, Marjorie Lamkin, Shane Leahy, Stephen Lindberg, Tom Lommel, Michael Long, Jonathan Longstaff, Ginny Loveday, Kevin D. Luebke, Michael Lydon, Matthew Maranda, Joel Marsh, Gleb Masaltsev, Chris McDaniel, Chris McGovern, Jim McKay, Mark Meredith, Mark Merida, Lou Michelli, David Middleton, Mike Mihalas, Mark A. Miller, Paige Miller, Ian Mills, Stacy Mills, David Milman, Daren Mitchell, TL Frasqueri-Molina, Scott Moore, David Morris, Tim Mottishaw, JoDee Murch, Joshua Murdock, William Myers, Walter Nau, Kevin Neff, Daniel "KBlin" Oliveira, Grigory Parovichnikov, Alan Patrick, Russ Paulsen, Matt Petruzzelli, Zachary Pickett, Chris Presnall, Nel Pulanco, Jack Reid, Joe Reilly, Renout van Rijn, Sam Robertson, Carlos Robles, Evan Rodarte, Matthew Roderick, Zane Romine, Nathan Ross, Dave Rosser, David Russell, Ruty Rutenberg, A.C. Ryder, Arthur Saucier, Benjamin Schindewolf, Ken Schreur, James Schweiss, the Seer, Jonathan Connor Self, Nicholas Sementelli, Arthur Severance, Ben Siekert, Jimmy Spiva, the Dead Squad, Francois P. Lefebvre Sr., Keaton Stamps, Matthew Talley, Dan Taylor, Kirsten A. Thomas, Laura Thompson, Jia Jian Tin, Kyle Turner, Justin Turner, Alex Vine, Yoerik de Voogd, Shane Walker, Matthew Warwick, Chris "Waffles" Wathen, Eric Weberg, Werebear, Gary West, Andy Wieland, Keith Williams, David Williamson, Travis Woodall, Arthur Wright, Keoki Young

ON THE COVER

Xanathar gazes lovingly upon its pet fish. Indeed, this cover, painted by Jason Rainville, features a great many of Xanathar's treasures and secrets. Can you find them all?

ON THE ALTERNATIVE COVER

Hydro74 takes us for a swim in this stylized dreamscape of Xanathar and its prized fish.

620C2209000001 EN
ISBN: 978-0-7869-6611-0
First Printing: November 2017

9 8 7 6 5 4

Disclaimer: No goldfish were harmed in the making of this book. Especially not Sylgar. Sylgar definitely did not die because we forgot to change his water. If you see Xanathar, make sure it knows that. Be perfectly clear Sylgar was not harmed. And we had nothing to do with it. Better yet, don't bring it up, and don't mention us.

Contents

INTRODUCTION

BENEATH THE BUSTLING CITY OF WATERDEEP, a beholder crime lord keeps tabs on everyone and everything—or so the beholder thinks. Known as Xanathar, this bizarre being believes it can gather information on everything in the DUNGEONS & DRAGONS multiverse. The beholder desires to know it all! But no matter what the beholder learns and what treasures it acquires, its most prized possession in all the multiverse remains its goldfish, Sylgar.

The first major rules expansion to the fifth edition of D&D, *Xanathar's Guide to Everything* provides a wealth of new options for the game. Xanathar might not be able to realize its dream to know everything, but this book does delve into every major part of the game: adventurers, their adventures, and the magic they wield.

USING THIS BOOK

Written for both players and Dungeon Masters, this book offers options to enhance campaigns in any world, whether you're adventuring in the Forgotten Realms, another official D&D setting, or a world of your own creation. The options here build on the official rules contained within the *Player's Handbook*, the *Monster Manual*, and the *Dungeon Master's Guide*. Think of this book as the companion to those volumes. It builds on their foundation, exploring pathways first laid in those publications. Nothing herein is required for a D&D campaign—this is not a fourth core rulebook—but we hope it will provide you new ways to enjoy the game.

Chapter 1 offers character options that expand on those offered in the *Player's Handbook*. Chapter 2 is a toolkit for the DM that provides new resources for running the game and designing adventures, all of it building on the *Monster Manual* and the *Dungeon Master's Guide*. Chapter 3 presents new spells for player characters and spellcasting monsters to unleash.

Appendix A provides guidance on running a shared campaign, similar to the activities staged by the D&D Adventurers League, and appendix B contains a host of tables that allow you to quickly generate names for the characters in your D&D stories.

As you peruse the many options herein, you'll come across observations from Xanathar itself. Like the beholder's roving mind, your reading will take you to places in the game familiar and new. May you enjoy the journey!

UNEARTHED ARCANA

Much of the material in this book originally appeared in Unearthed Arcana, a series of online articles we publish to explore rules that might officially become part of the game. Some Unearthed Arcana offerings don't end up resonating with fans and are set aside for the time being. The Unearthed Arcana material that inspired the options in the following chapters was well received and, thanks to feedback from thousands of you, has been refined into the official forms presented here.

What's that, Sylgar? No. Not yet, my fishy friend. They just got here. Perhaps after we chat a bit. I find a little conversation at the beginning helps digestion.

THE CORE RULES

This book relies on the rules in the three core rule-books. The game especially makes frequent use of the rules in chapters 7–10 of the *Player's Handbook*: "Using Ability Scores," "Adventuring," "Combat," and "Spellcasting." That book's appendix A is also crucial; it contains definitions of conditions, like invisible and prone. You don't need to know the rules by heart, but it's helpful to know where to find them when you need them.

If you're a DM, you should also know where to look things up in the *Dungeon Master's Guide*, especially the rules on how magic items work (see chapter 7 of that book). The introduction of the *Monster Manual* is your guide on how to use a monster's stat block.

THE DM ADJUDICATES THE RULES

One rule overrides all others: the DM is the final authority on how the rules work in play.

Rules are part of what makes D&D a game, rather than just improvised storytelling. The game's rules are meant to help organize, and even inspire, the action of a D&D campaign. The rules are a tool, and we want our tools to be as effective as possible. No matter how good those tools might be, they need a group of players to bring them to life and a DM to guide their use.

The DM is key. Many unexpected events can occur in a D&D campaign, and no set of rules could reasonably account for every contingency. If the rules tried to do so, the game would become a slog. An alternative would be for the rules to severely limit what characters can do, which would be contrary to the open-endedness of D&D. Here's the path the game takes: it lays a foundation of rules that a DM can build on, and it embraces the DM's role as the bridge between the things the rules address and the things they don't.

TEN RULES TO REMEMBER

A few rules in the core rulebooks sometimes trip up a new player or DM. Here are ten of those rules. Keeping them in mind will help you interpret the options in this book.

EXCEPTIONS SUPERSEDE GENERAL RULES

General rules govern each part of the game. For example, the combat rules tell you that melee weapon attacks use Strength and ranged weapon attacks use Dexterity. That's a general rule, and a general rule is in effect as long as something in the game doesn't explicitly say otherwise.

The game also includes elements—class features, spells, magic items, monster abilities, and the like—that sometimes contradict a general rule. When an exception and a general rule disagree, the exception wins. For example, if a feature says you can make melee weapon attacks using your Charisma, you can do so, even though that statement disagrees with the general rule.

ROUND DOWN

Whenever you divide or multiply a number in the game, round down if you end up with a fraction, even if the fraction is one-half or greater.

ADVANTAGE AND DISADVANTAGE

Even if more than one factor gives you advantage or disadvantage on a roll, you have it only once, and if you have advantage and disadvantage on the same roll, they cancel each other.

COMBINING DIFFERENT EFFECTS

Different game effects can affect a target at the same time. For example, two different benefits can give you a bonus to your Armor Class. But when two or more effects have the same proper name, only one of them (the most powerful one if their benefits aren't identical) applies while the durations of the effects overlap. For example, if *bless* is cast on you when you're still under the effect of an earlier *bless*, you gain the benefit of only one casting. Similarly, if you're in the radius of more than one Aura of Protection, you benefit only from the one that grants the highest bonus.

REACTION TIMING

Certain game features let you take a special action, called a reaction, in response to some event. Making opportunity attacks and casting the *shield* spell are two typical uses of reactions. If you're unsure when a reaction occurs in relation to its trigger, here's the rule: the reaction happens after its trigger completes, unless the description of the reaction explicitly says otherwise.

Once you take a reaction, you can't take another one until the start of your next turn.

RESISTANCE AND VULNERABILITY

Here's the order that you apply modifiers to damage: (1) any relevant damage immunity, (2) any addition or subtraction to the damage, (3) one relevant damage resistance, and (4) one relevant damage vulnerability.

Even if multiple sources give you resistance to a type of damage you're taking, you can apply resistance to it only once. The same is true of vulnerability.

PROFICIENCY BONUS

If your proficiency bonus applies to a roll, you can add the bonus only once to the roll, even if multiple things in the game say your bonus applies. Moreover, if more than one thing tells you to double or halve your bonus, you double it only once or halve it only once before applying it. Whether multiplied, divided, or left at its normal value, the bonus can be used only once per roll.

BONUS ACTION SPELLS

If you want to cast a spell that has a casting time of 1 bonus action, remember that you can't cast any other spells before or after it on the same turn, except for cantrips with a casting time of 1 action.

CONCENTRATION

As soon as you start casting a spell or using a special ability that requires concentration, your concentration on another effect ends instantly.

TEMPORARY HIT POINTS

Temporary hit points aren't cumulative. If you have temporary hit points and receive more of them, you don't add them together, unless a game feature says you can. Instead, you decide which temporary hit points to keep.

Chapter 1
Character Options

THE MAIN FIGURES IN ANY D&D CAMPAIGN are the characters created by the players. The heroics, folly, righteousness, and potential villainy of your characters are at the heart of the story. This chapter provides a variety of new options for them, focusing on additional subclasses for each of the classes in the *Player's Handbook*.

Each class offers a character-defining choice at 1st, 2nd, or 3rd level that unlocks a series of special features, not available to the class as a whole. That choice is called a subclass. Each class has a collective term that describes its subclasses; in the fighter, for instance, the subclasses are called martial archetypes, and in the paladin, they're sacred oaths. The table below identifies each of the subclasses in this book. In addition, the section for druids presents details on how the Wild Shape feature works, and the warlock receives a collection of new choices for the class's Eldritch Invocations feature.

Each of the class presentations leads off with advice on how to add depth and detail to your character's personality. You can use the tables in these sections as a source of inspiration, or roll a die to randomly determine a result if desired.

Following the subclasses, the section called "This Is Your Life" presents a series of tables for adding detail to your character's backstory.

The chapter concludes with a selection of feats for the races in the *Player's Handbook*, offering ways to delve deeper into a character's racial identity.

Subclasses

Class	Subclass	Level Available	Description
Barbarian	Path of the Ancestral Guardian	3rd	Calls on the spirits of honored ancestors to protect others
Barbarian	Path of the Storm Herald	3rd	Filled with a rage that channels the primal magic of the storm
Barbarian	Path of the Zealot	3rd	Fueled by a religious zeal that visits destruction on foes
Bard	College of Glamour	3rd	Wields the beguiling, glorious magic of the Feywild
Bard	College of Swords	3rd	Entertains and slays with daring feats of weapon prowess
Bard	College of Whispers	3rd	Plants fear and doubt in the minds of others
Cleric	Forge Domain	1st	Clad in heavy armor, serves a god of the forge or creation
Cleric	Grave Domain	1st	Opposes the blight of undeath
Druid	Circle of Dreams	2nd	Mends wounds, guards the weary, and strides through dreams
Druid	Circle of the Shepherd	2nd	Summons nature spirits to bolster friends and harry foes
Fighter	Arcane Archer	3rd	Imbues arrows with spectacular magical effects
Fighter	Cavalier	3rd	Defends allies and knocks down enemies, often on horseback
Fighter	Samurai	3rd	Combines resilience with courtly elegance and mighty strikes
Monk	Way of the Drunken Master	3rd	Confounds foes through a martial arts tradition inspired by the swaying of a drunkard
Monk	Way of the Kensei	3rd	Channels ki through a set of mastered weapons
Monk	Way of the Sun Soul	3rd	Transforms ki into bursts of fire and searing bolts of light
Paladin	Oath of Conquest	3rd	Strikes terror in enemies and crushes the forces of chaos
Paladin	Oath of Redemption	3rd	Offers redemption to the worthy and destruction to those who refuse mercy or righteousness
Ranger	Gloom Stalker	3rd	Unafraid of the dark, relentlessly stalks and ambushes foes
Ranger	Horizon Walker	3rd	Finds portals to other worlds and channels planar magic
Ranger	Monster Slayer	3rd	Hunts down creatures of the night and wielders of grim magic
Rogue	Inquisitive	3rd	Roots out secrets, akin to a masterful detective
Rogue	Mastermind	3rd	A master tactician, manipulates others
Rogue	Scout	3rd	Combines stealth with a knack for survival
Rogue	Swashbuckler	3rd	Delivers deadly strikes with speed and panache
Sorcerer	Divine Soul	1st	Harnesses magic bestowed by a god or other divine source
Sorcerer	Shadow Magic	1st	Wields the grim magic of the Shadowfell
Sorcerer	Storm Sorcery	1st	Crackles with the power of the storm
Warlock	The Celestial	1st	Forges a pact with a being from celestial realms
Warlock	The Hexblade	1st	Serves a shadowy entity that bestows dread curses
Wizard	War Magic	2nd	Mixes evocation and abjuration magic to dominate the battlefield

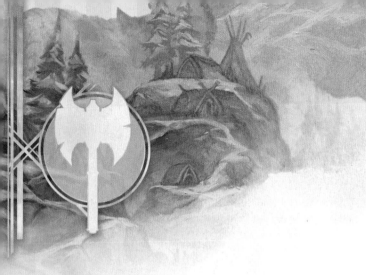

Rawr! I'm really angry! Funny, I don't feel any stronger. Maybe because I'm always angry, I'm always in top condition. Stands to reason.

Barbarian

I HAVE WITNESSED THE INDOMITABLE PERFORMANCE OF *barbarians on the field of battle, and it makes me wonder what force lies at the heart of their rage.*

—Seret, archwizard

The anger felt by a normal person resembles the rage of a barbarian in the same way that a gentle breeze is akin to a furious thunderstorm. The barbarian's driving force comes from a place that transcends mere emotion, making its manifestation all the more terrible. Whether the impetus for the fury comes entirely from within or from forging a link with a spirit animal, a raging barbarian becomes able to perform supernatural feats of strength and endurance. The outburst is temporary, but while it lasts, it takes over body and mind, driving the barbarian on despite peril and injury, until the last enemy falls.

It can be tempting to play a barbarian character that is a straightforward application of the classic archetype—a brute, and usually a dimwitted one at that, who rushes in where others fear to tread. But not all the barbarians in the world are cut from that cloth, so you can certainly put your own spin on things. Either way, consider adding some flourishes to make your barbarian stand out from all others; see the following sections for some ideas.

Personal Totems

Barbarians tend to travel light, carrying little in the way of personal effects or other unnecessary gear. The few possessions they do carry often include small items that have special significance. A personal totem is significant because it has a mystical origin or is tied to an important moment in the character's life—perhaps a remembrance from the barbarian's past or a harbinger of what lies ahead.

A personal totem of this sort might be associated with a barbarian's spirit animal, or might actually be the totem object for the animal, but such a connection is not essential. One who has a bear totem spirit, for instance, could still carry an eagle's feather as a personal totem.

Consider creating one or more personal totems for your character—objects that hold a special link to your character's past or future. Think about how a totem might affect your character's actions.

Personal Totems

d6	Totem
1	A tuft of fur from a solitary wolf that you befriended during a hunt
2	Three eagle feathers given to you by a wise shaman, who told you they would play a role in determining your fate
3	A necklace made from the claws of a young cave bear that you slew singlehandedly as a child
4	A small leather pouch holding three stones that represent your ancestors
5	A few small bones from the first beast you killed, tied together with colored wool
6	An egg-sized stone in the shape of your spirit animal that appeared one day in your belt pouch

Tattoos

The members of many barbarian clans decorate their bodies with tattoos, each of which represents a significant moment in the life of the bearer or the bearer's ancestors, or which symbolizes a feeling or an attitude. As with personal totems, a barbarian's tattoos might or might not be related to an animal spirit.

Each tattoo a barbarian displays contributes to that individual's identity. If your character wears tattoos, what do they look like, and what do they represent?

Tattoos

d6	Tattoo
1	The wings of an eagle are spread wide across your upper back.
2	Etched on the backs of your hands are the paws of a cave bear.
3	The symbols of your clan are displayed in viny patterns along your arms.
4	The antlers of an elk are inked across your back.
5	Images of your spirit animal are tattooed along your weapon arm and hand.
6	The eyes of a wolf are marked on your back to help you see and ward off evil spirits.

Superstitions

Barbarians vary widely in how they understand life. Some follow gods and look for guidance from those deities in the cycles of nature and the animals they encounter. These barbarians believe that spirits inhabit the plants and animals of the world, and the barbarians look to them for omens and power.

Other barbarians trust only in the blood that runs in their veins and the steel they hold in their hands. They have no use for the invisible world, instead relying on their senses to hunt and survive like the wild beasts they emulate.

Both of these attitudes can give rise to superstitions. These beliefs are often passed down within a family or shared among the members of a clan or a hunting group.

If your barbarian character has any superstitions, were they ingrained in you by your family, or are they the result of personal experience?

So ancestors are people who did the procreation thing to make more people before you were born? Like how many people? That's a lot of the procreation thing. Ew. You're disgusting.

SUPERSTITIONS

d6	Superstition
1	If you disturb the bones of the dead, you inherit all the troubles that plagued them in life.
2	Never trust a wizard. They're all devils in disguise, especially the friendly ones.
3	Dwarves have lost their spirits, and are almost like the undead. That's why they live underground.
4	Magical things bring trouble. Never sleep with a magic object within ten feet of you.
5	When you walk through a graveyard, be sure to wear silver, or a ghost might jump into your body.
6	If an elf looks you in the eyes, she's trying to read your thoughts.

PRIMAL PATHS

At 3rd level, a barbarian gains the Primal Path feature. The following options are available to a barbarian, in addition to those offered in the *Player's Handbook*: the Path of the Ancestral Guardian, the Path of the Storm Herald, and the Path of the Zealot.

PATH OF THE ANCESTRAL GUARDIAN

Some barbarians hail from cultures that revere their ancestors. These tribes teach that the warriors of the past linger in the world as mighty spirits, who can guide and protect the living. When a barbarian who follows this path rages, the barbarian contacts the spirit world and calls on these guardian spirits for aid.

Barbarians who draw on their ancestral guardians can better fight to protect their tribes and their allies. In order to cement ties to their ancestral guardians, barbarians who follow this path cover themselves in elaborate tattoos that celebrate their ancestors' deeds. These tattoos tell sagas of victories against terrible monsters and other fearsome rivals.

PATH OF THE ANCESTRAL GUARDIAN FEATURES

Barbarian Level	Feature
3rd	Ancestral Protectors
6th	Spirit Shield (2d6)
10th	Consult the Spirits, Spirit Shield (3d6)
14th	Vengeful Ancestors, Spirit Shield (4d6)

ANCESTRAL PROTECTORS

Starting when you choose this path at 3rd level, spectral warriors appear when you enter your rage. While you're raging, the first creature you hit with an attack on your turn becomes the target of the warriors, which hinder its attacks. Until the start of your next turn, that target has disadvantage on any attack roll that isn't against you, and when the target hits a creature other than you with an attack, that creature has resistance to the damage dealt by the attack. The effect on the target ends early if your rage ends.

SPIRIT SHIELD

Beginning at 6th level, the guardian spirits that aid you can provide supernatural protection to those you defend. If you are raging and another creature you can see within 30 feet of you takes damage, you can use your reaction to reduce that damage by 2d6.

When you reach certain levels in this class, you can reduce the damage by more: by 3d6 at 10th level and by 4d6 at 14th level.

CONSULT THE SPIRITS

At 10th level, you gain the ability to consult with your ancestral spirits. When you do so, you cast the *augury* or *clairvoyance* spell, without using a spell slot or material components. Rather than creating a spherical sensor, this use of *clairvoyance* invisibly summons one of your ancestral spirits to the chosen location. Wisdom is your spellcasting ability for these spells.

After you cast either spell in this way, you can't use this feature again until you finish a short or long rest.

VENGEFUL ANCESTORS

At 14th level, your ancestral spirits grow powerful enough to retaliate. When you use your Spirit Shield to reduce the damage of an attack, the attacker takes an amount of force damage equal to the damage that your Spirit Shield prevents.

PATH OF THE STORM HERALD

All barbarians harbor a fury within. Their rage grants them superior strength, durability, and speed. Barbarians who follow the Path of the Storm Herald learn to transform that rage into a mantle of primal magic, which swirls around them. When in a fury, a barbarian of this path taps into the forces of nature to create powerful magical effects.

Storm heralds are typically elite champions who train alongside druids, rangers, and others sworn to protect nature. Other storm heralds hone their craft in lodges in regions wracked by storms, in the frozen reaches at the world's end, or deep in the hottest deserts.

PATH OF THE STORM HERALD FEATURES

Barbarian Level	Feature
3rd	Storm Aura
6th	Storm Soul
10th	Shielding Storm
14th	Raging Storm

You know one of the great benefits of living underground? No weather. Don't mess this up for me.

STORM AURA

Starting at 3rd level, you emanate a stormy, magical aura while you rage. The aura extends 10 feet from you in every direction, but not through total cover.

Your aura has an effect that activates when you enter your rage, and you can activate the effect again on each of your turns as a bonus action. Choose desert, sea, or tundra. Your aura's effect depends on that chosen environment, as detailed below. You can change your environment choice whenever you gain a level in this class.

If your aura's effects require a saving throw, the DC equals 8 + your proficiency bonus + your Constitution modifier.

Desert. When this effect is activated, all other creatures in your aura take 2 fire damage each. The damage increases when you reach certain levels in this class, increasing to 3 at 5th level, 4 at 10th level, 5 at 15th level, and 6 at 20th level.

Sea. When this effect is activated, you can choose one other creature you can see in your aura. The target must make a Dexterity saving throw. The target takes 1d6 lightning damage on a failed save, or half as much damage on a successful one. The damage increases when you reach certain levels in this class, increasing to 2d6 at 10th level, 3d6 at 15th level, and 4d6 at 20th level.

Tundra. When this effect is activated, each creature of your choice in your aura gains 2 temporary hit points, as icy spirits inure it to suffering. The temporary hit points increase when you reach certain levels in this class, increasing to 3 at 5th level, 4 at 10th level, 5 at 15th level, and 6 at 20th level.

STORM SOUL

At 6th level, the storm grants you benefits even when your aura isn't active. The benefits are based on the environment you chose for your Storm Aura.

Desert. You gain resistance to fire damage, and you don't suffer the effects of extreme heat, as described in the *Dungeon Master's Guide*. Moreover, as an action, you can touch a flammable object that isn't being worn or carried by anyone else and set it on fire.

Sea. You gain resistance to lightning damage, and you can breathe underwater. You also gain a swimming speed of 30 feet.

Tundra. You gain resistance to cold damage, and you don't suffer the effects of extreme cold, as described in the *Dungeon Master's Guide*. Moreover, as an action, you can touch water and turn a 5-foot cube of it into ice, which melts after 1 minute. This action fails if a creature is in the cube.

SHIELDING STORM

At 10th level, you learn to use your mastery of the storm to protect others. Each creature of your choice has the damage resistance you gained from the Storm Soul feature while the creature is in your Storm Aura.

Raging Storm

At 14th level, the power of the storm you channel grows mightier, lashing out at your foes. The effect is based on the environment you chose for your Storm Aura.

Desert. Immediately after a creature in your aura hits you with an attack, you can use your reaction to force that creature to make a Dexterity saving throw. On a failed save, the creature takes fire damage equal to half your barbarian level.

Sea. When you hit a creature in your aura with an attack, you can use your reaction to force that creature to make a Strength saving throw. On a failed save, the creature is knocked prone, as if struck by a wave.

Tundra. Whenever the effect of your Storm Aura is activated, you can choose one creature you can see in the aura. That creature must succeed on a Strength saving throw, or its speed is reduced to 0 until the start of your next turn, as magical frost covers it.

Path of the Zealot

Some deities inspire their followers to pitch themselves into a ferocious battle fury. These barbarians are zealots—warriors who channel their rage into powerful displays of divine power.

A variety of gods across the worlds of D&D inspire their followers to embrace this path. Tempus from the Forgotten Realms and Hextor and Erythnul of Greyhawk are all prime examples. In general, the gods who inspire zealots are deities of combat, destruction, and violence. Not all are evil, but few are good.

Path of the Zealot Features

Barbarian Level	Feature
3rd	Divine Fury, Warrior of the Gods
6th	Fanatical Focus
10th	Zealous Presence
14th	Rage beyond Death

Divine Fury

Starting when you choose this path at 3rd level, you can channel divine fury into your weapon strikes. While you're raging, the first creature you hit on each of your turns with a weapon attack takes extra damage equal to 1d6 + half your barbarian level. The extra damage is necrotic or radiant; you choose the type of damage when you gain this feature.

Warrior of the Gods

At 3rd level, your soul is marked for endless battle. If a spell, such as *raise dead*, has the sole effect of restoring you to life (but not undeath), the caster doesn't need material components to cast the spell on you.

Fanatical Focus

Starting at 6th level, the divine power that fuels your rage can protect you. If you fail a saving throw while you're raging, you can reroll it, and you must use the new roll. You can use this ability only once per rage.

Zealous Presence

At 10th level, you learn to channel divine power to inspire zealotry in others. As a bonus action, you unleash a battle cry infused with divine energy. Up to ten other creatures of your choice within 60 feet of you that can hear you gain advantage on attack rolls and saving throws until the start of your next turn.

Once you use this feature, you can't use it again until you finish a long rest.

Rage beyond Death

Beginning at 14th level, the divine power that fuels your rage allows you to shrug off fatal blows.

While you're raging, having 0 hit points doesn't knock you unconscious. You still must make death saving throws, and you suffer the normal effects of taking damage while at 0 hit points. However, if you would die due to failing death saving throws, you don't die until your rage ends, and you die then only if you still have 0 hit points.

BARD

MUSIC IS THE FRUIT OF THE DIVINE TREE THAT VIBRATES with the Words of Creation. But the question I ask you is, can a bard go to the root of this tree? Can one tap into the source of that power? Ah, then what manner of music they would bring to this world!

—Fletcher Danairia, master bard

Bards bring levity during grave times; they impart wisdom to offset ignorance; and they make the ridiculous seem sublime. Bards are preservers of ancient history, their songs and tales perpetuating the memory of great events down through time—knowledge so important that it is memorized and passed along as oral history, to survive even when no written record remains.

It is also the bard's role to chronicle smaller and more contemporary events—the stories of today's heroes, including their feats of valor as well as their less than impressive failures.

Of course, the world has many people who can carry a tune or tell a good story, and there's much more to any adventuring bard than a glib tongue and a melodious voice. Yet what truly sets bards apart from others—and from one another—are the style and substance of their performances.

To grab and hold the attention of an audience, bards are typically flamboyant and outgoing when they perform. The most famous of them are essentially the D&D world's equivalent of pop stars. If you're playing a bard, consider using one of your favorite musicians as a role model for your character.

You can add some unique aspects to your bard character by considering the suggestions that follow.

DEFINING WORK

Every successful bard is renowned for at least one piece of performance art, typically a song or a poem that is popular with everyone who hears it. These performances are spoken about for years by those who view them, and some spectators have had their lives forever changed because of the experience.

If your character is just starting out, your ultimate defining work is likely in the future. But in order to make any sort of living at your profession, chances are you already have a piece or two in your repertoire that have proven to be audience pleasers.

DEFINING WORKS

d6	Defining Work
1	"The Three Flambinis," a ribald song concerning mistaken identities and unfettered desire
2	"Waltz of the Myconids," an upbeat tune that children in particular enjoy
3	"Asmodeus's Golden Arse," a dramatic poem you claim was inspired by your personal visit to Avernus
4	"The Pirates of Luskan," your firsthand account of being kidnapped by sea reavers as a child
5	"A Hoop, Two Pigeons, and a Hell Hound," a subtle parody of an incompetent noble
6	"A Fool in the Abyss," a comedic poem about a jester's travels among demons

INSTRUMENT

In a bard's quest for the ultimate performance and the highest acclaim, one's instrument is at least as important as one's vocal ability. The instrument's quality of manufacture is a critical factor, of course; the best ones make the best music, and some bards are continually on the lookout for an improvement. Perhaps just as important, though, is the instrument's own entertainment value; those that are bizarrely constructed or made of exotic materials are likely to leave a lasting impression on an audience.

You might have an "off the rack" instrument, perhaps because it's all you can afford right now. Or, if your first instrument was gifted to you, it might be of a more elaborate sort. Are you satisfied with the instrument you have, or do you aspire to replace it with something truly distinctive?

INSTRUMENTS

d6	Instrument
1	A masterfully crafted halfling fiddle
2	A mithral horn made by elves
3	A zither made with drow spider silk
4	An orcish drum
5	A wooden bullywug croak box
6	A tinker's harp of gnomish design

EMBARRASSMENT

Almost every bard has suffered at least one bad experience in front of an audience, and chances are you're no exception. No one becomes famous right away, after all; perhaps you had a few small difficulties early in your career, or maybe it took you a while to restore your reputation after one agonizing night when the fates conspired to bring about your theatrical ruin.

Music is stupid. Wait. I changed my mind. Music is fun. Play more music. No, I was right the first time. Music is stupid. But I won't maim you after all, in case I change my mind again.

The ways that a performance can go wrong are as varied as the fish in the sea. No matter what sort of disaster might occur, however, a bard has the courage and the confidence to rebound from it—either pressing on with the show (if possible) or promising to come back tomorrow with a new performance that's guaranteed to please.

Embarrassments

d6	Embarrassment
1	The time when your comedic song, "Big Tom's Hijinks"—which, by the way, you thought was brilliant—did not go over well with Big Tom
2	The matinee performance when a circus's owlbear got loose and terrorized the crowd
3	When your opening song was your enthusiastic but universally hated rendition of "Song of the Froghemoth"
4	The first and last public performance of "Mirt, Man about Town"
5	The time on stage when your wig caught fire and you threw it down—which set fire to the stage
6	When you sat on your lute by mistake during the final stanza of "Starlight Serenade"

A Bard's Muse

Naturally, every bard has a repertoire of songs and stories. Some bards are generalists who can draw from a wide range of topics for each performance, and who take pride in their versatility. Others adopt a more personal approach to their art, driven by their attachment to a muse—a particular concept that inspires much of what those bards do in front of an audience.

A bard who follows a muse generally does so to gain a deeper understanding of what that muse represents and how to best convey that understanding to others through performance.

If your bard character has a muse, it could be one of the three described here, or one of your own devising.

Nature. You feel a kinship with the natural world, and its beauty and mystery inspire you. For you, a tree is deeply symbolic, its roots delving into the dark unknown to draw forth the power of the earth, while its branches reach toward the sun to nourish their flowers and fruit. Nature is the ancient witness who has seen every kingdom rise and fall, even those whose names have been forgotten and wait to be rediscovered. The gods of nature share their secrets with druids and sages, opening their hearts and minds to new ways of seeing, and as with those individuals, you find that your creativity blossoms while you wander in an open field of waving grass or walk in silent reverence through a grove of ancient oaks.

Love. You are on a quest to identify the essence of true love. Though you do not disdain the superficial love of flesh and form, the deeper form of love that can inspire thousands or bring joy to one's every moment is what you are interested in. Love of this sort takes on many forms, and you can see its presence everywhere—from the sparkling of a beautiful gem to the song of a simple fisher thanking the sea for its bounty. You are on the trail of love, that most precious and mysterious of emotions, and your search fills your stories and your songs with vitality and passion.

Conflict. Drama embodies conflict, and the best stories have conflict as a key element. From the morning-after tale of a tavern brawl to the saga of an epic battle, from a lover's spat to a rift between powerful dynasties, conflict is what inspires tale-tellers like you to create your best work. Conflict can bring out the best in some people, causing their heroic nature to shine forth and transform the world, but it can cause others to gravitate toward darkness and fall under the sway of evil. You strive to experience or witness all forms of conflict, great and small, so as to study this eternal aspect of life and immortalize it in your words and music.

Illusions? How fugint. Before I destroy you, make one that looks like a really big goldfish—like as big as me! Hmm. that's too big. Goodbye!

BARD COLLEGES

At 3rd level, a bard gains the Bard College feature. The following options are available to a bard, in addition to those offered in the *Player's Handbook*: the College of Glamour, the College of Swords, and the College of Whispers.

COLLEGE OF GLAMOUR

The College of Glamour is the home of bards who mastered their craft in the vibrant realm of the Feywild or under the tutelage of someone who dwelled there. Tutored by satyrs, eladrin, and other fey, these bards learn to use their magic to delight and captivate others.

The bards of this college are regarded with a mixture of awe and fear. Their performances are the stuff of legend. These bards are so eloquent that a speech or song that one of them performs can cause captors to release the bard unharmed and can lull a furious dragon into complacency. The same magic that allows them to quell beasts can also bend minds. Villainous bards of this college can leech off a community for weeks, misusing their magic to turn their hosts into thralls. Heroic bards of this college instead use this power to gladden the downtrodden and undermine oppressors.

COLLEGE OF GLAMOUR FEATURES

Bard Level	Feature
3rd	Mantle of Inspiration, Enthralling Performance
6th	Mantle of Majesty
14th	Unbreakable Majesty

MANTLE OF INSPIRATION

When you join the College of Glamour at 3rd level, you gain the ability to weave a song of fey magic that imbues your allies with vigor and speed.

As a bonus action, you can expend one use of your Bardic Inspiration to grant yourself a wondrous appearance. When you do so, choose a number of creatures you can see and that can see you within 60 feet of you, up to a number equal to your Charisma modifier (minimum of one). Each of them gains 5 temporary hit points. When a creature gains these temporary hit points, it can immediately use its reaction to move up to its speed, without provoking opportunity attacks.

The number of temporary hit points increases when you reach certain levels in this class, increasing to 8 at 5th level, 11 at 10th level, and 14 at 15th level.

ENTHRALLING PERFORMANCE

Starting at 3rd level, you can charge your performance with seductive, fey magic.

If you perform for at least 1 minute, you can attempt to inspire wonder in your audience by singing, reciting a poem, or dancing. At the end of the performance, choose a number of humanoids within 60 feet of you who watched and listened to all of it, up to a number equal to your Charisma modifier (minimum of one). Each target must succeed on a Wisdom saving throw against your spell save DC or be charmed by you. While charmed in this way, the target idolizes you, it speaks glowingly of you to anyone who talks to it, and it hinders anyone who opposes you, although it avoids violence unless it was already inclined to fight on your behalf. This effect ends on a target after 1 hour, if it takes any damage, if you attack it, or if it witnesses you attacking or damaging any of its allies.

If a target succeeds on its saving throw, the target has no hint that you tried to charm it.

Once you use this feature, you can't use it again until you finish a short or long rest.

MANTLE OF MAJESTY

At 6th level, you gain the ability to cloak yourself in a fey magic that makes others want to serve you. As a bonus action, you cast *command*, without expending a spell slot, and you take on an appearance of unearthly beauty for 1 minute or until your concentration ends (as if you were concentrating on a spell). During this time, you can cast *command* as a bonus action on each of your turns, without expending a spell slot.

Any creature charmed by you automatically fails its saving throw against the *command* you cast with this feature.

Once you use this feature, you can't use it again until you finish a long rest.

UNBREAKABLE MAJESTY

At 14th level, your appearance permanently gains an otherworldly aspect that makes you look more lovely and fierce.

In addition, as a bonus action, you can assume a magically majestic presence for 1 minute or until you are incapacitated. For the duration, whenever any creature tries to attack you for the first time on a turn, the attacker must make a Charisma saving throw against your spell save DC. On a failed save, it can't attack you on this turn, and it must choose a new target for its attack or the attack is wasted. On a successful save, it can attack you on this turn, but it has disadvantage on any saving throw it makes against your spells on your next turn.

Once you assume this majestic presence, you can't do so again until you finish a short or long rest.

COLLEGE OF SWORDS

Bards of the College of Swords are called blades, and they entertain through daring feats of weapon prowess. Blades perform stunts such as sword swallowing, knife throwing and juggling, and mock combats. Though they use their weapons to entertain, they are also highly trained and skilled warriors in their own right.

Their talent with weapons inspires many blades to lead double lives. One blade might use a circus troupe as cover for nefarious deeds such as assassination, robbery, and blackmail. Other blades strike at the wicked, bringing justice to bear against the cruel and powerful. Most troupes are happy to accept a blade's talent for the excitement it adds to a performance, but few entertainers fully trust a blade in their ranks.

Blades who abandon their lives as entertainers have often run into trouble that makes maintaining their secret activities impossible. A blade caught stealing or engaging in vigilante justice is too great a liability for most troupes. With their weapon skills and magic, these blades either take up work as enforcers for thieves' guilds or strike out on their own as adventurers.

COLLEGE OF SWORDS FEATURES

Bard Level	Feature
3rd	Bonus Proficiencies, Fighting Style, Blade Flourish
6th	Extra Attack
14th	Master's Flourish

BONUS PROFICIENCIES

When you join the College of Swords at 3rd level, you gain proficiency with medium armor and the scimitar.

If you're proficient with a simple or martial melee weapon, you can use it as a spellcasting focus for your bard spells.

FIGHTING STYLE

At 3rd level, you adopt a style of fighting as your specialty. Choose one of the following options. You can't take a Fighting Style option more than once, even if something in the game lets you choose again.

Dueling. When you are wielding a melee weapon in one hand and no other weapons, you gain a +2 bonus to damage rolls with that weapon.

Two-Weapon Fighting. When you engage in two-weapon fighting, you can add your ability modifier to the damage of the second attack.

BLADE FLOURISH

At 3rd level, you learn to perform impressive displays of martial prowess and speed.

Whenever you take the Attack action on your turn, your walking speed increases by 10 feet until the end of the turn, and if a weapon attack that you make as part of this action hits a creature, you can use one of the follow-

ing Blade Flourish options of your choice. You can use only one Blade Flourish option per turn.

Defensive Flourish. You can expend one use of your Bardic Inspiration to cause the weapon to deal extra damage to the target you hit. The damage equals the number you roll on the Bardic Inspiration die. You also add the number rolled to your AC until the start of your next turn.

Slashing Flourish. You can expend one use of your Bardic Inspiration to cause the weapon to deal extra damage to the target you hit and to any other creature of your choice that you can see within 5 feet of you. The damage equals the number you roll on the Bardic Inspiration die.

Mobile Flourish. You can expend one use of your Bardic Inspiration to cause the weapon to deal extra damage to the target you hit. The damage equals the number you roll on the Bardic Inspiration die. You can also push the target up to 5 feet away from you, plus a number of feet equal to the number you roll on that die. You can then immediately use your reaction to move up to your walking speed to an unoccupied space within 5 feet of the target.

EXTRA ATTACK

Starting at 6th level, you can attack twice, instead of once, whenever you take the Attack action on your turn.

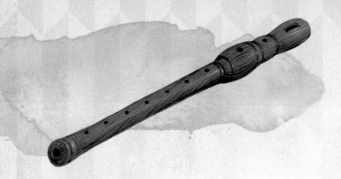

MASTER'S FLOURISH

Starting at 14th level, whenever you use a Blade Flourish option, you can roll a d6 and use it instead of expending a Bardic Inspiration die.

COLLEGE OF WHISPERS

Most folk are happy to welcome a bard into their midst. Bards of the College of Whispers use this to their advantage. They appear to be like other bards, sharing news, singing songs, and telling tales to the audiences they gather. In truth, the College of Whispers teaches its students that they are wolves among sheep. These bards use their knowledge and magic to uncover secrets and turn them against others through extortion and threats.

Many other bards hate the College of Whispers, viewing it as a parasite that uses a bard's reputation to acquire wealth and power. For this reason, members of this college rarely reveal their true nature. They typically claim to follow some other college, or they keep their actual calling secret in order to infiltrate and exploit royal courts and other settings of power.

COLLEGE OF WHISPERS FEATURES

Bard Level	Feature
3rd	Psychic Blades, Words of Terror
6th	Mantle of Whispers
14th	Shadow Lore

PSYCHIC BLADES

When you join the College of Whispers at 3rd level, you gain the ability to make your weapon attacks magically toxic to a creature's mind.

When you hit a creature with a weapon attack, you can expend one use of your Bardic Inspiration to deal an extra 2d6 psychic damage to that target. You can do so only once per round on your turn.

The psychic damage increases when you reach certain levels in this class, increasing to 3d6 at 5th level, 5d6 at 10th level, and 8d6 at 15th level.

WORDS OF TERROR

At 3rd level, you learn to infuse innocent-seeming words with an insidious magic that can inspire terror.

If you speak to a humanoid alone for at least 1 minute, you can attempt to seed paranoia in its mind. At the end of the conversation, the target must succeed on a Wisdom saving throw against your spell save DC or be frightened of you or another creature of your choice. The target is frightened in this way for 1 hour, until it is attacked or damaged, or until it witnesses its allies being attacked or damaged.

If the target succeeds on its saving throw, the target has no hint that you tried to frighten it.

Once you use this feature, you can't use it again until you finish a short or long rest.

MANTLE OF WHISPERS

At 6th level, you gain the ability to adopt a humanoid's persona. When a humanoid dies within 30 feet of you, you can magically capture its shadow using your reaction. You retain this shadow until you use it or you finish a long rest.

You can use the shadow as an action. When you do so, it vanishes, magically transforming into a disguise that appears on you. You now look like the dead person, but healthy and alive. This disguise lasts for 1 hour or until you end it as a bonus action.

While you're in the disguise, you gain access to all information that the humanoid would freely share with a casual acquaintance. Such information includes general details on its background and personal life, but doesn't include secrets. The information is enough that you can pass yourself off as the person by drawing on its memories.

Another creature can see through this disguise by succeeding on a Wisdom (Insight) check contested by your Charisma (Deception) check. You gain a +5 bonus to your check.

Once you capture a shadow with this feature, you can't capture another one with it until you finish a short or long rest.

SHADOW LORE

At 14th level, you gain the ability to weave dark magic into your words and tap into a creature's deepest fears.

As an action, you magically whisper a phrase that only one creature of your choice within 30 feet of you can hear. The target must make a Wisdom saving throw against your spell save DC. It automatically succeeds if it doesn't share a language with you or if it can't hear you. On a successful saving throw, your whisper sounds like unintelligible mumbling and has no effect.

On a failed saving throw, the target is charmed by you for the next 8 hours or until you or your allies attack it, damage it, or force it to make a saving throw. It interprets the whispers as a description of its most mortifying secret. You gain no knowledge of this secret, but the target is convinced you know it.

The charmed creature obeys your commands for fear that you will reveal its secret. It won't risk its life for you or fight for you, unless it was already inclined to do so. It grants you favors and gifts it would offer to a close friend.

When the effect ends, the creature has no understanding of why it held you in such fear.

Once you use this feature, you can't use it again until you finish a long rest.

Speak up! It's really hard to hear you over the screaming.
Nope. It's no use. I'll have to stop the screaming.
Disintegrations all around, then. ☀

CLERIC

TO BECOME A CLERIC IS TO BECOME A MESSENGER OF *the gods. The power the divine offers is great, but it always comes with tremendous responsibility.*

—Riggby the patriarch

Almost all the folk in the world who revere a deity live their lives without ever being directly touched by a divine being. As such, they can never know what it feels like to be a cleric—someone who is not only a devout worshiper, but who has also been invested with a measure of a deity's power.

The question has long been debated: Does a mortal become a cleric as a consequence of deep devotion to one's deity, thereby attracting the god's favor? Or is it the deity who sees the potential in a person and calls that individual into service? Ultimately, perhaps, the answer doesn't matter. However clerics come into being, the world needs clerics as much as clerics and deities need each other.

If you're playing a cleric character, the following sections offer ways to add some detail to that character's history and personality.

TEMPLE

Most clerics start their lives of service as priests in an order, then later realize that they have been blessed by their god with the qualities needed to become a cleric. To prepare for this new duty, candidates typically receive instruction from a cleric of a temple or another place of study devoted to their deity.

Some temples are cut off from the world so that their occupants can focus on devotions, while other temples open their doors to minister to and heal the masses. What is noteworthy about the temple you studied at?

TEMPLES

d6	Temple
1	Your temple is said to be the oldest surviving structure built to honor your god.
2	Acolytes of several like-minded deities all received instruction together in your temple.
3	You come from a temple famed for the brewery it operates. Some say you smell like one of its ales.
4	Your temple is a fortress and a proving ground that trains warrior-priests.
5	Your temple is a peaceful, humble place, filled with vegetable gardens and simple priests.
6	You served in a temple in the Outer Planes.

KEEPSAKE

Many clerics have items among their personal gear that symbolize their faith, remind them of their vows, or otherwise help to keep them on their chosen paths. Even though such an item is not imbued with divine power, it is vitally important to its owner because of what it represents.

KEEPSAKES

d6	Keepsake
1	The finger bone of a saint
2	A metal-bound book that tells how to hunt and destroy infernal creatures
3	A pig's whistle that reminds you of your humble and beloved mentor
4	A braid of hair woven from the tail of a unicorn
5	A scroll that describes how best to rid the world of necromancers
6	A runestone said to be blessed by your god

SECRET

No mortal soul is entirely free of second thoughts or doubt. Even a cleric must grapple with dark desires or the forbidden attraction of turning against the teachings of one's deity.

If you haven't considered this aspect of your character yet, see the table entries for some possibilities, or use them for inspiration. Your deep, dark secret might involve something you did (or are doing), or it could be rooted in the way you feel about the world and your role in it.

SECRETS

d6	Secret
1	An imp offers you counsel. You try to ignore the creature, but sometimes its advice is helpful.
2	You believe that, in the final analysis, the gods are nothing more than ultrapowerful mortal creatures.
3	You acknowledge the power of the gods, but you think that most events are dictated by pure chance.
4	Even though you can work divine magic, you have never truly felt the presence of a divine essence within yourself.
5	You are plagued by nightmares that you believe are sent by your god as punishment for some unknown transgression.
6	In times of despair, you feel that you are but a plaything of the gods, and you resent their remoteness.

I've got a minion that forges things. An ink-stained little twerp with excellent penmanship. So how do the hammers and fire help the process? Wouldn't the paper get burned? Oh, the fire must be for the wax seals!

CLERIC OF THE FORGE

DIVINE DOMAINS

At 1st level, a cleric gains the Divine Domain feature. The following domain options are available to a cleric, in addition to those offered in the *Player's Handbook*: Forge and Grave.

FORGE DOMAIN

The gods of the forge are patrons of artisans who work with metal, from a humble blacksmith who keeps a village in horseshoes and plow blades to the mighty elf artisan whose diamond-tipped arrows of mithral have felled demon lords. The gods of the forge teach that, with patience and hard work, even the most intractable metal can be transformed from a lump of ore to a beautifully wrought object. Clerics of these deities search for objects lost to the forces of darkness, liberate mines overrun by orcs, and uncover rare and wondrous materials necessary to create potent magic items. Followers of these gods take great pride in their work, and they are willing to craft and use heavy armor and powerful weapons to protect them. Deities of this domain include Gond, Reorx, Onatar, Moradin, Hephaestus, and Goibhniu.

FORGE DOMAIN FEATURES

Cleric Level	Feature
1st	Domain Spells, Bonus Proficiencies, Blessing of the Forge
2nd	Channel Divinity: Artisan's Blessing
6th	Soul of the Forge
8th	Divine Strike (1d8)
14th	Divine Strike (2d8)
17th	Saint of Forge and Fire

DOMAIN SPELLS

You gain domain spells at the cleric levels listed in the Forge Domain Spells table. See the Divine Domain class feature for how domain spells work.

FORGE DOMAIN SPELLS

Cleric Level	Spells
1st	*identify, searing smite*
3rd	*heat metal, magic weapon*
5th	*elemental weapon, protection from energy*
7th	*fabricate, wall of fire*
9th	*animate objects, creation*

SERVING A PANTHEON, PHILOSOPHY, OR FORCE

The typical cleric is an ordained servant of a particular god and chooses a Divine Domain associated with that deity. The cleric's magic flows from the god or the god's sacred realm, and often the cleric bears a holy symbol that represents that divinity.

Some clerics, especially in a world like Eberron, serve a whole pantheon, rather than a single deity. In certain campaigns, a cleric might instead serve a cosmic force, such as life or death, or a philosophy or concept, such as love, peace, or one of the nine alignments. Chapter 1 of the *Dungeon Master's Guide* explores options like these, in the section "Gods of Your World."

Talk with your DM about the divine options available in your campaign, whether they're gods, pantheons, philosophies, or cosmic forces. Whatever being or thing your cleric ends up serving, choose a Divine Domain that is appropriate for it, and if it doesn't have a holy symbol, work with your DM to design one.

The cleric's class features often refer to your deity. If you are devoted to a pantheon, cosmic force, or philosophy, your cleric features still work for you as written. Think of the references to a god as references to the divine thing you serve that gives you your magic.

Bonus Proficiencies

When you choose this domain at 1st level, you gain proficiency with heavy armor and smith's tools.

Blessing of the Forge

At 1st level, you gain the ability to imbue magic into a weapon or armor. At the end of a long rest, you can touch one nonmagical object that is a suit of armor or a simple or martial weapon. Until the end of your next long rest or until you die, the object becomes a magic item, granting a +1 bonus to AC if it's armor or a +1 bonus to attack and damage rolls if it's a weapon.

Once you use this feature, you can't use it again until you finish a long rest.

Channel Divinity: Artisan's Blessing

Starting at 2nd level, you can use your Channel Divinity to create simple items.

You conduct an hour-long ritual that crafts a nonmagical item that must include some metal: a simple or martial weapon, a suit of armor, ten pieces of ammunition, a set of tools, or another metal object (see chapter 5, "Equipment," in the *Player's Handbook* for examples of these items). The creation is completed at the end of the hour, coalescing in an unoccupied space of your choice on a surface within 5 feet of you.

The thing you create can be something that is worth no more than 100 gp. As part of this ritual, you must lay out metal, which can include coins, with a value equal to the creation. The metal irretrievably coalesces and transforms into the creation at the ritual's end, magically forming even nonmetal parts of the creation.

The ritual can create a duplicate of a nonmagical item that contains metal, such as a key, if you possess the original during the ritual.

Soul of the Forge

Starting at 6th level, your mastery of the forge grants you special abilities:

- You gain resistance to fire damage.
- While wearing heavy armor, you gain a +1 bonus to AC.

Divine Strike

At 8th level, you gain the ability to infuse your weapon strikes with the fiery power of the forge. Once on each of your turns when you hit a creature with a weapon attack, you can cause the attack to deal an extra 1d8 fire damage to the target. When you reach 14th level, the extra damage increases to 2d8.

I guess if you can't disintegrate them or eat them, burying dead bodies makes as much sense as anything else.

CLERIC OF THE GRAVE

Saint of Forge and Fire

At 17th level, your blessed affinity with fire and metal becomes more powerful:

- You gain immunity to fire damage.
- While wearing heavy armor, you have resistance to bludgeoning, piercing, and slashing damage from nonmagical attacks.

Grave Domain

Gods of the grave watch over the line between life and death. To these deities, death and the afterlife are a foundational part of the multiverse. To desecrate the peace of the dead is an abomination. Deities of the grave include Kelemvor, Wee Jas, the ancestral spirits of the Undying Court, Hades, Anubis, and Osiris. Followers of these deities seek to put wandering spirits to rest, destroy the undead, and ease the suffering of the dying. Their magic also allows them to stave off death for a time, particularly for a person who still has some great work to accomplish in the world. This is a delay of death, not a denial of it, for death will eventually get its due.

CIRCLE OF MORTALITY

At 1st level, you gain the ability to manipulate the line between life and death. When you would normally roll one or more dice to restore hit points with a spell to a creature at 0 hit points, you instead use the highest number possible for each die.

In addition, you learn the *spare the dying* cantrip, which doesn't count against the number of cleric cantrips you know. For you, it has a range of 30 feet, and you can cast it as a bonus action.

EYES OF THE GRAVE

At 1st level, you gain the ability to occasionally sense the presence of the undead, whose existence is an insult to the natural cycle of life. As an action, you can open your awareness to magically detect undead. Until the end of your next turn, you know the location of any undead within 60 feet of you that isn't behind total cover and that isn't protected from divination magic. This sense doesn't tell you anything about a creature's capabilities or identity.

You can use this feature a number of times equal to your Wisdom modifier (minimum of once). You regain all expended uses when you finish a long rest.

CHANNEL DIVINITY: PATH TO THE GRAVE

Starting at 2nd level, you can use your Channel Divinity to mark another creature's life force for termination.

As an action, you choose one creature you can see within 30 feet of you, cursing it until the end of your next turn. The next time you or an ally of yours hits the cursed creature with an attack, the creature has vulnerability to all of that attack's damage, and then the curse ends.

SENTINEL AT DEATH'S DOOR

At 6th level, you gain the ability to impede death's progress. As a reaction when you or a creature you can see within 30 feet of you suffers a critical hit, you can turn that hit into a normal hit. Any effects triggered by a critical hit are canceled.

You can use this feature a number of times equal to your Wisdom modifier (minimum of once). You regain all expended uses when you finish a long rest.

POTENT SPELLCASTING

Starting at 8th level, you add your Wisdom modifier to the damage you deal with any cleric cantrip.

KEEPER OF SOULS

Starting at 17th level, you can seize a trace of vitality from a parting soul and use it to heal the living. When an enemy you can see dies within 60 feet of you, you or one creature of your choice that is within 60 feet of you regains hit points equal to the enemy's number of Hit Dice. You can use this feature only if you aren't incapacitated. Once you use it, you can't do so again until the start of your next turn.

GRAVE DOMAIN FEATURES

Cleric Level	Feature
1st	Domain Spells, Circle of Mortality, Eyes of the Grave
2nd	Channel Divinity: Path to the Grave
6th	Sentinel at Death's Door
8th	Potent Spellcasting
17th	Keeper of Souls

DOMAIN SPELLS

You gain domain spells at the cleric levels listed in the Grave Domain Spells table. See the Divine Domain class feature for how domain spells work.

GRAVE DOMAIN SPELLS

Cleric Level	Spells
1st	bane, false life
3rd	gentle repose, ray of enfeeblement
5th	revivify, vampiric touch
7th	blight, death ward
9th	antilife shell, raise dead

DRUID

EVEN IN DEATH, EACH CREATURE PLAYS ITS PART IN *maintaining the Great Balance. But now an imbalance grows, a force that seeks to hold sway over nature. This is the destructive behavior of the mortal races. The farther away from nature their actions take them, the more corrupting their influence becomes. As druids, we seek mainly to protect and educate, to preserve the Great Balance, but there are times when we must rise up against danger and eradicate it.*

—Safhran, archdruid

Druids are the caretakers of the natural world, and it is said that in time a druid becomes the voice of nature, speaking the truth that is too subtle for the general populace to hear. Many who become druids find that they naturally gravitate toward nature; its forces, cycles, and movements fill their minds and spirits with wonder and insight. Many sages and wise folk have studied nature, writing volumes about its mystery and power, but druids are a special kind of being: at some point, they begin to embody these natural forces, producing magical phenomena that link them to the spirit of nature and the flow of life. Because of their strange and mysterious power, druids are often revered, shunned, or considered dangerous by the people around them.

Your druid character might be a true worshiper of nature, one who has always scorned civilization and found solace in the wild. Or your character could be a child of the city who now strives to bring the civilized world into harmony with the wilderness. You can use the sections that follow to flesh out your druid, regardless of how your character came to the profession.

TREASURED ITEM

Some druids carry one or more items that are sacred to them or have deep personal significance. Such items are not necessarily magical, but every one is an object whose meaning connects the druid's mind and heart to a profound concept or spiritual outlook.

When you decide what your character's treasured item is, think about giving it an origin story: how did you come by the item, and why is it important to you?

TREASURED ITEMS

d6	Item
1	A twig from the meeting tree that stands in the center of your village
2	A vial of water from the source of a sacred river
3	Special herbs tied together in a bundle
4	A small bronze bowl engraved with animal images
5	A rattle made from a dried gourd and holly berries
6	A miniature golden sickle handed down to you by your mentor

GUIDING ASPECT

Many druids feel a strong link to a specific aspect of the natural world, such as a body of water, an animal, a type of tree, or some other sort of plant. You identify with your chosen aspect; by its behavior or its very nature, it sets an example that you seek to emulate.

GUIDING ASPECTS

d6	Guiding Aspect
1	Yew trees remind you of renewing your mind and spirit, letting the old die and the new spring forth.
2	Oak trees represent strength and vitality. Meditating under an oak fills your body and mind with resolve and fortitude.
3	The river's endless flow reminds you of the great span of the world. You seek to act with the long-term interests of nature in mind.
4	The sea is a constant, churning cauldron of power and chaos. It reminds you that accepting change is necessary to sustain yourself in the world.
5	The birds in the sky are evidence that even the smallest creatures can survive if they remain above the fray.
6	As demonstrated by the actions of the wolf, an individual's strength is nothing compared to the power of the pack.

MENTOR

It's not unusual for would-be druids to seek out (or be sought out by) instructors or elders who teach them the basics of their magical arts. Most druids who learn from a mentor begin their training at a young age, and the mentor has a vital role in shaping a student's attitudes and beliefs.

If your character received training from someone else, who or what was that individual, and what was the nature of your relationship? Did your mentor imbue you with a particular outlook or otherwise influence your approach to achieving the goals of your chosen path?

I don't dream because I don't sleep. I'm always awake so no one can ever sneak up on me. If I dreamed, they would be bigger dreams than yours, though, because my head is bigger.

DRUID OF
THE CIRCLE
OF DREAMS

CIRCLE OF DREAMS

Druids who are members of the Circle of Dreams hail from regions that have strong ties to the Feywild and its dreamlike realms. The druids' guardianship of the natural world makes for a natural alliance between them and good-aligned fey. These druids seek to fill the world with dreamy wonder. Their magic mends wounds and brings joy to downcast hearts, and the realms they protect are gleaming, fruitful places, where dream and reality blur together and where the weary can find rest.

CIRCLE OF DREAMS FEATURES

Druid Level	Feature
2nd	Balm of the Summer Court
6th	Hearth of Moonlight and Shadow
10th	Hidden Paths
14th	Walker in Dreams

BALM OF THE SUMMER COURT

At 2nd level, you become imbued with the blessings of the Summer Court. You are a font of energy that offers respite from injuries. You have a pool of fey energy represented by a number of d6s equal to your druid level.

As a bonus action, you can choose one creature you can see within 120 feet of you and spend a number of those dice equal to half your druid level or less. Roll the spent dice and add them together. The target regains a number of hit points equal to the total. The target also gains 1 temporary hit point per die spent.

You regain all expended dice when you finish a long rest.

HEARTH OF MOONLIGHT AND SHADOW

At 6th level, home can be wherever you are. During a short or long rest, you can invoke the shadowy power of the Gloaming Court to help guard your respite. At the start of the rest, you touch a point in space, and an invisible, 30-foot-radius sphere of magic appears, centered on that point. Total cover blocks the sphere.

While within the sphere, you and your allies gain a +5 bonus to Dexterity (Stealth) and Wisdom (Perception) checks, and any light from open flames in the sphere (a campfire, torches, or the like) isn't visible outside it.

The sphere vanishes at the end of the rest or when you leave the sphere.

HIDDEN PATHS

Starting at 10th level, you can use the hidden, magical pathways that some fey use to traverse space in the blink of an eye. As a bonus action on your turn, you can teleport up to 60 feet to an unoccupied space you can see. Alternatively, you can use your action to teleport

MENTORS

d6	Mentor
1	Your mentor was a wise treant who taught you to think in terms of years and decades rather than days or months.
2	You were tutored by a dryad who watched over a slumbering portal to the Abyss. During your training, you were tasked with watching for hidden threats to the world.
3	Your tutor always interacted with you in the form of a falcon. You never saw the tutor's humanoid form.
4	You were one of several youngsters who were mentored by an old druid, until one of your fellow pupils betrayed your group and killed your master.
5	Your mentor has appeared to you only in visions. You have yet to meet this person, and you are not sure such a person exists in mortal form.
6	Your mentor was a werebear who taught you to treat all living things with equal regard.

DRUID CIRCLES

At 2nd level, a druid gains the Druid Circle feature. The following options are available to a druid, in addition to those offered in the *Player's Handbook*: the Circle of Dreams and the Circle of the Shepherd.

one willing creature you touch up to 30 feet to an unoccupied space you can see.

You can use this feature a number of times equal to your Wisdom modifier (minimum of once), and you regain all expended uses of it when you finish a long rest.

WALKER IN DREAMS

At 14th level, the magic of the Feywild grants you the ability to travel mentally or physically through dreamlands.

When you finish a short rest, you can cast one of the following spells, without expending a spell slot or requiring material components: *dream* (with you as the messenger), *scrying*, or *teleportation circle*.

This use of *teleportation circle* is special. Rather than opening a portal to a permanent teleportation circle, it opens a portal to the last location where you finished a long rest on your current plane of existence. If you haven't taken a long rest on your current plane, the spell fails but isn't wasted.

Once you use this feature, you can't use it again until you finish a long rest.

CIRCLE OF THE SHEPHERD

Druids of the Circle of the Shepherd commune with the spirits of nature, especially the spirits of beasts and the fey, and call to those spirits for aid. These druids recognize that all living things play a role in the natural world, yet they focus on protecting animals and fey creatures that have difficulty defending themselves. Shepherds, as they are known, see such creatures as their charges. They ward off monsters that threaten them, rebuke hunters who kill more prey than necessary, and prevent civilization from encroaching on rare animal habitats and on sites sacred to the fey. Many of these druids are happiest far from cities and towns, content to spend their days in the company of animals and the fey creatures of the wilds.

Members of this circle become adventurers to oppose forces that threaten their charges or to seek knowledge and power that will help them safeguard their charges better. Wherever these druids go, the spirits of the wilderness are with them.

DRUID OF THE CIRCLE OF THE SHEPHERD

CIRCLE OF THE SHEPHERD FEATURES

Druid Level	Feature
2nd	Speech of the Woods, Spirit Totem
6th	Mighty Summoner
10th	Guardian Spirit
14th	Faithful Summons

SPEECH OF THE WOODS

At 2nd level, you gain the ability to converse with beasts and many fey.

You learn to speak, read, and write Sylvan. In addition, beasts can understand your speech, and you gain the ability to decipher their noises and motions. Most beasts lack the intelligence to convey or understand sophisticated concepts, but a friendly beast could relay what it has seen or heard in the recent past. This ability doesn't grant you friendship with beasts, though you can combine this ability with gifts to curry favor with them as you would with any nonplayer character.

SPIRIT TOTEM

Starting at 2nd level, you can call forth nature spirits to influence the world around you. As a bonus action, you can magically summon an incorporeal spirit to a point you can see within 60 feet of you. The spirit creates an aura in a 30-foot radius around that point. It counts as neither a creature nor an object, though it has the spectral appearance of the creature it represents.

As a bonus action, you can move the spirit up to 60 feet to a point you can see.

The spirit persists for 1 minute or until you're incapacitated. Once you use this feature, you can't use it again until you finish a short or long rest.

The effect of the spirit's aura depends on the type of spirit you summon from the options below.

Bear Spirit. The bear spirit grants you and your allies its might and endurance. Each creature of your choice in the aura when the spirit appears gains temporary hit points equal to 5 + your druid level. In addition, you and your allies gain advantage on Strength checks and Strength saving throws while in the aura.

Hawk Spirit. The hawk spirit is a consummate hunter, aiding you and your allies with its keen sight. When a creature makes an attack roll against a target in the spirit's aura, you can use your reaction to grant advantage to that attack roll. In addition, you and your allies have advantage on Wisdom (Perception) checks while in the aura.

Unicorn Spirit. The unicorn spirit lends its protection to those nearby. You and your allies gain advantage on all ability checks made to detect creatures in the spirit's aura. In addition, if you cast a spell using a spell slot that restores hit points to any creature inside or outside the aura, each creature of your choice in the aura also regains hit points equal to your druid level.

MIGHTY SUMMONER

Starting at 6th level, beasts and fey that you conjure are more resilient than normal. Any beast or fey summoned or created by a spell that you cast gains the following benefits:

- The creature appears with more hit points than normal: 2 extra hit points per Hit Die it has.
- The damage from its natural weapons is considered magical for the purpose of overcoming immunity and resistance to nonmagical attacks and damage.

GUARDIAN SPIRIT

Beginning at 10th level, your Spirit Totem safeguards the beasts and fey that you call forth with your magic. When a beast or fey that you summoned or created with a spell ends its turn in your Spirit Totem aura, that creature regains a number of hit points equal to half your druid level.

FAITHFUL SUMMONS

Starting at 14th level, the nature spirits you commune with protect you when you are the most defenseless. If you are reduced to 0 hit points or are incapacitated against your will, you can immediately gain the benefits of *conjure animals* as if it were cast using a 9th-level spell slot. It summons four beasts of your choice that are challenge rating 2 or lower. The conjured beasts appear within 20 feet of you. If they receive no commands from you, they protect you from harm and attack your foes. The spell lasts for 1 hour, requiring no concentration, or until you dismiss it (no action required).

Once you use this feature, you can't use it again until you finish a long rest.

LEARNING BEAST SHAPES

The Wild Shape feature in the *Player's Handbook* lets you transform into a beast that you've seen. That rule gives you a tremendous amount of flexibility, making it easy to amass an array of beast form options for yourself, but you must abide by the limitations in the Beast Shapes table in that book.

When you gain Wild Shape as a 2nd-level druid, you might wonder which beasts you've already seen. The following tables organize beasts from the *Monster Manual* according to the beasts' most likely environments. Consider the environment your druid grew up in, then consult the appropriate table for a list of animals that your druid has probably seen by 2nd level.

These tables can also help you and your DM determine which animals you might see on your travels. In addition, the tables include each beast's challenge rating and note whether a beast has a flying or swimming speed. This information will help you determine whether you qualify to assume that beast's form.

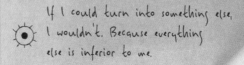
If I could turn into something else, I wouldn't. Because everything else is inferior to me.

The tables include all the individual beasts that are eligible for Wild Shape (up to a challenge rating of 1) or the Circle Forms feature of the Circle of the Moon (up to a challenge rating of 6).

ARCTIC

CR	Beast	Fly/Swim
0	Owl	Fly
1/8	Blood hawk	Fly
1/4	Giant owl	Fly
1	Brown bear	—
2	Polar bear	Swim
2	Saber-toothed tiger	—
6	Mammoth	—

COAST

CR	Beast	Fly/Swim
0	Crab	Swim
0	Eagle	Fly
1/8	Blood hawk	Fly
1/8	Giant crab	Swim
1/8	Poisonous snake	Swim
1/8	Stirge	Fly
1/4	Giant lizard	—
1/4	Giant wolf spider	—
1/4	Pteranodon	Fly
1	Giant eagle	Fly
1	Giant toad	Swim
2	Plesiosaurus	Swim

DESERT

CR	Beast	Fly/Swim
0	Cat	—
0	Hyena	—
0	Jackal	—
0	Scorpion	—
0	Vulture	Fly
1/8	Camel	—
1/8	Flying snake	Fly
1/8	Mule	—
1/8	Poisonous snake	Swim
1/8	Stirge	Fly
1/4	Constrictor snake	Swim
1/4	Giant lizard	—
1/4	Giant poisonous snake	Swim
1/4	Giant wolf spider	—
1	Giant hyena	—
1	Giant spider	—
1	Giant toad	Swim
1	Giant vulture	Fly
1	Lion	—
2	Giant constrictor snake	Swim
3	Giant scorpion	—

FOREST

CR	Beast	Fly/Swim
0	Baboon	—
0	Badger	—
0	Cat	—
0	Deer	—
0	Hyena	—
0	Owl	Fly
1/8	Blood hawk	Fly
1/8	Flying snake	Fly
1/8	Giant rat	—
1/8	Giant weasel	—
1/8	Poisonous snake	Swim
1/8	Mastiff	—
1/8	Stirge	Fly
1/4	Boar	—
1/4	Constrictor snake	Swim
1/4	Elk	—
1/4	Giant badger	—
1/4	Giant bat	Fly
1/4	Giant frog	Swim
1/4	Giant lizard	—
1/4	Giant owl	Fly
1/4	Giant poisonous snake	Swim
1/4	Giant wolf spider	—
1/4	Panther	—
1/4	Wolf	—
1/2	Ape	—
1/2	Black bear	—
1/2	Giant wasp	Fly
1	Brown bear	—
1	Dire wolf	—
1	Giant hyena	—
1	Giant spider	—
1	Giant toad	Swim
1	Tiger	—
2	Giant boar	—
2	Giant constrictor snake	Swim
2	Giant elk	—

GRASSLAND

CR	Beast	Fly/Swim
0	Cat	—
0	Deer	—
0	Eagle	Fly
0	Goat	—
0	Hyena	—
0	Jackal	—
0	Vulture	Fly
1/8	Blood hawk	Fly
1/8	Flying snake	Fly
1/8	Giant weasel	—
1/8	Poisonous snake	Swim
1/8	Stirge	Fly
1/4	Axe beak	—
1/4	Boar	—
1/4	Elk	—
1/4	Giant poisonous snake	Swim
1/4	Giant wolf spider	—
1/4	Panther (leopard)	—
1/4	Pteranodon	Fly
1/4	Riding horse	—
1/4	Wolf	—
1/2	Giant goat	—
1/2	Giant wasp	Fly
1	Giant eagle	Fly
1	Giant hyena	—
1	Giant vulture	Fly
1	Lion	—
1	Tiger	—
2	Allosaurus	—
2	Giant boar	—
2	Giant elk	—
2	Rhinoceros	—
3	Ankylosaurus	—
4	Elephant	—
5	Triceratops	—

Hill

CR	Beast	Fly/Swim
0	Baboon	—
0	Eagle	Fly
0	Goat	—
0	Hyena	—
0	Raven	Fly
0	Vulture	Fly
1/8	Blood hawk	Fly
1/8	Giant weasel	—
1/8	Mastiff	—
1/8	Mule	—
1/8	Poisonous snake	Swim
1/8	Stirge	Fly
1/4	Axe beak	—
1/4	Boar	—
1/4	Elk	—
1/4	Giant owl	Fly
1/4	Giant wolf spider	—
1/4	Panther (cougar)	—
1/4	Wolf	—
1/2	Giant goat	—
1	Brown bear	—
1	Dire wolf	—
1	Giant eagle	Fly
1	Giant hyena	—
1	Lion	—
2	Giant boar	—
2	Giant elk	—

Mountain

CR	Beast	Fly/Swim
0	Eagle	Fly
0	Goat	—
1/8	Blood hawk	Fly
1/8	Stirge	Fly
1/4	Pteranodon	Fly
1/2	Giant goat	—
1	Giant eagle	Fly
1	Lion	—
2	Giant elk	—
2	Saber-toothed tiger	—

Swamp

CR	Beast	Fly/Swim
0	Rat	—
0	Raven	Fly
1/8	Giant rat	—
1/8	Poisonous snake	Swim
1/8	Stirge	Fly
1/4	Constrictor snake	Swim
1/4	Giant frog	Swim
1/4	Giant lizard	—
1/4	Giant poisonous snake	Swim
1/2	Crocodile	Swim
1	Giant spider	—
1	Giant toad	Swim
2	Giant constrictor snake	Swim
5	Giant crocodile	Swim

Underdark

CR	Beast	Fly/Swim
0	Giant fire beetle	—
1/8	Giant rat	—
1/8	Stirge	Fly
1/4	Giant bat	Fly
1/4	Giant centipede	—
1/4	Giant lizard	—
1/4	Giant poisonous snake	Swim
1	Giant spider	—
1	Giant toad	Swim
2	Giant constrictor snake	Swim
2	Polar bear (cave bear)	Swim

Underwater

CR	Beast	Fly/Swim
0	Quipper	Swim
1/4	Constrictor snake	Swim
1/2	Giant sea horse	Swim
1/2	Reef shark	Swim
1	Giant octopus	Swim
2	Giant constrictor snake	Swim
2	Hunter shark	Swim
2	Plesiosaurus	Swim
3	Killer whale	Swim
5	Giant shark	Swim

FIGHTER

LET ME KNOW WHEN YOU'RE ALL DONE TALKING.

—Tordek

Of all the adventurers in the worlds of D&D, the fighter is perhaps the greatest paradox. On the one hand, a singular feature of the class is that no two fighters ply their craft in quite the same way; their weapons, armor, and tactics differ across a vast spectrum. On the other hand, regardless of the tools and methods one uses, at the heart of every fighter's motivation lies the same basic truth: it is better to wound than to be wounded.

Although some adventuring fighters risk their lives fighting for glory or treasure, others are primarily concerned with the welfare of others. They put more value on the well-being of the society, the village, or the group than on their own safety. Even if there's gold in the offing, the true reward for most fighters comes from sending enemies to their doom.

The sections below offer ways to add a little depth and a few personal touches to your fighter character.

HERALDIC SIGN

Fighters typically do battle for a cause. Some fight on behalf of kingdoms besieged by monsters, while others quest only for personal glory. In either case, a fighter often displays a heraldic sign that represents that cause, either adopting the symbol of a nation or a royal line, or creating a crest to represent one's self-interest.

Your character could be affiliated with an organization or a cause, and thus might already travel under a banner of some sort. If that's not the case, consider devising a heraldic sign that symbolizes an aspect of your nature or speaks to what you see as your purpose in the world.

Sticks and stones may break my bones, but swords will never hurt me—as long as I stay really high and shoot down at an angle.

HERALDIC SIGNS

d6	Sign
1	A rampant golden dragon on a green field, representing valor and a quest for wealth
2	The fist of a storm giant clutching lightning before a storm cloud, symbolizing wrath and power
3	Crossed greatswords in front of a castle gate, signifying the defense of a city or kingdom
4	A skull with a dagger through it, representing the doom you bring to your enemies
5	A phoenix in a ring of fire, an expression of an indomitable spirit
6	Three drops of blood beneath a horizontal sword blade on a black background, symbolizing three foes you have sworn to kill

INSTRUCTOR

Some fighters are natural-born combatants who have a talent for surviving in battle. Others learned the basics of their combat prowess in their formative years from spending time in a military or some other martial organization, when they were taught by the leaders of the group.

A third type of fighter comes from the ranks of those who received one-on-one instruction from an accomplished veteran of the craft. That instructor was, or perhaps still is, well versed in a certain aspect of combat that relates to the student's background.

If you decide that your character had an individual instructor, what is that person's specialty? Do you emulate your instructor in how you fight, or did you take the instructor's teachings and adapt them to your own purposes?

INSTRUCTORS

d6	Instructor
1	**Gladiator.** Your instructor was a slave who fought for freedom in the arena, or one who willingly chose the gladiator's life to earn money and fame.
2	**Military.** Your trainer served with a group of soldiers and knows much about working as a team.
3	**City Watch.** Crowd control and peacekeeping are your instructor's specialties.
4	**Tribal Warrior.** Your instructor grew up in a tribe, where fighting for one's life was practically an everyday occurrence.
5	**Street Fighter.** Your trainer excels at urban combat, combining close-quarters work with silence and efficiency.
6	**Weapon Master.** Your mentor helped you to become one with your chosen weapon, by imparting highly specialized knowledge of how to wield it most effectively.

Arrows are the worst. They go much farther than eye rays. That's why I stay indoors all the time. Besides, the sky is totally overrated.

SIGNATURE STYLE

Many fighters distinguish themselves from their peers by adopting and perfecting a particular style or method of waging combat. Although this style might be a natural outgrowth of a fighter's personality, that's not always the case—someone's approach to the world in general does not necessarily dictate how that person operates when lives are on the line.

Do you have a combat style that mirrors your outlook on life, or is something else inside you unleashed when weapons are drawn?

SIGNATURE STYLES

d6	Style
1	**Elegant.** You move with precise grace and total control, never using more energy than you need.
2	**Brutal.** Your attacks rain down like hammer blows, meant to splinter bone or send blood flying.
3	**Cunning.** You dart in to attack at just the right moment and use small-scale tactics to tilt the odds in your favor.
4	**Effortless.** You rarely perspire or display anything other than a stoic expression in battle.
5	**Energetic.** You sing and laugh during combat as your spirit soars. You are happiest when you have a foe in front of you and a weapon in hand.
6	**Sinister.** You scowl and sneer while fighting, and you enjoy mocking your foes as you defeat them.

MARTIAL ARCHETYPES

At 3rd level, a fighter gains the Martial Archetype feature. The following options are available to a fighter, in addition to those offered in the *Player's Handbook*: the Arcane Archer, the Cavalier, and the Samurai.

ARCANE ARCHER

An Arcane Archer studies a unique elven method of archery that weaves magic into attacks to produce supernatural effects. Arcane Archers are some of the most elite warriors among the elves. They stand watch over the fringes of elven domains, keeping a keen eye out for trespassers and using magic-infused arrows to defeat monsters and invaders before they can reach elven settlements. Over the centuries, the methods of these elf archers have been learned by members of other races who can also balance arcane aptitude with archery.

ARCANE ARCHER FEATURES

Fighter Level	Feature
3rd	Arcane Archer Lore, Arcane Shot (2 options)
7th	Curving Shot, Magic Arrow, Arcane Shot (3 options)
10th	Arcane Shot (4 options)
15th	Ever-Ready Shot, Arcane Shot (5 options)
18th	Arcane Shot (6 options, improved shots)

ARCANE ARCHER LORE

At 3rd level, you learn magical theory or some of the secrets of nature—typical for practitioners of this elven martial tradition. You choose to gain proficiency in either the Arcana or the Nature skill, and you choose to learn either the *prestidigitation* or the *druidcraft* cantrip.

ARCANE SHOT

At 3rd level, you learn to unleash special magical effects with some of your shots. When you gain this feature, you learn two Arcane Shot options of your choice (see "Arcane Shot Options" below).

Once per turn when you fire a magic arrow from a shortbow or longbow as part of the Attack action, you can apply one of your Arcane Shot options to that arrow. You decide to use the option when the arrow hits a creature, unless the option doesn't involve an attack roll. You have two uses of this ability, and you regain all expended uses of it when you finish a short or long rest.

You gain an additional Arcane Shot option of your choice when you reach certain levels in this class: 7th, 10th, 15th, and 18th level. Each option also improves when you become an 18th-level fighter.

MAGIC ARROW

At 7th level, you gain the ability to infuse arrows with magic. Whenever you fire a nonmagical arrow from a shortbow or longbow, you can make it magical for the purpose of overcoming resistance and immunity to nonmagical attacks and damage. The magic fades from the arrow immediately after it hits or misses its target.

CURVING SHOT

At 7th level, you learn how to direct an errant arrow toward a new target. When you make an attack roll with a magic arrow and miss, you can use a bonus action to reroll the attack roll against a different target within 60 feet of the original target.

EVER-READY SHOT

Starting at 15th level, your magical archery is available whenever battle starts. If you roll initiative and have no uses of Arcane Shot remaining, you regain one use of it.

ARCANE SHOT OPTIONS

The Arcane Shot feature lets you choose options for it at certain levels. The options are presented here in alphabetical order. They are all magical effects, and each one is associated with one of the schools of magic.

If an option requires a saving throw, your Arcane Shot save DC equals 8 + your proficiency bonus + your Intelligence modifier.

LEFT TO RIGHT: SAMURAI, CAVALIER, AND ARCANE ARCHER

Banishing Arrow. You use abjuration magic to try to temporarily banish your target to a harmless location in the Feywild. The creature hit by the arrow must also succeed on a Charisma saving throw or be banished. While banished in this way, the target's speed is 0, and it is incapacitated. At the end of its next turn, the target reappears in the space it vacated or in the nearest unoccupied space if that space is occupied.

After you reach 18th level in this class, a target also takes 2d6 force damage when the arrow hits it.

Beguiling Arrow. Your enchantment magic causes this arrow to temporarily beguile its target. The creature hit by the arrow takes an extra 2d6 psychic damage, and choose one of your allies within 30 feet of the target. The target must succeed on a Wisdom saving throw, or it is charmed by the chosen ally until the start of your next turn. This effect ends early if the chosen ally attacks the charmed target, deals damage to it, or forces it to make a saving throw.

The psychic damage increases to 4d6 when you reach 18th level in this class.

Bursting Arrow. You imbue your arrow with force energy drawn from the school of evocation. The energy detonates after your attack. Immediately after the arrow hits the creature, the target and all other creatures within 10 feet of it take 2d6 force damage each.

The force damage increases to 4d6 when you reach 18th level in this class.

Enfeebling Arrow. You weave necromantic magic into your arrow. The creature hit by the arrow takes an extra 2d6 necrotic damage. The target must also succeed on a Constitution saving throw, or the damage dealt by its weapon attacks is halved until the start of your next turn.

The necrotic damage increases to 4d6 when you reach 18th level in this class.

Grasping Arrow. When this arrow strikes its target, conjuration magic creates grasping, poisonous brambles, which wrap around the target. The creature hit by the arrow takes an extra 2d6 poison damage, its speed is reduced by 10 feet, and it takes 2d6 slashing damage the first time on each turn it moves 1 foot or more without teleporting. The target or any creature that can reach it can use its action to remove the brambles with a successful Strength (Athletics) check against your Arcane Shot save DC. Otherwise, the brambles last for 1 minute or until you use this option again.

The poison damage and slashing damage both increase to 4d6 when you reach 18th level in this class.

Piercing Arrow. You use transmutation magic to give your arrow an ethereal quality. When you use this option, you don't make an attack roll for the attack. Instead, the arrow shoots forward in a line, which is 1 foot wide and 30 feet long, before disappearing. The arrow passes harmlessly through objects, ignoring cover. Each creature in that line must make a Dexterity saving throw. On a failed save, a creature takes damage as if it were hit by the arrow, plus an extra 1d6 piercing damage. On a successful save, a target takes half as much damage.

The piercing damage increases to 2d6 when you reach 18th level in this class.

Seeking Arrow. Using divination magic, you grant your arrow the ability to seek out a target. When you use this option, you don't make an attack roll for the attack. Instead, choose one creature you have seen in the past minute. The arrow flies toward that creature, moving around corners if necessary and ignoring three-quarters cover and half cover. If the target is within the weapon's range and there is a path large enough for the arrow to travel to the target, the target must make a Dexterity saving throw. Otherwise, the arrow disappears after traveling as far as it can. On a failed save, the target takes damage as if it were hit by the arrow, plus an extra 1d6 force damage, and you learn the target's current location. On a successful save, the target takes half as much damage, and you don't learn its location.

The force damage increases to 2d6 when you reach 18th level in this class.

Shadow Arrow. You weave illusion magic into your arrow, causing it to occlude your foe's vision with shadows. The creature hit by the arrow takes an extra 2d6 psychic damage, and it must succeed on a Wisdom saving throw or be unable to see anything farther than 5 feet away until the start of your next turn.

The psychic damage increases to 4d6 when you reach 18th level in this class.

CAVALIER

The archetypal Cavalier excels at mounted combat. Usually born among the nobility and raised at court, a Cavalier is equally at home leading a cavalry charge or exchanging repartee at a state dinner. Cavaliers also learn how to guard those in their charge from harm, often serving as the protectors of their superiors and of the weak. Compelled to right wrongs or earn prestige, many of these fighters leave their lives of comfort to embark on glorious adventure.

CAVALIER FEATURES

Fighter Level	Feature
3rd	Bonus Proficiency, Born to the Saddle, Unwavering Mark
7th	Warding Maneuver
10th	Hold the Line
15th	Ferocious Charger
18th	Vigilant Defender

BONUS PROFICIENCY

When you choose this archetype at 3rd level, you gain proficiency in one of the following skills of your choice: Animal Handling, History, Insight, Performance, or Persuasion. Alternatively, you learn one language of your choice.

BORN TO THE SADDLE

Starting at 3rd level, your mastery as a rider becomes apparent. You have advantage on saving throws made to avoid falling off your mount. If you fall off your mount and descend no more than 10 feet, you can land on your feet if you're not incapacitated.

Finally, mounting or dismounting a creature costs you only 5 feet of movement, rather than half your speed.

UNWAVERING MARK

Starting at 3rd level, you can menace your foes, foiling their attacks and punishing them for harming others. When you hit a creature with a melee weapon attack, you can mark the creature until the end of your next turn. This effect ends early if you are incapacitated or you die, or if someone else marks the creature.

While it is within 5 feet of you, a creature marked by you has disadvantage on any attack roll that doesn't target you.

In addition, if a creature marked by you deals damage to anyone other than you, you can make a special melee weapon attack against the marked creature as a bonus action on your next turn. You have advantage on the attack roll, and if it hits, the attack's weapon deals extra damage to the target equal to half your fighter level.

Regardless of the number of creatures you mark, you can make this special attack a number of times equal to your Strength modifier (minimum of once), and you regain all expended uses of it when you finish a long rest.

WARDING MANEUVER

At 7th level, you learn to fend off strikes directed at you, your mount, or other creatures nearby. If you or a creature you can see within 5 feet of you is hit by an attack, you can roll 1d8 as a reaction if you're wielding a melee weapon or a shield. Roll the die, and add the number rolled to the target's AC against that attack. If the attack still hits, the target has resistance against the attack's damage.

You can use this feature a number of times equal to your Constitution modifier (minimum of once), and you regain all expended uses of it when you finish a long rest.

HOLD THE LINE

At 10th level, you become a master of locking down your enemies. Creatures provoke an opportunity attack from you when they move 5 feet or more while within your reach, and if you hit a creature with an opportunity attack, the target's speed is reduced to 0 until the end of the current turn.

So there are different names for different sorts of people who swing swords? Why? Let me try: big sword swinger and tiny sword swinger. No, that sounds like it's the size of the sword that matters. How about: big meat bag with a sword and little meat bag with a sword!

FEROCIOUS CHARGER

Starting at 15th level, you can run down your foes, whether you're mounted or not. If you move at least 10 feet in a straight line right before attacking a creature and you hit it with the attack, that target must succeed on a Strength saving throw (DC 8 + your proficiency bonus + your Strength modifier) or be knocked prone. You can use this feature only once on each of your turns.

VIGILANT DEFENDER

Starting at 18th level, you respond to danger with extraordinary vigilance. In combat, you get a special reaction that you can take once on every creature's turn, except your turn. You can use this special reaction only to make an opportunity attack, and you can't use it on the same turn that you take your normal reaction.

SAMURAI

The Samurai is a fighter who draws on an implacable fighting spirit to overcome enemies. A Samurai's resolve is nearly unbreakable, and the enemies in a Samurai's path have two choices: yield or die fighting.

SAMURAI FEATURES

Fighter Level	Feature
3rd	Bonus Proficiency, Fighting Spirit (5 temp. hp)
7th	Elegant Courtier
10th	Tireless Spirit, Fighting Spirit (10 temp. hp)
15th	Rapid Strike, Fighting Spirit (15 temp. hp)
18th	Strength before Death

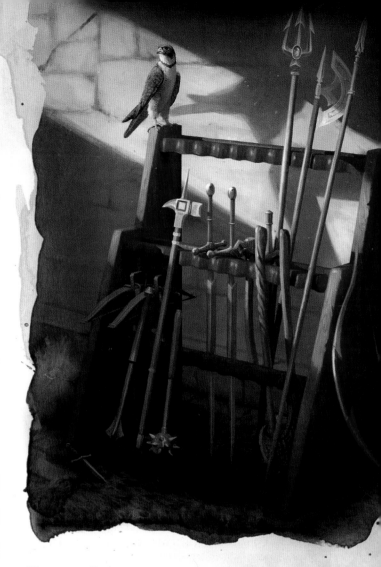

BONUS PROFICIENCY

When you choose this archetype at 3rd level, you gain proficiency in one of the following skills of your choice: History, Insight, Performance, or Persuasion. Alternatively, you learn one language of your choice.

FIGHTING SPIRIT

Starting at 3rd level, your intensity in battle can shield you and help you strike true. As a bonus action on your turn, you can give yourself advantage on weapon attack rolls until the end of the current turn. When you do so, you also gain 5 temporary hit points. The number of temporary hit points increases when you reach certain levels in this class, increasing to 10 at 10th level and 15 at 15th level.

You can use this feature three times, and you regain all expended uses of it when you finish a long rest.

ELEGANT COURTIER

Starting at 7th level, your discipline and attention to detail allow you to excel in social situations. Whenever you make a Charisma (Persuasion) check, you gain a bonus to the check equal to your Wisdom modifier.

Your self-control also causes you to gain proficiency in Wisdom saving throws. If you already have this proficiency, you instead gain proficiency in Intelligence or Charisma saving throws (your choice).

TIRELESS SPIRIT

Starting at 10th level, when you roll initiative and have no uses of Fighting Spirit remaining, you regain one use.

RAPID STRIKE

Starting at 15th level, you learn to trade accuracy for swift strikes. If you take the Attack action on your turn and have advantage on an attack roll against one of the targets, you can forgo the advantage for that roll to make an additional weapon attack against that target, as part of the same action. You can do so no more than once per turn.

STRENGTH BEFORE DEATH

Starting at 18th level, your fighting spirit can delay the grasp of death. If you take damage that reduces you to 0 hit points and doesn't kill you outright, you can use your reaction to delay falling unconscious, and you can immediately take an extra turn, interrupting the current turn. While you have 0 hit points during that extra turn, taking damage causes death saving throw failures as normal, and three death saving throw failures can still kill you. When the extra turn ends, you fall unconscious if you still have 0 hit points.

Once you use this feature, you can't use it again until you finish a long rest.

I bet I could be a monk if I wanted. What? Why are you laughing?

MONK

DO NOT MISTAKE MY SILENCE FOR ACCEPTANCE OF YOUR *villainy. While you blustered and threatened, I've planned four different ways to snap your neck with my bare hands.*

—Ember, grand master of flowers

Monks walk a path of contradiction. They study their art as a wizard does, and like a wizard, they wear no armor and typically eschew weapons. Yet they are deadly combatants, their abilities on a par with those of a raging barbarian or a superbly trained fighter. Monks embrace this seeming contradiction, for it speaks to the core of all monastic study. By coming to know oneself completely, one learns much of the wider world.

A monk's focus on inner mastery leads many such individuals to become detached from society, more concerned with their personal experience than with happenings elsewhere. Adventuring monks are a rare breed of an already rare type of character, taking their quest for perfection beyond the walls of the monastery into the world at large.

Playing a monk character offers many intriguing opportunities to try something different. To distinguish your monk character even further, consider the options in the sections that follow.

MONASTERY

A monk studies in a monastery in preparation for a life of asceticism. Most of those who enter a monastery make it their home for the rest of their lives, with the exception of adventurers and others who have reason to leave. For those individuals, a monastery might serve as a refuge between excursions to the world or as a source of support in times of need.

What sort of place was your monastery, and where is it located? Did attending it contribute to your experience in an unusual or distinctive way?

MONASTERIES

d6	Monastery
1	Your monastery is carved out of a mountainside, where it looms over a treacherous pass.
2	Your monastery is high in the branches of an immense tree in the Feywild.
3	Your monastery was founded long ago by a cloud giant and is inside a cloud castle that can be reached only by flying.
4	Your monastery is built beside a volcanic system of hot springs, geysers, and sulfur pools. You regularly received visits from azer traders.
5	Your monastery was founded by gnomes and is an underground labyrinth of tunnels and rooms.
6	Your monastery was carved from an iceberg in the frozen reaches of the world.

MONASTIC ICON

Even in the monastic lifestyle, which eschews materialism and personal possessions, symbolism plays an important part in defining the identity of an order. Some monastic orders treat certain creatures with special regard, either because the creature is tied to the order's history or because it serves as an example of a quality the monks seek to emulate.

If your character's monastery had a special icon, you might wear a crude image of the creature somewhere inconspicuous on your clothing to serve as an identifying mark. Or perhaps your order's icon does not have a physical form but is expressed through a gesture or a posture that you adopt, and which other monks might know how to interpret.

MONASTIC ICONS

d6	Icon
1	**Monkey.** Quick reflexes and the ability to travel through the treetops are two of the reasons why your order admires the monkey.
2	**Dragon Turtle.** The monks of your seaside monastery venerate the dragon turtle, reciting ancient prayers and offering garlands of flowers to honor this living spirit of the sea.
3	**Ki-rin.** Your monastery sees its main purpose as watching over and protecting the land in the manner of the ki-rin.
4	**Owlbear.** The monks of your monastery revere a family of owlbears and have coexisted with them for generations.
5	**Hydra.** Your order singles out the hydra for its ability to unleash several attacks simultaneously.
6	**Dragon.** A dragon once laired within your monastery. Its influence remains long after its departure.

LEFT TO RIGHT: DRUNKEN MASTER, KENSEI, AND SUN SOUL

MASTER

During your studies, you were likely under the tutelage of a master who imparted to you the precepts of the order. Your master was the one most responsible for shaping your understanding of the martial arts and your attitude toward the world. What sort of person was your master, and how did your relationship with your master affect you?

MASTERS

d6	Master
1	Your master was a tyrant whom you had to defeat in single combat to complete your instruction.
2	Your master was kindly and taught you to pursue the cause of peace.
3	Your master was merciless in pushing you to your limits. You nearly lost an eye during one especially brutal practice session.
4	Your master seemed goodhearted while tutoring you, but betrayed your monastery in the end.
5	Your master was cold and distant. You suspect that the two of you might be related.
6	Your master was kind and generous, never critical of your progress. Nevertheless, you feel you never fully lived up to the expectations placed on you.

MONASTIC TRADITIONS

At 3rd level, a monk gains the Monastic Tradition feature. The following options are available to a monk, in addition to those offered in the *Player's Handbook*: the Way of the Drunken Master, the Way of the Kensei, and the Way of the Sun Soul.

WAY OF THE DRUNKEN MASTER

The Way of the Drunken Master teaches its students to move with the jerky, unpredictable movements of a drunkard. A drunken master sways, tottering on unsteady feet, to present what seems like an incompetent combatant who proves frustrating to engage. The drunken master's erratic stumbles conceal a carefully executed dance of blocks, parries, advances, attacks, and retreats.

A drunken master often enjoys playing the fool to bring gladness to the despondent or to demonstrate humility to the arrogant, but when battle is joined, the drunken master can be a maddening, masterful foe.

WAY OF THE DRUNKEN MASTER FEATURES

Monk Level	Feature
3rd	Bonus Proficiencies, Drunken Technique
6th	Tipsy Sway
11th	Drunkard's Luck
17th	Intoxicated Frenzy

WAY OF THE KENSEI

Monks of the Way of the Kensei train relentlessly with their weapons, to the point where the weapon becomes an extension of the body. Founded on a mastery of sword fighting, the tradition has expanded to include many different weapons.

A kensei sees a weapon in much the same way a calligrapher or painter regards a pen or brush. Whatever the weapon, the kensei views it as a tool used to express the beauty and precision of the martial arts. That such mastery makes a kensei a peerless warrior is but a side effect of intense devotion, practice, and study.

WAY OF THE KENSEI FEATURES

Monk Level	Feature
3rd	Path of the Kensei (2 weapons)
6th	One with the Blade, Path of the Kensei (3 weapons)
11th	Sharpen the Blade, Path of the Kensei (4 weapons)
17th	Unerring Accuracy, Path of the Kensei (5 weapons)

PATH OF THE KENSEI

When you choose this tradition at 3rd level, your special martial arts training leads you to master the use of certain weapons. This path also includes instruction in the deft strokes of calligraphy or painting. You gain the following benefits.

Kensei Weapons. Choose two types of weapons to be your kensei weapons: one melee weapon and one ranged weapon. Each of these weapons can be any simple or martial weapon that lacks the heavy and special properties. The longbow is also a valid choice. You gain proficiency with these weapons if you don't already have it. Weapons of the chosen types are monk weapons for you. Many of this tradition's features work only with your kensei weapons. When you reach 6th, 11th, and 17th level in this class, you can choose another type of weapon—either melee or ranged—to be a kensei weapon for you, following the criteria above.

Agile Parry. If you make an unarmed strike as part of the Attack action on your turn and are holding a kensei weapon, you can use it to defend yourself if it is a melee weapon. You gain a +2 bonus to AC until the start of your next turn, while the weapon is in your hand and you aren't incapacitated.

Kensei's Shot. You can use a bonus action on your turn to make your ranged attacks with a kensei weapon more deadly. When you do so, any target you hit with a ranged attack using a kensei weapon takes an extra 1d4 damage of the weapon's type. You retain this benefit until the end of the current turn.

Way of the Brush. You gain proficiency with your choice of calligrapher's supplies or painter's supplies.

ONE WITH THE BLADE

At 6th level, you extend your ki into your kensei weapons, granting you the following benefits.

BONUS PROFICIENCIES

When you choose this tradition at 3rd level, you gain proficiency in the Performance skill if you don't already have it. Your martial arts technique mixes combat training with the precision of a dancer and the antics of a jester. You also gain proficiency with brewer's supplies if you don't already have it.

DRUNKEN TECHNIQUE

At 3rd level, you learn how to twist and turn quickly as part of your Flurry of Blows. Whenever you use Flurry of Blows, you gain the benefit of the Disengage action, and your walking speed increases by 10 feet until the end of the current turn.

TIPSY SWAY

Starting at 6th level, you can move in sudden, swaying ways. You gain the following benefits.

Leap to Your Feet. When you're prone, you can stand up by spending 5 feet of movement, rather than half your speed.

Redirect Attack. When a creature misses you with a melee attack roll, you can spend 1 ki point as a reaction to cause that attack to hit one creature of your choice, other than the attacker, that you can see within 5 feet of you.

DRUNKARD'S LUCK

Starting at 11th level, you always seem to get a lucky bounce at the right moment. When you make an ability check, an attack roll, or a saving throw and have disadvantage on the roll, you can spend 2 ki points to cancel the disadvantage for that roll.

INTOXICATED FRENZY

At 17th level, you gain the ability to make an overwhelming number of attacks against a group of enemies. When you use your Flurry of Blows, you can make up to three additional attacks with it (up to a total of five Flurry of Blows attacks), provided that each Flurry of Blows attack targets a different creature this turn.

Magic Kensei Weapons. Your attacks with your kensei weapons count as magical for the purpose of overcoming resistance and immunity to nonmagical attacks and damage.

Deft Strike. When you hit a target with a kensei weapon, you can spend 1 ki point to cause the weapon to deal extra damage to the target equal to your Martial Arts die. You can use this feature only once on each of your turns.

SHARPEN THE BLADE

At 11th level, you gain the ability to augment your weapons further with your ki. As a bonus action, you can expend up to 3 ki points to grant one kensei weapon you touch a bonus to attack and damage rolls when you attack with it. The bonus equals the number of ki points you spent. This bonus lasts for 1 minute or until you use this feature again. This feature has no effect on a magic weapon that already has a bonus to attack and damage rolls.

UNERRING ACCURACY

At 17th level, your mastery of weapons grants you extraordinary accuracy. If you miss with an attack roll using a monk weapon on your turn, you can reroll it. You can use this feature only once on each of your turns.

WAY OF THE SUN SOUL

Monks of the Way of the Sun Soul learn to channel their life energy into searing bolts of light. They teach that meditation can unlock the ability to unleash the indomitable light shed by the soul of every living creature.

WAY OF THE SUN SOUL FEATURES

Monk Level	Feature
3rd	Radiant Sun Bolt
6th	Searing Arc Strike
11th	Searing Sunburst
17th	Sun Shield

RADIANT SUN BOLT

Starting when you choose this tradition at 3rd level, you can hurl searing bolts of magical radiance.

You gain a new attack option that you can use with the Attack action. This special attack is a ranged spell attack with a range of 30 feet. You are proficient with it, and you add your Dexterity modifier to its attack and damage rolls. Its damage is radiant, and its damage die is a d4. This die changes as you gain monk levels, as shown in the Martial Arts column of the Monk table.

When you take the Attack action on your turn and use this special attack as part of it, you can spend 1 ki point to make the special attack twice as a bonus action.

When you gain the Extra Attack feature, this special attack can be used for any of the attacks you make as part of the Attack action.

SEARING ARC STRIKE

At 6th level, you gain the ability to channel your ki into searing waves of energy. Immediately after you take the Attack action on your turn, you can spend 2 ki points to cast the *burning hands* spell as a bonus action.

You can spend additional ki points to cast *burning hands* as a higher-level spell. Each additional ki point you spend increases the spell's level by 1. The maximum number of ki points (2 plus any additional points) that you can spend on the spell equals half your monk level.

SEARING SUNBURST

At 11th level, you gain the ability to create an orb of light that erupts into a devastating explosion. As an action, you magically create an orb and hurl it at a point you choose within 150 feet, where it erupts into a sphere of radiant light for a brief but deadly instant.

Each creature in that 20-foot-radius sphere must succeed on a Constitution saving throw or take 2d6 radiant damage. A creature doesn't need to make the save if the creature is behind total cover that is opaque.

You can increase the sphere's damage by spending ki points. Each point you spend, to a maximum of 3, increases the damage by 2d6.

SUN SHIELD

At 17th level, you become wreathed in a luminous, magical aura. You shed bright light in a 30-foot radius and dim light for an additional 30 feet. You can extinguish or restore the light as a bonus action.

If a creature hits you with a melee attack while this light shines, you can use your reaction to deal radiant damage to the creature. The radiant damage equals 5 + your Wisdom modifier.

PALADIN

THE TRUE WORTH OF A PALADIN IS MEASURED NOT IN *foes defeated or dungeons plundered. It is measured in lives saved and hearts turned to the causes of mercy and justice.*

—Isteval

A paladin is a living embodiment of an oath—a promise or a vow made manifest in the person of a holy warrior who has the skill and the determination to see the cause through to the end. Some paladins devote themselves expressly to protecting the innocent and spreading justice in the world, while others resolve to attain that goal by conquering those who stand defiant and bringing them under the rule of law.

Although no paladin in the world could be described as typical, a number of them are narrow-minded do-gooders who refuse to tolerate even the smallest deviation from their own outlook. Paladins who take up the adventuring life, however, rarely remain so rigid in their attitudes—if only to keep from alienating their companions.

You can flesh out your paladin character by using the suggestions below. It's important to keep in mind that most paladins aren't robots. They have doubts and prejudices and harbor contradictory thoughts just as any other character does. Some are compelled by an internal motivation that might sometimes be at odds with the principles of their oaths.

PERSONAL GOAL

The precepts of a paladin's oath provide purpose to the character and dictate an ultimate goal or an overall intent that the paladin abides by and advances. Aside from that, some paladins are driven by a personal goal that either complements or transcends the dictates of their oaths. Paladins who swear different oaths might have the same personal goal, differing only in how they apply that goal to their actions when upholding their oaths.

If your paladin character has a personal goal, it might be drawn from some life event and thus not directly tied to the oath.

PERSONAL GOALS

d6	Goal
1	**Peace.** You fight so that future generations will not have to.
2	**Revenge.** Your oath is the vehicle through which you will right an ancient wrong.
3	**Duty.** You will live up to what you have sworn to do, or die trying.
4	**Leadership.** You will win a great battle that bards will sing about, and in so doing, you will become an example to inspire others.
5	**Faith.** You know your path is righteous, or else the gods would not have set you upon it.
6	**Glory.** You will lead the world into a grand new era, one that will be branded with your name.

SYMBOL

Paladins are mindful of the influence of symbols, and many of them adopt or design an artistic device that bears a distinctive image. Your symbol exemplifies the oath you have taken and communicates that message to those around you, friend and foe alike.

Your symbol might be displayed on a banner, a flag, or your clothing for all to see. Or it could be less obvious, such as a trinket or a token that you carry concealed on your person.

SYMBOLS

d6	Symbol
1	A dragon, emblematic of your nobility in peace and your ferocity in combat
2	A clenched fist, because you are always ready to fight for your beliefs
3	An upraised open hand, indicating your preference for diplomacy over combat
4	A red heart, showing the world your commitment to justice
5	A black heart, signifying that emotions such as pity do not sway your dedication to your oath
6	An unblinking eye, meaning that you are ever alert to all threats against your cause

NEMESIS

Their adherence to a sacred oath demands that paladins take an active stance in carrying their beliefs into the world. This activity naturally leads to conflict with creatures or entities that oppose those beliefs. Among those opponents, one often stands out as a paladin's most persistent or most formidable foe—a nemesis whose presence or influence is a constant factor in a paladin's life.

Your paladin character might have an enemy that dates from the days before you took up your path. Or you could be a target because when you became a paladin, you immediately attracted the attention of those that would do you in. If you have a nemesis, who or what is it? Whom among your enemies do you consider to be the biggest threat to achieving your goals?

NEMESES

d6	Nemesis
1	A mighty orc war chief who threatens to overrun and destroy everything you hold sacred
2	A fiend or a celestial, the agent of a power of the Outer Planes, who has been charged with corrupting or redeeming you, as appropriate
3	A dragon whose servants dog your steps
4	A high priest who sees you as a misguided fool and wants you to abandon your religion
5	A rival paladin who trained with you but became an oath-breaker and holds you responsible
6	A vampire who has sworn revenge against all paladins after being defeated by one

TEMPTATION

Although paladins are dedicated to their oaths, they are mortals, and thus they are flawed. Many of them exhibit a type of behavior or hold to an attitude that is not in keeping with the highest ideals of their calling.

What is the temptation that your character succumbs to or finds it difficult to resist?

TEMPTATIONS

d6	Temptation
1	**Fury.** When your anger is roused, you have trouble thinking straight, and you fear you might do something you'll regret.
2	**Pride.** Your deeds are noteworthy, and no one takes note of them more often than you.
3	**Lust.** You can't resist an attractive face and a pleasant smile.
4	**Envy.** You are mindful of what some famous folk have accomplished, and you feel inadequate when your deeds don't compare to theirs.
5	**Despair.** You consider the great strength of the enemies you must defeat, and at times you see no way to achieve final victory.
6	**Greed.** Regardless of how much glory and treasure you amass, it's never enough for you.

SACRED OATHS

At 3rd level, a paladin gains the Sacred Oath feature. The following options are available to a paladin, in addition to those offered in the *Player's Handbook*: the Oath of Conquest and the Oath of Redemption.

PALADIN OF CONQUEST

OATH OF CONQUEST

The Oath of Conquest calls to paladins who seek glory in battle and the subjugation of their enemies. It isn't enough for these paladins to establish order. They must crush the forces of chaos. Sometimes called knight tyrants or iron mongers, those who swear this oath gather into grim orders that serve gods or philosophies of war and well-ordered might.

Some of these paladins go so far as to consort with the powers of the Nine Hells, valuing the rule of law over the balm of mercy. The archdevil Bel, warlord of Avernus, counts many of these paladins—called hell knights—as his most ardent supporters. Hell knights cover their armor with trophies taken from fallen enemies, a grim warning to any who dare oppose them and the decrees of their lords. These knights are often most fiercely resisted by other paladins of this oath, who believe that the hell knights have wandered too far into darkness.

TENETS OF CONQUEST

A paladin who takes this oath has the tenets of conquest seared on the upper arm.

Douse the Flame of Hope. It is not enough to merely defeat an enemy in battle. Your victory must be so overwhelming that your enemies' will to fight is shattered forever. A blade can end a life. Fear can end an empire.

Rule with an Iron Fist. Once you have conquered, tolerate no dissent. Your word is law. Those who obey it shall be favored. Those who defy it shall be punished as an example to all who might follow.

Strength Above All. You shall rule until a stronger one arises. Then you must grow mightier and meet the challenge, or fall to your own ruin.

OATH OF CONQUEST FEATURES

Paladin Level	Feature
3rd	Oath Spells, Channel Divinity
7th	Aura of Conquest (10 ft.)
15th	Scornful Rebuke
18th	Aura of Conquest (30 ft.)
20th	Invincible Conqueror

OATH SPELLS

You gain oath spells at the paladin levels listed in the Oath of Conquest Spells table. See the Sacred Oath class feature for how oath spells work.

OATH OF CONQUEST SPELLS

Paladin Level	Spells
3rd	armor of Agathys, command
5th	hold person, spiritual weapon
9th	bestow curse, fear
13th	dominate beast, stoneskin
17th	cloudkill, dominate person

CHANNEL DIVINITY

When you take this oath at 3rd level, you gain the following two Channel Divinity options. See the Sacred Oath class feature for how Channel Divinity works.

Conquering Presence. You can use your Channel Divinity to exude a terrifying presence. As an action, you force each creature of your choice that you can see within 30 feet of you to make a Wisdom saving throw. On a failed save, a creature becomes frightened of you for 1 minute. The frightened creature can repeat this saving throw at the end of each of its turns, ending the effect on itself on a success.

Guided Strike. You can use your Channel Divinity to strike with supernatural accuracy. When you make an attack roll, you can use your Channel Divinity to gain a +10 bonus to the roll. You make this choice after you see the roll, but before the DM says whether the attack hits or misses.

AURA OF CONQUEST

Starting at 7th level, you constantly emanate a menacing aura while you're not incapacitated. The aura extends 10 feet from you in every direction, but not through total cover.

If a creature is frightened of you, its speed is reduced to 0 while in the aura, and that creature takes psychic damage equal to half your paladin level if it starts its turn there.

At 18th level, the range of this aura increases to 30 feet.

SCORNFUL REBUKE

Starting at 15th level, those who dare to strike you are psychically punished for their audacity. Whenever a creature hits you with an attack, that creature takes psychic damage equal to your Charisma modifier (minimum of 1) if you're not incapacitated.

INVINCIBLE CONQUEROR

At 20th level, you gain the ability to harness extraordinary martial prowess. As an action, you can magically become an avatar of conquest, gaining the following benefits for 1 minute:

- You have resistance to all damage.
- When you take the Attack action on your turn, you can make one additional attack as part of that action.
- Your melee weapon attacks score a critical hit on a roll of 19 or 20 on the d20.

Once you use this feature, you can't use it again until you finish a long rest.

OATH OF REDEMPTION

The Oath of Redemption sets a paladin on a difficult path, one that requires a holy warrior to use violence only as a last resort. Paladins who dedicate themselves to this oath believe that any person can be redeemed and that the path of benevolence and justice is one that anyone can walk. These paladins face evil creatures in the hope of turning their foes to the light, and they slay their enemies only when such a deed will clearly save other lives. Paladins who follow this path are known as redeemers.

While redeemers are idealists, they are no fools. Redeemers know that undead, demons, devils, and other supernatural threats can be inherently evil. Against such foes, paladins who swear this oath bring the full wrath of their weapons and spells to bear. Yet the redeemers still pray that, one day, even creatures of wickedness will invite their own redemption.

TENETS OF REDEMPTION

The tenets of the Oath of Redemption hold a paladin to a high standard of peace and justice.

Peace. Violence is a weapon of last resort. Diplomacy and understanding are the paths to long-lasting peace.

Innocence. All people begin life in an innocent state, and it is their environment or the influence of dark forces that drives them to evil. By setting the proper example, and working to heal the wounds of a deeply flawed world, you can set anyone on a righteous path.

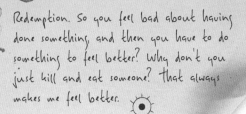

Redemption. So you feel bad about having done something, and then you have to do something to feel better? Why don't you just kill and eat someone? That always makes me feel better.

Patience. Change takes time. Those who have walked the path of the wicked must be given reminders to keep them honest and true. Once you have planted the seed of righteousness in a creature, you must work day after day to allow that seed to survive and flourish.

Wisdom. Your heart and mind must stay clear, for eventually you will be forced to admit defeat. While every creature can be redeemed, some are so far along the path of evil that you have no choice but to end their lives for the greater good. Any such action must be carefully weighed and the consequences fully understood, but once you have made the decision, follow through with it knowing your path is just.

OATH OF REDEMPTION FEATURES

Paladin Level	Feature
3rd	Oath Spells, Channel Divinity
7th	Aura of the Guardian (10 ft.)
15th	Protective Spirit
18th	Aura of the Guardian (30 ft.)
20th	Emissary of Redemption

OATH SPELLS

You gain oath spells at the paladin levels listed in the Oath of Redemption Spells table. See the Sacred Oath class feature for how oath spells work.

OATH OF REDEMPTION SPELLS

Paladin Level	Spells
3rd	sanctuary, sleep
5th	calm emotions, hold person
9th	counterspell, hypnotic pattern
13th	Otiluke's resilient sphere, stoneskin
17th	hold monster, wall of force

CHANNEL DIVINITY

When you take this oath at 3rd level, you gain the following two Channel Divinity options.

Emissary of Peace. You can use your Channel Divinity to augment your presence with divine power. As a bonus action, you grant yourself a +5 bonus to Charisma (Persuasion) checks for the next 10 minutes.

Rebuke the Violent. You can use your Channel Divinity to rebuke those who use violence. Immediately after an attacker within 30 feet of you deals damage with an attack against a creature other than you, you can use your reaction to force the attacker to make a Wisdom saving throw. On a failed save, the attacker takes radiant damage equal to the damage it just dealt. On a successful save, it takes half as much damage.

AURA OF THE GUARDIAN

Starting at 7th level, you can shield others from harm at the cost of your own health. When a creature within 10 feet of you takes damage, you can use your reaction to magically take that damage, instead of that creature taking it. This feature doesn't transfer any other effects that might accompany the damage, and this damage can't be reduced in any way.

At 18th level, the range of this aura increases to 30 feet.

PROTECTIVE SPIRIT

Starting at 15th level, a holy presence mends your wounds in battle. You regain hit points equal to 1d6 + half your paladin level if you end your turn in combat with fewer than half of your hit points remaining and you aren't incapacitated.

EMISSARY OF REDEMPTION

At 20th level, you become an avatar of peace, which gives you two benefits:

- You have resistance to all damage dealt by other creatures (their attacks, spells, and other effects).
- Whenever a creature hits you with an attack, it takes radiant damage equal to half the damage you take from the attack.

If you attack a creature, cast a spell on it, or deal damage to it by any means but this feature, neither benefit works against that creature until you finish a long rest.

I'm a monster. Are you going to try to kill me? Didn't think so. Go kill some goblins or something. On second thought, goblins aren't monsters—they're people. So maybe you should call yourself a people killer.

RANGER

I SPEND A LOT OF MY LIFE AWAY FROM CIVILIZATION, *keeping to its fringes to protect it. Don't assume that because I don't bend the knee to your king that I haven't done more to protect him than all his knights put together.*

—Soveliss

Rangers are free-minded wanderers and seekers who patrol the edges of civilized territory, turning back the denizens of the wild lands beyond. It is a thankless job, since their efforts are rarely understood and almost never rewarded. Yet rangers persist in their duties, never doubting that their work makes the world a safer place.

A relationship with civilization informs every ranger's personality and history. Some rangers see themselves as enforcers of the law and bringers of justice on civilization's frontier, answering to no sovereign power. Others are survivalists who eschew civilization altogether. They vanquish monsters to keep themselves safe while they live in and travel through the perilous wild areas of the world. If their efforts also benefit the kingdoms and other civilized realms that they avoid, so be it.

If you're creating or playing a ranger character, the following sections offer ideas for embellishing the character and enhancing your roleplaying experience.

VIEW OF THE WORLD

A ranger's view of the world begins (and sometimes ends) with that character's outlook toward civilized folk and the places they occupy. Some rangers have an attitude toward civilization that's deeply rooted in disdain, while others pity the people they have sworn to protect—though on the battlefield, it's impossible to tell the difference between one ranger and another. Indeed, to those who have seen them operate and been the beneficiaries of their prowess, it scarcely matters why rangers do what they do. That said, no two rangers are likely to express their opinions on any matter in the same way.

If you haven't yet thought about the details of your character's worldview, consider putting a finer point on things by summarizing that viewpoint in a short statement (such as the entries on the following table). How might that feeling affect the way you conduct yourself?

VIEWS OF THE WORLD

d6	View
1	Towns and cities are the best places for those who can't survive on their own.
2	The advancement of civilization is the best way to thwart chaos, but its reach must be monitored.
3	Towns and cities are a necessary evil, but once the wilderness is purged of supernatural threats, we will need them no more.
4	Walls are for cowards, who huddle behind them while others do the work of making the world safe.
5	Visiting a town is not unpleasant, but after a few days I feel the irresistible call to return to the wild.
6	Cities breed weakness by isolating folk from the harsh lessons of the wild.

HOMELAND

All rangers, regardless of how they came to take up the profession, have a strong connection to the natural world and its various terrains. For some rangers, the wilderness is where they grew up, either as a result of being born there or moving there at a young age. For other rangers, civilization was originally home, but the wilderness became a second homeland.

Think of your character's backstory and decide what terrain feels most like home, whether or not you were born there. What does that terrain say about your personality? Does it influence which spells you choose to learn? Have your experiences there shaped who your favored enemies are?

HOMELANDS

d6	Homeland
1	You patrolled an ancient forest, darkened and corrupted by several crossings to the Shadowfell.
2	As part of a group of nomads, you acquired the skills for surviving in the desert.
3	Your early life in the Underdark prepared you for the challenges of combating its denizens.
4	You dwelled on the edge of a swamp, in an area imperiled by land creatures as well as aquatic ones.
5	Because you grew up among the peaks, finding the best path through the mountains is second nature to you.
6	You wandered the far north, learning how to protect yourself and prosper in a realm overrun by ice.

LEFT TO RIGHT: HORIZON WALKER, MONSTER SLAYER, AND GLOOM STALKER

SWORN ENEMY

Every ranger begins with a favored enemy (or two). The determination of a favored enemy might be tied to a specific event in the character's early life, or it might be entirely a matter of choice.

What spurred your character to select a particular enemy? Was the choice made because of tradition or curiosity, or do you have a grudge to settle?

SWORN ENEMIES

d6	Enemy
1	You seek revenge on nature's behalf for the great transgressions your foe has committed.
2	Your forebears or predecessors fought these creatures, and so shall you.
3	You bear no enmity toward your foe. You stalk such creatures as a hunter tracks down a wild animal.
4	You find your foe fascinating, and you collect books of tales and history concerning it.
5	You collect tokens of your fallen enemies to remind you of each kill.
6	You respect your chosen enemy, and you see your battles as a test of respective skills.

RANGER ARCHETYPES

At 3rd level, a ranger gains the Ranger Archetype feature. The following options are available to a ranger, in addition to those offered in the *Player's Handbook*: the Gloom Stalker, the Horizon Walker, and the Monster Slayer.

GLOOM STALKER

Gloom Stalkers are at home in the darkest places: deep under the earth, in gloomy alleyways, in primeval forests, and wherever else the light dims. Most folk enter such places with trepidation, but a Gloom Stalker ventures boldly into the darkness, seeking to ambush threats before they can reach the broader world. Such rangers are often found in the Underdark, but they will go any place where evil lurks in the shadows.

GLOOM STALKER FEATURES

Ranger Level	Feature
3rd	Gloom Stalker Magic, Dread Ambusher, Umbral Sight
7th	Iron Mind
11th	Stalker's Flurry
15th	Shadowy Dodge

GLOOM STALKER MAGIC

Starting at 3rd level, you learn an additional spell when you reach certain levels in this class, as shown in the Gloom Stalker Spells table. The spell counts as a ranger spell for you, but it doesn't count against the number of ranger spells you know.

GLOOM STALKER SPELLS

Ranger Level	Spell
3rd	disguise self
5th	rope trick
9th	fear
13th	greater invisibility
17th	seeming

DREAD AMBUSHER

At 3rd level, you master the art of the ambush. You can give yourself a bonus to your initiative rolls equal to your Wisdom modifier.

At the start of your first turn of each combat, your walking speed increases by 10 feet, which lasts until the end of that turn. If you take the Attack action on that turn, you can make one additional weapon attack as part of that action. If that attack hits, the target takes an extra 1d8 damage of the weapon's damage type.

UMBRAL SIGHT

At 3rd level, you gain darkvision out to a range of 60 feet. If you already have darkvision from your race, its range increases by 30 feet.

You are also adept at evading creatures that rely on darkvision. While in darkness, you are invisible to any creature that relies on darkvision to see you in that darkness.

IRON MIND

By 7th level, you have honed your ability to resist the mind-altering powers of your prey. You gain proficiency in Wisdom saving throws. If you already have this proficiency, you instead gain proficiency in Intelligence or Charisma saving throws (your choice).

STALKER'S FLURRY

At 11th level, you learn to attack with such unexpected speed that you can turn a miss into another strike. Once on each of your turns when you miss with a weapon attack, you can make another weapon attack as part of the same action.

SHADOWY DODGE

Starting at 15th level, you can dodge in unforeseen ways, with wisps of supernatural shadow around you. Whenever a creature makes an attack roll against you and doesn't have advantage on the roll, you can use your reaction to impose disadvantage on it. You must use this feature before you know the outcome of the attack roll.

HORIZON WALKER

Horizon Walkers guard the world against threats that originate from other planes or that seek to ravage the mortal realm with otherworldly magic. They seek out planar portals and keep watch over them, venturing to the Inner Planes and the Outer Planes as needed to pursue their foes. These rangers are also friends to any forces in the multiverse—especially benevolent dragons, fey, and elementals—that work to preserve life and the order of the planes.

HORIZON WALKER FEATURES

Ranger Level	Feature
3rd	Horizon Walker Magic, Detect Portal, Planar Warrior (1d8)
7th	Ethereal Step
11th	Distant Strike, Planar Warrior (2d8)
15th	Spectral Defense

HORIZON WALKER MAGIC

Starting at 3rd level, you learn an additional spell when you reach certain levels in this class, as shown in the Horizon Walker Spells table. The spell counts as a ranger spell for you, but it doesn't count against the number of ranger spells you know.

HORIZON WALKER SPELLS

Ranger Level	Spell
3rd	protection from evil and good
5th	misty step
9th	haste
13th	banishment
17th	teleportation circle

DETECT PORTAL

At 3rd level, you gain the ability to magically sense the presence of a planar portal. As an action, you detect the distance and direction to the closest planar portal within 1 mile of you.

Once you use this feature, you can't use it again until you finish a short or long rest.

See the "Planar Travel" section in chapter 2 of the *Dungeon Master's Guide* for examples of planar portals.

PLANAR WARRIOR

At 3rd level, you learn to draw on the energy of the multiverse to augment your attacks.

As a bonus action, choose one creature you can see within 30 feet of you. The next time you hit that creature on this turn with a weapon attack, all damage dealt by the attack becomes force damage, and the creature takes an extra 1d8 force damage from the attack. When you reach 11th level in this class, the extra damage increases to 2d8.

ETHEREAL STEP

At 7th level, you learn to step through the Ethereal Plane. As a bonus action, you can cast the *etherealness* spell with this feature, without expending a spell slot, but the spell ends at the end of the current turn.

Once you use this feature, you can't use it again until you finish a short or long rest.

DISTANT STRIKE

At 11th level, you gain the ability to pass between the planes in the blink of an eye. When you take the Attack action, you can teleport up to 10 feet before each attack to an unoccupied space you can see.

If you attack at least two different creatures with the action, you can make one additional attack with it against a third creature.

SPECTRAL DEFENSE

At 15th level, your ability to move between planes enables you to slip through the planar boundaries to lessen the harm done to you during battle. When you take damage from an attack, you can use your reaction to give yourself resistance to all of that attack's damage on this turn.

MONSTER SLAYER

You have dedicated yourself to hunting down creatures of the night and wielders of grim magic. A Monster Slayer seeks out vampires, dragons, evil fey, fiends, and other magical threats. Trained in supernatural techniques to overcome such monsters, slayers are experts at unearthing and defeating mighty, mystical foes.

MONSTER SLAYER FEATURES

Ranger Level	Feature
3rd	Monster Slayer Magic, Hunter's Sense, Slayer's Prey
7th	Supernatural Defense
11th	Magic-User's Nemesis
15th	Slayer's Counter

MONSTER SLAYER MAGIC

Starting at 3rd level, you learn an additional spell when you reach certain levels in this class, as shown in the Monster Slayer Spells table. The spell counts as a ranger spell for you, but it doesn't count against the number of ranger spells you know.

MONSTER SLAYER SPELLS

Ranger Level	Spell
3rd	*protection from evil and good*
5th	*zone of truth*
9th	*magic circle*
13th	*banishment*
17th	*hold monster*

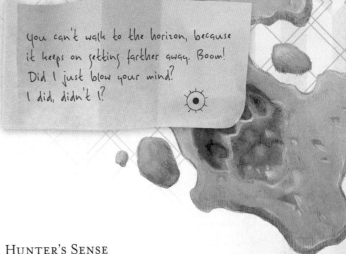

You can't walk to the horizon, because it keeps on getting farther away. Boom! Did I just blow your mind? I did, didn't I?

HUNTER'S SENSE

At 3rd level, you gain the ability to peer at a creature and magically discern how best to hurt it. As an action, choose one creature you can see within 60 feet of you. You immediately learn whether the creature has any damage immunities, resistances, or vulnerabilities and what they are. If the creature is hidden from divination magic, you sense that it has no damage immunities, resistances, or vulnerabilities.

You can use this feature a number of times equal to your Wisdom modifier (minimum of once). You regain all expended uses of it when you finish a long rest.

SLAYER'S PREY

Starting at 3rd level, you can focus your ire on one foe, increasing the harm you inflict on it. As a bonus action, you designate one creature you can see within 60 feet of you as the target of this feature. The first time each turn that you hit that target with a weapon attack, it takes an extra 1d6 damage from the weapon.

This benefit lasts until you finish a short or long rest. It ends early if you designate a different creature.

SUPERNATURAL DEFENSE

At 7th level, you gain extra resilience against your prey's assaults on your mind and body. Whenever the target of your Slayer's Prey forces you to make a saving throw and whenever you make an ability check to escape that target's grapple, add 1d6 to your roll.

MAGIC-USER'S NEMESIS

At 11th level, you gain the ability to thwart someone else's magic. When you see a creature casting a spell or teleporting within 60 feet of you, you can use your reaction to try to magically foil it. The creature must succeed on a Wisdom saving throw against your spell save DC, or its spell or teleport fails and is wasted.

Once you use this feature, you can't use it again until you finish a short or long rest.

SLAYER'S COUNTER

At 15th level, you gain the ability to counterattack when your prey tries to sabotage you. If the target of your Slayer's Prey forces you to make a saving throw, you can use your reaction to make one weapon attack against the quarry. You make this attack immediately before making the saving throw. If your attack hits, your save automatically succeeds, in addition to the attack's normal effects.

thieves are the worst. I hate anyone that handles my stuff when I'm not looking, especially if they don't put it back where they found it.

ROGUE

PEOPLE FORGET THAT THE ENTIRE POINT OF VENTURING *down into a dusty tomb is to bring back the prizes hidden away there. Fighting is for fools. Dead men can't spend their fortunes.*

—Barnabas Bladecutter

When brute force won't get the job done, or when magic isn't available or appropriate, the rogue rises to the fore. With skills tied to stealth, subterfuge, and trickery, rogues can get into and out of trouble in ways that few other characters can emulate.

Some rogues who turn to adventuring are former criminals who have decided that dodging monsters is preferable to remaining one step ahead of the law. Others are professional killers in search of a profitable application of their talents between contracts. Some simply love the thrill of overcoming any challenge that stands in their way.

On adventures, a rogue is likely to mix an outwardly cautious approach—few rogues enjoy combat—with a ravenous hunger for loot. Most of the time, in a rogue's mind, taking up arms against a creature is not about killing the creature but about becoming the new owner of its treasure.

The following sections explore certain facets of what it means to be a rogue, which you can use to add depth to your character.

GUILTY PLEASURE

Most of what rogues do revolves around obtaining treasure and preventing others from doing the same. Little gets in the way of attaining those goals, except that many rogues are enticed away from that path by a compulsion that clouds their thinking—an irresistible need that must be satisfied, even if doing so is risky.

A rogue's guilty pleasure could be the acquisition of a physical item, something to be experienced, or a way of conducting oneself at certain times. One rogue might not be able to pass up any loot made of silver, for instance, even if said loot is hanging around the neck of a castle guard. Another one can't go through a day in the city without lifting a purse or two, just to keep in practice.

What's the one form of temptation that your rogue character can't resist when the opportunity presents itself, even if giving into it might mean trouble for you and your companions?

GUILTY PLEASURES

d6	Pleasure
1	Large gems
2	A smile from a pretty face
3	A new ring for your finger
4	The chance to deflate someone's ego
5	The finest food and drink
6	Adding to your collection of exotic coins

ADVERSARY

Naturally, those who enforce the law are bound to come up against those who break it, and it's the rare rogue who isn't featured on at least one wanted poster. Beyond that, it's in the nature of their profession that rogues often come into contact with criminal elements, whether out of choice or necessity. Some of those people can be adversaries too, and they're likely to be harder to deal with than the average member of the city watch.

If your character's backstory doesn't already include a personage of this sort, you could work with your DM to come up with a reason why an adversary has appeared in your life. Perhaps you've been the subject of scrutiny for a while from someone who wants to use you for nefarious purposes and has just now become known to you. Such an incident could be the basis for an upcoming adventure.

Does your rogue character have an adversary who also happens to be a criminal? If so, how is this relationship affecting your life?

ADVERSARIES

d6	Adversary
1	The pirate captain on whose ship you once served; what you call moving on, the captain calls mutiny
2	A master spy to whom you unwittingly fed bad information, which led to the assassination of the wrong target
3	The master of the local thieves' guild, who wants you to join the organization or leave town
4	An art collector who uses illegal means to acquire masterpieces
5	A fence who uses you as a messenger to set up illicit meetings
6	The proprietor of an illegal pit fighting arena where you once took bets

LEFT TO RIGHT: SWASHBUCKLER, MASTERMIND, INQUISITIVE, AND SCOUT

BENEFACTOR

Few rogues make it far in life before needing someone's help, which means thereafter owing that benefactor a significant debt.

If your character's backstory doesn't already include a personage of this sort, you could work with your DM to determine why a benefactor has appeared in your life. Perhaps you benefited from something your benefactor did for you without realizing who was responsible, and that person has now just become known to you. Who helped you in the past, whether or not you knew it at the time, and what do you owe that person as recompense?

BENEFACTORS

d6	Benefactor
1	A smuggler kept you from getting caught but lost a valuable shipment in doing so. Now you owe that person an equally valuable favor.
2	The Beggar King has hidden you from your pursuers many times, in return for future considerations.
3	A magistrate once kept you out of jail in return for information on a powerful crime lord.
4	Your parents used their savings to bail you out of trouble in your younger days and are now destitute.
5	A dragon didn't eat you when it had a chance, and in return you promised to set aside choice pieces of treasure for it.
6	A druid once helped you out of a tight spot; now any random animal you see could be that benefactor, perhaps come to claim a return favor.

ROGUISH ARCHETYPES

At 3rd level, a rogue gains the Roguish Archetype feature. The following options are available to a rogue, in addition to those offered in the *Player's Handbook*: the Inquisitive, the Mastermind, the Scout, and the Swashbuckler.

INQUISITIVE

As an archetypal Inquisitive, you excel at rooting out secrets and unraveling mysteries. You rely on your sharp eye for detail, but also on your finely honed ability to read the words and deeds of other creatures to determine their true intent. You excel at defeating creatures that hide among and prey upon ordinary folk, and your mastery of lore and your keen deductions make you well equipped to expose and end hidden evils.

INQUISITIVE FEATURES

Rogue Level	Feature
3rd	Ear for Deceit, Eye for Detail, Insightful Fighting
9th	Steady Eye
13th	Unerring Eye
17th	Eye for Weakness

EAR FOR DECEIT

When you choose this archetype at 3rd level, you develop a talent for picking out lies. Whenever you make a Wisdom (Insight) check to determine whether a creature is lying, treat a roll of 7 or lower on the d20 as an 8.

Oh, please. If anyone is a mastermind around here, it's me. You're like a master doofus or a master dummy. No, you are!

Eye for Detail

Starting at 3rd level, you can use a bonus action to make a Wisdom (Perception) check to spot a hidden creature or object or to make an Intelligence (Investigation) check to uncover or decipher clues.

Insightful Fighting

At 3rd level, you gain the ability to decipher an opponent's tactics and develop a counter to them. As a bonus action, you can make a Wisdom (Insight) check against a creature you can see that isn't incapacitated, contested by the target's Charisma (Deception) check. If you succeed, you can use your Sneak Attack against that target even if you don't have advantage on the attack roll, but not if you have disadvantage on it.

This benefit lasts for 1 minute or until you successfully use this feature against a different target.

Steady Eye

Starting at 9th level, you have advantage on any Wisdom (Perception) or Intelligence (Investigation) check if you move no more than half your speed on the same turn.

Unerring Eye

Beginning at 13th level, your senses are almost impossible to foil. As an action, you sense the presence of illusions, shapechangers not in their original form, and other magic designed to deceive the senses within 30 feet of you, provided you aren't blinded or deafened. You sense that an effect is attempting to trick you, but you gain no insight into what is hidden or into its true nature.

You can use this feature a number of times equal to your Wisdom modifier (minimum of once), and you regain all expended uses of it when you finish a long rest.

Eye for Weakness

At 17th level, you learn to exploit a creature's weaknesses by carefully studying its tactics and movement. While your Insightful Fighting feature applies to a creature, your Sneak Attack damage against that creature increases by 3d6.

Mastermind

Your focus is on people and on the influence and secrets they have. Many spies, courtiers, and schemers follow this archetype, leading lives of intrigue. Words are your weapons as often as knives or poison, and secrets and favors are some of your favorite treasures.

Mastermind Features

Rogue Level	Feature
3rd	Master of Intrigue, Master of Tactics
9th	Insightful Manipulator
13th	Misdirection
17th	Soul of Deceit

Master of Intrigue

When you choose this archetype at 3rd level, you gain proficiency with the disguise kit, the forgery kit, and one gaming set of your choice. You also learn two languages of your choice.

Additionally, you can unerringly mimic the speech patterns and accent of a creature that you hear speak for at least 1 minute, enabling you to pass yourself off as a native speaker of a particular land, provided that you know the language.

Master of Tactics

Starting at 3rd level, you can use the Help action as a bonus action. Additionally, when you use the Help action to aid an ally in attacking a creature, the target of that attack can be within 30 feet of you, rather than within 5 feet of you, if the target can see or hear you.

Insightful Manipulator

Starting at 9th level, if you spend at least 1 minute observing or interacting with another creature outside combat, you can learn certain information about its capabilities compared to your own. The DM tells you if the creature is your equal, superior, or inferior in regard to two of the following characteristics of your choice:

- Intelligence score
- Wisdom score
- Charisma score
- Class levels (if any)

At the DM's option, you might also realize you know a piece of the creature's history or one of its personality traits, if it has any.

Misdirection

Beginning at 13th level, you can sometimes cause another creature to suffer an attack meant for you. When you are targeted by an attack while a creature within 5 feet of you is granting you cover against that attack, you can use your reaction to have the attack target that creature instead of you.

Soul of Deceit

Starting at 17th level, your thoughts can't be read by telepathy or other means, unless you allow it. You can present false thoughts by succeeding on a Charisma (Deception) check contested by the mind reader's Wisdom (Insight) check.

Additionally, no matter what you say, magic that would determine if you are telling the truth indicates you are being truthful if you so choose, and you can't be compelled to tell the truth by magic.

Scout

You are skilled in stealth and surviving far from the streets of a city, allowing you to scout ahead of your companions during expeditions. Rogues who embrace this archetype are at home in the wilderness and among barbarians and rangers, and many Scouts serve as the eyes and ears of war bands. Ambusher, spy, bounty hunter—these are just a few of the roles that Scouts assume as they range the world.

Scout Features

Rogue Level	Feature
3rd	Skirmisher, Survivalist
9th	Superior Mobility
13th	Ambush Master
17th	Sudden Strike

Skirmisher

Starting at 3rd level, you are difficult to pin down during a fight. You can move up to half your speed as a reaction when an enemy ends its turn within 5 feet of you. This movement doesn't provoke opportunity attacks.

Survivalist

When you choose this archetype at 3rd level, you gain proficiency in the Nature and Survival skills if you don't already have it. Your proficiency bonus is doubled for any ability check you make that uses either of those proficiencies.

Superior Mobility

At 9th level, your walking speed increases by 10 feet. If you have a climbing or swimming speed, this increase applies to that speed as well.

Ambush Master

Starting at 13th level, you excel at leading ambushes and acting first in a fight.

You have advantage on initiative rolls. In addition, the first creature you hit during the first round of a combat becomes easier for you and others to strike; attack rolls against that target have advantage until the start of your next turn.

Sudden Strike

Starting at 17th level, you can strike with deadly speed. If you take the Attack action on your turn, you can make one additional attack as a bonus action. This attack can benefit from your Sneak Attack even if you have already used it this turn, but you can't use your Sneak Attack against the same target more than once in a turn.

Swashbuckler

You focus your training on the art of the blade, relying on speed, elegance, and charm in equal parts. While some warriors are brutes clad in heavy armor, your method of fighting looks almost like a performance. Duelists and pirates typically belong to this archetype.

A Swashbuckler excels in single combat, and can fight with two weapons while safely darting away from an opponent.

Swashbuckler Features

Rogue Level	Feature
3rd	Fancy Footwork, Rakish Audacity
9th	Panache
13th	Elegant Maneuver
17th	Master Duelist

Fancy Footwork

When you choose this archetype at 3rd level, you learn how to land a strike and then slip away without reprisal. During your turn, if you make a melee attack against a creature, that creature can't make opportunity attacks against you for the rest of your turn.

Rakish Audacity

Starting at 3rd level, your confidence propels you into battle. You can give yourself a bonus to your initiative rolls equal to your Charisma modifier.

You also gain an additional way to use your Sneak Attack; you don't need advantage on the attack roll to use your Sneak Attack against a creature if you are within 5 feet of it, no other creatures are within 5 feet of you, and you don't have disadvantage on the attack roll. All the other rules for Sneak Attack still apply to you.

Panache

At 9th level, your charm becomes extraordinarily beguiling. As an action, you can make a Charisma (Persuasion) check contested by a creature's Wisdom (Insight) check. The creature must be able to hear you, and the two of you must share a language.

If you succeed on the check and the creature is hostile to you, it has disadvantage on attack rolls against targets other than you and can't make opportunity attacks against targets other than you. This effect lasts for 1 minute, until one of your companions attacks the target or affects it with a spell, or until you and the target are more than 60 feet apart.

If you succeed on the check and the creature isn't hostile to you, it is charmed by you for 1 minute. While charmed, it regards you as a friendly acquaintance. This effect ends immediately if you or your companions do anything harmful to it.

Elegant Maneuver

Starting at 13th level, you can use a bonus action on your turn to gain advantage on the next Dexterity (Acrobatics) or Strength (Athletics) check you make during the same turn.

Master Duelist

Beginning at 17th level, your mastery of the blade lets you turn failure into success in combat. If you miss with an attack roll, you can roll it again with advantage. Once you do so, you can't use this feature again until you finish a short or long rest.

What's a swashbuckler? Do you swash buckles or buckle swashes? You can't tell me you don't think that word is funny.

Divine? Arcane? What difference does it make where magic comes from? You've got it or you don't. Fortunately, I've got loads of the stuff.

Sorcerer

PRACTICE AND STUDY ARE FOR AMATEURS. TRUE POWER *is a birthright.*

—Hennet, scion of Tiamat

When it comes to drawing forth their abilities in times of need, sorcerers have it easy compared to other characters. Their power not only rests within them, but it likely takes some effort to keep it at bay. Every sorcerer is born to the role, or stumbles into it through cosmic chance. Unlike other characters, who must actively learn, embrace, and pursue their talents, sorcerers have their power thrust upon them.

Because the idea of an innately magical being traveling among them does not sit well with many folk, sorcerers tend to breed mistrust and suspicion in others they come across. Nonetheless, many sorcerers succeed in overcoming that prejudice through deeds that benefit their less magically gifted contemporaries.

Sorcerers are often defined by the events surrounding the manifestation of their power. For those who receive it as an expected birthright, its appearance is a cause for celebration. Other sorcerers are treated as outcasts, banished from their homes after the sudden, terrifying arrival of their abilities.

Playing a sorcerer character can be as rewarding as it is challenging. The sections below offer suggestions on how to flesh out and personalize your persona.

Arcane Origin

Some sorcerers understand where their power came from, based on how their abilities manifested. Others can only speculate, since their powers came to them in a way that suggests no particular cause.

Does your character know the source of your magical power? Does it tie back to some distant relative, a cosmic event, or blind chance? If your sorcerer doesn't know where their power arose from, your DM can use this table (or select an origin) and reveal it to you when the information plays a role in the campaign.

Arcane Origins

d6	Origin
1	Your power arises from your family's bloodline. You are related to some powerful creature, or you inherited a blessing or a curse.
2	You are the reincarnation of a being from another plane of existence.
3	A powerful entity entered the world. Its magic changed you.
4	Your birth was prophesied in an ancient text, and you are foretold to use your power for terrible ends.
5	You are the product of generations of careful, selective breeding.
6	You were made in a vat by an alchemist.

Reaction

When a new sorcerer enters the world, either at birth or later when one's power becomes evident, the consequences of that event depend greatly on how its witnesses react to what they have seen.

When your sorcerer's powers appeared, how did the world around you respond? Were other people supportive, fearful, or somewhere in between?

Reactions

d6	Reaction
1	Your powers are seen as a great blessing by those around you, and you are expected to use them in service to your community.
2	Your powers caused destruction and even a death when they became evident, and you were treated as a criminal.
3	Your neighbors hate and fear your power, causing them to shun you.
4	You came to the attention of a sinister cult that plans on exploiting your abilities.
5	People around you believe that your powers are a curse levied on your family for a past transgression.
6	Your powers are believed to be tied to an ancient line of mad kings that supposedly ended in a bloody revolt over a century ago.

Supernatural Mark

A sorcerer at rest is almost indistinguishable from a normal person; it's only when their magic flies forth that sorcerers reveal their true nature. Even so, many sorcerers have a subtle but telling physical trait that sets them apart from other folk.

If your sorcerer has a supernatural mark, it might be one that's easily concealed, or it could be a source of pride that you keep on constant display.

SUPERNATURAL MARKS

d6	Mark
1	Your eyes are an unusual color, such as red.
2	You have an extra toe on one foot.
3	One of your ears is noticeably larger than the other.
4	Your hair grows at a prodigious rate.
5	You wrinkle your nose repeatedly while you are chewing.
6	A red splotch appears on your neck once a day, then vanishes after an hour.

SIGN OF SORCERY

As the world well knows, some sorcerers are better than others at controlling their spellcasting. Sometimes a wild display of magic gone awry emanates from a sorcerer who casts a spell. But even when one's magic goes off as planned, the act of casting is often accompanied by a telltale sign that makes it clear where that magical energy came from.

When your sorcerer character casts a spell, does the effort reveal itself in a sign of sorcery? Is this sign tied to your origin or some other aspect of who you are, or is it a seemingly random phenomenon?

SIGNS OF SORCERY

d6	Sign
1	You deliver the verbal components of your spells in the booming voice of a titan.
2	For a moment after you cast a spell, the area around you grows dark and gloomy.
3	You sweat profusely while casting a spell and for a few seconds thereafter.
4	Your hair and garments are briefly buffeted about, as if by a breeze, whenever you call forth a spell.
5	If you are standing when you cast a spell, you rise six inches into the air and gently float back down.
6	Illusory blue flames wreathe your head as you begin your casting, then abruptly disappear.

Sorcerous Origins

At 1st level, a sorcerer gains the Sorcerous Origin feature. The following options are available to a sorcerer, in addition to those offered in the *Player's Handbook*: Divine Soul, Shadow Magic, and Storm Sorcery.

Why do so many celestial things have bird wings and infernal things have bat wings? It seems arbitrary. There should be a bat angel!

Divine Soul

Sometimes the spark of magic that fuels a sorcerer comes from a divine source that glimmers within the soul. Having such a blessed soul is a sign that your innate magic might come from a distant but powerful familial connection to a divine being. Perhaps your ancestor was an angel, transformed into a mortal and sent to fight in a god's name. Or your birth might align with an ancient prophecy, marking you as a servant of the gods or a chosen vessel of divine magic.

A Divine Soul, with a natural magnetism, is seen as a threat by some religious hierarchies. As an outsider who commands sacred power, a Divine Soul can undermine an existing order by claiming a direct tie to the divine.

In some cultures, only those who can claim the power of a Divine Soul may command religious power. In these lands, ecclesiastical positions are dominated by a few bloodlines and preserved over generations.

Divine Soul Features

Sorcerer Level	Feature
1st	Divine Magic, Favored by the Gods
6th	Empowered Healing
14th	Otherworldly Wings
18th	Unearthly Recovery

Divine Magic

Your link to the divine allows you to learn spells from the cleric class. When your Spellcasting feature lets you learn or replace a sorcerer cantrip or a sorcerer spell of 1st level or higher, you can choose the new spell from the cleric spell list or the sorcerer spell list. You must otherwise obey all the restrictions for selecting the spell, and it becomes a sorcerer spell for you.

In addition, choose an affinity for the source of your divine power: good, evil, law, chaos, or neutrality. You learn an additional spell based on that affinity, as shown below. It is a sorcerer spell for you, but it doesn't count against your number of sorcerer spells known. If you later replace this spell, you must replace it with a spell from the cleric spell list.

Affinity	Spell
Good	*cure wounds*
Evil	*inflict wounds*
Law	*bless*
Chaos	*bane*
Neutrality	*protection from evil and good*

Favored by the Gods

Starting at 1st level, divine power guards your destiny. If you fail a saving throw or miss with an attack roll, you can roll 2d4 and add it to the total, possibly changing the outcome. Once you use this feature, you can't use it again until you finish a short or long rest.

Empowered Healing

Starting at 6th level, the divine energy coursing through you can empower healing spells. Whenever you or an ally within 5 feet of you rolls dice to determine the number of hit points a spell restores, you can spend 1 sorcery point to reroll any number of those dice once, provided you aren't incapacitated. You can use this feature only once per turn.

Otherworldly Wings

Starting at 14th level, you can use a bonus action to manifest a pair of spectral wings from your back. While the wings are present, you have a flying speed of 30 feet. The wings last until you're incapacitated, you die, or you dismiss them as a bonus action.

The affinity you chose for your Divine Magic feature determines the appearance of the spectral wings: eagle wings for good or law, bat wings for evil or chaos, and dragonfly wings for neutrality.

Unearthly Recovery

At 18th level, you gain the ability to overcome grievous injuries. As a bonus action when you have fewer than half of your hit points remaining, you can regain a number of hit points equal to half your hit point maximum.

Once you use this feature, you can't use it again until you finish a long rest.

Shadow Magic

You are a creature of shadow, for your innate magic comes from the Shadowfell itself. You might trace your lineage to an entity from that place, or perhaps you were exposed to its fell energy and transformed by it.

The power of shadow magic casts a strange pall over your physical presence. The spark of life that sustains you is muffled, as if it struggles to remain viable against the dark energy that imbues your soul. At your option, you can pick from or roll on the Shadow Sorcerer Quirks table to create a quirk for your character.

Shadow Sorcerer Quirks

d6	Quirk
1	You are always icy cold to the touch.
2	When you are asleep, you don't appear to breathe (though you must still breathe to survive).
3	You barely bleed, even when badly injured.
4	Your heart beats once per minute. This event sometimes surprises you.
5	You have trouble remembering that living creatures and corpses should be treated differently.
6	You blinked. Once. Last week.

Shadow Magic Features

Sorcerer Level	Feature
1st	Eyes of the Dark, Strength of the Grave
3rd	Eyes of the Dark (*darkness*)
6th	Hound of Ill Omen
14th	Shadow Walk
18th	Umbral Form

Eyes of the Dark

Starting at 1st level, you have darkvision with a range of 120 feet.

When you reach 3rd level in this class, you learn the *darkness* spell, which doesn't count against your number of sorcerer spells known. In addition, you can cast it by spending 2 sorcery points or by expending a spell slot. If you cast it with sorcery points, you can see through the darkness created by the spell.

Strength of the Grave

Starting at 1st level, your existence in a twilight state between life and death makes you difficult to defeat. When damage reduces you to 0 hit points, you can make a Charisma saving throw (DC 5 + the damage taken). On a success, you instead drop to 1 hit point. You can't use this feature if you are reduced to 0 hit points by radiant damage or by a critical hit.

After the saving throw succeeds, you can't use this feature again until you finish a long rest.

Hound of Ill Omen

At 6th level, you gain the ability to call forth a howling creature of darkness to harass your foes. As a bonus action, you can spend 3 sorcery points to magically summon a hound of ill omen to target one creature you can see within 120 feet of you. The hound uses the dire wolf's statistics (see the *Monster Manual* or appendix C in the *Player's Handbook*), with the following changes:

- The hound is size Medium, not Large, and it counts as a monstrosity, not a beast.
- It appears with a number of temporary hit points equal to half your sorcerer level.
- It can move through other creatures and objects as if they were difficult terrain. The hound takes 5 force damage if it ends its turn inside an object.
- At the start of its turn, the hound automatically knows its target's location. If the target was hidden, it is no longer hidden from the hound.

The hound appears in an unoccupied space of your choice within 30 feet of the target. Roll initiative for the hound. On its turn, it can move only toward its target by the most direct route, and it can use its action only to attack its target. The hound can make opportunity attacks,

but only against its target. Additionally, while the hound is within 5 feet of the target, the target has disadvantage on saving throws against any spell you cast. The hound disappears if it is reduced to 0 hit points, if its target is reduced to 0 hit points, or after 5 minutes.

Shadow Walk

At 14th level, you gain the ability to step from one shadow into another. When you are in dim light or darkness, as a bonus action, you can magically teleport up to 120 feet to an unoccupied space you can see that is also in dim light or darkness.

Umbral Form

Starting at 18th level, you can spend 6 sorcery points as a bonus action to magically transform yourself into a shadowy form. In this form, you have resistance to all damage except force and radiant damage, and you can move through other creatures and objects as if they were difficult terrain. You take 5 force damage if you end your turn inside an object.

You remain in this form for 1 minute. It ends early if you are incapacitated, if you die, or if you dismiss it as a bonus action.

Storm Sorcery

Your innate magic comes from the power of elemental air. Many with this power can trace their magic back to a near-death experience caused by the Great Rain, but perhaps you were born during a howling gale so powerful that folk still tell stories of it, or your lineage might include the influence of potent air creatures such as djinn. Whatever the case, the magic of the storm permeates your being.

Sometimes I disintegrate my shadow when I see it, because I think it's a different beholder.

Storm sorcerers are invaluable members of a ship's crew. Their magic allows them to exert control over wind and weather in their immediate area. Their abilities also prove useful in repelling attacks by sahuagin, pirates, and other waterborne threats.

STORM SORCERY FEATURES

Sorcerer Level	Feature
1st	Wind Speaker, Tempestuous Magic
6th	Heart of the Storm, Storm Guide
14th	Storm's Fury
18th	Wind Soul

WIND SPEAKER

The arcane magic you command is infused with elemental air. You can speak, read, and write Primordial. Knowing this language allows you to understand and be understood by those who speak its dialects: Aquan, Auran, Ignan, and Terran.

TEMPESTUOUS MAGIC

Starting at 1st level, you can use a bonus action on your turn to cause whirling gusts of elemental air to briefly surround you, immediately before or after you cast a spell of 1st level or higher. Doing so allows you to fly up to 10 feet without provoking opportunity attacks.

HEART OF THE STORM

At 6th level, you gain resistance to lightning and thunder damage. In addition, whenever you start casting a spell of 1st level or higher that deals lightning or thunder damage, stormy magic erupts from you. This eruption causes creatures of your choice that you can see within 10 feet of you to take lightning or thunder damage (choose each time this ability activates) equal to half your sorcerer level.

STORM GUIDE

At 6th level, you gain the ability to subtly control the weather around you.

If it is raining, you can use an action to cause the rain to stop falling in a 20-foot-radius sphere centered on you. You can end this effect as a bonus action.

If it is windy, you can use a bonus action each round to choose the direction that the wind blows in a 100-foot-radius sphere centered on you. The wind blows in that direction until the end of your next turn. This feature doesn't alter the speed of the wind.

STORM'S FURY

Starting at 14th level, when you are hit by a melee attack, you can use your reaction to deal lightning damage to the attacker. The damage equals your sorcerer level. The attacker must also make a Strength saving throw against your sorcerer spell save DC. On a failed save, the attacker is pushed in a straight line up to 20 feet away from you.

WIND SOUL

At 18th level, you gain immunity to lightning and thunder damage.

You also gain a magical flying speed of 60 feet. As an action, you can reduce your flying speed to 30 feet for 1 hour and choose a number of creatures within 30 feet of you equal to 3 + your Charisma modifier. The chosen creatures gain a magical flying speed of 30 feet for 1 hour. Once you reduce your flying speed in this way, you can't do so again until you finish a short or long rest.

What is it with people and the weather? It's just the sky weeping and shouting because it's so far away from me.

PATRON ATTITUDES

d6	Attitude
1	Your patron has guided and helped your family for generations and is kindly toward you.
2	Each interaction with your capricious patron is a surprise, whether pleasant or painful.
3	Your patron is the spirit of a long-dead hero who sees your pact as a way for it to continue to influence the world.
4	Your patron is a strict disciplinarian but treats you with a measure of respect.
5	Your patron tricked you into a pact and treats you as a slave.
6	You are mostly left to your own devices with no interference from your patron. Sometimes you dread the demands it will make when it does appear.

SPECIAL TERMS OF THE PACT

A pact can range from a loose agreement to a formal contract with lengthy, detailed clauses and lists of requirements. The terms of a pact—what a warlock must do to receive a patron's favor—are always dictated by the patron. On occasion, those terms include a special proviso that might seem odd or whimsical, but warlocks take these dictates as seriously as they do the other requirements of their pacts.

Does your character have a pact that requires you to change your behavior in an unusual or seemingly frivolous way? Even if your patron hasn't imposed such a duty on you already, that's not to say it couldn't still happen.

SPECIAL TERMS

d6	Term
1	When directed, you must take immediate action against a specific enemy of your patron.
2	Your pact tests your willpower; you are required to abstain from alcohol and other intoxicants.
3	At least once a day, you must inscribe or carve your patron's name or symbol on the wall of a building.
4	You must occasionally conduct bizarre rituals to maintain your pact.
5	You can never wear the same outfit twice, since your patron finds such predictability to be boring.
6	When you use an eldritch invocation, you must speak your patron's name aloud or risk incurring its displeasure.

WARLOCK

You think me mad? I think true insanity is being content to live a life of mortal drudgery when knowledge and power is there for the taking in the realm beyond.

—Xarren, herald of Acamar

Warlocks are finders and keepers of secrets. They push at the edge of our understanding of the world, always seeking to expand their expertise. Where sages or wizards might heed a clear sign of danger and end their research, a warlock plunges ahead, heedless of the cost. Thus, it takes a peculiar mixture of intelligence, curiosity, and recklessness to produce a warlock. Many folk would describe that combination as evidence of madness. Warlocks see it as a demonstration of bravery.

Warlocks are defined by two elements that work in concert to forge their path into this class. The first element is the event or circumstances that led to a warlock's entering into a pact with a planar entity. The second one is the nature of the entity a warlock is bound to. Unlike clerics, who typically embrace a deity and that god's ethos, a warlock might have no love for a patron, or vice versa.

The sections that follow provide ways to embellish a warlock character that could generate some intriguing story and roleplaying opportunities.

PATRON'S ATTITUDE

Every relationship is a two-way street, but in the case of warlocks and their patrons it's not necessarily true that both sides of the street are the same width or made of the same stuff. The feeling that a warlock holds for their patron, whether positive or negative, might be reciprocated by the patron, or the two participants in the pact might view one another with opposing emotions.

When you determine the attitude your warlock character holds toward your patron, also consider how things look from the patron's perspective. How does your patron behave toward you? Is your patron a friend and ally, or an enemy that grants you power only because you forced a pact upon it?

WARLOCK OF
THE CELESTIAL

OTHERWORLDLY PATRONS

At 1st level, a warlock gains the Otherworldly Patron feature. The following options are available to a warlock, in addition to those offered in the *Player's Handbook*: the Celestial and the Hexblade.

THE CELESTIAL

Your patron is a powerful being of the Upper Planes. You have bound yourself to an ancient empyrean, solar, ki-rin, unicorn, or other entity that resides in the planes of everlasting bliss. Your pact with that being allows you to experience the barest touch of the holy light that illuminates the multiverse.

Being connected to such power can cause changes in your behavior and beliefs. You might find yourself driven to annihilate the undead, to defeat fiends, and to protect the innocent. At times, your heart might also be filled with a longing for the celestial realm of your patron, and a desire to wander that paradise for the rest of your days. But you know that your mission is among mortals for now, and that your pact binds you to bring light to the dark places of the world.

CELESTIAL FEATURES

Warlock Level	Feature
1st	Expanded Spell List, Bonus Cantrips, Healing Light
6th	Radiant Soul
10th	Celestial Resilience
14th	Searing Vengeance

EXPANDED SPELL LIST

The Celestial lets you choose from an expanded list of spells when you learn a warlock spell. The following spells are added to the warlock spell list for you.

CELESTIAL EXPANDED SPELLS

Spell Level	Spells
1st	*cure wounds, guiding bolt*
2nd	*flaming sphere, lesser restoration*
3rd	*daylight, revivify*
4th	*guardian of faith, wall of fire*
5th	*flame strike, greater restoration*

BONUS CANTRIPS

At 1st level, you learn the *light* and *sacred flame* cantrips. They count as warlock cantrips for you, but they don't count against your number of cantrips known.

HEALING LIGHT

At 1st level, you gain the ability to channel celestial energy to heal wounds. You have a pool of d6s that you spend to fuel this healing. The number of dice in the pool equals 1 + your warlock level.

As a bonus action, you can heal one creature you can see within 60 feet of you, spending dice from the pool. The maximum number of dice you can spend at once equals your Charisma modifier (minimum of one die).

BINDING MARK

Some patrons make a habit of, and often enjoy, marking the warlocks under their sway in some fashion. A binding mark makes it clear—to those who know about such things—that the individual in question is bound to the patron's service. A warlock might take advantage of such a mark, claiming it as proof of one's pact, or might want to keep it under wraps (if possible) to avoid the difficulties it might bring.

If your warlock's pact comes with a binding mark, how you feel about displaying it probably depends on the nature of your relationship with the one who gave it to you. Is the mark a source of pride or something you are secretly ashamed of?

BINDING MARKS

d6	Mark
1	One of your eyes looks the same as one of your patron's eyes.
2	Each time you wake up, the small blemish on your face appears in a different place.
3	You display outward symptoms of a disease but suffer no ill effects from it.
4	Your tongue is an unnatural color.
5	You have a vestigial tail.
6	Your nose glows in the dark.

Roll the dice you spend, add them together, and restore a number of hit points equal to the total.

Your pool regains all expended dice when you finish a long rest.

RADIANT SOUL

Starting at 6th level, your link to the Celestial allows you to serve as a conduit for radiant energy. You have resistance to radiant damage, and when you cast a spell that deals radiant or fire damage, you can add your Charisma modifier to one radiant or fire damage roll of that spell against one of its targets.

CELESTIAL RESILIENCE

Starting at 10th level, you gain temporary hit points whenever you finish a short or long rest. These temporary hit points equal your warlock level + your Charisma modifier. Additionally, choose up to five creatures you can see at the end of the rest. Those creatures each gain temporary hit points equal to half your warlock level + your Charisma modifier.

SEARING VENGEANCE

Starting at 14th level, the radiant energy you channel allows you to resist death. When you have to make a death saving throw at the start of your turn, you can instead spring back to your feet with a burst of radiant energy. You regain hit points equal to half your hit point maximum, and then you stand up if you so choose. Each creature of your choice that is within 30 feet of you takes radiant damage equal to 2d8 + your Charisma modifier, and it is blinded until the end of the current turn.

Once you use this feature, you can't use it again until you finish a long rest.

THE HEXBLADE

You have made your pact with a mysterious entity from the Shadowfell—a force that manifests in sentient magic weapons carved from the stuff of shadow. The mighty sword *Blackrazor* is the most notable of these weapons, which have been spread across the multiverse over the ages. The shadowy force behind these weapons can offer power to warlocks who form pacts with it. Many hexblade warlocks create weapons that emulate those formed in the Shadowfell. Others forgo such arms, content to weave the dark magic of that plane into their spellcasting.

Because the Raven Queen is known to have forged the first of these weapons, many sages speculate that she and the force are one and that the weapons, along with hexblade warlocks, are tools she uses to manipulate events on the Material Plane to her inscrutable ends.

HEXBLADE FEATURES

Warlock Level	Feature
1st	Expanded Spell List, Hexblade's Curse, Hex Warrior
6th	Accursed Specter
10th	Armor of Hexes
14th	Master of Hexes

EXPANDED SPELL LIST

The Hexblade lets you choose from an expanded list of spells when you learn a warlock spell. The following spells are added to the warlock spell list for you.

HEXBLADE EXPANDED SPELLS

Spell Level	Spells
1st	*shield, wrathful smite*
2nd	*blur, branding smite*
3rd	*blink, elemental weapon*
4th	*phantasmal killer, staggering smite*
5th	*banishing smite, cone of cold*

HEXBLADE'S CURSE

Starting at 1st level, you gain the ability to place a baleful curse on someone. As a bonus action, choose one creature you can see within 30 feet of you. The target is cursed for 1 minute. The curse ends early if the target dies, you die, or you are incapacitated. Until the curse ends, you gain the following benefits:

- You gain a bonus to damage rolls against the cursed target. The bonus equals your proficiency bonus.
- Any attack roll you make against the cursed target is a critical hit on a roll of 19 or 20 on the d20.
- If the cursed target dies, you regain hit points equal to your warlock level + your Charisma modifier (minimum of 1 hit point).

You can't use this feature again until you finish a short or long rest.

HEX WARRIOR

At 1st level, you acquire the training necessary to effectively arm yourself for battle. You gain proficiency with medium armor, shields, and martial weapons.

The influence of your patron also allows you to mystically channel your will through a particular weapon. Whenever you finish a long rest, you can touch one weapon that you are proficient with and that lacks the two-handed property. When you attack with that weapon, you can use your Charisma modifier, instead of Strength or Dexterity, for the attack and damage rolls. This benefit lasts until you finish a long rest. If you later

WARLOCK OF THE HEXBLADE

gain the Pact of the Blade feature, this benefit extends to every pact weapon you conjure with that feature, no matter the weapon's type.

ACCURSED SPECTER

Starting at 6th level, you can curse the soul of a person you slay, temporarily binding it to your service. When you slay a humanoid, you can cause its spirit to rise from its corpse as a specter, the statistics for which are in the *Monster Manual*. When the specter appears, it gains temporary hit points equal to half your warlock level. Roll initiative for the specter, which has its own turns. It obeys your verbal commands, and it gains a special bonus to its attack rolls equal to your Charisma modifier (minimum of +0).

The specter remains in your service until the end of your next long rest, at which point it vanishes to the afterlife.

Once you bind a specter with this feature, you can't use the feature again until you finish a long rest.

ARMOR OF HEXES

At 10th level, your hex grows more powerful. If the target cursed by your Hexblade's Curse hits you with an attack roll, you can use your reaction to roll a d6. On a 4 or higher, the attack instead misses you, regardless of its roll.

MASTER OF HEXES

Starting at 14th level, you can spread your Hexblade's Curse from a slain creature to another creature. When

the creature cursed by your Hexblade's Curse dies, you can apply the curse to a different creature you can see within 30 feet of you, provided you aren't incapacitated. When you apply the curse in this way, you don't regain hit points from the death of the previously cursed creature.

ELDRITCH INVOCATIONS

At 2nd level, a warlock gains the Eldritch Invocations feature. Here are new options for that feature, in addition to the options in the *Player's Handbook*.

If an eldritch invocation has a prerequisite, you must meet it to learn the invocation. You can learn the invocation at the same time that you meet its prerequisite. A level prerequisite refers to your level in this class.

ASPECT OF THE MOON
Prerequisite: Pact of the Tome feature

You no longer need to sleep and can't be forced to sleep by any means. To gain the benefits of a long rest, you can spend all 8 hours doing light activity, such as reading your Book of Shadows and keeping watch.

CLOAK OF FLIES
Prerequisite: 5th level

As a bonus action, you can surround yourself with a magical aura that looks like buzzing flies. The aura extends 5 feet from you in every direction, but not through total cover. It lasts until you're incapacitated or you dismiss it as a bonus action.

The aura grants you advantage on Charisma (Intimidation) checks but disadvantage on all other Charisma checks. Any other creature that starts its turn in the aura takes poison damage equal to your Charisma modifier (minimum of 0 damage).

Once you use this invocation, you can't use it again until you finish a short or long rest.

ELDRITCH SMITE
Prerequisite: 5th level, Pact of the Blade feature

Once per turn when you hit a creature with your pact weapon, you can expend a warlock spell slot to deal an extra 1d8 force damage to the target, plus another 1d8 per level of the spell slot, and you can knock the target prone if it is Huge or smaller.

GHOSTLY GAZE
Prerequisite: 7th level

As an action, you gain the ability to see through solid objects to a range of 30 feet. Within that range, you have darkvision if you don't already have it. This special sight lasts for 1 minute or until your concentration ends (as if you were concentrating on a spell). During that time, you perceive objects as ghostly, transparent images.

Once you use this invocation, you can't use it again until you finish a short or long rest.

GIFT OF THE DEPTHS
Prerequisite: 5th level

You can breathe underwater, and you gain a swimming speed equal to your walking speed.

You can also cast *water breathing* once without expending a spell slot. You regain the ability to do so when you finish a long rest.

GIFT OF THE EVER-LIVING ONES
Prerequisite: Pact of the Chain feature

Whenever you regain hit points while your familiar is within 100 feet of you, treat any dice rolled to determine the hit points you regain as having rolled their maximum value for you.

GRASP OF HADAR
Prerequisite: eldritch blast cantrip

Once on each of your turns when you hit a creature with your *eldritch blast*, you can move that creature in a straight line 10 feet closer to you.

IMPROVED PACT WEAPON
Prerequisite: Pact of the Blade feature

You can use any weapon you summon with your Pact of the Blade feature as a spellcasting focus for your warlock spells.

In addition, the weapon gains a +1 bonus to its attack and damage rolls, unless it is a magic weapon that already has a bonus to those rolls.

Finally, the weapon you conjure can be a shortbow, longbow, light crossbow, or heavy crossbow.

LANCE OF LETHARGY
Prerequisite: eldritch blast cantrip

Once on each of your turns when you hit a creature with your *eldritch blast*, you can reduce that creature's speed by 10 feet until the end of your next turn.

MADDENING HEX
Prerequisite: 5th level, hex *spell or a warlock feature that curses*

As a bonus action, you cause a psychic disturbance around the target cursed by your *hex* spell or by a warlock feature of yours, such as Hexblade's Curse or Sign of Ill Omen. When you do so, you deal psychic damage to the cursed target and each creature of your choice that you can see within 5 feet of it. The psychic damage equals your Charisma modifier (minimum of 1 damage). To use this invocation, you must be able to see the cursed target, and it must be within 30 feet of you.

RELENTLESS HEX
Prerequisite: 7th level, hex *spell or a warlock feature that curses*

Your curse creates a temporary bond between you and your target. As a bonus action, you can magically tele-

port up to 30 feet to an unoccupied space you can see within 5 feet of the target cursed by your *hex* spell or by a warlock feature of yours, such as Hexblade's Curse or Sign of Ill Omen. To teleport in this way, you must be able to see the cursed target.

SHROUD OF SHADOW
Prerequisite: 15th level

You can cast *invisibility* at will, without expending a spell slot.

TOMB OF LEVISTUS
Prerequisite: 5th level

As a reaction when you take damage, you can entomb yourself in ice, which melts away at the end of your next turn. You gain 10 temporary hit points per warlock level, which take as much of the triggering damage as possible. Immediately after you take the damage, you gain vulnerability to fire damage, your speed is reduced to 0, and you are incapacitated. These effects, including any remaining temporary hit points, all end when the ice melts.

Once you use this invocation, you can't use it again until you finish a short or long rest.

TRICKSTER'S ESCAPE
Prerequisite: 7th level

You can cast *freedom of movement* once on yourself without expending a spell slot. You regain the ability to do so when you finish a long rest.

Wizard

WIZARDRY REQUIRES UNDERSTANDING. THE KNOWLEDGE *of how and why magic works, and our efforts to broaden that understanding, have brought about the key advances in civilization over the centuries.*

—Gimble the illusionist

Only a select few people in the world are wielders of magic. Of all those, wizards stand at the pinnacle of the craft. Even the least of them can manipulate forces that flout the laws of nature, and the most accomplished among them can cast spells with world-shaking effects.

The price that wizards pay for their mastery is that most valuable of commodities: time. It takes years of study, instruction, and experimentation to learn how to harness magical energy and carry spells around in one's own mind. For adventuring wizards and other spellcasters who aspire to the highest echelons of the profession, the studying never ends, nor does the quest for knowledge and power.

If you're playing a wizard, take advantage of the opportunity to make your character more than just a stereotypical spell-slinger. Use the advice that follows to add some intriguing details to how your wizard interacts with the world.

Spellbook

Your wizard character's most prized possession—your spellbook—might be an innocuous-looking volume whose covers show no hint of what's inside. Or you might display some flair, as many wizards do, by carrying a spellbook of an unusual sort. If you don't own such an item already, one of your goals might be to find a spellbook that sets you apart by its appearance or its means of manufacture.

Spellbooks

d6	Spellbook
1	A tome with pages that are thin sheets of metal, spells etched into them with acid
2	Long straps of leather on which spells are written, wrapped around a staff for ease of transport
3	A battered tome filled with pictographs that only you can understand
4	Small stones inscribed with spells and kept in a cloth bag
5	A scorched book, ravaged by dragon fire, with the script of your spells barely visible on its pages
6	A tome full of black pages whose writing is visible only in dim light or darkness

Ambition

Few aspiring wizards undertake the study of magic without some personal goal in mind. Many wizards use their spells as a tool to produce a tangible benefit, in material goods or in status, for themselves or their companions. For others, the theoretical aspect of magic might have a strong appeal, pushing those wizards to seek out knowledge that supports new theories of the arcane or confirms old ones.

Beyond the obvious, why does your wizard character study magic, and what do you want to achieve? If you haven't given these questions much thought, you can do so now, and the answers you come up with will likely affect how your future unfolds.

Ambitions

d6	Ambition
1	You will prove that the gods aren't as powerful as folk believe.
2	Immortality is the end goal of your studies.
3	If you can fully understand magic, you can unlock its use for all and usher in an era of equality.
4	Magic is a dangerous tool. You use it to protect what you treasure.
5	Arcane power must be taken away from those who would abuse it.
6	You will become the greatest wizard the world has seen in generations.

ECCENTRICITY

Endless hours of solitary study and research can have a negative effect on anyone's social skills. Wizards, who are a breed apart to begin with, are no exception. An odd mannerism or two is not necessarily a drawback, though; an eccentricity of this sort is usually harmless and could provide a source of amusement or serve as a calling card of sorts.

If your character has an eccentricity, is it a physical tic or a mental one? Are you well known in some circles because of it? Do you fight to overcome it, or do you embrace this minor claim to fame of yours?

ECCENTRICITIES

d6	Eccentricity
1	You have the habit of tapping your foot incessantly, which often annoys those around you.
2	Your memory is quite good, but you have no trouble pretending to be absentminded when it suits your purposes.
3	You never enter a room without looking to see what's hanging from the ceiling.
4	Your most prized possession is a dead worm that you keep inside a potion vial.
5	When you want people to leave you alone, you start talking to yourself. That usually does the trick.
6	Your fashion sense and grooming, or more accurately lack thereof, sometimes cause others to assume you are a beggar.

ARCANE TRADITION

At 2nd level, a wizard gains the Arcane Tradition feature. The following War Magic option is available to a wizard, in addition to the options offered in the *Player's Handbook*.

WAR MAGIC

A variety of arcane colleges specialize in training wizards for war. The tradition of War Magic blends principles of evocation and abjuration, rather than specializing in either of those schools. It teaches techniques that empower a caster's spells, while also providing methods for wizards to bolster their own defenses.

Followers of this tradition are known as war mages. They see their magic as both a weapon and armor, a resource superior to any piece of steel. War mages act fast in battle, using their spells to seize tactical control of a situation. Their spells strike hard, while their defensive skills foil their opponents' attempts to counterattack. War mages are also adept at turning other spellcasters' magical energy against them.

WAR MAGE

In great battles, a war mage often works with evokers, abjurers, and other types of wizards. Evokers, in particular, sometimes tease war mages for splitting their attention between offense and defense. A war mage's typical response: "What good is being able to throw a mighty *fireball* if I die before I can cast it?"

WAR MAGIC FEATURES

Wizard Level	Feature
2nd	Arcane Deflection, Tactical Wit
6th	Power Surge
10th	Durable Magic
14th	Deflecting Shroud

ARCANE DEFLECTION

At 2nd level, you have learned to weave your magic to fortify yourself against harm. When you are hit by an attack or you fail a saving throw, you can use your reaction to gain a +2 bonus to your AC against that attack or a +4 bonus to that saving throw.

When you use this feature, you can't cast spells other than cantrips until the end of your next turn.

Tactical Wit

Starting at 2nd level, your keen ability to assess tactical situations allows you to act quickly in battle. You can give yourself a bonus to your initiative rolls equal to your Intelligence modifier.

Power Surge

Starting at 6th level, you can store magical energy within yourself to later empower your damaging spells. In its stored form, this energy is called a power surge.

You can store a maximum number of power surges equal to your Intelligence modifier (minimum of one). Whenever you finish a long rest, your number of power surges resets to one. Whenever you successfully end a spell with *dispel magic* or *counterspell*, you gain one power surge, as you steal magic from the spell you foiled. If you end a short rest with no power surges, you gain one power surge.

Once per turn when you deal damage to a creature or object with a wizard spell, you can spend one power surge to deal extra force damage to that target. The extra damage equals half your wizard level.

Durable Magic

Beginning at 10th level, the magic you channel helps ward off harm. While you maintain concentration on a spell, you have a +2 bonus to AC and all saving throws.

Deflecting Shroud

At 14th level, your Arcane Deflection becomes infused with deadly magic. When you use your Arcane Deflection feature, you can cause magical energy to arc from you. Up to three creatures of your choice that you can see within 60 feet of you each take force damage equal to half your wizard level.

This Is Your Life

The character creation rules in the *Player's Handbook* provide all the information you need to define your character in preparation for a life of adventuring. What they don't do is account for all the circumstances that shaped your character during the years between your birth and the start of your career as a member of a class.

What did your character accomplish or experience before deciding to become an adventurer? What were the circumstances of your birth? How large is your family, and what sorts of relationships do you have with your relatives? Which people were the greatest influences on you during your formative years, for better or worse?

To answer these questions and more, you can use the tables and the advice in this section to compose a well-developed backstory for your character—an autobiography of sorts—that you can use to inform how you roleplay the character. Your DM can draw from this material as the campaign proceeds, creating situations and scenarios that build off your previous life experiences.

Ideas, Not Rules

Even though these pages are full of tables and die rolls, they don't make up a rules system—in fact, the opposite is true. You can use as much or as little of this material as you desire, and you can make decisions in any order you want.

For instance, you might not want these tables to help you decide who your parents and siblings are, because that's among the information you've already come up with. But you can still use other parts, such as the section on life events, to provide added depth and detail.

How and When to Use the Tables

If you're comfortable with letting the dice decide a certain fact about your character, go ahead and roll. If not, you can take charge and make the decision, choosing from among the possibilities on a table. Of course, you also have the option of disregarding the result of a die roll if it conflicts with another result. Likewise, if the text instructs you to roll on a table, that's not meant to be taken literally. You can always make your own choice.

Although these tables are meant to augment the step-by-step character creation process in the *Player's Handbook*, they don't occupy a specific place in that process. You can use some of them early on—for instance, it's possible to determine your parents and other family members immediately after deciding your character's race—but you could also wait until later in the process. You might prefer to establish more facts about your character's game identity—such as your class, ability scores, and alignment—before supplementing that information with what's offered here.

Section by Section

This material is divided into four sections, each addressing a different aspect of your character's backstory.

Origins. To find out who and where you came from, use the "Origins" section. When you're done, you will have a summary of facts about your parents, your siblings, and the circumstances under which you grew up.

A YOUNG STREET URCHIN PILFERS A POUCH AND, TO HER SURPRISE, BECOMES THE NEW OWNER OF A SPELLBOOK

Personal Decisions. After you have selected your character's background and class, use the appropriate tables to determine how you came to make those choices.

Life Events. Your character's existence until now, no matter how brief or uneventful, has been marked by one or more life events—memorable happenings that have had an effect on who you are today.

Supplemental Tables. Your life has intersected with the lives of plenty of other people, all the way from your infancy to today. When a result mentions such a person, you can use the supplemental tables (page 72) to add needed details—such as race, class, or occupation—to that person. Some tables in the other sections direct you to one or more of the supplemental tables, and you can also use them any other time you see fit.

Origins

The usual first step in creating your character's life story is to determine your early circumstances. Who were your parents? Where were you born? Did you have any siblings? Who raised you? You can address these questions by using the following tables.

Parents

You had parents, of course, even if they didn't raise you. To determine what you know about these people, use the Parents table. If you want, you can roll separately on the table for your mother and your father. Use the supplemental tables as desired (particularly Class, Occupation, and Alignment) to learn more about your parents.

PARENTS

d100	Parents
01–95	You know who your parents are or were.
96–00	You do not know who your parents were.

Nonhuman Parents. If your character is a half-elf, a half-orc, or a tiefling, you can use one of the tables below to determine the race of each of your parents. When you have a result, randomly determine which part of the result refers to your father and which to your mother.

HALF-ELF PARENTS

d8	Parents
1–5	One parent was an elf and the other was a human.
6	One parent was an elf and the other was a half-elf.
7	One parent was a human and the other was a half-elf.
8	Both parents were half-elves.

HALF-ORC PARENTS

d8	Parents
1–3	One parent was an orc and the other was a human.
4–5	One parent was an orc and the other was a half-orc.
6–7	One parent was a human and the other was a half-orc.
8	Both parents were half-orcs.

TIEFLING PARENTS

d8	Parents
1–4	Both parents were humans, their infernal heritage dormant until you came along.
5–6	One parent was a tiefling and the other was a human.
7	One parent was a tiefling and the other was a devil.
8	One parent was a human and the other was a devil.

BIRTHPLACE

After establishing your parentage, you can determine where you were born by using the Birthplace table. (Modify the result or roll again if you get a result that's inconsistent with what you know about your parents.) Once you have a result, roll percentile dice. On a roll of 00, a strange event coincided with your birth: the moon briefly turning red, all the milk within a mile spoiling, the water in the area freezing solid in midsummer, all the iron in the home rusting or turning to silver, or some other unusual event of your choice.

BIRTHPLACE

d100	Location
01–50	Home
51–55	Home of a family friend
56–63	Home of a healer or midwife
64–65	Carriage, cart, or wagon
66–68	Barn, shed, or other outbuilding
69–70	Cave
71–72	Field
73–74	Forest
75–77	Temple
78	Battlefield
79–80	Alley or street
81–82	Brothel, tavern, or inn
83–84	Castle, keep, tower, or palace
85	Sewer or rubbish heap
86–88	Among people of a different race
89–91	On board a boat or a ship
92–93	In a prison or in the headquarters of a secret organization
94–95	In a sage's laboratory
96	In the Feywild
97	In the Shadowfell
98	On the Astral Plane or the Ethereal Plane
99	On an Inner Plane of your choice
00	On an Outer Plane of your choice

SIBLINGS

You might be an only child or one of many children. Your siblings could be cherished friends or hated rivals. Roll on the Number of Siblings table to determine how many brothers or sisters you have. If you are a dwarf or an elf, subtract 2 from your roll. Then, roll on the Birth Order table for each sibling to determine that person's age relative to yours (older, younger, or born at the same time).

Occupation. For each sibling of suitable age, roll on the Occupation supplemental table to determine what that person does for a living.

Alignment. You can choose your siblings' alignments or roll on the Alignment supplemental table.

Status. By now, each of your siblings might be alive and well, alive and not so well, in dire straits, or dead. Roll on the Status supplemental table.

Relationship. You can roll on the Relationship supplemental table to determine how your siblings feel about you. They might all have the same attitude toward you, or some might view you differently from how the others do.

Other Details. You can decide any other details you like about each sibling, including gender, personality, and place in the world.

Number of Siblings

d10	Siblings
2 or lower	None
3–4	1d3
5–6	1d4 + 1
7–8	1d6 + 2
9–10	1d8 + 3

Birth Order

2d6	Birth Order
2	Twin, triplet, or quadruplet
3–7	Older
8–12	Younger

Family and Friends

Who raised you, and what was life like for you when you were growing up? You might have been raised by your parents, by relatives, or in an orphanage. Or you could have spent your childhood on the streets of a crowded city with only your fellow runaways and orphans to keep you company.

Use the Family table to determine who raised you. If you know who your parents are but you get a result that does not mention one or both of them, use the Absent Parent table to determine what happened.

Next, refer to the Family Lifestyle table to determine the general circumstances of your upbringing. (Chapter 5 of the *Player's Handbook* has more information about lifestyles.) The result on that table includes a number that is applied to your roll on the Childhood Home table, which tells you where you spent your early years. Wrap up this section by using the Childhood Memories table, which tells you how you were treated by other youngsters as you were growing up.

Supplemental Tables. You can roll on the Relationship table to determine how your family members or other important figures in your life feel about you. You can also use the Race, Occupation, and Alignment tables to learn more about the family members or guardians who raised you.

Family

d100	Family
01	None
02	Institution, such as an asylum
03	Temple
04–05	Orphanage
06–07	Guardian
08–15	Paternal or maternal aunt, uncle, or both; or extended family such as a tribe or clan
16–25	Paternal or maternal grandparent(s)
26–35	Adoptive family (same or different race)
36–55	Single father or stepfather
56–75	Single mother or stepmother
76–00	Mother and father

YEARS LATER, WHILE SERVING ON A SHIP'S CREW, SHE CALLS ON A BIT OF HER MAGIC TO HELP RIG A MAST

Absent Parent

d4	Fate
1	Your parent died (roll on the Cause of Death supplemental table).
2	Your parent was imprisoned, enslaved, or otherwise taken away.
3	Your parent abandoned you.
4	Your parent disappeared to an unknown fate.

Family Lifestyle

3d6	Lifestyle*
3	Wretched (−40)
4–5	Squalid (−20)
6–8	Poor (−10)
9–12	Modest (+0)
13–15	Comfortable (+10)
16–17	Wealthy (+20)
18	Aristocratic (+40)

*Use the number in this result as a modifier to your roll on the Childhood Home table.

THOUGH SHE SURVIVED THE SINKING OF HER SHIP, SHE LOST
ALL HER WORLDLY GOODS—EXCEPT FOR HER SPELLBOOK

CHILDHOOD HOME

d100*	Home
0 or lower	On the streets
1–20	Rundown shack
21–30	No permanent residence; you moved around a lot
31–40	Encampment or village in the wilderness
41–50	Apartment in a rundown neighborhood
51–70	Small house
71–90	Large house
91–110	Mansion
111 or higher	Palace or castle

*After making this roll, apply the modifier from the Family Lifestyle table to arrive at the result.

CHILDHOOD MEMORIES

3d6 + Cha mod	Memory
3 or lower	I am still haunted by my childhood, when I was treated badly by my peers.
4–5	I spent most of my childhood alone, with no close friends.
6–8	Others saw me as being different or strange, and so I had few companions.
9–12	I had a few close friends and lived an ordinary childhood.
13–15	I had several friends, and my childhood was generally a happy one.
16–17	I always found it easy to make friends, and I loved being around people.
18 or higher	Everyone knew who I was, and I had friends everywhere I went.

PERSONAL DECISIONS

Your character's life takes a particular course depending on the choices you make for the character's background and class.

BACKGROUND

Roll on the appropriate table in this section as soon as you decide your background, or at any later time if you choose. If a background includes a special decision point, such as a folk hero's defining event or the specialty of a criminal or a sage, it's best to make that determination before using the pertinent table below.

ACOLYTE

d6	I became an acolyte because ...
1	I ran away from home at an early age and found refuge in a temple.
2	My family gave me to a temple, since they were unable or unwilling to care for me.
3	I grew up in a household with strong religious convictions. Entering the service of one or more gods seemed natural.
4	An impassioned sermon struck a chord deep in my soul and moved me to serve the faith.
5	I followed a childhood friend, a respected acquaintance, or someone I loved into religious service.
6	After encountering a true servant of the gods, I was so inspired that I immediately entered the service of a religious group.

CHARLATAN

d6	I became a charlatan because ...
1	I was left to my own devices, and my knack for manipulating others helped me survive.
2	I learned early on that people are gullible and easy to exploit.
3	I often got in trouble, but I managed to talk my way out of it every time.
4	I took up with a confidence artist, from whom I learned my craft.
5	After a charlatan fleeced my family, I decided to learn the trade so I would never be fooled by such deception again.
6	I was poor or I feared becoming poor, so I learned the tricks I needed to keep myself out of poverty.

CRIMINAL

d6	I became a criminal because ...
1	I resented authority in my younger days and saw a life of crime as the best way to fight against tyranny and oppression.
2	Necessity forced me to take up the life, since it was the only way I could survive.
3	I fell in with a gang of reprobates and ne'er-do-wells, and I learned my specialty from them.
4	A parent or relative taught me my criminal specialty to prepare me for the family business.
5	I left home and found a place in a thieves' guild or some other criminal organization.
6	I was always bored, so I turned to crime to pass the time and discovered I was quite good at it.

ENTERTAINER

d6	I became an entertainer because ...
1	Members of my family made ends meet by performing, so it was fitting for me to follow their example.
2	I always had a keen insight into other people, enough so that I could make them laugh or cry with my stories or songs.
3	I ran away from home to follow a minstrel troupe.
4	I saw a bard perform once, and I knew from that moment on what I was born to do.
5	I earned coin by performing on street corners and eventually made a name for myself.
6	A traveling entertainer took me in and taught me the trade.

FOLK HERO

d6	I became a folk hero because ...
1	I learned what was right and wrong from my family.
2	I was always enamored by tales of heroes and wished I could be something more than ordinary.
3	I hated my mundane life, so when it was time for someone to step up and do the right thing, I took my chance.
4	A parent or one of my relatives was an adventurer, and I was inspired by that person's courage.
5	A mad old hermit spoke a prophecy when I was born, saying that I would accomplish great things.
6	I have always stood up for those who are weaker than I am.

GUILD ARTISAN

d6	I became a guild artisan because ...
1	I was apprenticed to a master who taught me the guild's business.
2	I helped a guild artisan keep a secret or complete a task, and in return I was taken on as an apprentice.

d6	I became a guild artisan because ...
3	One of my family members who belonged to the guild made a place for me.
4	I was always good with my hands, so I took the opportunity to learn a trade.
5	I wanted to get away from my home situation and start a new life.
6	I learned the essentials of my craft from a mentor but had to join the guild to finish my training.

HERMIT

d6	I became a hermit because ...
1	My enemies ruined my reputation, and I fled to the wilds to avoid further disparagement.
2	I am comfortable with being isolated, as I seek inner peace.
3	I never liked the people I called my friends, so it was easy for me to strike out on my own.
4	I felt compelled to forsake my past, but did so with great reluctance, and sometimes I regret making that decision.
5	I lost everything—my home, my family, my friends. Going it alone was all I could do.
6	Society's decadence disgusted me, so I decided to leave it behind.

NOBLE

d6	I became a noble because ...
1	I come from an old and storied family, and it fell to me to preserve the family name.
2	My family has been disgraced, and I intend to clear our name.
3	My family recently came by its title, and that elevation thrust us into a new and strange world.
4	My family has a title, but none of my ancestors have distinguished themselves since we gained it.
5	My family is filled with remarkable people. I hope to live up to their example.
6	I hope to increase my family's power and influence.

OUTLANDER

d6	I became an outlander because ...
1	I spent a lot of time in the wilderness as a youngster, and I came to love that way of life.
2	From a young age, I couldn't abide the stink of the cities and preferred to spend my time in nature.
3	I came to understand the darkness that lurks in the wilds, and I vowed to combat it.
4	My people lived on the edges of civilization, and I learned the methods of survival from my family.
5	After a tragedy I retreated to the wilderness, leaving my old life behind.
6	My family moved away from civilization, and I learned to adapt to my new environment.

SAGE

d6	I became a sage because ...
1	I was naturally curious, so I packed up and went to a university to learn more about the world.
2	My mentor's teachings opened my mind to new possibilities in that field of study.
3	I was always an avid reader, and I learned much about my favorite topic on my own.
4	I discovered an old library and pored over the texts I found there. That experience awakened a hunger for more knowledge.
5	I impressed a wizard who told me I was squandering my talents and should seek out an education to take advantage of my gifts.
6	One of my parents or a relative gave me a basic education that whetted my appetite, and I left home to build on what I had learned.

SAILOR

d6	I became a sailor because ...
1	I was press-ganged by pirates and forced to serve on their ship until I finally escaped.
2	I wanted to see the world, so I signed on as a deckhand for a merchant ship.
3	One of my relatives was a sailor who took me to sea.
4	I needed to escape my community quickly, so I stowed away on a ship. When the crew found me, I was forced to work for my passage.
5	Reavers attacked my community, so I found refuge on a ship until I could seek vengeance.
6	I had few prospects where I was living, so I left to find my fortune elsewhere.

SOLDIER

d6	I became a soldier because ...
1	I joined the militia to help protect my community from monsters.
2	A relative of mine was a soldier, and I wanted to carry on the family tradition.
3	The local lord forced me to enlist in the army.
4	War ravaged my homeland while I was growing up. Fighting was the only life I ever knew.
5	I wanted fame and fortune, so I joined a mercenary company, selling my sword to the highest bidder.
6	Invaders attacked my homeland. It was my duty to take up arms in defense of my people.

URCHIN

d6	I became an urchin because ...
1	Wanderlust caused me to leave my family to see the world. I look after myself.
2	I ran away from a bad situation at home and made my own way in the world.

d6	I became an urchin because ...
3	Monsters wiped out my village, and I was the sole survivor. I had to find a way to survive.
4	A notorious thief looked after me and other orphans, and we spied and stole to earn our keep.
5	One day I woke up on the streets, alone and hungry, with no memory of my early childhood.
6	My parents died, leaving no one to look after me. I raised myself.

CLASS TRAINING

If you haven't chosen your class yet, do so now, keeping in mind your background and all the other details you have established so far. Once you've made your selection, roll a d6 and find the number you rolled on the appropriate table in this section, which describes how you came to be a member of that class.

The class sections earlier in this chapter have further story suggestions, which you can use in concert with the material here.

BARBARIAN

d6	I became a barbarian because ...
1	My devotion to my people lifted me in battle, making me powerful and dangerous.
2	The spirits of my ancestors called on me to carry out a great task.
3	I lost control in battle one day, and it was as if something else was manipulating my body, forcing it to kill every foe I could reach.
4	I went on a spiritual journey to find myself and instead found a spirit animal to guide, protect, and inspire me.
5	I was struck by lightning and lived. Afterward, I found a new strength within me that let me push beyond my limitations.
6	My anger needed to be channeled into battle, or I risked becoming an indiscriminate killer.

BARD

d6	I became a bard because ...
1	I awakened my latent bardic abilities through trial and error.
2	I was a gifted performer and attracted the attention of a master bard who schooled me in the old techniques.
3	I joined a loose society of scholars and orators to learn new techniques of performance and magic.
4	I felt a calling to recount the deeds of champions and heroes, to bring them alive in song and story.
5	I joined one of the great colleges to learn old lore, the secrets of magic, and the art of performance.
6	I picked up a musical instrument one day and instantly discovered that I could play it.

CLERIC

d6	I became a cleric because ...
1	A supernatural being in service to the gods called me to become a divine agent in the world.
2	I saw the injustice and horror in the world and felt moved to take a stand against them.
3	My god gave me an unmistakable sign. I dropped everything to serve the divine.
4	Although I was always devout, it wasn't until I completed a pilgrimage that I knew my true calling.
5	I used to serve in my religion's bureaucracy but found I needed to work in the world, to bring the message of my faith to the darkest corners of the land.
6	I realize that my god works through me, and I do as commanded, even though I don't know why I was chosen to serve.

DRUID

d6	I became a druid because ...
1	I saw too much devastation in the wild places, too much of nature's splendor ruined by the despoilers. I joined a circle of druids to fight back against the enemies of nature.
2	I found a place among a group of druids after I fled a catastrophe.
3	I have always had an affinity for animals, so I explored my talent to see how I could best use it.
4	I befriended a druid and was moved by druidic teachings. I decided to follow my friend's guidance and give something back to the world.
5	While I was growing up, I saw spirits all around me—entities no one else could perceive. I sought out the druids to help me understand the visions and communicate with these beings.
6	I have always felt disgust for creatures of unnatural origin. For this reason, I immersed myself in the study of the druidic mysteries and became a champion of the natural order.

FIGHTER

d6	I became a fighter because ...
1	I wanted to hone my combat skills, and so I joined a war college.
2	I squired for a knight who taught me how to fight, care for a steed, and conduct myself with honor. I decided to take up that path for myself.
3	Horrible monsters descended on my community, killing someone I loved. I took up arms to destroy those creatures and others of a similar nature.
4	I joined the army and learned how to fight as part of a group.
5	I grew up fighting, and I refined my talents by defending myself against people who crossed me.
6	I could always pick up just about any weapon and know how to use it effectively.

TODAY, HER HUMBLE ORIGINS FAR BEHIND HER, SHE HAS BECOME A WIZARD OF GREAT RENOWN WITH A FLAIR FOR THE HIGH SEAS

MONK

d6	I became a monk because ...
1	I was chosen to study at a secluded monastery. There, I was taught the fundamental techniques required to eventually master a tradition.
2	I sought instruction to gain a deeper understanding of existence and my place in the world.
3	I stumbled into a portal to the Shadowfell and took refuge in a strange monastery, where I learned how to defend myself against the forces of darkness.
4	I was overwhelmed with grief after losing someone close to me, and I sought the advice of philosophers to help me cope with my loss.
5	I could feel that a special sort of power lay within me, so I sought out those who could help me call it forth and master it.
6	I was wild and undisciplined as a youngster, but then I realized the error of my ways. I applied to a monastery and became a monk as a way to live a life of discipline.

Paladin

d6	I became a paladin because ...
1	A fantastical being appeared before me and called on me to undertake a holy quest.
2	One of my ancestors left a holy quest unfulfilled, so I intend to finish that work.
3	The world is a dark and terrible place. I decided to serve as a beacon of light shining out against the gathering shadows.
4	I served as a paladin's squire, learning all I needed to swear my own sacred oath.
5	Evil must be opposed on all fronts. I feel compelled to seek out wickedness and purge it from the world.
6	Becoming a paladin was a natural consequence of my unwavering faith. In taking my vows, I became the holy sword of my religion.

Ranger

d6	I became a ranger because ...
1	I found purpose while I honed my hunting skills by bringing down dangerous animals at the edge of civilization.
2	I always had a way with animals, able to calm them with a soothing word and a touch.
3	I suffer from terrible wanderlust, so being a ranger gave me a reason not to remain in one place for too long.
4	I have seen what happens when the monsters come out from the dark. I took it upon myself to become the first line of defense against the evils that lie beyond civilization's borders.
5	I met a grizzled ranger who taught me woodcraft and the secrets of the wild lands.
6	I served in an army, learning the precepts of my profession while blazing trails and scouting enemy encampments.

Rogue

d6	I became a rogue because ...
1	I've always been nimble and quick of wit, so I decided to use those talents to help me make my way in the world.
2	An assassin or a thief wronged me, so I focused my training on mastering the skills of my enemy to better combat foes of that sort.
3	An experienced rogue saw something in me and taught me several useful tricks.
4	I decided to turn my natural lucky streak into the basis of a career, though I still realize that improving my skills is essential.
5	I took up with a group of ruffians who showed me how to get what I want through sneakiness rather than direct confrontation.
6	I'm a sucker for a shiny bauble or a sack of coins, as long as I can get my hands on it without risking life and limb.

Sorcerer

d6	I became a sorcerer because ...
1	When I was born, all the water in the house froze solid, the milk spoiled, or all the iron turned to copper. My family is convinced that this event was a harbinger of stranger things to come for me.
2	I suffered a terrible emotional or physical strain, which brought forth my latent magical power. I have fought to control it ever since.
3	My immediate family never spoke of my ancestors, and when I asked, they would change the subject. It wasn't until I started displaying strange talents that the full truth of my heritage came out.
4	When a monster threatened one of my friends, I became filled with anxiety. I lashed out instinctively and blasted the wretched thing with a force that came from within me.
5	Sensing something special in me, a stranger taught me how to control my gift.
6	After I escaped from a magical conflagration, I realized that though I was unharmed, I was not unchanged. I began to exhibit unusual abilities that I am just beginning to understand.

Warlock

d6	I became a warlock because ...
1	While wandering around in a forbidden place, I encountered an otherworldly being that offered to enter into a pact with me.
2	I was examining a strange tome I found in an abandoned library when the entity that would become my patron suddenly appeared before me.

d6	I became a warlock because ...
3	I stumbled into the clutches of my patron after I accidentally stepped through a magical doorway.
4	When I was faced with a terrible crisis, I prayed to any being who would listen, and the creature that answered became my patron.
5	My future patron visited me in my dreams and offered great power in exchange for my service.
6	One of my ancestors had a pact with my patron, so that entity was determined to bind me to the same agreement.

WIZARD

d6	I became a wizard because ...
1	An old wizard chose me from among several candidates to serve an apprenticeship.
2	When I became lost in a forest, a hedge wizard found me, took me in, and taught me the rudiments of magic.
3	I grew up listening to tales of great wizards and knew I wanted to follow their path. I strove to be accepted at an academy of magic and succeeded.
4	One of my relatives was an accomplished wizard who decided I was smart enough to learn the craft.
5	While exploring an old tomb, library, or temple, I found a spellbook. I was immediately driven to learn all I could about becoming a wizard.
6	I was a prodigy who demonstrated mastery of the arcane arts at an early age. When I became old enough to set out on my own, I did so to learn more magic and expand my power.

LIFE EVENTS

No matter how long you've been alive, you have experienced at least one signature event that has markedly influenced your character. Life events include wondrous happenings and tragedies, conflicts and successes, and encounters with the unusual. They can help to explain why your character became an adventurer, and some might still affect your life even after they are long over.

The older a character is, the greater the chance for multiple life events, as shown on the Life Events by Age table. If you have already chosen your character's starting age, see the entry in the Life Events column that corresponds to how old you are. Otherwise, you can roll dice to determine your current age and number of life events randomly.

After you know the number of life events your character has experienced, roll once on the Life Events table for each of them. Many of the results on that table direct you to one of the secondary tables that follow. Once you have determined all of your character's life events, you can arrange them in any chronological order you see fit.

LIFE EVENTS BY AGE

d100	Current Age	Life Events
01–20	20 years or younger	1
21–59	21–30 years	1d4
60–69	31–40 years	1d6
70–89	41–50 years	1d8
90–99	51–60 years	1d10
00	61 years or older	1d12

LIFE EVENTS

d100	Event
01–10	You suffered a tragedy. Roll on the Tragedies table.
11–20	You gained a bit of good fortune. Roll on the Boons table.
21–30	You fell in love or got married. If you get this result more than once, you can choose to have a child instead. Work with your DM to determine the identity of your love interest.
31–40	You made an enemy of an adventurer. Roll a d6. An odd number indicates you are to blame for the rift, and an even number indicates you are blameless. Use the supplemental tables and work with your DM to determine this hostile character's identity and the danger this enemy poses to you.
41–50	You made a friend of an adventurer. Use the supplemental tables and work with your DM to add more detail to this friendly character and establish how your friendship began.
51–70	You spent time working in a job related to your background. Start the game with an extra 2d6 gp.
71–75	You met someone important. Use the supplemental tables to determine this character's identity and how this individual feels about you. Work out additional details with your DM as needed to fit this character into your backstory.
76–80	You went on an adventure. Roll on the Adventures table to see what happened to you. Work with your DM to determine the nature of the adventure and the creatures you encountered.
81–85	You had a supernatural experience. Roll on the Supernatural Events table to find out what it was.
86–90	You fought in a battle. Roll on the War table to learn what happened to you. Work with your DM to come up with the reason for the battle and the factions involved. It might have been a small conflict between your community and a band of orcs, or it could have been a major battle in a larger war.
91–95	You committed a crime or were wrongly accused of doing so. Roll on the Crime table to determine the nature of the offense and on the Punishment table to see what became of you.
96–99	You encountered something magical. Roll on the Arcane Matters table.
00	Something truly strange happened to you. Roll on the Weird Stuff table.

Secondary Tables

These tables add detail to many of the results on the Life Events table. The tables are in alphabetical order.

Adventures

d100	Outcome
01–10	You nearly died. You have nasty scars on your body, and you are missing an ear, 1d3 fingers, or 1d4 toes.
11–20	You suffered a grievous injury. Although the wound healed, it still pains you from time to time.
21–30	You were wounded, but in time you fully recovered.
31–40	You contracted a disease while exploring a filthy warren. You recovered from the disease, but you have a persistent cough, pockmarks on your skin, or prematurely gray hair.
41–50	You were poisoned by a trap or a monster. You recovered, but the next time you must make a saving throw against poison, you make the saving throw with disadvantage.
51–60	You lost something of sentimental value to you during your adventure. Remove one trinket from your possessions.
61–70	You were terribly frightened by something you encountered and ran away, abandoning your companions to their fate.
71–80	You learned a great deal during your adventure. The next time you make an ability check or a saving throw, you have advantage on the roll.
81–90	You found some treasure on your adventure. You have 2d6 gp left from your share of it.
91–99	You found a considerable amount of treasure on your adventure. You have 1d20 + 50 gp left from your share of it.
00	You came across a common magic item (of the DM's choice).

Arcane Matters

d10	Magical Event
1	You were charmed or frightened by a spell.
2	You were injured by the effect of a spell.
3	You witnessed a powerful spell being cast by a cleric, a druid, a sorcerer, a warlock, or a wizard.
4	You drank a potion (of the DM's choice).
5	You found a *spell scroll* (of the DM's choice) and succeeded in casting the spell it contained.
6	You were affected by teleportation magic.
7	You turned invisible for a time.
8	You identified an illusion for what it was.
9	You saw a creature being conjured by magic.
10	Your fortune was read by a diviner. Roll twice on the Life Events table, but don't apply the results. Instead, the DM picks one event as a portent of your future (which might or might not come true).

Boons

d10	Boon
1	A friendly wizard gave you a *spell scroll* containing one cantrip (of the DM's choice).
2	You saved the life of a commoner, who now owes you a life debt. This individual accompanies you on your travels and performs mundane tasks for you, but will leave if neglected, abused, or imperiled. Determine details about this character by using the supplemental tables and working with your DM.
3	You found a riding horse.
4	You found some money. You have 1d20 gp in addition to your regular starting funds.
5	A relative bequeathed you a simple weapon of your choice.
6	You found something interesting. You gain one additional trinket.
7	You once performed a service for a local temple. The next time you visit the temple, you can receive healing up to your hit point maximum.
8	A friendly alchemist gifted you with a *potion of healing* or a flask of acid, as you choose.
9	You found a treasure map.
10	A distant relative left you a stipend that enables you to live at the comfortable lifestyle for 1d20 years. If you choose to live at a higher lifestyle, you reduce the price of the lifestyle by 2 gp during that time period.

Crime

d8	Crime
1	Murder
2	Theft
3	Burglary
4	Assault
5	Smuggling
6	Kidnapping
7	Extortion
8	Counterfeiting

Punishment

d12	Punishment
1–3	You did not commit the crime and were exonerated after being accused.
4–6	You committed the crime or helped do so, but nonetheless the authorities found you not guilty.
7–8	You were nearly caught in the act. You had to flee and are wanted in the community where the crime occurred.
9–12	You were caught and convicted. You spent time in jail, chained to an oar, or performing hard labor. You served a sentence of 1d4 years or succeeded in escaping after that much time.

SUPERNATURAL EVENTS

d100	Event
01–05	You were ensorcelled by a fey and enslaved for 1d6 years before you escaped.
06–10	You saw a demon and ran away before it could do anything to you.
11–15	A devil tempted you. Make a DC 10 Wisdom saving throw. On a failed save, your alignment shifts one step toward evil (if it's not evil already), and you start the game with an additional 1d20 + 50 gp.
16–20	You woke up one morning miles from your home, with no idea how you got there.
21–30	You visited a holy site and felt the presence of the divine there.
31–40	You witnessed a falling red star, a face appearing in the frost, or some other bizarre happening. You are certain that it was an omen of some sort.
41–50	You escaped certain death and believe it was the intervention of a god that saved you.
51–60	You witnessed a minor miracle.
61–70	You explored an empty house and found it to be haunted.
71–75	You were briefly possessed. Roll a d6 to determine what type of creature possessed you: 1, celestial; 2, devil; 3, demon; 4, fey; 5, elemental; 6, undead.
76–80	You saw a ghost.
81–85	You saw a ghoul feeding on a corpse.
86–90	A celestial or a fiend visited you in your dreams to give a warning of dangers to come.
91–95	You briefly visited the Feywild or the Shadowfell.
96–00	You saw a portal that you believe leads to another plane of existence.

TRAGEDIES

d12	Tragedy
1–2	A family member or a close friend died. Roll on the Cause of Death supplemental table to find out how.
3	A friendship ended bitterly, and the other person is now hostile to you. The cause might have been a misunderstanding or something you or the former friend did.
4	You lost all your possessions in a disaster, and you had to rebuild your life.
5	You were imprisoned for a crime you didn't commit and spent 1d6 years at hard labor, in jail, or shackled to an oar in a slave galley.
6	War ravaged your home community, reducing everything to rubble and ruin. In the aftermath, you either helped your town rebuild or moved somewhere else.
7	A lover disappeared without a trace. You have been looking for that person ever since.

d12	Tragedy
8	A terrible blight in your home community caused crops to fail, and many starved. You lost a sibling or some other family member.
9	You did something that brought terrible shame to you in the eyes of your family. You might have been involved in a scandal, dabbled in dark magic, or offended someone important. The attitude of your family members toward you becomes indifferent at best, though they might eventually forgive you.
10	For a reason you were never told, you were exiled from your community. You then either wandered in the wilderness for a time or promptly found a new place to live.
11	A romantic relationship ended. Roll a d6. An odd number means it ended with bad feelings, while an even number means it ended amicably.
12	A current or prospective romantic partner of yours died. Roll on the Cause of Death supplemental table to find out how. If the result is murder, roll a d12. On a 1, you were responsible, whether directly or indirectly.

WAR

d12	War Outcome
1	You were knocked out and left for dead. You woke up hours later with no recollection of the battle.
2–3	You were badly injured in the fight, and you still bear the awful scars of those wounds.
4	You ran away from the battle to save your life, but you still feel shame for your cowardice.
5–7	You suffered only minor injuries, and the wounds all healed without leaving scars.

d12	War Outcome
8–9	You survived the battle, but you suffer from terrible nightmares in which you relive the experience.
10–11	You escaped the battle unscathed, though many of your friends were injured or lost.
12	You acquitted yourself well in battle and are remembered as a hero. You might have received a medal for your bravery.

Weird Stuff

d12	What Happened
1	You were turned into a toad and remained in that form for 1d4 weeks.
2	You were petrified and remained a stone statue for a time until someone freed you.
3	You were enslaved by a hag, a satyr, or some other being and lived in that creature's thrall for 1d6 years.
4	A dragon held you as a prisoner for 1d4 months until adventurers killed it.
5	You were taken captive by a race of evil humanoids such as drow, kuo-toa, or quaggoths. You lived as a slave in the Underdark until you escaped.
6	You served a powerful adventurer as a hireling. You have only recently left that service. Use the supplemental tables and work with your DM to determine the basic details about your former employer.
7	You went insane for 1d6 years and recently regained your sanity. A tic or some other bit of odd behavior might linger.
8	A lover of yours was secretly a silver dragon.
9	You were captured by a cult and nearly sacrificed on an altar to the foul being the cultists served. You escaped, but you fear they will find you.
10	You met a demigod, an archdevil, an archfey, a demon lord, or a titan, and you lived to tell the tale.
11	You were swallowed by a giant fish and spent a month in its gullet before you escaped.
12	A powerful being granted you a *wish*, but you squandered it on something frivolous.

Supplemental Tables

The supplemental tables below give you a way to randomly determine characteristics and other facts about individuals who are part of your character's life. Use these tables when directed to do so by another table, or when you simply want to come up with a piece of information quickly. The tables are in alphabetical order.

Alignment

3d6	Alignment
3	Chaotic evil (50%) or chaotic neutral (50%)
4–5	Lawful evil
6–8	Neutral evil
9–12	Neutral

3d6	Alignment
13–15	Neutral good
16–17	Lawful good (50%) or lawful neutral (50%)
18	Chaotic good (50%) or chaotic neutral (50%)

Cause of Death

d12	Cause of Death
1	Unknown
2	Murdered
3	Killed in battle
4	Accident related to class or occupation
5	Accident unrelated to class or occupation
6–7	Natural causes, such as disease or old age
8	Apparent suicide
9	Torn apart by an animal or a natural disaster
10	Consumed by a monster
11	Executed for a crime or tortured to death
12	Bizarre event, such as being hit by a meteorite, struck down by an angry god, or killed by a hatching slaad egg

Class

d100	Class
01–07	Barbarian
08–14	Bard
15–29	Cleric
30–36	Druid
37–52	Fighter
53–58	Monk
59–64	Paladin
65–70	Ranger
71–84	Rogue
85–89	Sorcerer
90–94	Warlock
95–00	Wizard

Occupation

d100	Occupation
01–05	Academic
06–10	Adventurer (roll on the Class table)
11	Aristocrat
12–26	Artisan or guild member
27–31	Criminal
32–36	Entertainer
37–38	Exile, hermit, or refugee
39–43	Explorer or wanderer
44–55	Farmer or herder
56–60	Hunter or trapper
61–75	Laborer
76–80	Merchant
81–85	Politician or bureaucrat
86–90	Priest
91–95	Sailor
96–00	Soldier

RACE

d100	Race
01–40	Human
41–50	Dwarf
51–60	Elf
61–70	Halfling
71–75	Dragonborn
76–80	Gnome
81–85	Half-elf
86–90	Half-orc
91–95	Tiefling
96–00	DM's choice

RELATIONSHIP

3d4	Attitude
3–4	Hostile
5–10	Friendly
11–12	Indifferent

STATUS

3d6	Status
3	Dead (roll on the Cause of Death table)
4–5	Missing or unknown
6–8	Alive, but doing poorly due to injury, financial trouble, or relationship difficulties
9–12	Alive and well
13–15	Alive and quite successful
16–17	Alive and infamous
18	Alive and famous

WHAT'S NEXT?

When you're finished using these tables, you'll have a collection of facts and notes that—at a minimum—encapsulate what your character has been doing in the world up till now. Sometimes that might be all the information you want, but you don't have to stop there.

By using your creativity to stitch all these bits together into a continuous narrative, you can create a full-fledged autobiography for your character in as little as a few sentences—an excellent example of how the whole is greater than the sum of its parts.

Did you get a couple of results on the tables that don't outright contradict each other but also don't seem to fit together smoothly? If so, now is your chance to explain what happened to you. For instance, let's say you were born in a castle, but your childhood home was in the wilderness. It could be that your parents traveled from their forest home to seek help from a midwife at the castle when your mother was close to giving birth. Or your parents might have been members of the castle's staff before you were born, but they were released from service soon after you came into the world.

In addition to deepening your own roleplaying experience, your character's history presents your DM with opportunities to weave those elements into the story of the campaign. Any way you look at it, adding definition to your character's pre-adventuring life is time well spent.

RACIAL FEATS

Leveling up in a class is the main way a character evolves during a campaign. Some DMs also allow the use of feats to customize a character. Feats are an optional rule in chapter 6, "Customization Options," of the *Player's Handbook*. The DM decides whether they're used and may also decide that some feats are available in a campaign and others aren't.

This section introduces a collection of special feats that allow you to explore your character's race further. These feats are each associated with a race from the *Player's Handbook*, as summarized in the Racial Feats table. A racial feat represents either a deepening connection to your race's culture or a physical transformation that brings you closer to an aspect of your race's lineage.

The cause of a particular transformation is up to you and your DM. A transformational feat can symbolize a latent quality that has emerged as you age, or a transformation might be the result of an event in the campaign, such as exposure to powerful magic or visiting a place of ancient significance to your race. Transformations are a fundamental motif of fantasy literature and folklore. Figuring out why your character has changed can be a rich addition to your campaign's story.

RACIAL FEATS

Race	Feat
Dragonborn	Dragon Fear
Dragonborn	Dragon Hide
Dwarf	Dwarven Fortitude
Dwarf	Squat Nimbleness
Elf	Elven Accuracy
Elf (drow)	Drow High Magic
Elf (high)	Fey Teleportation
Elf (wood)	Wood Elf Magic
Gnome	Fade Away
Gnome	Squat Nimbleness
Half-elf	Elven Accuracy
Half-elf	Prodigy
Half-orc	Orcish Fury
Half-orc	Prodigy
Halfling	Bountiful Luck
Halfling	Second Chance
Halfling	Squat Nimbleness
Human	Prodigy
Tiefling	Flames of Phlegethos
Tiefling	Infernal Constitution

The feats are presented below in alphabetical order.

BOUNTIFUL LUCK

Prerequisite: Halfling

Your people have extraordinary luck, which you have learned to mystically lend to your companions when you see them falter. You're not sure how you do it; you just wish it, and it happens. Surely a sign of fortune's favor!

When an ally you can see within 30 feet of you rolls a 1 on the d20 for an attack roll, an ability check, or a saving throw, you can use your reaction to let the ally reroll the die. The ally must use the new roll.

When you use this ability, you can't use your Lucky racial trait before the end of your next turn.

DRAGON FEAR

Prerequisite: Dragonborn

When angered, you can radiate menace. You gain the following benefits:

- Increase your Strength, Constitution, or Charisma score by 1, to a maximum of 20.
- Instead of exhaling destructive energy, you can expend a use of your Breath Weapon trait to roar, forcing each creature of your choice within 30 feet of you to make a Wisdom saving throw (DC 8 + your proficiency bonus + your Charisma modifier). A target automatically succeeds on the save if it can't hear or see you. On a failed save, a target becomes frightened of you for 1 minute. If the frightened target takes any damage, it can repeat the saving throw, ending the effect on itself on a success.

DRAGON HIDE

Prerequisite: Dragonborn

You manifest scales and claws reminiscent of your draconic ancestors. You gain the following benefits:

- Increase your Strength, Constitution, or Charisma score by 1, to a maximum of 20.
- Your scales harden. While you aren't wearing armor, you can calculate your AC as 13 + your Dexterity modifier. You can use a shield and still gain this benefit.
- You grow retractable claws from the tips of your fingers. Extending or retracting the claws requires no action. The claws are natural weapons, which you can use to make unarmed strikes. If you hit with them, you deal slashing damage equal to 1d4 + your Strength modifier, instead of the normal bludgeoning damage for an unarmed strike.

DROW HIGH MAGIC

Prerequisite: Elf (drow)

You learn more of the magic typical of dark elves. You learn the *detect magic* spell and can cast it at will, without expending a spell slot. You also learn *levitate* and *dispel magic*, each of which you can cast once without expending a spell slot. You regain the ability to cast those two spells in this way when you finish a long rest. Charisma is your spellcasting ability for all three spells.

DWARVEN FORTITUDE

Prerequisite: Dwarf

You have the blood of dwarf heroes flowing through your veins. You gain the following benefits:

- Increase your Constitution score by 1, to a maximum of 20.

- Whenever you take the Dodge action in combat, you can spend one Hit Die to heal yourself. Roll the die, add your Constitution modifier, and regain a number of hit points equal to the total (minimum of 1).

ELVEN ACCURACY

Prerequisite: Elf or half-elf

The accuracy of elves is legendary, especially that of elf archers and spellcasters. You have uncanny aim with attacks that rely on precision rather than brute force. You gain the following benefits:

- Increase your Dexterity, Intelligence, Wisdom, or Charisma score by 1, to a maximum of 20.
- Whenever you have advantage on an attack roll using Dexterity, Intelligence, Wisdom, or Charisma, you can reroll one of the dice once.

FADE AWAY

Prerequisite: Gnome

Your people are clever, with a knack for illusion magic. You have learned a magical trick for fading away when you suffer harm. You gain the following benefits:

- Increase your Dexterity or Intelligence score by 1, to a maximum of 20.
- Immediately after you take damage, you can use a reaction to magically become invisible until the end of your next turn or until you attack, deal damage, or force someone to make a saving throw. Once you use this ability, you can't do so again until you finish a short or long rest.

FEY TELEPORTATION

Prerequisite: Elf (high)

Your study of high elven lore has unlocked fey power that few other elves possess, except your eladrin cousins. Drawing on your fey ancestry, you can momentarily stride through the Feywild to shorten your path from one place to another. You gain the following benefits:

- Increase your Intelligence or Charisma score by 1, to a maximum of 20.
- You learn to speak, read, and write Sylvan.
- You learn the *misty step* spell and can cast it once without expending a spell slot. You regain the ability to cast it in this way when you finish a short or long rest. Intelligence is your spellcasting ability for this spell.

FLAMES OF PHLEGETHOS

Prerequisite: Tiefling

You learn to call on hellfire to serve your commands. You gain the following benefits:

- Increase your Intelligence or Charisma score by 1, to a maximum of 20.
- When you roll fire damage for a spell you cast, you can reroll any roll of 1 on the fire damage dice, but you must use the new roll, even if it is another 1.
- Whenever you cast a spell that deals fire damage, you can cause flames to wreathe you until the end of your

next turn. The flames don't harm you or your possessions, and they shed bright light out to 30 feet and dim light for an additional 30 feet. While the flames are present, any creature within 5 feet of you that hits you with a melee attack takes 1d4 fire damage.

INFERNAL CONSTITUTION

Prerequisite: Tiefling

Fiendish blood runs strong in you, unlocking a resilience akin to that possessed by some fiends. You gain the following benefits:

- Increase your Constitution score by 1, to a maximum of 20.
- You have resistance to cold damage and poison damage.
- You have advantage on saving throws against being poisoned.

ORCISH FURY

Prerequisite: Half-orc

Your inner fury burns tirelessly. You gain the following benefits:

- Increase your Strength or Constitution score by 1, to a maximum of 20.
- When you hit with an attack using a simple or martial weapon, you can roll one of the weapon's damage dice an additional time and add it as extra damage of the weapon's damage type. Once you use this ability, you can't use it again until you finish a short or long rest.
- Immediately after you use your Relentless Endurance trait, you can use your reaction to make one weapon attack.

PRODIGY

Prerequisite: Half-elf, half-orc, or human

You have a knack for learning new things. You gain the following benefits:

- You gain one skill proficiency of your choice, one tool proficiency of your choice, and fluency in one language of your choice.
- Choose one skill in which you have proficiency. You gain expertise with that skill, which means your proficiency bonus is doubled for any ability check you make with it. The skill you choose must be one that isn't already benefiting from a feature, such as Expertise, that doubles your proficiency bonus.

SECOND CHANCE

Prerequisite: Halfling

Fortune favors you when someone tries to strike you. You gain the following benefits:

- Increase your Dexterity, Constitution, or Charisma score by 1, to a maximum of 20.
- When a creature you can see hits you with an attack roll, you can use your reaction to force that creature to reroll. Once you use this ability, you can't use it again until you roll initiative at the start of combat or until you finish a short or long rest.

SQUAT NIMBLENESS

Prerequisite: Dwarf or a Small race

You are uncommonly nimble for your race. You gain the following benefits:

- Increase your Strength or Dexterity score by 1, to a maximum of 20.
- Increase your walking speed by 5 feet.
- You gain proficiency in the Acrobatics or Athletics skill (your choice).
- You have advantage on any Strength (Athletics) or Dexterity (Acrobatics) check you make to escape from being grappled.

WOOD ELF MAGIC

Prerequisite: Elf (wood)

You learn the magic of the primeval woods, which are revered and protected by your people. You learn one druid cantrip of your choice. You also learn the *longstrider* and *pass without trace* spells, each of which you can cast once without expending a spell slot. You regain the ability to cast these two spells in this way when you finish a long rest. Wisdom is your spellcasting ability for all three spells.

CHAPTER 2
DUNGEON MASTER'S TOOLS

S THE DUNGEON MASTER, YOU OVERSEE the game and weave together the story experienced by your players. You're the one who keeps it all going, and this chapter is for you. It gives you new rules options, as well as some refined tools for creating and running adventures and campaigns. It is a supplement to the tools and advice offered in the *Dungeon Master's Guide.*

The chapter opens with optional rules meant to help you run certain parts of the game more smoothly. The chapter then goes into greater depth on several topics—encounter building, random encounters, traps, magic items, and downtime—which largely relate to how you create and stage your adventures.

The material in this chapter is meant to make your life easier. Ignore anything you find here that doesn't help you, and don't hesitate to customize the things that you do use. The game's rules exist to serve you and the games you run. As always, make them your own.

SIMULTANEOUS EFFECTS

Most effects in the game happen in succession, following an order set by the rules or the DM. In rare cases, effects can happen at the same time, especially at the start or end of a creature's turn. If two or more things happen at the same time on a character or monster's turn, the person at the game table—whether player or DM—who controls that creature decides the order in which those things happen. For example, if two effects occur at the end of a player character's turn, the player decides which of the two effects happens first.

FALLING

Falling from a great height is a significant risk for adventurers and their foes. The rule given in the *Player's Handbook* is simple: at the end of a fall, you take 1d6 bludgeoning damage for every 10 feet you fell, to a maximum of 20d6. You also land prone, unless you somehow avoid taking damage from the fall. Here are two optional rules that expand on that simple rule.

RATE OF FALLING

The rule for falling assumes that a creature immediately drops the entire distance when it falls. But what if a creature is at a high altitude when it falls, perhaps on the back of a griffon or on board an airship? Realistically, a fall from such a height can take more than a few seconds, extending past the end of the turn when the fall occurred. If you'd like high-altitude falls to be properly time-consuming, use the following optional rule.

When you fall from a great height, you instantly descend up to 500 feet. If you're still falling on your next turn, you descend up to 500 feet at the end of that turn. This process continues until the fall ends, either because you hit the ground or the fall is otherwise halted.

FLYING CREATURES AND FALLING

A flying creature in flight falls if it is knocked prone, if its speed is reduced to 0 feet, or if it otherwise loses the ability to move, unless it can hover or it is being held aloft by magic, such as the *fly* spell.

If you'd like a flying creature to have a better chance of surviving a fall than a non-flying creature does, use this rule: subtract the creature's current flying speed from the distance it fell before calculating falling damage. This rule is helpful to a flier that is knocked prone but is still conscious and has a current flying speed that is greater than 0 feet. The rule is designed to simulate the creature flapping its wings furiously or taking similar measures to slow the velocity of its fall.

If you use the rule for rate of falling in the previous section, a flying creature descends 500 feet on the turn when it falls, just as other creatures do. But if that creature starts any of its later turns still falling and is prone, it can halt the fall on its turn by spending half its flying speed to counter the prone condition (as if it were standing up in midair).

SLEEP

Just as in the real world, D&D characters spend many hours sleeping, most often as part of a long rest. Most monsters also need to sleep. While a creature sleeps, it is subjected to the unconscious condition. Here are a few rules that expand on that basic fact.

WAKING SOMEONE

A creature that is naturally sleeping, as opposed to being in a magically or chemically induced sleep, wakes up if it takes any damage or if someone else uses an action to shake or slap the creature awake. A sudden loud noise—such as yelling, thunder, or a ringing bell—also awakens someone that is sleeping naturally.

Whispers don't disturb sleep, unless a sleeper's passive Wisdom (Perception) score is 20 or higher and the whispers are within 10 feet of the sleeper. Speech at a normal volume awakens a sleeper if the environment is otherwise silent (no wind, birdsong, crickets, street sounds, or the like) and the sleeper has a passive Wisdom (Perception) score of 15 or higher.

SLEEPING IN ARMOR

Sleeping in light armor has no adverse effect on the wearer, but sleeping in medium or heavy armor makes it difficult to recover fully during a long rest.

When you finish a long rest during which you slept in medium or heavy armor, you regain only one quarter of your spent Hit Dice (minimum of one die). If you have any levels of exhaustion, the rest doesn't reduce your exhaustion level.

Going without a Long Rest

A long rest is never mandatory, but going without sleep does have its consequences. If you want to account for the effects of sleep deprivation on characters and creatures, use these rules.

Whenever you end a 24-hour period without finishing a long rest, you must succeed on a DC 10 Constitution saving throw or suffer one level of exhaustion.

It becomes harder to fight off exhaustion if you stay awake for multiple days. After the first 24 hours, the DC increases by 5 for each consecutive 24-hour period without a long rest. The DC resets to 10 when you finish a long rest.

Adamantine Weapons

Adamantine is an ultrahard metal found in meteorites and extraordinary mineral veins. In addition to being used to craft *adamantine armor*, the metal is also used for weapons.

Melee weapons and ammunition made of or coated with adamantine are unusually effective when used to break objects. Whenever an adamantine weapon or piece of ammunition hits an object, the hit is a critical hit.

The adamantine version of a melee weapon or of ten pieces of ammunition costs 500 gp more than the normal version, whether the weapon or ammunition is made of the metal or coated with it.

Tying Knots

The rules are purposely open-ended concerning mundane tasks like tying knots, but sometimes knowing how well a knot was fashioned is important in a dramatic scene when someone is trying to untie a knot or slip out of one. Here's an optional rule for determining the effectiveness of a knot.

The creature who ties the knot makes an Intelligence (Sleight of Hand) check when doing so. The total of the check becomes the DC for an attempt to untie the knot with an Intelligence (Sleight of Hand) check or to slip out of it with a Dexterity (Acrobatics) check.

This rule intentionally links Sleight of Hand with Intelligence, rather than Dexterity. This is an example of how to apply the rule in the "Variant: Skills with Different Abilities" section in chapter 7 of the *Player's Handbook*.

Tool Proficiencies

Tool proficiencies are a useful way to highlight a character's background and talents. At the game table, though, the use of tools sometimes overlaps with the use of skills, and it can be unclear how to use them together in certain situations. This section offers various ways that tools can be used in the game.

Tools and Skills Together

Tools have more specific applications than skills. The History skill applies to any event in the past. A tool such as a forgery kit is used to make fake objects and little else. Thus, why would a character who has the opportunity to acquire one or the other want to gain a tool proficiency instead of proficiency in a skill?

To make tool proficiencies more attractive choices for the characters, you can use the methods outlined below.

Advantage. If the use of a tool and the use of a skill both apply to a check, and a character is proficient with the tool and the skill, consider allowing the character to make the check with advantage. This simple benefit can go a long way toward encouraging players to pick up tool proficiencies. In the tool descriptions that follow, this benefit is often expressed as additional insight (or something similar), which translates into an increased chance that the check will be a success.

Added Benefit. In addition, consider giving characters who have both a relevant skill and a relevant tool proficiency an added benefit on a successful check. This benefit might be in the form of more detailed information or could simulate the effect of a different sort of successful check. For example, a character proficient with mason's tools makes a successful Wisdom (Perception) check to find a secret door in a stone wall. Not only does the character notice the door's presence, but you decide that the tool proficiency entitles the character to an automatic success on an Intelligence (Investigation) check to determine how to open the door.

Tool Descriptions

The following sections go into detail about the tools presented in the *Player's Handbook*, offering advice on how to use them in a campaign.

Components. The first paragraph in each description gives details on what a set of supplies or tools is made up of. A character who is proficient with a tool knows how to use all of its component parts.

Skills. Every tool potentially provides advantage on a check when used in conjunction with certain skills, provided a character is proficient with the tool and the skill. As DM, you can allow a character to make a check using the indicated skill with advantage. Paragraphs that begin with skill names discuss these possibilities. In each of these paragraphs, the benefits apply only to someone who has proficiency with the tool, not someone who simply owns it.

With respect to skills, the system is mildly abstract in terms of what a tool proficiency represents; essentially, it assumes that a character who has proficiency with a tool also has learned about facets of the trade or profession that are not necessarily associated with the use of the tool.

In addition, you can consider giving a character extra information or an added benefit on a skill check. The text provides some examples and ideas when this opportunity is relevant.

Special Use. Proficiency with a tool usually brings with it a particular benefit in the form of a special use, as described in this paragraph.

Sample DCs. A table at the end of each section lists activities that a tool can be used to perform, and suggested DCs for the necessary ability checks.

ALCHEMIST'S SUPPLIES

Alchemist's supplies enable a character to produce useful concoctions, such as acid or alchemist's fire.

Components. Alchemist's supplies include two glass beakers, a metal frame to hold a beaker in place over an open flame, a glass stirring rod, a small mortar and pestle, and a pouch of common alchemical ingredients, including salt, powdered iron, and purified water.

Arcana. Proficiency with alchemist's supplies allows you to unlock more information on Arcana checks involving potions and similar materials.

Investigation. When you inspect an area for clues, proficiency with alchemist's supplies grants additional insight into any chemicals or other substances that might have been used in the area.

Alchemical Crafting. You can use this tool proficiency to create alchemical items. A character can spend money to collect raw materials, which weigh 1 pound for every 50 gp spent. The DM can allow a character to make a check using the indicated skill with advantage. As part of a long rest, you can use alchemist's supplies to make one dose of acid, alchemist's fire, antitoxin, oil, perfume, or soap. Subtract half the value of the created item from the total gp worth of raw materials you are carrying.

ALCHEMIST'S SUPPLIES

Activity	DC
Create a puff of thick smoke	10
Identify a poison	10
Identify a substance	15
Start a fire	15
Neutralize acid	20

BREWER'S SUPPLIES

Brewing is the art of producing beer. Not only does beer serve as an alcoholic beverage, but the process of brewing purifies water. Crafting beer takes weeks of fermentation, but only a few hours of work.

Components. Brewer's supplies include a large glass jug, a quantity of hops, a siphon, and several feet of tubing.

History. Proficiency with brewer's supplies gives you additional insight on Intelligence (History) checks concerning events that involve alcohol as a significant element.

Medicine. This tool proficiency grants additional insight when you treat anyone suffering from alcohol poisoning or when you can use alcohol to dull pain.

Persuasion. A stiff drink can help soften the hardest heart. Your proficiency with brewer's supplies can help you ply someone with drink, giving them just enough alcohol to mellow their mood.

Potable Water. Your knowledge of brewing enables you to purify water that would otherwise be undrinkable. As part of a long rest, you can purify up to 6 gallons of water, or 1 gallon as part of a short rest.

BREWER'S SUPPLIES

Activity	DC
Detect poison or impurities in a drink	10
Identify alcohol	15
Ignore effects of alcohol	20

CALLIGRAPHER'S SUPPLIES

Calligraphy treats writing as a delicate, beautiful art. Calligraphers produce text that is pleasing to the eye, using a style that is difficult to forge. Their supplies also give them some ability to examine scripts and determine if they are legitimate, since a calligrapher's training involves long hours of studying writing and attempting to replicate its style and design.

Components. Calligrapher's supplies include ink, a dozen sheets of parchment, and three quills.

Arcana. Although calligraphy is of little help in deciphering the content of magical writings, proficiency with these supplies can aid in identifying who wrote a script of a magical nature.

History. This tool proficiency can augment the benefit of successful checks made to analyze or investigate ancient writings, scrolls, or other texts, including runes etched in stone or messages in frescoes or other displays.

Decipher Treasure Map. This tool proficiency grants you expertise in examining maps. You can make an Intelligence check to determine a map's age, whether a map includes any hidden messages, or similar facts.

CALLIGRAPHER'S SUPPLIES

Activity	DC
Identify writer of nonmagical script	10
Determine writer's state of mind	15
Spot forged text	15
Forge a signature	20

CARPENTER'S TOOLS

Skill at carpentry enables a character to construct wooden structures. A carpenter can build a house, a shack, a wooden cabinet, or similar items.

Components. Carpenter's tools include a saw, a hammer, nails, a hatchet, a square, a ruler, an adze, a plane, and a chisel.

History. This tool proficiency aids you in identifying the use and the origin of wooden buildings and other large wooden objects.

Investigation. You gain additional insight when inspecting areas within wooden structures, because you know tricks of construction that can conceal areas from discovery.

Perception. You can spot irregularities in wooden walls or floors, making it easier to find trap doors and secret passages.

Stealth. You can quickly assess the weak spots in a wooden floor, making it easier to avoid the places that creak and groan when they're stepped on.

Fortify. With 1 minute of work and raw materials, you can make a door or window harder to force open. Increase the DC needed to open it by 5.

Temporary Shelter. As part of a long rest, you can construct a lean-to or a similar shelter to keep your group dry and in the shade for the duration of the rest. Because it was fashioned quickly from whatever wood was available, the shelter collapses 1d3 days after being assembled.

CARPENTER'S TOOLS

Activity	DC
Build a simple wooden structure	10
Design a complex wooden structure	15
Find a weak point in a wooden wall	15
Pry apart a door	20

CARTOGRAPHER'S TOOLS

Using cartographer's tools, you can create accurate maps to make travel easier for yourself and those who come after you. These maps can range from large-scale depictions of mountain ranges to diagrams that show the layout of a dungeon level.

Components. Cartographer's tools consist of a quill, ink, parchment, a pair of compasses, calipers, and a ruler.

Arcana, History, Religion. You can use your knowledge of maps and locations to unearth more detailed information when you use these skills. For instance, you might spot hidden messages in a map, identify when the map was made to determine if geographical features have changed since then, and so forth.

Nature. Your familiarity with physical geography makes it easier for you to answer questions or solve issues relating to the terrain around you.

Survival. Your understanding of geography makes it easier to find paths to civilization, to predict areas where villages or towns might be found, and to avoid becoming lost. You have studied so many maps that common patterns, such as how trade routes evolve and where settlements arise in relation to geographic locations, are familiar to you.

Craft a Map. While traveling, you can draw a map as you go in addition to engaging in other activity.

CARTOGRAPHER'S TOOLS

Activity	DC
Determine a map's age and origin	10
Estimate direction and distance to a landmark	15
Discern that a map is fake	15
Fill in a missing part of a map	20

COBBLER'S TOOLS

Although the cobbler's trade might seem too humble for an adventurer, a good pair of boots will see a character across rugged wilderness and through deadly dungeons.

Components. Cobbler's tools consist of a hammer, an awl, a knife, a shoe stand, a cutter, spare leather, and thread.

Arcana, History. Your knowledge of shoes aids you in identifying the magical properties of enchanted boots or the history of such items.

Investigation. Footwear holds a surprising number of secrets. You can learn where someone has recently visited by examining the wear and the dirt that has accumulated on their shoes. Your experience in repairing shoes makes it easier for you to identify where damage might come from.

Maintain Shoes. As part of a long rest, you can repair your companions' shoes. For the next 24 hours, up to six creatures of your choice who wear shoes you worked on can travel up to 10 hours a day without making saving throws to avoid exhaustion.

Craft Hidden Compartment. With 8 hours of work, you can add a hidden compartment to a pair of shoes. The compartment can hold an object up to 3 inches long and 1 inch wide and deep. You make an Intelligence check using your tool proficiency to determine the Intelligence (Investigation) check DC needed to find the compartment.

COBBLER'S TOOLS

Activity	DC
Determine a shoe's age and origin	10
Find a hidden compartment in a boot heel	15

COOK'S UTENSILS

Adventuring is a hard life. With a cook along on the journey, your meals will be much better than the typical mix of hardtack and dried fruit.

Components. Cook's utensils include a metal pot, knives, forks, a stirring spoon, and a ladle.

History. Your knowledge of cooking techniques allows you to assess the social patterns involved in a culture's eating habits.

Medicine. When administering treatment, you can transform medicine that is bitter or sour into a pleasing concoction.

Survival. When foraging for food, you can make do with ingredients you scavenge that others would be unable to transform into nourishing meals.

Prepare Meals. As part of a short rest, you can prepare a tasty meal that helps your companions regain their strength. You and up to five creatures of your choice regain 1 extra hit point per Hit Die spent during a short rest, provided you have access to your cook's utensils and sufficient food.

COOK'S UTENSILS

Activity	DC
Create a typical meal	10
Duplicate a meal	10
Spot poison or impurities in food	15
Create a gourmet meal	15

DISGUISE KIT

The perfect tool for anyone who wants to engage in trickery, a disguise kit enables its owner to adopt a false identity.

Components. A disguise kit includes cosmetics, hair dye, small props, and a few pieces of clothing.

Deception. In certain cases, a disguise can improve your ability to weave convincing lies.

Intimidation. The right disguise can make you look more fearsome, whether you want to scare someone away by posing as a plague victim or intimidate a gang of thugs by taking the appearance of a bully.

Performance. A cunning disguise can enhance an audience's enjoyment of a performance, provided the disguise is properly designed to evoke the desired reaction.

Persuasion. Folk tend to trust a person in uniform. If you disguise yourself as an authority figure, your efforts to persuade others are often more effective.

Create Disguise. As part of a long rest, you can create a disguise. It takes you 1 minute to don such a disguise once you have created it. You can carry only one such disguise on you at a time without drawing undue attention, unless you have a *bag of holding* or a similar method to keep them hidden. Each disguise weighs 1 pound.

At other times, it takes 10 minutes to craft a disguise that involves moderate changes to your appearance, and 30 minutes for one that requires more extensive changes.

DISGUISE KIT

Activity	DC
Cover injuries or distinguishing marks	10
Spot a disguise being used by someone else	15
Copy a humanoid's appearance	20

FORGERY KIT

A forgery kit is designed to duplicate documents and to make it easier to copy a person's seal or signature.

Components. A forgery kit includes several different types of ink, a variety of parchments and papers, several quills, seals and sealing wax, gold and silver leaf, and small tools to sculpt melted wax to mimic a seal.

Arcana. A forgery kit can be used in conjunction with the Arcana skill to determine if a magic item is real or fake.

Deception. A well-crafted forgery, such as papers proclaiming you to be a noble or a writ that grants you safe passage, can lend credence to a lie.

History. A forgery kit combined with your knowledge of history improves your ability to create fake historical documents or to tell if an old document is authentic.

Investigation. When you examine objects, proficiency with a forgery kit is useful for determining how an object was made and whether it is genuine.

Other Tools. Knowledge of other tools makes your forgeries that much more believable. For example, you could combine proficiency with a forgery kit and proficiency with cartographer's tools to make a fake map.

Quick Fake. As part of a short rest, you can produce a forged document no more than one page in length. As part of a long rest, you can produce a document that is up to four pages long. Your Intelligence check using a forgery kit determines the DC for someone else's Intelligence (Investigation) check to spot the fake.

FORGERY KIT

Activity	DC
Mimic handwriting	15
Duplicate a wax seal	20

GAMING SET

Proficiency with a gaming set applies to one type of game, such as Three-Dragon Ante or games of chance that use dice.

Components. A gaming set has all the pieces needed to play a specific game or type of game, such as a complete deck of cards or a board and tokens.

History. Your mastery of a game includes knowledge of its history, as well as of important events it was connected to or prominent historical figures involved with it.

Insight. Playing games with someone is a good way to gain understanding of their personality, granting you a better ability to discern their lies from their truths and read their mood.

Sleight of Hand. Sleight of Hand is a useful skill for cheating at a game, as it allows you to swap pieces, palm cards, or alter a die roll. Alternatively, engrossing a target in a game by manipulating the components with dexterous movements is a great distraction for a pickpocketing attempt.

GAMING SET

Activity	DC
Catch a player cheating	15
Gain insight into an opponent's personality	15

GLASSBLOWER'S TOOLS

Someone who is proficient with glassblower's tools has not only the ability to shape glass, but also specialized knowledge of the methods used to produce glass objects.

Components. The tools include a blowpipe, a small marver, blocks, and tweezers. You need a source of heat to work glass.

Arcana, History. Your knowledge of glassmaking techniques aids you when you examine glass objects, such as potion bottles or glass items found in a treasure hoard. For instance, you can study how a glass potion bottle has been changed by its contents to help determine a potion's effects. (A potion might leave behind a residue, deform the glass, or stain it.)

Investigation. When you study an area, your knowledge can aid you if the clues include broken glass or glass objects.

Identify Weakness. With 1 minute of study, you can identify the weak points in a glass object. Any damage dealt to the object by striking a weak spot is doubled.

GLASSBLOWER'S TOOLS

Activity	DC
Identify source of glass	10
Determine what a glass object once held	20

HERBALISM KIT

Proficiency with an herbalism kit allows you to identify plants and safely collect their useful elements.

Components. An herbalism kit includes pouches to store herbs, clippers and leather gloves for collecting plants, a mortar and pestle, and several glass jars.

Arcana. Your knowledge of the nature and uses of herbs can add insight to your magical studies that deal with plants and your attempts to identify potions.

Investigation. When you inspect an area overgrown with plants, your proficiency can help you pick out details and clues that others might miss.

Medicine. Your mastery of herbalism improves your ability to treat illnesses and wounds by augmenting your methods of care with medicinal plants.

Nature and Survival. When you travel in the wild, your skill in herbalism makes it easier to identify plants and spot sources of food that others might overlook.

Identify Plants. You can identify most plants with a quick inspection of their appearance and smell.

HERBALISM KIT

Activity	DC
Find plants	15
Identify poison	20

JEWELER'S TOOLS

Training with jeweler's tools includes the basic techniques needed to beautify gems. It also gives you expertise in identifying precious stones.

Components. Jeweler's tools consist of a small saw and hammer, files, pliers, and tweezers.

Arcana. Proficiency with jeweler's tools grants you knowledge about the reputed mystical uses of gems.

This insight proves handy when you make Arcana checks related to gems or gem-encrusted items.

Investigation. When you inspect jeweled objects, your proficiency with jeweler's tools aids you in picking out clues they might hold.

Identify Gems. You can identify gems and determine their value at a glance.

JEWELER'S TOOLS

Activity	DC
Modify a gem's appearance	15
Determine a gem's history	20

LAND AND WATER VEHICLES

Proficiency with land vehicles covers a wide range of options, from chariots and howdahs to wagons and carts. Proficiency with water vehicles covers anything that navigates waterways. Proficiency with vehicles grants the knowledge needed to handle vehicles of that type, along with knowledge of how to repair and maintain them.

In addition, a character proficient with water vehicles is knowledgeable about anything a professional sailor would be familiar with, such as information about the sea and islands, tying knots, and assessing weather and sea conditions.

Arcana. When you study a magic vehicle, this tool proficiency aids you in uncovering lore or determining how the vehicle operates.

Investigation, Perception. When you inspect a vehicle for clues or hidden information, your proficiency aids you in noticing things that others might miss.

Vehicle Handling. When piloting a vehicle, you can apply your proficiency bonus to the vehicle's AC and saving throws.

VEHICLES

Activity	DC
Navigate rough terrain or waters	10
Assess a vehicle's condition	15
Take a tight corner at high speed	20

LEATHERWORKER'S TOOLS

Knowledge of leatherworking extends to lore concerning animal hides and their properties. It also confers knowledge of leather armor and similar goods.

Components. Leatherworker's tools include a knife, a small mallet, an edger, a hole punch, thread, and leather scraps.

Arcana. Your expertise in working with leather grants you added insight when you inspect magic items crafted from leather, such as boots and some cloaks.

Investigation. You gain added insight when studying leather items or clues related to them, as you draw on your knowledge of leather to pick out details that others would overlook.

Identify Hides. When looking at a hide or a leather item, you can determine the source of the leather and any special techniques used to treat it. For example, you can spot the difference between leather crafted using dwarven methods and leather crafted using halfling methods.

Leatherworker's Tools

Activity	DC
Modify a leather item's appearance	10
Determine a leather item's history	20

Mason's Tools

Mason's tools allow you to craft stone structures, including walls and buildings crafted from brick.

Components. Mason's tools consist of a trowel, a hammer, a chisel, brushes, and a square.

History. Your expertise aids you in identifying a stone building's date of construction and purpose, along with insight into who might have built it.

Investigation. You gain additional insight when inspecting areas within stone structures.

Perception. You can spot irregularities in stone walls or floors, making it easier to find trap doors and secret passages.

Demolition. Your knowledge of masonry allows you to spot weak points in brick walls. You deal double damage to such structures with your weapon attacks.

Mason's Tools

Activity	DC
Chisel a small hole in a stone wall	10
Find a weak point in a stone wall	15

Musical Instruments

Proficiency with a musical instrument indicates you are familiar with the techniques used to play it. You also have knowledge of some songs commonly performed with that instrument.

History. Your expertise aids you in recalling lore related to your instrument.

Performance. Your ability to put on a good show is improved when you incorporate an instrument into your act.

Compose a Tune. As part of a long rest, you can compose a new tune and lyrics for your instrument. You might use this ability to impress a noble or spread scandalous rumors with a catchy tune.

Musical Instrument

Activity	DC
Identify a tune	10
Improvise a tune	20

Navigator's Tools

Proficiency with navigator's tools helps you determine a true course based on observing the stars. It also grants you insight into charts and maps while developing your sense of direction.

Components. Navigator's tools include a sextant, a compass, calipers, a ruler, parchment, ink, and a quill.

Survival. Knowledge of navigator's tools helps you avoid becoming lost and also grants you insight into the most likely location for roads and settlements.

Sighting. By taking careful measurements, you can determine your position on a nautical chart and the time of day.

Navigator's Tools

Activity	DC
Plot a course	10
Discover your position on a nautical chart	15

Painter's Supplies

Proficiency with painter's supplies represents your ability to paint and draw. You also acquire an understanding of art history, which can aid you in examining works of art.

Components. Painter's supplies include an easel, canvas, paints, brushes, charcoal sticks, and a palette.

Arcana, History, Religion. Your expertise aids you in uncovering lore of any sort that is attached to a work of art, such as the magical properties of a painting or the origins of a strange mural found in a dungeon.

Investigation, Perception. When you inspect a painting or a similar work of visual art, your knowledge of the practices behind creating it can grant you additional insight.

Painting and Drawing. As part of a short or long rest, you can produce a simple work of art. Although your work might lack precision, you can capture an image or a scene, or make a quick copy of a piece of art you saw.

Painter's Supplies

Activity	DC
Paint an accurate portrait	10
Create a painting with a hidden message	20

Poisoner's Kit

A poisoner's kit is a favored resource for thieves, assassins, and others who engage in skulduggery. It allows you to apply poisons and create them from various materials. Your knowledge of poisons also helps you treat them.

Components. A poisoner's kit includes glass vials, a mortar and pestle, chemicals, and a glass stirring rod.

History. Your training with poisons can help you when you try to recall facts about infamous poisonings.

Investigation, Perception. Your knowledge of poisons has taught you to handle those substances carefully, giving you an edge when you inspect poisoned objects or try to extract clues from events that involve poison.

Medicine. When you treat the victim of a poison, your knowledge grants you added insight into how to provide the best care to your patient.

Nature, Survival. Working with poisons enables you to acquire lore about which plants and animals are poisonous.

Handle Poison. Your proficiency allows you to handle and apply a poison without risk of exposing yourself to its effects.

Poisoner's Tools

Activity	DC
Spot a poisoned object	10
Determine the effects of a poison	20

Arcana and History. Your expertise lends you additional insight when examining metal objects, such as weapons.

Investigation. You can spot clues and make deductions that others might overlook when an investigation involves armor, weapons, or other metalwork.

Repair. With access to your tools and an open flame hot enough to make metal pliable, you can restore 10 hit points to a damaged metal object for each hour of work.

SMITH'S TOOLS

Activity	DC
Sharpen a dull blade	10
Repair a suit of armor	15
Sunder a nonmagical metal object	15

THIEVES' TOOLS

Perhaps the most common tools used by adventurers, thieves' tools are designed for picking locks and foiling traps. Proficiency with the tools also grants you a general knowledge of traps and locks.

Components. Thieves' tools include a small file, a set of lock picks, a small mirror mounted on a metal handle, a set of narrow-bladed scissors, and a pair of pliers.

History. Your knowledge of traps grants you insight when answering questions about locations that are renowned for their traps.

Investigation and Perception. You gain additional insight when looking for traps, because you have learned a variety of common signs that betray their presence.

Set a Trap. Just as you can disable traps, you can also set them. As part of a short rest, you can create a trap using items you have on hand. The total of your check becomes the DC for someone else's attempt to discover or disable the trap. The trap deals damage appropriate to the materials used in crafting it (such as poison or a weapon) or damage equal to half the total of your check, whichever the DM deems appropriate.

THIEVES' TOOLS

Activity	DC
Pick a lock	Varies
Disable a trap	Varies

TINKER'S TOOLS

A set of tinker's tools is designed to enable you to repair many mundane objects. Though you can't manufacture much with tinker's tools, you can mend torn clothes, sharpen a worn sword, and patch a tattered suit of chain mail.

Components. Tinker's tools include a variety of hand tools, thread, needles, a whetstone, scraps of cloth and leather, and a small pot of glue.

History. You can determine the age and origin of objects, even if you have only a few pieces remaining from the original.

Investigation. When you inspect a damaged object, you gain knowledge of how it was damaged and how long ago.

POTTER'S TOOLS

Potter's tools are used to create a variety of ceramic objects, most typically pots and similar vessels.

Components. Potter's tools include potter's needles, ribs, scrapers, a knife, and calipers.

History. Your expertise aids you in identifying ceramic objects, including when they were created and their likely place or culture of origin.

Investigation, Perception. You gain additional insight when inspecting ceramics, uncovering clues others would overlook by spotting minor irregularities.

Reconstruction. By examining pottery shards, you can determine an object's original, intact form and its likely purpose.

POTTER'S TOOLS

Activity	DC
Determine what a vessel once held	10
Create a serviceable pot	15
Find a weak point in a ceramic object	20

SMITH'S TOOLS

Smith's tools allow you to work metal, heating it to alter its shape, repair damage, or work raw ingots into useful items.

Components. Smith's tools include hammers, tongs, charcoal, rags, and a whetstone.

Repair. You can restore 10 hit points to a damaged object for each hour of work. For any object, you need access to the raw materials required to repair it. For metal objects, you need access to an open flame hot enough to make the metal pliable.

TINKER'S TOOLS

Activity	DC
Temporarily repair a disabled device	10
Repair an item in half the time	15
Improvise a temporary item using scraps	20

WEAVER'S TOOLS

Weaver's tools allow you to create cloth and tailor it into articles of clothing.

Components. Weaver's tools include thread, needles, and scraps of cloth. You know how to work a loom, but such equipment is too large to transport.

Arcana, History. Your expertise lends you additional insight when examining cloth objects, including cloaks and robes.

Investigation. Using your knowledge of the process of creating cloth objects, you can spot clues and make deductions that others would overlook when you examine tapestries, upholstery, clothing, and other woven items.

Repair. As part of a short rest, you can repair a single damaged cloth object.

Craft Clothing. Assuming you have access to sufficient cloth and thread, you can create an outfit for a creature as part of a long rest.

WEAVER'S TOOLS

Activity	DC
Repurpose cloth	10
Mend a hole in a piece of cloth	10
Tailor an outfit	15

WOODCARVER'S TOOLS

Woodcarver's tools allow you to craft intricate objects from wood, such as wooden tokens or arrows.

Components. Woodcarver's tools consist of a knife, a gouge, and a small saw.

Arcana, History. Your expertise lends you additional insight when you examine wooden objects, such as figurines or arrows.

Nature. Your knowledge of wooden objects gives you some added insight when you examine trees.

Repair. As part of a short rest, you can repair a single damaged wooden object.

Craft Arrows. As part of a short rest, you can craft up to five arrows. As part of a long rest, you can craft up to twenty. You must have enough wood on hand to produce them.

WOODCARVER'S TOOLS

Activity	DC
Craft a small wooden figurine	10
Carve an intricate pattern in wood	15

SPELLCASTING

This section expands on the spellcasting rules presented in the *Player's Handbook* and the *Dungeon Master's Guide*, providing clarifications and new options.

PERCEIVING A CASTER AT WORK

Many spells create obvious effects: explosions of fire, walls of ice, teleportation, and the like. Other spells, such as *charm person*, display no visible, audible, or otherwise perceptible sign of their effects, and could easily go unnoticed by someone unaffected by them. As noted in the *Player's Handbook*, you normally don't know that a spell has been cast unless the spell produces a noticeable effect.

But what about the act of casting a spell? Is it possible for someone to perceive that a spell is being cast in their presence? To be perceptible, the casting of a spell must involve a verbal, somatic, or material component. The form of a material component doesn't matter for the purposes of perception, whether it's an object specified in the spell's description, a component pouch, or a spellcasting focus.

If the need for a spell's components has been removed by a special ability, such as the sorcerer's Subtle Spell feature or the Innate Spellcasting trait possessed by many creatures, the casting of the spell is imperceptible. If an imperceptible casting produces a perceptible effect, it's normally impossible to determine who cast the spell in the absence of other evidence.

IDENTIFYING A SPELL

Sometimes a character wants to identify a spell that someone else is casting or that was already cast. To do so, a character can use their reaction to identify a spell as it's being cast, or they can use an action on their turn to identify a spell by its effect after it is cast.

If the character perceived the casting, the spell's effect, or both, the character can make an Intelligence (Arcana) check with the reaction or action. The DC equals 15 + the spell's level. If the spell is cast as a class spell and the character is a member of that class, the check is made with advantage. For example, if the spellcaster casts a spell as a cleric, another cleric has advantage on the check to identify the spell. Some spells aren't associated with any class when they're cast, such as when a monster uses its Innate Spellcasting trait.

This Intelligence (Arcana) check represents the fact that identifying a spell requires a quick mind and familiarity with the theory and practice of casting. This is true even for a character whose spellcasting ability is Wisdom or Charisma. Being able to cast spells doesn't by itself make you adept at deducing exactly what others are doing when they cast their spells.

INVALID SPELL TARGETS

A spell specifies what a caster can target with it: any type of creature, a creature of a certain type (humanoid or beast, for instance), an object, an area, the caster, or something else. But what happens if a spell targets something that isn't a valid target? For example,

someone might cast *charm person* on a creature be-
lieved to be a humanoid, not knowing that the target is
in fact a vampire. If this issue comes up, handle it using
the following rule.

If you cast a spell on someone or something that can't
be affected by the spell, nothing happens to that target,
but if you used a spell slot to cast the spell, the slot is
still expended. If the spell normally has no effect on a
target that succeeds on a saving throw, the invalid target
appears to have succeeded on its saving throw, even
though it didn't attempt one (giving no hint that the creature is in fact an invalid target). Otherwise, you perceive
that the spell did nothing to the target.

AREAS OF EFFECT ON A GRID

The *Dungeon Master's Guide* includes the following
short rule for using areas of effect on a grid.

Choose an intersection of squares as the point of
origin of an area of effect, then follow the rules for that
kind of area as normal (see the "Areas of Effect" section
in chapter 10 of the *Player's Handbook*). If an area of effect is circular and covers at least half a square, it affects
that square.

That rule works, but it can require a fair amount of
on-the-spot adjudication. This section offers two alternatives for determining the exact location of an area: the
template method and the token method. Both of these
methods assume you're using a grid and miniatures of
some sort. Because these methods can yield different
results for the number of squares in a given area, it's
not recommended that they be combined at the table—
choose whichever method you and your players find easier or more intuitive.

TEMPLATE METHOD

The template method uses two-dimensional shapes
that represent different areas of effect. The aim of the
method is to accurately portray the length and width
of each area on the grid and to leave little doubt about
which creatures are affected by it. You'll need to make
these templates or find premade ones.

Making a Template. Making a template is simple. Get
a piece of paper or card stock, and cut it in the shape of
the area of effect you're using. Every 5 feet of the area
equals 1 inch of the template's size. For example, the
20-foot-radius sphere of the *fireball* spell, which has a
40-foot diameter, would translate into a circular template with an 8-inch diameter.

Using a Template. To use an area-of-effect template,
apply it to the grid. If the terrain is flat, you can lay it on
the surface; otherwise, hold the template above the surface and take note of which squares it covers or partially
covers. If any part of a square is under the template, that
square is included in the area of effect. If a creature's
miniature is in an affected square, that creature is in
the area. Being adjacent to the edge of the template
isn't enough for a square to be included in the area of
effect; the square must be entirely or partly covered by
the template.

You can also use this method without a grid. If you do
so, a creature is included in an area of effect if any part
of the miniature's base is overlapped by the template.

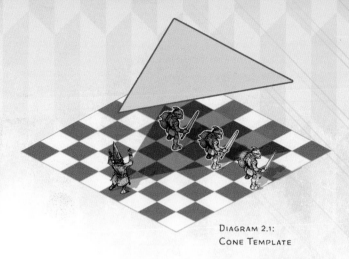

DIAGRAM 2.1:
CONE TEMPLATE

DIAGRAM 2.2:
SPHERE TEMPLATE

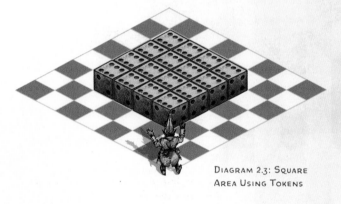

DIAGRAM 2.3: SQUARE
AREA USING TOKENS

DIAGRAM 2.4: SQUARE
AREA WITH TOTAL COVER

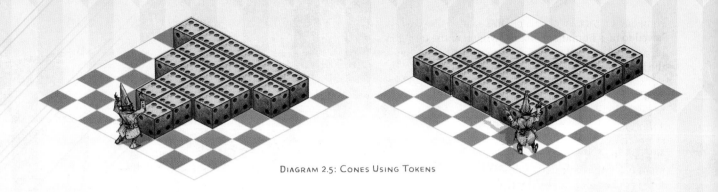

DIAGRAM 2.5: CONES USING TOKENS

DIAGRAM 2.6: LINES USING TOKENS

When you place a template, follow all the rules in the *Player's Handbook* for placing the associated area of effect. If an area of effect, such as a cone or a line, originates from a spellcaster, the template should extend out from the caster and be positioned however the caster likes within the bounds of the rules.

Diagrams 2.1 and 2.2 show the template method in action.

TOKEN METHOD

The token method is meant to make areas of effect tactile and fun. To use this method, grab some dice or other tokens, which you're going to use to represent your areas of effect.

Rather than faithfully representing the shapes of the different areas of effect, this method gives you a way to create square-edged versions of them on a grid easily, as described in the following subsections.

Using Tokens. Every 5-foot square of an area of effect becomes a die or other token that you place on the grid. Each token goes inside a square, not at an intersection of lines. If an area's token is in a square, that square is included in the area of effect. It's that simple.

Diagrams 2.3 through 2.6 show this method in action, using dice as the tokens.

Circles. This method depicts everything using squares, and a circular area of effect becomes square in it, whether the area is a sphere, cylinder, or radius. For instance, the 10-foot radius of *flame strike*, which has a diameter of 20 feet, is expressed as a square that is 20 feet on a side, as shown in diagram 2.3. Diagram 2.4 shows that area with total cover inside it.

Cones. A cone is represented by rows of tokens on the grid, extending from the cone's point of origin. In the rows, the squares are adjoining side by side or corner to corner, as shown in diagram 2.5. To determine the number of rows a cone contains, divide its length by 5. For example, a 30-foot cone contains six rows.

Here's how to create the rows. Starting with a square adjacent to the cone's point of origin, place one token. The square can be orthogonally or diagonally adjacent to the point of origin. In every row beyond that one, place as many tokens as you placed in the previous row, plus one more token. Place this row's tokens so that their squares each share a side with a square in the previous row. If the cone is orthogonally adjacent to the point of origin, you'll have one more token to place in the row; place it on one end or the other of the row you just created (you don't have to pick the side chosen in diagram 2.5). Keep placing tokens in this way until you've created all of the cone's rows.

Lines. A line can extend from its source orthogonally or diagonally, as shown in diagram 2.6.

ENCOUNTER BUILDING

This section introduces new guidelines on building combat encounters for an adventure. They are an alternative to the rules in "Creating Encounters" in chapter 3 of the *Dungeon Master's Guide*. This approach uses the same math that underlies the rules presented in that book, but it makes a few adjustments to the way that math is presented to produce a more flexible system.

This encounter-building system assumes that, as DM, you want to have a clear understanding of the threat posed by a group of monsters. It will be useful to you if you want to emphasize combat in your adventure, if you want to ensure that a foe isn't too deadly for a group of characters, and if you want to understand the relationship between a character's level and a monster's challenge rating.

Building an encounter using these guidelines follows a series of steps.

STEP 1: ASSESS THE CHARACTERS

To build an encounter using this system, first take stock of the player characters. This system uses the characters' levels to determine the numbers and challenge ratings of creatures you can pit them against without making a fight too hard or too easy. Even though character level is important, you should also take note of each character's hit point maximum and saving throw modifiers, as well as how much damage the mightiest characters can deal with a single attack. Character level and challenge rating are good for defining the difficulty of an encounter, but they don't tell the whole story. You'll make use of these additional character statistics when you select monsters for an encounter in step 4.

STEP 2: CHOOSE ENCOUNTER SIZE

Determine whether you want to create a battle that pits one creature against the characters, or if you want to use multiple monsters. If the fight is against a single opponent, your best candidate for that foe is one of the game's legendary creatures, which are designed to fill this need. If the battle involves multiple monsters, decide roughly how many creatures you want to use before continuing with step 3.

STEP 3: DETERMINE NUMBERS AND CHALLENGE RATINGS

The process for building fights that feature only one legendary monster is simple. The Solo Monster Challenge Rating table shows you which challenge rating (CR) to use for a legendary creature opposing a party of four to six characters, creating a satisfying but difficult battle. For example, for a party of five 9th-level characters, a CR 12 legendary creature makes an optimal encounter.

For a more perilous battle, match up the characters with a legendary creature whose challenge rating is 1 or 2 higher than optimal. For an easy fight, use a legendary creature whose challenge rating is 3 or more lower than the challenge rating for an optimal encounter.

SOLO MONSTER CHALLENGE RATING

Character Level	Party Size		
	6 Characters	5 Characters	4 Characters
1st	2	2	1
2nd	4	3	2
3rd	5	4	3
4th	6	5	4
5th	9	8	7
6th	10	9	8
7th	11	10	9
8th	12	11	10
9th	13	12	11
10th	14	13	12
11th	15	14	13
12th	17	16	15
13th	18	17	16
14th	19	18	17
15th	20	19	18
16th	21	20	19
17th	22	21	20
18th	22	21	20
19th	23	22	21
20th	24	23	22

If your encounter features multiple monsters, balancing it takes a little more work. Refer to the Multiple Monsters tables, which are broken up by level ranges, providing information for how to balance encounters for characters of 1st–5th level, 6th–10th level, 11th–15th level, and 16th–20th level.

First, you need to note the challenge rating for each creature the party will face. Then, to create your encounter, find the level of each character on the appropriate table. Each table shows what a single character of a given level is equivalent to in terms of challenge rating—a value represented by a ratio that compares numbers of characters to a single monster ranked by challenge rating. The first number in each expression is the number of characters of the given level. The second number tells how many monsters of the listed challenge rating those characters are equivalent to.

For example, reading the row for 1st-level characters from the 1st–5th Level table, we see that one 1st-level character is the equivalent of two CR 1/8 monsters or one CR 1/4 monster. The ratio reverses for higher challenge ratings, where a single monster is more powerful than a single 1st-level character. One CR 1/2 creature is equivalent to three 1st-level characters, while one CR 1 opponent is equivalent to five.

Let's say you have a party of four 3rd-level characters. Using the table, you can see that one CR 2 foe is a good match for the entire party, but that the characters will likely have a hard time handling a CR 3 creature.

Using the same guidelines, you can mix and match challenge ratings to put together a group of creatures to oppose four 3rd-level characters. For example, you could select one CR 1 creature. That's worth two 3rd-level characters, leaving you with two characters' worth of monsters to allocate. You could then add two CR 1/4 monsters to account for one other character and one CR 1/2 monster to account for the final character. In total, your encounter has one CR 1, one CR 1/2, and two CR 1/4 creatures.

For groups in which the characters are of different levels, you have two options. You can group all characters of the same level together, match them with monsters, and then combine all the creatures into one encounter. Alternatively, you can determine the group's average level and treat each character as being of that level for the purpose of selecting appropriate monsters.

The above guidelines are designed to create a fight that will challenge a party while still being winnable. If you want to create an easier encounter that will challenge characters but not threaten to defeat them, you can treat the party as if it were roughly one-third

smaller than it is. For example, to make an easy encounter for a party of five characters, put them up against monsters that would be a tough fight for three characters. Likewise, you can treat the party as up to half again larger to build a battle that is potentially deadly, though still not likely to be an automatic defeat. A party of four characters facing an encounter designed for six characters would fall into this category.

WEAK MONSTERS AND HIGH-LEVEL CHARACTERS

To save space on the tables and keep them simple, some of the lower challenge ratings are missing from the higher-level tables. For low challenge ratings not appearing on the table, assume a 1:12 ratio, indicating that twelve creatures of those challenge ratings are equivalent to one character of a specific level.

STEP 4: SELECT MONSTERS

After using the tables from the previous step to determine the challenge ratings of the monsters in your encounter, you're ready to pick individual monsters. This process is more of an art than a science.

In addition to assessing monsters by challenge rating, it's important to look at how certain monsters might

Managing a lot of minions is hard.
You end up getting mad and eating half of them.
It's easier if you can keep an eye on each one.
So stick with ten, eleven tops.

MULTIPLE MONSTERS: 1ST–5TH LEVEL

Character Level	Challenge Rating								
	1/8	1/4	1/2	1	2	3	4	5	6
1st	1:2	1:1	3:1	5:1	—	—	—	—	—
2nd	1:3	1:2	1:1	3:1	6:1	—	—	—	—
3rd	1:5	1:2	1:1	2:1	4:1	6:1	—	—	—
4th	1:8	1:4	1:2	1:1	2:1	4:1	6:1	—	—
5th	1:12	1:8	1:4	1:2	1:1	2:1	3:1	5:1	6:1

MULTIPLE MONSTERS: 6TH–10TH LEVEL

Character Level	Challenge Rating												
	1/8	1/4	1/2	1	2	3	4	5	6	7	8	9	10
6th	1:12	1:9	1:5	1:2	1:1	2:1	2:1	4:1	5:1	6:1	—	—	—
7th	1:12	1:12	1:6	1:3	1:1	1:1	2:1	3:1	4:1	5:1	—	—	—
8th	1:12	1:12	1:7	1:4	1:2	1:1	2:1	3:1	3:1	4:1	6:1	—	—
9th	1:12	1:12	1:8	1:4	1:2	1:1	1:1	2:1	3:1	4:1	5:1	6:1	—
10th	1:12	1:12	1:10	1:5	1:2	1:1	1:1	2:1	2:1	3:1	4:1	5:1	6:1

MULTIPLE MONSTERS: 11TH–15TH LEVEL

Character Level	Challenge Rating														
	1	2	3	4	5	6	7	8	9	10	11	12	13	14	15
11th	1:6	1:3	1:2	1:1	2:1	2:1	2:1	3:1	4:1	5:1	6:1	—	—	—	—
12th	1:8	1:3	1:2	1:1	1:1	2:1	2:1	3:1	3:1	4:1	5:1	6:1	—	—	—
13th	1:9	1:4	1:2	1:2	1:1	1:1	2:1	2:1	3:1	3:1	4:1	5:1	6:1	—	—
14th	1:10	1:4	1:3	1:2	1:1	1:1	2:1	2:1	3:1	3:1	4:1	4:1	5:1	6:1	—
15th	1:12	1:5	1:3	1:2	1:1	1:1	1:1	2:1	2:1	3:1	3:1	4:1	5:1	5:1	6:1

MULTIPLE MONSTERS: 16TH–20TH LEVEL

Character Level	Challenge Rating																		
	2	3	4	5	6	7	8	9	10	11	12	13	14	15	16	17	18	19	20
16th	1:5	1:3	1:2	1:1	1:1	1:1	2:1	2:1	2:1	3:1	4:1	4:1	5:1	5:1	6:1	—	—	—	—
17th	1:7	1:4	1:3	1:2	1:1	1:1	1:1	2:1	2:1	2:1	3:1	3:1	4:1	4:1	5:1	6:1	—	—	—
18th	1:7	1:5	1:3	1:2	1:1	1:1	1:1	2:1	2:1	2:1	3:1	3:1	4:1	4:1	5:1	6:1	6:1	—	—
19th	1:8	1:5	1:3	1:2	1:2	1:1	1:1	1:1	2:1	2:1	2:1	3:1	3:1	4:1	4:1	5:1	6:1	6:1	—
20th	1:9	1:6	1:4	1:2	1:2	1:1	1:1	1:1	1:1	2:1	2:1	2:1	3:1	3:1	4:1	4:1	5:1	5:1	6:1

stack up against your group. Hit points, attacks, and saving throws are all useful indicators. Compare the damage a monster can deal to the hit point maximum of each character. Be wary of any monster that is capable of dropping a character with a single attack, unless you are designing the fight to be especially deadly.

In the same way, compare the monsters' hit points to the damage output of the party's strongest characters, again looking for targets that can be killed with one blow. Having a significant number of foes drop in the first rounds of combat can make an encounter too easy.

Likewise, look at whether a monster's deadliest abilities call for saving throws that most of the party members are weak with, and compare the characters' offensive abilities to the monsters' saving throws.

If the only creatures you can choose from at the desired challenge rating aren't a good match for the characters' statistics, don't be afraid to go back to step 3. By altering your challenge rating targets and adjusting the number of creatures in the encounter, you can come up with different options for building the encounter.

STEP 5: ADD FLAVOR

The events that unfold during an encounter have to do with a lot more than swinging weapons and casting spells. The most interesting confrontations also take into account the personality or behavior of the monsters, perhaps determining whether they can be communicated with or whether they're all acting in concert. Other possible factors include the nature of the physical environment, such as whether it includes obstacles or other features that might come into play, and the ever-present possibility of something unexpected taking place.

If you already have ideas for how to flesh out your encounter in these ways, go right ahead and finish your creation. Otherwise, take a look at the following sections for some basic advice on adding flavor elements to the simple mechanics of the fight.

Monster Personality

To address the question of a monster's personality, you can use the tables in chapter 4 of the *Dungeon Master's Guide*, use the Monster Personality table below, or simply jot down a few notes based on a creature's *Monster Manual* description. During the battle, you can use these ideas to inform how you portray the monsters and their actions. To keep things simple, you can assign the same personality traits to an entire group of monsters. For example, one bandit gang might be an unruly mob of braggarts, while the members of another gang are always on edge and ready to flee at the first sign of danger.

Monster Personality

d8	Personality
1	Cowardly; looking to surrender
2	Greedy; wants treasure
3	Braggart; makes a show of bravery but runs from danger
4	Fanatic; ready to die fighting
5	Rabble; poorly trained and easily rattled
6	Brave; stands its ground
7	Joker; taunts its enemies
8	Bully; refuses to believe it can lose

Monster Relationships

Do rivalries, hatreds, or attachments exist among the monsters in an encounter? If so, you can use such relationships to inform the monsters' behavior during combat. The death of a much-revered leader might throw its followers into a frenzy. On the other hand, a monster might decide to flee if its spouse is killed, or a mistreated toady might be eager to surrender and betray its master in return for its life.

Monster Relationships

d6	Relationship
1	Has a rival; wants one random ally to suffer
2	Is abused by others; hangs back, betrays at first opportunity
3	Is worshiped; allies will die for it
4	Is outcast by group; its allies ignore it
5	Is outcast by choice; cares only for itself
6	Is seen as a bully; its allies want to see it defeated

Terrain and Traps

A few elements that make a battlefield something other than a large area of flat ground can go a long way toward spicing up an encounter. Consider setting your encounter in an area that would provide challenges even if a fight were not taking place there. What potential perils or other features might draw the characters' attention, either before or during the fight? Why are monsters lurking in this area to begin with—does it offer good hiding places, for instance?

To add details to an encounter area at random, look to the tables in appendix A of the *Dungeon Master's Guide* to determine room and area features, potential hazards, obstacles, traps, and more.

Random Events

Consider what might happen in an encounter area if the characters were to never enter it. Do the guards serve in shifts? What other characters or monsters might visit? Do creatures gather there to eat or gossip? Are there any natural phenomena—such as strong winds, earth tremors, or rain squalls—that sometimes take place in the area? Random events can add a fun element of the unexpected to an encounter. Just when you think a fight's outcome is evident, an unforeseen event can make things more compelling.

A number of the tables in the *Dungeon Master's Guide* can suggest random events. The tables used for encounter location, weird locales, and wilderness weather in chapter 5 of that book are a good starting point for outdoor encounters. The tables in appendix A can be useful for indoor and outdoor encounters—especially the tables for obstacles, traps, and tricks. Finally, consult the random encounter tables in the next section of this book for inspiration.

Quick Matchups

The guidelines above assume that you are concerned about balance in your combat encounters and have enough time to prepare them. If you don't have much time, or if you want simpler but less precise guidelines, the Quick Matchups table below offers an alternative.

This table gives you a way to match a character of a certain level with a number of monsters. The table lists the challenge ratings to use for including one, two, and four monsters per character for each level. For instance, looking at the 3rd-level entry on the table, you can see that a CR 1/2 monster is equivalent to one 3rd-level character, as are two CR 1/4 monsters and four CR 1/8 ones.

Quick Matchups

Character Level	1 Monster	2 Monsters	4 Monsters
1st	1/4	1/8	—
2nd	1/2	1/4	—
3rd	1/2	1/4	1/8
4th	1	1/2	1/4
5th	2	1	1/2
6th	2	1	1/2
7th	3	1	1/2
8th	3	2	1
9th	4	2	1
10th	4	2	1
11th	4	3	2
12th	5	3	2
13th	6	4	2
14th	6	4	2
15th	7	4	3
16th	7	4	3
17th	8	5	3
18th	8	5	3
19th	9	6	4
20th	10	6	4

Random Encounters: A World of Possibilities

Chapter 3 of the *Dungeon Master's Guide* provides guidance on using random encounters in your game. This section builds on that guidance, offering a host of random encounter tables for you to use when you determine that a random encounter is going to take place.

Using the monster lists in appendix B of that book as a basis, we've built a set of tables for each environment category: arctic, coastal, desert, forest, grassland, hill, mountain, swamp, Underdark, underwater, and urban. Within each category, separate tables are provided for each of the four tiers of play: levels 1–4, 5–10, 11–16, and 17–20.

Even though you can use these tables "out of the box," the advice in the *Dungeon Master's Guide* still holds true: tailoring such tables to your game can reinforce the themes and flavor of your campaign. We encourage you to customize this material to make it your own.

In the tables, a name in bold refers to a stat block in the *Monster Manual*.

Flight, or Fight, or … ?

Each of the results on these tables represents a certain kind of challenge or potential challenge.

If you let the dice have their way and the result is a large number of monsters, the generated encounter might be too difficult or dangerous for the characters in their present circumstances. They might want to flee to avoid contact, or not to approach any closer after perceiving the monsters from a distance.

Of course, you also have the freedom to adjust the numbers, but it's important to remember that not every encounter involving a monster needs to result in combat. An encounter might indeed be the prelude to a battle, a parley, or some other interaction. What happens next depends on what the characters try, or what you decide is bound to occur.

The tables also include entries for what the *Dungeon Master's Guide* calls "encounters of a less monstrous nature." Many of these results cry out to be customized or detailed, which offers you an opportunity to connect them to the story of your campaign. And in so doing, you've taken a step toward making your own personalized encounter table. Now, keep going!

Arctic Encounters (Levels 1–4)

d100	Encounter
01	1 giant owl
02–05	1d6 + 3 kobolds
06–08	1d4 + 3 trappers (commoners)
09–10	1 owl
11–12	2d4 blood hawks
13–17	2d6 bandits
18–20	1d3 winged kobolds with 1d6 kobolds
21–25	The partially eaten carcass of a mammoth, from which 1d4 weeks of rations can be harvested
26–29	2d8 hunters (tribal warriors)
30–35	1 half-ogre
36–40	Single-file tracks in the snow that stop abruptly
41–45	1d3 ice mephits
46–50	1 brown bear
51–53	1d6 + 1 orcs
54–55	1 polar bear
56–57	1d6 scouts
58–60	1 saber-toothed tiger
61–65	A frozen pond with a jagged hole in the ice that appears recently made
66–68	1 berserker
69–70	1 ogre
71–72	1 griffon
73–75	1 druid
76–80	3d4 refugees (commoners) fleeing from orcs
81	1d3 veterans
82	1d4 orogs
83	2 brown bears
84	1 orc Eye of Gruumsh with 2d8 orcs
85	1d3 winter wolves
86–87	1d4 yetis
88	1 half-ogre
89	1d3 manticores
90	1 bandit captain with 2d6 bandits
91	1 revenant
92–93	1 troll
94–95	1 werebear
96–97	1 young remorhaz
98	1 mammoth
99	1 young white dragon
00	1 frost giant

Arctic Encounters (Levels 5–10)

d100	Encounter
01–05	2 saber-toothed tigers
06–07	1d4 half-ogres
08–10	1d3 + 1 brown bears
11–15	1d3 polar bears
16–20	2d4 berserkers
21–25	A half-orc druid tending to an injured polar bear. If the characters assist the druid, she gives them a vial of antitoxin.
26–30	2d8 scouts
31–35	2d4 ice mephits
36–40	2d6 + 1 zombies aboard a galleon trapped in the ice. Searching the ship yields 2d20 days of rations.
41–45	1 manticore
46–50	2d6 + 3 orcs
51–53	1d6 + 2 ogres

d100	Encounter
54–55	2d4 **griffons**
56–57	1d4 **veterans**
58–60	1 **bandit captain** with 1 **druid**, 1d3 **berserkers**, and 2d10 + 5 **bandits**
61–65	1d4 hours of extreme cold (see chapter 5 of the *Dungeon Master's Guide*)
66–68	1 **young remorhaz**
69–72	1 **orc Eye of Gruumsh** with 1d6 **orogs** and 2d8 + 6 **orcs**
73–75	1 **revenant**
76–80	A howl that echoes over the land for 1d3 minutes
81–82	1d3 **mammoths**
83–84	1 **young white dragon**
85–86	2d4 **winter wolves**
87–88	1d6 + 2 **yetis**
89–90	1d2 **frost giants**
91–92	1d3 **werebears**
93–94	1d4 **trolls**
95–96	1 **abominable yeti**
97–98	1 **remorhaz**
99	1 **roc**
00	2d4 **young remorhazes**

ARCTIC ENCOUNTERS (LEVELS 11–16)

d100	Encounter
01	1 **abominable yeti**
02–04	1d6 **revenants**
05–10	1d4 + 1 **werebears**
11–20	1d3 **young white dragons**
21–25	A blizzard that reduces visibility to 5 feet for 1d6 hours
26–35	1 **roc**
36–40	A herd of 3d20 + 60 caribou (**deer**) moving through the snow
41–50	1d4 **mammoths**
51–60	1d8 + 1 **trolls**
61–65	A mile-wide frozen lake in which the preserved corpses of strange creatures can be seen
66–75	2d4 **young remorhazes**
76–80	A crumbling ice castle littered with the frozen bodies of blue-skinned humanoids
81–90	1 **adult white dragon**
91–96	1d8 + 1 **frost giants**
97–99	1d4 **remorhazes**
00	1 **ancient white dragon**

ARCTIC ENCOUNTERS (LEVELS 17–20)

d100	Encounter
01–02	2d10 **revenants**
03–04	2d8 **trolls**
05–06	2d10 **werebears**
07–08	1 **frost giant**
09–10	2d4 **young remorhazes**
11–20	1d4 **frost giants**
21–25	A circular patch of black ice on the ground. The air temperature around the patch is warmer than in the surrounding area, and characters who inspect the ice find bits of machinery frozen within.
26–35	1 **ancient white dragon**
36–40	An adventurer frozen 6 feet under the ice; 50% chance the corpse has a rare magic item of the DM's choice
41–50	1d3 **abominable yetis**
51–60	1d4 **remorhazes**
61–65	A 500-foot-high wall of ice that is 300 feet thick and spread across 1d4 miles
66–75	1d4 **rocs**
76–80	The likeness of a stern woman with long, flowing hair, carved into the side of a mountain
81–90	1d10 **frost giants** with 2d4 **polar bears**
91–96	1d3 **adult white dragons**
97–99	2d4 **abominable yetis**
00	1 **ancient white dragon** with 1d3 **young white dragons**

COASTAL ENCOUNTERS (LEVELS 1–4)

d100	Encounter
01	1 **pseudodragon**
02–05	2d8 **crabs**
06–10	2d6 **fishers** (**commoners**)
11	1d3 **poisonous snakes**
12–13	1d6 **guards** protecting a stranded **noble**
14–15	2d4 **scouts**
16–18	2d10 **merfolk**
19–20	1d6 + 2 **sahuagin**
21–25	1d4 **ghouls** feeding on corpses aboard the wreckage of a merchant ship. A search uncovers 2d6 bolts of ruined silk, a 50-foot length of rope, and a barrel of salted herring.
26–27	1d4 **winged kobolds** with 1d6 + 1 **kobolds**
28–29	2d6 **tribal warriors**
30–31	3d4 **kobolds**
32–33	2d4 + 5 **blood hawks**
34–35	1d8 + 1 **pteranodons**
36–40	A few dozen baby turtles struggling to make their way to the sea
41–42	1d6 + 2 **giant lizards**

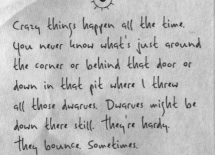

Crazy things happen all the time. You never know what's just around the corner or behind that door or down in that pit where I threw all those dwarves. Dwarves might be down there still. They're hardy. They bounce. Sometimes.

d100	Encounter
43–44	1d6 + 4 giant crabs
45–46	2d4 stirges
47–48	2d6 + 3 bandits
49–53	2d4 sahuagin
54–55	1d6 + 2 scouts
56–60	1 sea hag
61–65	A momentary formation in the waves that looks like an enormous humanoid face
66–70	1 druid
71–75	1d4 harpies
76–80	A lone hermit (acolyte) sitting on the beach, contemplating the meaning of the multiverse
81	1d4 berserkers
82	1d6 giant eagles
83	2d4 giant toads
84	1d4 ogres or 1d4 merrow
85	3d6 sahuagin
86	1d4 veterans
87	1d2 plesiosauruses
88	1 bandit captain with 2d6 bandits
89	1d3 manticores
90	1 banshee
91–92	1d4 + 3 griffons
93–94	1 sahuagin priestess with 1d3 merrow and 2d6 sahuagin
95–96	1 sahuagin baron
97–98	1 water elemental
99	1 cyclops
00	1 young bronze dragon

COASTAL ENCOUNTERS (LEVELS 5–10)

d100	Encounter
01	2d8 giant wolf spiders
02–03	3d6 pteranodons
04–05	2d4 scouts
06–07	1d6 + 2 sahuagin
08	1 sea hag
09–10	1d4 + 1 giant toads
11–15	3d6 sahuagin
16–20	2d6 giant eagles
21–25	A pseudodragon chasing gulls through the air
26–29	1d2 druids
30–32	2d4 + 1 giant toads
33–35	1 commoner singing a dirge (day only) or 1 banshee (night only)

d100	Encounter
36–40	A stoppered bottle containing an illegible note and half buried in the sand
41–43	3 sea hags
44–46	1d8 + 1 harpies
47–50	1d4 plesiosauruses
51–53	1d4 manticores
54–56	2d4 ogres
57–60	1d10 griffons
61–65	A battle at sea between two galleons
66–70	1d4 + 3 merrow
71–75	A pirate crew consisting of 1 bandit captain, 1 druid, 2 berserkers, and 2d12 bandits, all searching for buried treasure
76–80	A severed humanoid hand tangled in a net
81–82	1 water elemental
83–84	1 cyclops
85–86	1d4 banshees (night only)
87–88	2d4 veterans
89–90	1 young bronze dragon
91–93	1d3 cyclopes
94–95	1 young blue dragon
96	1 sahuagin baron with 1d3 sahuagin priestesses and 2d8 sahuagin
97	1 djinni
98	1 roc
99	1 marid
00	1 storm giant

COASTAL ENCOUNTERS (LEVELS 11–16)

d100	Encounter
01	1d4 banshees (night only)
02–04	1 cyclops
05–08	1d6 + 2 manticores
09–10	1d8 + 2 veterans
11–20	1 young blue dragon
21–25	A nest of 1d6 dragon turtle eggs
26–35	1d4 sahuagin barons
36–40	A trident partially buried in the sand
41–50	1 young bronze dragon
51–55	1 marid
56–60	1d6 water elementals
61–65	2d6 ghasts crawling over 1d6 wrecked ships and feeding on the dead
66–70	1 djinni
71–75	1d3 young bronze dragons
76–80	A beached whale, dead and bloated. If it takes any damage, it explodes, and each creature within 30 feet of it must make a DC 15 Dexterity saving throw, taking 5d6 bludgeoning damage on a failed save, or half as much damage on a successful one.
81–82	2d4 cyclopes
83–84	1 storm giant
85–86	1d3 young blue dragons

Danger is everywhere. Always keep one eye open. That's much easier for me than it is for you.

d100	Encounter
87–88	1 **adult bronze dragon**
89–90	1 **adult blue dragon**
91–93	1d3 **rocs**
94–97	1 **dragon turtle**
98–99	1 **ancient bronze dragon**
00	1 **ancient blue dragon**

COASTAL ENCOUNTERS (LEVELS 17–20)

d100	Encounter
01–10	1 **roc**
11–20	1 **storm giant**
21–25	An **adult bronze dragon** fighting an **adult blue dragon** to the death
26–40	2d6 **cyclopes**
41–50	1 **adult bronze dragon** or 1 **adult blue dragon**
51–60	1d3 **djinn** or 1d3 **marids**
61–70	1 **dragon turtle**
71–75	1d3 **rocs**
76–80	1d6 + 2 **waterspouts** that dance on the water before stopping abruptly
81–90	1d6 **young blue dragons**
91–96	1 **ancient bronze dragon**
97–99	1 **ancient blue dragon**
00	1d3 + 1 **storm giants**

DESERT ENCOUNTERS (LEVELS 1–4)

d100	Encounter
01	3d8 **scorpions**
02	2d4 **vultures**
03	1 abandoned **mule**
04	2d6 **commoners** with 2d4 **camels** bound for a distant city
05	1d6 **flying snakes**
06	2d6 **hyenas** or 2d6 **jackals**
07	1d6 **guards** escorting a **noble** to the edge of the desert, all of them astride **camels**
08	1d6 **cats**
09	1 **pseudodragon**
10	1d4 **poisonous snakes**
11–13	2d4 **stirges**
14–15	1d6 + 2 **giant wolf spiders**
16–17	1 **scout**
18–20	2d4 **giant poisonous snakes**
21–25	Single-file tracks marching deeper into the desert
26–27	4d4 **kobolds**
28–29	1 **jackalwere**
30–31	3d6 **tribal warriors**

d100	Encounter
32–33	1d6 **giant lizards**
34–35	1 **swarm of insects**
36–40	An oasis surrounded by palm trees and containing the remnants of an old camp
41–44	3d6 **bandits**
45–46	1d4 **constrictor snakes**
47–48	2d4 **winged kobolds**
49–50	1 **dust mephit**
51–52	1d3 + 1 **giant toads**
53–54	1d4 **giant spiders**
55	1 **druid**
56–57	2d4 **hobgoblins**
58	1 **wight**
59–60	1 **ogre**
61–65	A brass lamp lying on the ground
66–67	1d4 **giant vultures**
68	1 **phase spider**
69	1 **giant constrictor snake**
70–71	1 **gnoll pack lord** with 1d3 **giant hyenas**
72	1d6 + 2 **gnolls**
73–74	1 **mummy**
75	1d3 **half-ogres**
76–80	A pile of humanoid bones wrapped in rotting cloth
81–82	1 **lamia**
83	1 **hobgoblin captain** with 2d6 **hobgoblins**
84	2d4 **death dogs**
85–86	1d4 **giant scorpions**
87	1 **yuan-ti malison** with 1d4 + 1 **yuan-ti purebloods**
88–89	1 **bandit captain** with 1 **druid** and 3d6 **bandits**
90	2d4 **thri-kreen**
91	1 **air elemental**
92	1d3 **couatls**
93	1 **fire elemental**
94	1d4 **gnoll fangs of Yeenoghu**
95	1 **revenant**
96	1d4 **weretigers**
97	1 **cyclops**
98	1 **young brass dragon**
99	1 **medusa**
00	1 **yuan-ti abomination**

Desert Encounters (Levels 5–10)

d100	Encounter
01	1d6 **scouts**
02	2d4 **jackalweres**
03	2d6 **hobgoblins**
04	1d4 + 3 **dust mephits**
05	1d6 **swarms of insects**
06	1 **giant constrictor snake**
07–08	1 **lion**
09–10	2d4 **gnolls**
11–12	2d6 **giant toads**
13–17	1 **mummy**

d100	Encounter
18–20	1d8 + 1 **giant vultures**
21–25	A stone obelisk partly buried in the sand
26–28	1 **ogre** with 1d3 **half-ogres**
29–35	1d10 **giant hyenas**
36–40	1d6 + 1 empty tents
41–43	1d6 + 2 **thri-kreen**
44–46	2d4 **yuan-ti purebloods**
47–50	1d6 + 3 **death dogs**
51–52	1d4 **giant scorpions**
53	1 **fire elemental**
54–55	1 **hobgoblin captain** with 3d4 **hobgoblins**
56	1d6 + 2 **ogres**
57–58	1d4 **lamias**
59–60	1 **air elemental**
61–65	A meteorite resting at the bottom of a glassy crater
66	1d4 + 1 **wights**
67–68	1 **young brass dragon**
69–70	1 **bandit captain** with 1d3 **berserkers** and 3d6 **bandits**
71–72	1 **cyclops**
73	1d4 **couatls**
74–75	1d4 **yuan-ti malisons**
76–80	Strong winds that kick up dust and reduce visibility to 1d6 feet for 1d4 hours
81–83	1 **revenant** with 1d3 **wights**
84–85	1d8 + 1 **phase spiders**
86–87	1d6 + 2 **weretigers**
88–90	2d4 **gnoll fangs of Yeenoghu**
91	1 **young blue dragon**
92	1d4 **cyclopes**
93	1d3 **yuan-ti abominations**
94	1d4 **medusas**
95	1 **guardian naga**
96	1d3 **young brass dragons**
97	1 **efreeti**
98	1 **roc**
99	1 **gynosphinx**
00	1 **adult brass dragon**

Desert Encounters (Levels 11–16)

d100	Encounter
01	1 **young brass dragon**
02–05	4d6 **gnolls**
06–10	3d10 **giant hyenas**
11–12	1d8 + 1 **lamias**
13–14	2d4 **gnoll fangs of Yeenoghu**
15–17	1d6 + 2 **giant scorpions**
18–20	2d4 **phase spiders**
21–25	A desert caravan consisting of 1d6 merchants (**nobles**) with 2d6 **guards**
26–27	1d6 + 1 **couatls**
28–30	1d4 **fire elementals**
31–32	1 **hobgoblin captain** with 3d10 + 10 **hobgoblins**
33–35	2d4 **wights**

d100	Encounter
36–40	1d6 square miles of desert glass
41–42	1 young blue dragon
43–45	1d6 + 2 weretigers
46–48	1d4 air elementals
49–50	1d6 + 1 yuan-ti malisons
51–55	1d4 medusas
56–60	1d4 revenants with 3d12 skeletons
61–65	A plundered pyramid
66–70	1d4 young brass dragons
71–75	1d3 yuan-ti abominations
76–78	1d6 + 2 cyclopes
79–82	1 adult brass dragon
83–85	1 purple worm
86	1d2 young blue dragons
87–88	1 mummy lord
89	1d3 guardian nagas
90	1 adult blue dragon
91	1d2 gynosphinxes
92–93	1d3 efreet
94	1 androsphinx
95	1d4 rocs
96–97	1 adult blue dracolich
98–99	1 ancient brass dragon
00	1 ancient blue dragon

Desert Encounters (Levels 17–20)

d100	Encounter
01–05	1 adult brass dragon
06–10	1d2 yuan-ti abominations with 2d10 + 5 yuan-ti malisons and 4d6 + 6 yuan-ti purebloods
11–14	1d6 + 2 medusas
15–18	1d2 purple worms
19–22	2d4 cyclopes
23–25	An abandoned city made from white marble, empty during the day. At night, harmless apparitions roam the streets, replaying the final moments of their lives.
26–30	1d3 young blue dragons
31–35	1 mummy lord
36–40	1d4 hours of extreme heat (see chapter 5 of the *Dungeon Master's Guide*)
41–50	1d3 guardian nagas
51–60	1d4 efreet
61–63	An old signpost identifying a single destination, called Pazar
64–72	1d4 rocs
73–80	1d3 gynosphinxes
81–85	1 adult blue dracolich
86–90	1 androsphinx
91–96	1 ancient brass dragon
97–99	1 ancient blue dragon
00	1d4 adult brass dragons

Forest Encounters (Levels 1–4)

d100	Encounter
01	1 giant owl
02	1d4 cats
03	2d4 woodcutters (commoners)
04	1 badger or 1d4 poisonous snakes
05	2d8 baboons
06	1d6 + 3 hyenas
07	1 owl
08	1 pseudodragon
09	1 panther
10	1 giant poisonous snake
11	1d6 + 2 boars
12	1d4 + 1 giant lizards
13	1 ape or 1 tiger
14	2d6 tribal warriors with 1d6 mastiffs
15	1d6 + 2 giant bats or 3d6 flying snakes
16	1 scout or 2d4 guards with 1d8 mastiffs
17	1d8 + 1 winged kobolds
18	1d3 constrictor snakes
19	1d10 + 5 giant rats or 2d6 + 3 giant weasels
20	1d4 + 1 needle blights with 1d6 + 3 twig blights
21–25	A lost, weeping child. If the characters take the child home, the parents reward them with 1d3 *potions of healing*.
26	1d8 + 1 giant frogs
27	4d4 kobolds
28	1d3 black bears
29	3d6 stirges
30	1 satyr
31	2d4 kenku
32	1d3 vine blights with 1d12 awakened shrubs
33	1d4 swarms of ravens
34	1 faerie dragon (yellow or younger)
35	1d4 + 2 giant badgers
36–40	A young woodcutter (scout) racing through the forest to rescue a lost friend
41	2d4 blink dogs
42	1d8 + 1 sprites
43	1d6 + 2 elk
44	1d4 lizardfolk or 3d6 bandits
45	1d4 + 4 wolves
46	2d4 giant wolf spiders
47	1 swarm of insects or 2d8 blood hawks
48	1d6 + 2 pixies
49	1 brown bear
50	1d4 + 3 goblins
51	1d3 dryads
52	1 awakened tree

d100	Encounter
53	1 phase spider
54	1d6 harpies
55	1 ettercap or 1d8 + 1 orcs
56	1 goblin boss with 2d6 + 1 goblins
57	1 ankheg
58	1 giant constrictor snake
59	1d4 bugbears or 2d4 hobgoblins
60	1 pegasus
61–65	A stream of cool, clean water flowing between the trees
66	1d4 half-ogres or 1 ogre
67	1 faerie dragon (green or older)
68	1 werewolf or 1d8 + 1 worgs
69	1 druid harvesting mistletoe
70	1 will-o'-wisp
71	1d4 dire wolves or 1 giant boar
72	1d10 giant wasps
73	1 owlbear or 1 giant elk
74	2d6 gnolls
75	1d6 giant toads
76–80	1d6 web cocoons hanging from the branches, holding withered carcasses

d100	Encounter
81	1 wereboar or 1d4 giant boars
82	1d6 + 2 giant spiders
83	1d4 centaurs or 1d4 giant elk
84	1 orc Eye of Gruumsh with 2d4 + 2 orcs
85	1 gnoll fang of Yeenoghu
86	1d4 gricks
87	1 bandit captain with 2d6 + 3 bandits
88	1d4 wererats
89	1 couatl (day) or 1 banshee (night)
90	1 gnoll pack lord with 1d4 giant hyenas
91	2d4 berserkers or 1d4 veterans
92	1 lizardfolk shaman with 1d3 swarms of poisonous snakes and 1d10 + 2 lizardfolk
93	1d4 displacer beasts
94	1d3 green hags
95	1 hobgoblin captain with 2d6 hobgoblins and 1d4 giant boars
96	1 yuan-ti malison with 1d6 + 1 yuan-ti purebloods
97	1d3 weretigers
98	1 gorgon or 1 unicorn
99	1 shambling mound
00	1 yuan-ti abomination

FOREST ENCOUNTERS (LEVELS 5–10)

d100	Encounter
01	2d4 **vine blights**
02	2d6 **hobgoblins** or 2d6 **orcs**
03	2d4 **apes** or 2d4 **satyrs**
04	1d3 **will-o'-wisps**
05	1d4 **swarms of poisonous snakes**
06	1 orc **Eye of Gruumsh** with 1d3 **orogs** and 1d8 + 2 **orcs**
07	1d3 **constrictor snakes** or 1d4 **tigers**
08	1 **goblin boss** with 3d6 **goblins**
09	1 **faerie dragon** (any age)
10	1 **brown bear** or 1d6 + 2 **black bears**
11–13	1d4 **giant boars**
14–15	1d8 + 1 **giant spiders**
16–17	1 **lizardfolk shaman** with 2d4 **lizardfolk**
18	1d10 **giant toads**
19	1d4 **ankhegs**
20	1d3 **awakened trees** (day) or 1 **banshee** (night)
21–25	A small shack almost hidden by the deep forest. The interior is empty aside from a large cast-iron oven.
26	1 **couatl**
27–28	1d4 **ogres** or 1d6 + 2 **half-ogres**
29–30	1 **gnoll pack lord** with 1d4 + 1 **giant hyenas**
31–32	1d6 **wererats**
33	1d4 **gricks**
34	1d8 + 1 **yuan-ti purebloods**
35	1d6 **pegasi**
36–40	An old stone archway of obvious elven design. Any character who passes under it makes Wisdom (Perception) checks with advantage for 1 hour.
41–42	1d6 + 2 **dryads**
43	1d4 **giant elk**
44	1d8 + 1 **harpies**
45–46	1 **bandit captain** with 1 **druid** and 1d6 + 5 **bandits**
47–48	2d4 **dire wolves**
49–50	2d4 **bugbears**
51–52	2d4 **centaurs**
53–54	3d10 **blink dogs**
55–56	1d4 **owlbears**
57–58	1d8 + 1 **berserkers**
59–60	1d3 **green hags**
61–65	A clear pool of water with 1d6 sleeping animals lying around its edge
66–67	1d4 **werewolves**
68–69	1 **werebear**
70–71	1d8 + 1 **ettercaps**
72–73	2d10 **elk**
74–75	1d4 **veterans**
76–80	An old tree with a wizened face carved into the trunk
81	1d4 **wereboars**
82	2d4 **displacer beasts**
83	1d4 **shambling mounds**
84	1 **hobgoblin captain** with 3d10 **hobgoblins** and 4d12 **goblins**
85	1 **yuan-ti abomination**
86	1d8 + 1 **phase spiders**
87	1d4 **trolls**
88	2d4 **yuan-ti malisons**
89	1 **oni**
90	1d4 **unicorns**
91	1d6 + 2 **weretigers**
92	1 **young green dragon**
93	1d4 **gorgons**
94	1d6 + 2 **gnoll fangs of Yeenoghu**
95	1 **treant**
96	1d4 **revenants**
97	1 **grick alpha** with 1d6 + 1 **gricks**
98	1d4 **giant apes**
99	1 **guardian naga**
00	1 **adult gold dragon**

FOREST ENCOUNTERS (LEVELS 11–16)

d100	Encounter
01–03	1 **werebear**
04–05	1d4 **druids** performing a ritual for the dead (day only) or 1d4 **banshees** (night only)
06–07	1d3 **couatls**
08–10	1d3 **gnoll fangs of Yeenoghu** with 2d6 + 3 **gnolls**
11–15	2d4 **displacer beasts**
16–20	1d6 + 2 **veterans**
21–25	A pool of clear, still water. Gold coins litter the bottom, but they disappear if removed from the pool.
26–30	1d4 + 1 **green hags** with 1d3 **owlbears**
31–35	1d6 + 2 **werewolves**
36–40	A small woodland shrine dedicated to a mysterious cult named the Siswa
41–45	1d6 + 2 **phase spiders**
46–50	2d4 **yuan-ti malisons**
51–52	1d3 **werebears**
53–54	1d4 **revenants**
55–56	1 **young green dragon**
57–58	1d4 **trolls**
59–60	1d6 + 2 **wereboars**
61–65	A group of seven people (**commoners**) wearing animal masks and ambling through the woods
66–67	1d4 **gorgons**
68–69	1d3 **shambling mounds**
70–71	1 **treant**
72–73	1d4 **unicorns**
74–75	1d6 + 2 **weretigers**
76–80	Peals of silvery laughter that echo from a distance
81–82	1 **guardian naga**
83–84	1 **young gold dragon**

d100	Encounter
85–86	1 **grick alpha** with 2d4 **gricks**
87–88	1d3 **yuan-ti abominations**
89–90	1 **adult green dragon**
91–93	1d8 + 1 **giant apes**
94–96	2d4 **oni**
97–99	1d3 **treants**
00	1 **ancient green dragon**

Forest Encounters (Levels 17–20)

d100	Encounter
01–05	1 **young green dragon**
06–10	1 **treant**
11–13	1 **guardian naga**
14–16	1d10 **revenants**
17–19	1d8 + 1 **unicorns**
20–22	1d3 **grick alphas**
23–25	For a few hundred feet, wherever the characters step, flowers bloom and emit soft light.
26–28	1 **young gold dragon**
29–31	1d6 + 2 **shambling mounds**
32–34	2d4 **werebears**
35–37	1d4 **oni**
38–40	4d6 + 10 **elves** living in a small community in the treetops
41–43	1d6 + 2 **gorgons**
44–46	2d4 **trolls**
47–49	1d4 **giant apes**
50–52	1d3 **yuan-ti abominations**
53–62	1d3 **young green dragons**
63–65	A 50-foot-tall stone statue of an elf warrior with hand raised, palm out, as if to forbid travelers from coming this way
66–75	1d4 **treants**
76–80	A cairn set atop a low hill
81–90	1 **adult gold dragon**
91–96	1 **ancient green dragon**
97–99	2d4 + 1 **treants**
00	1 **ancient gold dragon**

Grassland Encounters (Levels 1–5)

d100	Encounter
01	1 **hobgoblin captain** with 1d4 + 1 **hobgoblins**
02	1 **chimera**
03	1 **gorgon**
04	1d2 **couatls**
05	1 **ankylosaurus**
06	1 **weretiger**
07	1d3 **allosauruses**
08–09	1d3 **elephants**

d100	Encounter
10–14	A circle of standing stones within which the air is utterly still, no matter how hard the wind blows outside
15–16	1 **phase spider**
17–18	1 **gnoll pack lord** with 1d4 **giant hyenas**
19–20	1 **orog** or 1 **pegasus**
21–22	1 **ankheg**
23–24	1d3 **rhinoceroses**
25–28	1d3 **cockatrices**
29–32	1d6 + 2 **giant wasps** or 1d4 + 3 **swarms of insects**
33–36	1d4 **jackalweres** or 1d4 **scouts**
37–40	1d8 **giant goats** or 1d8 **worgs**
41–44	2d4 **hobgoblins**, 2d4 **orcs**, or 2d4 **gnolls**
45–46	1d2 **giant poisonous snakes**
47–48	1d6 + 2 **elk** or 1d6 + 2 **riding horses**
49–50	2d4 **goblins**
51–52	1d3 **boars**
53–54	1 **panther** (leopard) or 1 **lion**
55–58	1d6 + 3 **goblins** riding **wolves**
59–62	2d6 **giant wolf spiders** or 1 **giant eagle**
63–65	1d8 + 4 **pteranodons**
66–69	3d6 **wolves**
70–74	2d4 + 2 **axe beaks**
75–76	1 **giant boar** or 1d2 **tigers**
77–78	1 **ogre** or 1d3 **bugbears**
79–80	1 **giant elk**, or 1 **gnoll pack lord** with 1d3 **giant hyenas**
81–82	1d3 **giant vultures** or 1d3 **hippogriffs**
83–84	1 **goblin boss** with 1d6 + 2 **goblins** and 1d4 + 3 **wolves**, or 1d3 **thri-kreen**
85–89	1d3 **druids** patrolling the wilds
90–91	1d6 **scarecrows** or 1 **wereboar**
92–93	1d3 **centaurs** or 1d3 **griffons**
94	1d3 **gnoll fangs of Yeenoghu**, or 1 **orc Eye of Gruumsh** with 2d4 + 1 **orcs**
95–96	1 **triceratops**
97	1 **cyclops** or 1 **bulette**
98–99	1d4 **manticores**
00	1 **tyrannosaurus rex**

Grassland Encounters (Levels 6–10)

d100	Encounter
01	1d3 **gorgons**
02	1d4 **cyclopes**
03–04	1d3 **gnoll fangs of Yeenoghu**
05–06	1 **chimera**
07–09	1d4 + 1 **veterans** on **riding horses**
10–11	A tornado that touches down 1d6 miles away, tearing up the land for 1 mile before it dissipates
12–13	1d3 **manticores**
14–15	2d4 **ankhegs**
16–17	1d8 + 1 **centaurs**
18–19	1d6 + 2 **griffons**

d100	Encounter
20–21	1d6 **elephants**
22–24	A stretch of land littered with rotting war machines, bones, and banners of forgotten armies
25–28	1d8 + 1 **bugbears**
29–32	1 **gnoll pack lord** with 1d4 + 1 **giant hyenas**
33–36	2d4 **scarecrows**
37–40	1d12 **lions**
41–44	1d10 **thri-kreen**
45–46	1 **allosaurus**
47–48	1 **tiger**
49–50	1d2 **giant eagles** or 1d2 **giant vultures**
51–52	1 **goblin boss** with 2d4 **goblins**
53–54	1d2 **pegasi**
55–58	1 **ankylosaurus**
59–62	1d2 **couatls**
63–66	1 **orc Eye of Gruumsh** with 1d8 + 1 **orcs**
67–70	2d4 **hippogriffs**
71–74	1d4 + 1 **rhinoceroses**
75–76	1 **hobgoblin captain** with 2d6 **hobgoblins**
77–78	1d3 **phase spiders**
79–80	1d6 + 2 **giant boars**
81–82	2d4 **giant elk**
83–84	1d4 **ogres** and 1d4 **orogs**
85–87	A hot wind that carries the stench of rot
88–90	1d3 **weretigers**
91–92	1 **bulette**
93–94	A tribe of 2d20 + 20 nomads (**tribal warriors**) on **riding horses** following a herd of antelope (**deer**). The nomads are willing to trade food, leather, and information for weapons.
95–96	1d6 + 2 **wereboars**
97	1 **young gold dragon**
98–99	1d4 **triceratops**
00	1d3 **tyrannosaurus rexes**

Grassland Encounters (Levels 11–16)

d100	Encounter
01–05	3d6 **wereboars**
06–10	2d10 **gnoll fangs of Yeenoghu**
11–15	1d4 **bulettes**
16–17	An old road of paved stones, partly reclaimed by wilderness, that travels for 1d8 miles in either direction before ending
18–27	1d12 **couatls**
28–30	A witch (**mage**) dwelling in a crude hut. She offers *potions of healing*, antitoxins, and other consumable items for sale in exchange for food and news.
31–40	2d10 **elephants**
41–46	2d4 **weretigers**
47–56	1d8 + 1 **cyclopes**
57–61	1d3 **chimeras**
62–66	5 **triceratops**
67–69	A giant hole 50 feet across that descends nearly 500 feet before opening into an empty cave

d100	Encounter
70–79	1d4 + 3 **gorgons**
80–88	1d3 **young gold dragons**
89–90	A circular section of grass nearly a quarter-mile across that appears to have been pressed down; 1d4 more such circles connected by lines can be seen from overhead.
91–96	2d4 **tyrannosaurus rexes**
97–99	1 **adult gold dragon**
00	1 **ancient gold dragon**

Grassland Encounters (Levels 17–20)

d100	Encounter
01–10	2d6 **triceratops**
11–20	1d10 **gorgons**
21–25	2d6 **hyenas** feeding on the carcass of a dead dinosaur
26–35	3d6 **bulettes**
36–40	A fiery chariot that races across the sky
41–50	1d3 **young gold dragons**
51–60	2d4 **cyclopes**
61–65	A valley where all the grass has died and the ground is littered with stumps and fallen tree trunks, all petrified
66–75	2d10 **bugbears** with 4d6 **goblins** and 2d10 **wolves**
76–80	A friendly adventuring party of 1d6 + 1 characters of varying races, classes, and levels (average level 1d6 + 2). They share information about their recent travels.
81–90	1d12 **chimeras**
91–96	1d6 + 2 **tyrannosaurus rexes**
97–99	1 **adult gold dragon**
00	1 **ancient gold dragon**

Hill Encounters (Levels 1–4)

d100	Encounter
01	1 **eagle**
02–03	2d4 **baboons**
04–06	1d6 **bandits**
07	1d4 **vultures**
08	1d10 **commoners**
09	1 **raven**
10	1 **poisonous snake**
11–13	2d6 **bandits** or 2d6 **tribal warriors**
14	2d8 **goats**
15	1d6 + 4 **blood hawks**
16	1d4 + 3 **giant weasels**
17–18	1d3 **guards** with 1d2 **mastiffs** and 1 **mule**
19–20	1d6 + 5 **hyenas**
21–22	2d4 **stirges**

d100	Encounter
23–25	An empty cave littered with bones
26	1 pseudodragon or 1d3 giant owls
27	1 lion or 1 panther (cougar)
28–30	2d8 kobolds
31	1 hippogriff
32–34	2d4 goblins
35	1 worg
36	1d3 swarms of bats or 1d3 swarms of ravens
37	1 giant eagle
38–40	An old dwarf sitting on a stump, whittling a piece of wood
41	1d4 elk
42	1d4 winged kobolds with 1d6 kobolds
43	1d6 + 2 giant wolf spiders
44–45	2d4 wolves
46	1 swarm of insects
47	1d8 + 1 axe beaks
48–49	1 brown bear or 1d3 boars
50	1 scout
51	1 ogre
52–53	2d4 gnolls
54	1 giant elk
55	1d3 + 1 harpies
56	1 werewolf
57–58	2d4 orcs
59	1d4 half-ogres
60	1 druid or 1 veteran
61–63	The corpse of an adventurer that carries an intact explorer's pack and lies atop a longsword
64	1 green hag
65–66	1d3 dire wolves
67–68	A small cemetery containing 2d6 graves
69–70	1 hobgoblin captain with 2d4 hobgoblins
71	2d4 giant goats
72	1 manticore
73–74	1d6 + 2 hobgoblins
75	1 phase spider
76–78	A pile of droppings from a very large bird
79	1 gnoll fang of Yeenoghu
80	1d3 giant boars
81	1 gnoll pack lord with 1d3 giant hyenas
82	1 bandit captain with 2d4 bandits
83	1 orc Eye of Gruumsh with 1d8 + 2 orcs
84	1d3 orogs or 1d4 berserkers
85–86	1 ettin or 1 wereboar
87–88	1 goblin boss with 2d6 goblins
89	1d3 griffons
90	1d3 perytons or 1d4 pegasi
91–96	1d3 trolls
97–99	1 cyclops
00	1 stone giant

Hill Encounters (Levels 5–10)

d100	Encounter
01	1d4 pegasi or 1d3 perytons
02	1d6 + 2 giant goats
03	1 manticore
04	1d8 +1 gnolls or 1d8 + 1 hobgoblins
05	1d4 lions
06	1d6 + 2 worgs
07	1d4 brown bears
08	3d6 axe beaks
09	1 half-ogre with 2d6 orcs
10	2d10 winged kobolds
11–12	1 goblin boss with 1d4 dire wolves and 2d6 goblins
13	1d6 giant elk
14–15	1d8 + 1 giant eagles
16–17	1d4 phase spiders
18–19	1 gnoll pack lord with 2d4 giant hyenas
20	2d4 hippogriffs
21–25	A 15-foot-tall stone statue of a dwarf warrior that has been tipped over on its side
26–27	2d4 orogs
28–29	1d4 + 1 griffons
30–31	1d6 + 2 harpies
32–33	1 orc Eye of Gruumsh with 2d6 + 3 orcs
34–35	1d4 + 3 giant boars
36–40	A stone door set into the side of a steep hill, opening onto 15 feet of descending stairs that end at a cave-in
41–42	1d3 green hags
43–44	1d4 werewolves
45–46	1d6 + 2 ogres
47–48	1 hobgoblin captain with 2d8 hobgoblins
49–50	1 bandit captain with 3d6 bandits
51–54	1 chimera
55–58	1d4 ettins
59–62	1d6 + 2 veterans with 2d6 berserkers
63–65	An abandoned wooden hut
66–69	1 galeb duhr
70–73	1 bulette
74–77	1 wyvern
78–80	2d6 + 10 goats with 1 herder (tribal warrior)
81–82	1d3 hill giants
83–84	2d4 wereboars
85–86	1d4 revenants
87–88	1d2 gorgons
89–90	1d8 + 1 gnoll fangs of Yeenoghu
91–93	1d4 cyclopes
94–96	1 young red dragon
97–98	1d4 stone giants
99	1d3 young copper dragons
00	1 roc

Hill Encounters (Levels 11–16)

d100	Encounter
01	2d8 **manticores** or 2d8 **phase spiders**
02–04	1d6 **green hags** with 1d6 **wyverns**
05–07	1 **hobgoblin captain** with 1 **hill giant** and 4d10 **hobgoblins**
08–10	2d6 + 3 **werewolves**
11–14	1d6 + 2 **ettins**
15–18	1d3 **bulettes**
19–22	1d4 **werebears**
23–24	A stream of smoke emerging from a small chimney in the hillside
25–28	1d4 **wyverns**
29–32	1d8 + 1 **wereboars**
33–36	1d3 **revenants**
37–38	A mild earthquake that shakes the region for 1d20 seconds
39–42	1d3 **chimeras**
43–46	1d4 **gorgons**
47–50	1d6 + 2 **gnoll fangs of Yeenoghu**
51–54	1d4 **hill giants**
55–58	1 **young red dragon**
59–62	1d3 + 1 **galeb duhr**
63–65	2d10 dwarf miners (**commoners**), whistling as they march toward their mine
66–69	1d3 **young copper dragons**
70–73	1d4 **trolls**
74–77	1d3 **cyclopes**
78–80	1d3 **nobles** with 1d4 **scouts** prospecting for gold
81–85	1 **adult copper dragon**
86–90	2d4 **stone giants**
91–96	1d4 **rocs**
97–99	1 **adult red dragon**
00	1 **ancient copper dragon**

Hill Encounters (Levels 17–20)

d100	Encounter
01	1d2 **rocs**
02–05	1 **young red dragon**
06–10	2d6 **ettins**
11–15	1d4 **bulettes**
16–20	1d10 **revenants**
21–25	The white outline of an enormous horse carved into the side of a high hill
26–30	1d6 + 1 **gorgons**
31–35	2d4 + 1 **trolls**
36–40	The scorched remains of 2d10 humanoids littering a hillside
41–45	2d4 **hill giants**
46–50	1d6 + 2 **werebears**
51–55	2d4 **galeb duhr**
56–60	1d4 + 2 **wyverns**
61–65	A massive boulder partly buried in the earth as if it fell or was thrown there

d100	Encounter
66–70	1 **adult copper dragon**
71–75	1d6 + 3 **cyclopes**
76–80	The stub of an old stone tower jutting from the top of a hill
81–85	2d4 **stone giants**
86–90	1 **adult red dragon**
91–96	1 **ancient copper dragon**
97–99	1 **ancient red dragon**
00	1d2 **adult red dragons** with 1d3 **young red dragons**

Mountain Encounters (Levels 1–4)

d100	Encounter
01–02	1 **eagle**
03–05	1d3 **swarms of bats**
06–08	1d6 **goats**
09–11	1d10 + 5 **tribal warriors**
12–14	1d6 + 3 **pteranodons**
15–17	1d8 + 1 **winged kobolds**
18–20	1 **lion**
21–24	Stairs chiseled into the side of the mountain that climb 3d20 + 40 feet before ending abruptly
25–27	2d10 **stirges**
28–30	2d4 **aarakocra**
31–33	2d6 **dwarf soldiers** (**guards**) with 1d6 **mules** laden with iron ore
34–36	1 **giant eagle**
37–38	A small shrine dedicated to a lawful neutral god, perched on a stone outcropping
39–41	2d8 + 1 **blood hawks**
42–44	1 **giant goat**
45–47	3d4 **kobolds**
48–50	1 **half-ogre**
51–53	1 **berserker**
54–55	1 **orog**
56	1 **hell hound**
57	1 **druid**
58–59	1 **peryton**
60–61	1d2 **hippogriffs**
62	1 **manticore**
63–64	1d6 + 2 **scouts**
65–67	Enormous footprints left by a giant, which head into the mountain peaks
68–73	2d4 **orcs**
74–75	1 **giant elk**
76–77	1 **veteran**
78–79	1 **orc Eye of Gruumsh**
80	1d4 **harpies**
81	1 **ogre**
82	1 **griffon**
83	1 **basilisk**

d100	Encounter
84–85	1 **saber-toothed tiger**
86–90	A sparkling stream of water spilling from a crevice
91	1d2 **ettins**
92	1 **cyclops**
93	1 **troll**
94	1 **galeb duhr**
95	1 **air elemental**
96	1 **bulette**
97	1 **chimera**
98	1 **wyvern**
99	1 **stone giant**
00	1 **frost giant**

Mountain Encounters (Levels 5–10)

d100	Encounter
01–02	2d8 + 1 **aarakocra**
03–04	1 **lion** or 1 **saber-toothed tiger**
05–06	1d8 + 1 **giant goats**
07–08	1d4 + 3 **dwarf trailblazers** (**scouts**)
09–10	1d6 + 2 **orcs**
11–15	1d10 **giant eagles**
16–20	1d8 + 1 **hippogriffs**
21–25	1d8 fissures venting steam that partially obscures a 20-foot cube above each fissure
26–30	1 **basilisk**
31–35	1d12 **half-ogres**
36–40	A ravine blocked by a 100-foot-high wall, which has an opening in the center where a gate used to be
41–45	1 **manticore**
46–50	2d4 **harpies**
51–52	1 **galeb duhr**
53–54	1 **bulette**
55–56	1d10 **berserkers**
57–58	1d3 **hell hounds**
59–60	1d8 + 1 **veterans**
61–65	A distant mountain whose peak resembles a tooth
66–69	1d4 **ettins**
70–73	1 **wyvern**
74–75	1 **orc Eye of Gruumsh** with 1d6 **orogs** and 3d6 + 10 **orcs**
76–80	A row of 1d10 + 40 stakes upon which the bodies of kobolds, dwarves, or orcs are impaled
81–83	1 **fire giant**
84–85	1 **young silver dragon**
86–87	1d4 **air elementals**
88–90	1d4 **trolls**
91–92	1d3 + 1 **cyclopes**
93–94	1d4 **chimeras**
95–96	1 **cloud giant**
97	1 **roc**
98	1d4 **stone giants**
99	1 **young red dragon**
00	1d4 **frost giants**

Mountain Encounters (Levels 11–16)

d100	Encounter
01–02	1d8 + 1 **basilisks**
03–04	2d4 **hell hounds**
05–06	1d3 **chimeras**
07–08	1 **galeb duhr**
09–10	2d6 **veterans**
11–15	1 **young silver dragon**
16–20	2d4 **trolls**
21–25	1 **red dragon** gliding through the sky above the highest mountaintops
26–30	1d8 + 1 **manticores**
31–35	1d4 **cyclopes**
36–40	Heavy snowfall that lasts for 1d6 hours
41–45	1d10 **air elementals**
46–50	1d6 + 2 **bulettes**
51–55	1d4 **stone giants**
56–60	1 **fire giant**
61–65	2 **stone giants** playing catch with a boulder a few hundred feet away
66–70	1d8 + 1 **ettins**
71–75	1d3 **frost giants**
76–80	A wide crevasse, its depths shrouded in mist
81–85	1d4 **cloud giants**
86–90	1 **adult silver dragon**
91–96	1 **adult red dragon**
97–98	1d4 **rocs**
99	1 **ancient silver dragon**
00	1 **ancient red dragon**

Mountain Encounters (Levels 17–20)

d100	Encounter
01–05	1d10 **bulettes**
06–10	1d8 + 1 **chimeras**
11–15	1 **adult silver dragon**
16–20	1d8 + 1 **wyverns**
21–25	A massive boat perched atop a mountain
26–30	2d4 **galeb duhr**
31–35	1d4 **frost giants**
36–40	A wooded valley haunted by secretive and reclusive elves who tell warily of their master: a mad wizard who lives in the heart of the valley
41–45	1d10 **air elementals**
46–50	1d6 + 3 **trolls**
51–55	1 **adult red dragon**
56–60	1d4 **cloud giants**
61–65	A waterfall hundreds of feet high that drops into a clear pool
66–70	1d3 **fire giants**
71–75	2d4 **stone giants**
76–80	A force of 100 dwarves (**veterans**) standing guard at a mountain pass, permitting no passage until a traveler pays 100 gp (if on foot) or 200 gp (if mounted)

d100	Encounter
81–85	1d4 **rocs**
86–90	1d4 **young red dragons**
91–96	1 **ancient silver dragon**
97–00	1 **ancient red dragon**

Swamp Encounters (Levels 1–4)

d100	Encounter
01	1d4 **poisonous snakes**
02–05	3d6 **rats**
06–10	2d8 **ravens**
11–12	3d6 **giant rats**
13	1d10 + 5 **tribal warriors**
14–15	1d8 + 1 **giant lizards**
16–17	1 **crocodile**
18–19	1 **swarm of insects**
20	1 **giant spider**
21–22	1d4 + 1 mud huts partially sunken in murky water
23–25	2d8 + 1 **kobolds**
26	2d4 **mud mephits**
27–29	1d6 + 2 **giant poisonous snakes**
30	2d4 **winged kobolds**
31–32	1 **scout**
33–34	The corpse of an adventurer tangled in the weeds. Looting the body turns up an explorer's pack and perhaps (50% chance) a random common magic item.
35–38	1 **giant toad**
39–41	1d6 + 2 **constrictor snakes**
42–44	2d4 **giant frogs**
45	1d8 + 1 **swarms of rats** or 1d6 + 2 **swarms of ravens**
46–48	2d10 **stirges**
49–52	2d6 + 3 **bullywugs**
53–54	1d8 + 1 **orcs**
55–56	1d4 **yuan-ti purebloods**
57	1 **druid**
58–59	1 **yuan-ti malison**
60–62	1 **giant constrictor snake**
63–64	A high-pitched shriek that lasts for 1d4 minutes
65–67	2d4 **lizardfolk**
68–69	1d4 **ghouls**
70–71	1 **will-o'-wisp**
72	1 **wight**
73	1 **ghast**
74–75	1 **swarm of poisonous snakes**
76–77	A foul stench bubbling up from brackish waters
78–80	1d4 + 2 **ogres**
81–83	1 **shambling mound**
84–86	1 **lizardfolk shaman** with 1d6 **giant lizards** and 2d10 **lizardfolk**

d100	Encounter
87	1 **troll**
88–89	1d4 **green hags**
90–91	1 **revenant**
92–93	1 **giant crocodile**
94–95	1 **orc Eye of Gruumsh** with 1d3 **orogs** and 2d6 + 3 **orcs**
96–97	1 **young black dragon**
98	1 **yuan-ti abomination**
99	1d4 **water elementals**
00	1 **hydra**

SWAMP ENCOUNTERS (LEVELS 5–10)

d100	Encounter
01	1 **green hag**
02–03	2d4 **giant lizards** or 2d4 **giant poisonous snakes**
04–05	2d8 **winged kobolds**
06–07	1d10 + 1 **bullywugs** with 1d8 + 1 **giant frogs**
08–09	1 **druid**
10	1d8 + 1 **swarms of insects**
11–13	1d12 **ghouls**
14–16	2d8 **scouts**
17–19	2d10 **orcs**
20–22	2d4 **giant spiders**
23–24	Tainted water that exposes creatures that move through it to sight rot (see "Diseases" in chapter 8 of the *Dungeon Master's Guide*)
25–27	1d6 + 2 **giant toads**
28–30	3d6 **lizardfolk**
31–33	1d8 + 1 **yuan-ti purebloods**
34–36	1d4 + 1 **swarms of poisonous snakes**
37–38	A bloated humanoid corpse floating facedown in the water
39–41	1 **shambling mound**
42–44	1d4 + 1 **will-o'-wisps**
45–47	2d6 **crocodiles**
48–50	1d4 + 1 **giant constrictor snakes**
51–54	1 **lizardfolk shaman** with 1d3 **swarms of poisonous snakes** and 1d8 + 2 **lizardfolk**
55–58	1d8 + 1 **ogres**
59–62	2d4 **ghasts**
63–65	An altar partially sunk into the mud, devoted to a god that is part human and part frog
66–69	1 **giant crocodile**
70–73	1 **shambling mound**
74–77	1 **orc Eye of Gruumsh** with 1d3 **ogres** and 2d10 + 5 **orcs**
78–80	A torrential rain that lasts 1d6 minutes and puts out all unprotected flames within 1 mile
81–82	1 **young black dragon**
83–84	1d4 **green hags** with 1d6 + 1 **ogres**
85–86	1 **yuan-ti abomination**
87–88	1d4 + 1 **wights**

d100	Encounter
89–90	1d6 + 1 **yuan-ti malisons**
91–93	1d4 + 1 **trolls**
94–96	1d10 **revenants**
97–99	1d8 + 1 **water elementals**
00	1d3 **hydras**

SWAMP ENCOUNTERS (LEVELS 11–20)

d100	Encounter
01–10	1d4 **giant crocodiles**
11–15	1d3 **yuan-ti abominations**
16–20	1d6 + 1 **green hags**
21–25	A large, spreading tree from which 2d6 armored knights hang by the neck
26–30	2d4 **wights**
31–35	1d8 + 1 **yuan-ti malisons**
36–40	Fog that rolls across the terrain, making the area within 1d3 miles heavily obscured for 1d4 hours
41–45	1d4 **revenants**
46–50	1d6 **shambling mounds**
51–55	1d10 **water elementals**
56–60	1d4 **young black dragons**
61–65	An eerie, bat-headed idol almost completely covered by vines
66–70	1d8 + 2 **trolls**
71–75	1d3 **hydras**
76–80	The sound of drums beating several miles away
81–96	1 **adult black dragon**
97–00	1 **ancient black dragon**

UNDERDARK ENCOUNTERS (LEVELS 1–4)

d100	Encounter
01	1 **mind flayer arcanist**
02	1d3 + 1 **giant poisonous snakes**
03	1d3 **giant lizards**
04	2d4 **giant fire beetles**
05	1d8 + 1 **flumphs**
06	1 **shrieker**
07	1d12 **giant rats**
08	2d4 **kobolds**
09	1d8 + 1 **stirges**
10	2d4 humans (**tribal warriors**) seeking the way to the surface, fleeing their Underdark oppressors
11–12	1d10 **troglodytes**
13–14	1d2 **gray oozes**
15–16	3d6 **stirges**
17–18	1d3 **magma mephits**
19–20	1d10 **goblins**
21–22	Orc graffiti on the walls, suggesting something rude about the mother of someone named Krusk

d100	Encounter
23–24	1 swarm of insects
25	1 deep gnome
26–28	1d8 + 1 drow
29–30	1d4 violet fungi
31–32	1d12 kuo-toa
33	1 rust monster
34–35	A rubble-strewn passage that appears to have been recently cleared after a cave-in
36–37	1d8 + 1 giant bats
38–39	3d6 kobolds
40–41	2d4 grimlocks
42–43	1d4 + 3 swarms of bats
44	1 dwarf prospector (scout) looking for gold
45	1 carrion crawler or 1 gelatinous cube
46	1d8 darkmantles or 2d4 piercers
47	1 hell hound
48	1d3 specters
49	1d4 bugbears
50	1d10 + 5 winged kobolds
51	1d4 fire snakes
52	2d8 + 1 troglodytes
53	1d6 giant spiders
54	3d6 kuo-toa
55	1 goblin boss with 2d4 goblins
56	4d4 grimlocks
57	1 ochre jelly
58	2d10 giant centipedes
59	1 nothic or 1 giant toad
60	1d4 myconid adults with 5d4 myconid sprouts
61	1 minotaur skeleton or 1 minotaur
62	3d6 drow
63	1 mimic or 1 doppelganger
64	1d6 + 3 hobgoblins
65	1 intellect devourer or 1 spectator
66	1d8 + 1 orcs
67–68	A faint tapping coming from inside a nearby wall
69	1 gibbering mouther or 1 water weird
70	1d12 gas spores
71	1 giant constrictor snake
72	1d10 shadows
73	1d3 grells
74	1d4 wights
75	1d8 + 1 quaggoth spore servants
76	1d2 gargoyles
77	1d4 ogres or 1d3 ettins
78	1d4 dwarf explorers (veterans)
79–80	An abandoned miners' camp spattered with blood and littered with the contents of 1d3 dungeoneer's packs
81	1 chuul or 1 salamander
82	1d4 phase spiders or 1d3 hook horrors
83	5d4 duergar
84	1 ghost or 1 flameskull or 1 wraith

d100	Encounter
85	1 druid with 1 polar bear (cave bear)
86	1 hobgoblin captain with 1d4 half-ogres and 2d10 hobgoblins
87	1 earth elemental or 1 black pudding
88	1 kuo-toa monitor with 1d8 + 1 kuo-toa whips
89	1 quaggoth thonot with 1d3 quaggoths
90	1 beholder zombie or 1 bone naga
91	1 orc Eye of Gruumsh with 1d4 orogs and 2d8 orcs
92	1d4 ghasts with 1d10 ghouls
93–95	A reeking puddle where slimy water has dripped from the ceiling
96	1 otyugh or 1 roper
97	1 vampire spawn
98	1 chimera
99	1 mind flayer
00	1 spirit naga

Underdark Encounters (Levels 5–10)

d100	Encounter
01	3d6 swarms of bats
02	1d4 giant spiders or 1d4 giant toads
03	1 mimic
04	2d4 gray oozes
05	2d10 orcs or 3d6 troglodytes
06	3d6 grimlocks
07	1d6 + 2 magma mephits
08	1 goblin boss with 2d4 goblins
09	2d4 darkmantles
10	2d8 + 1 drow
11	2d10 piercers
12	1d4 minotaur skeletons
13–14	3d6 deep gnomes
15	1 druid with 1 polar bear (cave bear)
16–17	3d6 orcs
18	1 bone naga
19–20	2d6 bugbears
21–25	Luminescent fungi growing on the walls of a moist cave, filling it with dim light
26	2d4 specters
27	1d12 + 4 shadows
28	1d3 gibbering mouthers
29–30	4d4 hobgoblins
31–32	1d4 carrion crawlers
33–34	1 black pudding
35	1d4 ochre jellies
36–40	A patch of mold that appears yellow when light is directed toward it
41	1d4 nothics
42–43	2d8 + 1 gas spores
44–45	1d3 gelatinous cubes
46	1 ghost
47–48	1 flameskull
49–50	2d8 duergar

d100	Encounter
51	1 wraith
52	1 umber hulk
53	1 xorn
54	1d6 + 2 dwarf hunters (**veterans**) searching for trolls
55	1 **hobgoblin captain** with 3d10 **hobgoblins**
56	1 roper
57	1 **kuo-toa monitor** with 1d4 **kuo-toa whips** and 1d8 + 1 **kuo-toa**
58	1d3 **water weirds**
59	1d4 **ghasts** with 1d10 **ghouls**
60	1 otyugh
61–62	A merchant caravan consisting of 1 **drow mage**, 2 **drow elite warriors**, and 2d10 **quaggoths**
63	1d4 **wights**
64	1d4 **doppelgangers**
65	2d8 **fire snakes**
66	1d4 **spectators**
67	1 **orc Eye of Gruumsh** with 1d4 **orogs** and 2d10 + 3 **orcs**
68	1d3 **vampire spawn**
69	1d4 **hook horrors** or 1d4 **minotaurs**
70	3d6 **quaggoth spore servants**
71–72	1d3 **grells**
73	1d6 + 1 **intellect devourers**
74	1d10 **gargoyles**
75	1 **beholder zombie**
76–77	1 **quaggoth thonot** with 2d4 **quaggoths**
78	1d6 **ettins** or 1d4 **trolls**
79	1d8 + 1 **phase spiders**
80	1 **fomorian** or 1d3 **cyclopes**
81	1d4 **earth elementals**
82	3d6 **ogres**
83	1d4 + 1 **chuuls**
84	1d10 **hell hounds**
85	1d3 **drow elite warriors**
86	1d4 **chimeras**
87	1d4 **salamanders**
88	1 **cloaker**
89	2d4 **wights**
90	1d4 **driders**
91	1 **fire giant**
92	1 **grick alpha** with 2d4 **gricks**
93	1 **mind flayer arcanist**
94	1d4 **drow mages**
95	1 **spirit naga**
96	1d4 **mind flayers**
97	1 **behir**
98	1 **aboleth**
99	1 **dao** or 1 **stone giant**
00	1 **beholder**

Underdark Encounters (Levels 11–16)

d100	Encounter
01–02	3d6 **carrion crawlers**
03–04	1d6 + 1 **gelatinous cubes**
05–06	1d8 + 2 **gibbering mouthers**
07–08	2d8 **minotaur skeletons**
09–10	2d6 **ochre jellies**
11–12	2d4 **doppelgangers**
13–14	1d4 **quaggoth thonots** with 1d10 + 2 **quaggoths**
15–16	1d3 **ropers**
17–18	3d6 **gargoyles**
19–20	1d10 **mimics**
21–25	A 100-foot-long ravine, 4d10 feet wide and 5d20 + 200 feet deep
26–27	1 **hobgoblin captain** with 3d10 **hobgoblins**
28–29	2d4 **spectators**
30–31	3d6 **ghasts**
32–33	2d8 **intellect devourers**
34–35	1d3 **orc Eyes of Gruumsh** with 2d4 **orogs** and 2d10 **orcs**
36–40	A large cave containing 2d10 extraordinarily detailed statues of various creatures
41–42	1d8 + 1 **kuo-toa monitors**
43–44	2d4 **water weirds**
45–46	2d10 **gricks**
47–48	3d6 **nothics**
49–50	2d8 + 1 **ogres**
51–52	1d6 + 2 **chuuls**
53–54	1d8 + 1 **ettins**
55	3d6 **grells**
56	2d4 **flameskulls**
57	2d12 dwarf soldiers (**veterans**) on patrol
58	2d8 **hell hounds**
59	1d10 **ghosts**
60	3d4 **wights**
61	3d6 **phase spiders**
62	1d8 + 1 **bone nagas**
63–65	A shrill scream followed by dark laughter
66	1d4 **chimeras**
67	1d10 **black puddings**
68	3d6 **minotaurs**
69	2d4 **otyughs**
70	1d6 + 1 **beholder zombies**
71	4d4 **hook horrors**
72	1d8 + 1 **umber hulks**
73	2d4 **salamanders**
74	1d3 **grick alphas**
75	1d6 + 2 **xorn**
76–80	A ruined village that once belonged to deep gnomes. A search has a 50% chance of uncovering 1d3 *potions of healing* and a 25% chance of finding a random common magic item.
81	2d4 **earth elementals**
82	1d3 **spirit nagas**

d100	Encounter
83	1d8 + 1 **cyclops**
84	1d6 + 2 **trolls**
85	2d4 **stone giants**
86	2d4 **wraiths**
87	1d4 **fomorians**
88	1d3 **drow mages** with 1d4 **drow elite warriors**
89	1d10 **vampire spawn**
90	1d3 **cloakers**
91	1d4 **fire giants**
92	1 **mind flayer arcanist** with 1d6 + 1 **mind flayers**
93	1d4 **dao**
94	1d8 + 1 **driders**
95	1d3 **behirs**
96	1d4 **aboleths**
97	1 **beholder**
98	1 **young red shadow dragon**
99	1 **death tyrant**
00	1 **purple worm**

Underdark Encounters (Levels 17–20)

d100	Encounter
01	1d4 **grick alphas**
02	2d8 **spectators**
03–04	3d6 **minotaurs** or 2d8 **kuo-toa monitors**
05–06	2d8 **grells**
07–08	2d10 **phase spiders**
09–10	4d4 **hell hounds**
11–12	1d6 + 2 **ropers**
13–14	2d10 **wights**
15–16	3d6 **doppelgangers**
17–18	1d8 + 1 **chimeras**
19–20	1d4 **cloakers**
21	1d4 **hobgoblin captains** with 5d10 **hobgoblins**
22–23	1d8 + 1 **earth elementals**
24–25	2d4 **vampire spawn**
26–27	3d6 **minotaurs**
28–30	A 30-foot-tall inverted black pyramid floating 1 inch above the floor in a large cave
31–32	1d10 **beholder zombies**
33–34	1d4 **mind flayer arcanists**
35–36	1d6 + 2 **otyughs**
37–38	1d12 **trolls**
39–40	1d10 **wraiths**
41–43	A beautiful obsidian sculpture of a panther lying on the floor
44–45	1d4 **drow mages** with 1d6 **drow elite warriors**
46–47	1d4 **spirit nagas**
48–49	1d8 + 1 **salamanders**
50–51	2d4 **umber hulks**
52–53	1d10 **xorn**
54–56	1 **young red shadow dragon**
57–59	2d4 **fomorians**
60–62	1d8 + 1 **driders**

d100	Encounter
63–65	1d20 + 20 **spiders** crawling on the walls of a web-filled cave
66–68	1d4 **fire giants**
69–70	1d10 **mind flayers**
71–73	2d4 **stone giants**
74–76	1d12 **cyclops**
77–80	A large cave in which stands a 50-foot-tall idol of Blibdoolpoolp
81–85	1d3 **dao**
86–90	1d4 **beholders**
91–93	1d4 **behirs**
94–96	1 **death tyrant**
97–99	1d3 **purple worms**
00	2d4 **aboleths**

Underwater Encounters (Levels 1–4)

d100	Encounter
01–10	3d6 **quippers**
11–14	2d4 **steam mephits**
15–18	1d4 **sahuagin**
19–22	2d6 **merfolk**
23–25	2d4 corpses of drowned sailors tangled in kelp
26–29	2d4 **constrictor snakes**
30–33	1d4 **reef sharks**
34–37	1 **swarm of quippers**
38–40	A bed of enormous clams
41–45	1d10 **merfolk** with 1d3 **giant sea horses**
46–50	1 **giant octopus**
51–55	1 **merrow**
56–60	1 **plesiosaurus**
61–65	2d10 pieces of corroded brass dinnerware littering the bottom
66–70	1 **giant constrictor snake**
71–75	1 **sea hag**
76–80	A school of silvery fish darting through the water
81–85	1d4 **hunter sharks**
86–90	1 **sahuagin priestess** with 2d4 **sahuagin**
91–96	1d4 **killer whales**
97–98	1 **giant shark**
99	1 **water elemental**
00	1 **sahuagin baron**

Underwater Encounters (Levels 5–10)

d100	Encounter
01–02	3d6 **steam mephits**
03–04	1d10 **sahuagin**
05–06	1 **giant octopus**
07–08	3d6 **constrictor snakes**
09–10	2d10 **merfolk** with 1d4 **giant sea horses**
11–15	1d4 **sea hags**
16–20	2d4 **swarms of quippers**
21–25	A sunken galleon with a 50% chance of a random treasure hoard inside (roll on the Treasure Hoard: Challenge 5–10 table in chapter 7 of the *Dungeon Master's Guide*)
26–30	1d4 **plesiosauruses**
31–35	3d6 **reef sharks**
36–40	An abandoned bathysphere
41–50	1d4 **giant constrictor snakes**
51–55	2d4 **hunter sharks**
56–60	1d3 **sahuagin priestesses** with 2d10 **sahuagin**
61–65	An empty castle made from coral
66–70	1d4 **killer whales**
71–75	1d10 **merrow**
76–80	An eerie statue of a squatting humanoid, with bat wings on its back and tentacles sprouting from its face
81–85	1d4 **water elementals**
86–90	1 **sahuagin baron** with 2d8 **sahuagin**
91–96	1d4 **giant sharks**
97–99	1 **marid**
00	1 **storm giant**

Underwater Encounters (Levels 11–20)

d100	Encounter
01–10	1 **sahuagin baron** with 1d4 **sahuagin priestesses** and 2d10 **sahuagin**
11–35	1d10 **killer whales**
36–40	A ghost ship passing overhead, containing 2d6 + 10 **ghosts**
41–60	1d6 **giant sharks**
61–65	A 1-mile-radius sphere of effervescent water that allows air-breathing creatures to breathe water while in the sphere
66–75	1d10 **water elementals**
76–80	A shimmering, blue-green portal to the Elemental Plane of Water
81–90	1d4 **marids**
91–96	1d3 **storm giants**
97–99	1 **dragon turtle**
00	1 **kraken**

Urban Encounters (Levels 1–4)

d100	Encounter
01	1d6 **cats**
02–03	1 **commoner** with 1d6 **goats**
04–05	2d10 **rats**
06	1 **raven** perched on a signpost
07	1 **commoner** on a **draft horse**
08	2d4 **mastiffs**
09	1d2 **commoners** leading 1d4 **mules** or 1d4 **ponies**
10	1 **pseudodragon**
11	1 **spy**
12–13	1d8 + 1 **acolytes**
14	1d6 + 6 **flying snakes**
15	3d6 **kobolds**
16	2d4 **giant centipedes**
17	1d8 + 1 **skeletons**
18–19	1d6 + 2 **swarms of rats**
20	1d12 **zombies**
21–25	A peddler weighed down with a load of pots, pans, and other basic supplies
26	1 **giant wasp**
27–28	1 **warhorse**
29	2d8 **cultists**
30–31	3d4 **giant rats**
32	2d8 **stirges**
33	1d3 + 2 **giant poisonous snakes**
34	1d4 + 2 **swarms of bats**
35	2d4 **winged kobolds**
36–40	A wagon loaded with apples that has a broken wheel and holds up traffic
41	1 **crocodile**
42–43	1 **swarm of insects**
44–45	3d6 **bandits**
46–47	1d3 + 2 **nobles** on **riding horses** with an escort of 1d10 **guards**
48	2d4 **kenku**
49	1d6 + 2 **smoke mephits**
50	1d8 + 1 **swarms of ravens**
51–52	1 **wererat**
53–54	1d3 **half-ogres**
55–56	1 **mimic**
57–58	1d4 **ghouls**
59–60	1d4 **specters**
61–62	1d10 **shadows**
63–65	Someone empties a chamber pot onto the street from a second-floor window
66–67	1 **ghast**
68–69	1 **priest**
70–71	1 **will-o'-wisp**
72–73	1d3 **giant spiders**

d100	Encounter
74–75	1d4 yuan-ti purebloods
76–77	2d4 thugs
78–80	A doomsayer who preaches the end of the world from a street corner
81	1 cambion
82	1 vampire spawn
83	1 couatl
84	1 ghost
85	1 succubus or 1 incubus
86	1 bandit captain with 3d6 bandits
87	1d4 + 1 cult fanatics
88	1 knight or 1 veteran
89	1 water weird
90	1 wight
91	1 mage
92	1 shield guardian
93	1 gladiator
94	1 revenant
95	2d4 gargoyles
96	1d4 doppelgangers
97	1 oni
98	1 invisible stalker
99	1d8 + 1 phase spiders
00	1 assassin

Urban Encounters (Levels 5–10)

d100	Encounter
01–02	1d10 kenku
03–04	2d6 giant centipedes

d100	Encounter
05–06	2d8 skeletons
07–08	1d6 swarms of bats and 1d6 swarms of rats
09–10	3d6 winged kobolds
11–13	2d4 specters
14–16	1d4 wights
17–19	4d4 acolytes on draft horses
20–22	3d6 giant centipedes
23–25	A talkative urchin, badgering passersby to serve as their guide through the community for a price of 1 sp
26–28	1d10 spies
29–31	3d6 crocodiles
32–34	1d6 + 2 swarms of insects
35–37	2d4 smoke mephits
38–40	A noble shouts "Stop! Thief!" at a fleeing scoundrel (bandit)
41–43	1 succubus or 1 incubus
44–46	1d10 half-ogres
47–49	2d10 giant wasps
50–51	4d10 zombies
52–53	1d4 knights on warhorses
54–55	1d4 + 1 water weirds
56–57	1d8 + 1 mimics
58–59	2d8 giant spiders
60–61	3d6 shadows
62–65	An actor leans out from a second-story window to call to passersby, announcing a show
66–67	1 bandit captain with 3d8 bandits
68–69	1d10 will-o'-wisps
70–71	2d4 priests

d100	Encounter
72–74	3d6 **yuan-ti purebloods**
75–76	2d10 **thugs**
77–80	A fortune-teller reads cards for those who pay a price of 1 sp
81	1d3 **gladiators**
82	1d4 + 1 **couatls**
83	1d8 **ghosts**
84	2d4 **doppelgangers**
85	1d6 +2 **phase spiders**
86	2d4 **veterans**
87	1d8 **ghasts** with 2d6 **ghouls**
88	3d6 **gargoyles**
89	2d10 **cult fanatics**
90	3d6 **wererats**
91	1 **assassin**
92	1d3 **invisible stalkers**
93	1 **gray slaad**
94	1 **young silver dragon**
95	1d4 **cambions** or 1d4 **revenants**
96	3d6 **wights**
97	1 **archmage**
98	2d4 **vampire spawn** or 1d4 **oni**
99	1 **mage** with 1 **shield guardian**
00	1 **rakshasa** or 1 **vampire**

Urban Encounters (Levels 11–16)

d100	Encounter
01	1 **mimic**
02–05	1 **bandit captain** with 5d10 **bandits**, all on **riding horses**
06–10	1d10 **knights** on **warhorses** (one knight is a **doppelganger**)
11–13	1d8 **succubi** or 1d8 **incubi**
14–16	3d6 **cult fanatics**
17–19	1d10 **wights**
20–22	3d6 **wererats**
23–25	A distant boom followed by a plume of smoke rising from the other side of the community
26–28	1d8 + 1 **ghosts**
29–31	2d10 **gargoyles**
32–34	1d6 + 2 **water weirds**
35–37	1d4 + 4 **will-o'-wisps**
38–40	Street performers putting on a puppet show, involving two puppets beating each other with sticks to the amusement of the gathered crowd
41–43	2d4 **couatls**
44–46	2d8 **ghasts**
47–51	1d8 + 1 **veterans**
52–55	3d4 **priests**
56–58	2d4 **cambions**
59–61	1d10 **revenants**
62–65	2d4 **phase spiders**

d100	Encounter
66–69	A scruffy **commoner** that ducks into an alley to make a purchase from a suspicious-looking figure
70–72	1d8 **invisible stalkers**
73–75	1d8 + 1 **gladiators**
76–80	Two farmers trading blows over the price of potatoes (50% chance for one farmer to be a retired **assassin**)
81–82	1d4 **young silver dragons**
83–84	1d4 **assassins**
85–86	1d8 **oni**
87–88	1d4 **mages** with 1d4 **shield guardians**
89–90	1d10 **vampire spawn**
91–92	1 **adult silver dragon**
93–94	1d4 **gray slaadi**
95–96	1 **spellcaster vampire** or 1 **warrior vampire**
97	1 **archmage** speeding down the street on a **riding horse**, blasting 1d4 **guards** with spells
98	1 **rakshasa**
99	1 **vampire**
00	1 **ancient silver dragon**

Urban Encounters (Levels 17–20)

d100	Encounter
01–05	1d10 **invisible stalkers**
06–10	1d10 **revenants**
11–14	1d6 + 2 **gladiators**
15–18	2d4 **cambions**
19–22	2d6 **succubi** or 2d6 **incubi**
23–25	A witch (**archmage**) who zooms overhead on a *broom of flying*
26–30	1d4 **gray slaadi**
31–35	2d8 **couatls**
36–40	A distraught parent who rushes up to people, begging for help for a child who fell into the sewer
41–45	1d3 **young silver dragons**
46–50	3d6 **ghosts**
51–55	1 **adult silver dragon**
56–60	1d4 **mages** with 1d4 **shield guardians**
61–65	An aggressive merchant who hawks wares to passersby, claiming to be the purveyor of the finest silks in all the land
66–70	1 **ancient silver dragon**
71–75	3d6 **vampire spawn**
76–80	A patrol of 2d10 **guards** marching up the street, searching for someone or something
81–85	1d10 **assassins**
86–90	1d4 + 1 **gray slaadi**
91–93	1d10 **oni**
94–96	1 **spellcaster vampire** or 1 **warrior vampire**
97	1d4 **archmages**
98	1d3 **rakshasas**
99	1d4 **vampires**
00	1 **tarrasque**

Traps Revisited

The rules for traps in the *Dungeon Master's Guide* provide the basic information you need to manage traps at the game table. The material here takes a different, more elaborate approach—describing traps in terms of their game mechanics and offering guidance on creating traps of your own using these new rules.

Rather than characterize traps as mechanical or magical, these rules separate traps into two other categories: simple and complex.

Simple Traps

A simple trap activates and is thereafter harmless or easily avoided. A hidden pit dug at the entrance of a goblin lair, a poison needle that pops from a lock, and a crossbow rigged to fire when an intruder steps on a pressure plate are all simple traps.

Elements of a Simple Trap

The description of a simple trap begins with a line that gives the trap's level and the severity of the threat it poses. Following a general note on what the trap looks like and how it functions are three paragraphs that tell how the trap works in the game.

Level and Threat. A trap's level is actually a range of levels, equivalent to one of the tiers of play (levels 1–4, 5–10, 11–16, and 17–20), indicating the appropriate time to use the trap in your campaign. Additionally, each trap poses either a moderate, dangerous, or deadly threat, based on its particular details.

Trigger. A simple trap activates when an event occurs that triggers it. This entry in a trap's description gives the location of the trigger and the activity that causes the trap to activate.

Effect. A trap's effect occurs after it activates. The trap might fire a dart, unleash a cloud of poison gas, cause a hidden enclosure to open, and so on. This entry specifies what the trap targets, its attack bonus or saving throw DC, and what happens on a hit or a failed saving throw.

Countermeasures. Traps can be detected or defeated in a variety of ways by using ability checks or magic. This entry in a trap's description gives the means for counteracting the trap. It also specifies what happens, if anything, on a failed attempt to disable it.

Running a Simple Trap

To prepare for using a simple trap in play, start by making note of the characters' passive Wisdom (Perception) scores. Most traps allow Wisdom (Perception) checks to detect their triggers or other elements that can tip off their presence. If you stop to ask players for this information, they might suspect a hidden danger.

When a trap is triggered, apply its effects as specified in its description.

If the characters discover a trap, be open to adjudicating their ideas for defeating it. The trap's description is a starting point for countermeasures, rather than a complete definition.

To make it easier for you to describe what happens next, the players should be specific about how they want to defeat the trap. Simply stating the desire to make a check isn't helpful for you. Ask the players where their characters are positioned and what they intend to do to defeat the trap.

EXAMPLE SIMPLE TRAPS

The following simple traps can be used to populate your adventures or as models for your own creations.

BEAR TRAP

Simple trap (level 1–4, dangerous threat)

A bear trap resembles a set of iron jaws that springs shut when stepped on, clamping down on a creature's leg. The trap is spiked in the ground, leaving the victim immobilized.

Trigger. A creature that steps on the bear trap triggers it.

Effect. The trap makes an attack against the triggering creature. The attack has a +8 attack bonus and deals 5 (1d10) piercing damage on a hit. This attack can't gain advantage or disadvantage. A creature hit by the trap has its speed reduced to 0. It can't move until it breaks free of the trap, which requires a successful DC 15 Strength check by the creature or another creature adjacent to the trap.

Countermeasures. A successful DC 10 Wisdom (Perception) check reveals the trap. A successful DC 10 Dexterity check using thieves' tools disables it.

CROSSBOW TRAP

Simple trap (level 1–4, dangerous threat)

The crossbow trap is a favorite of kobolds and other creatures that rely on traps to defend their lairs. It consists of a trip wire strung across a hallway and connected to a pair of hidden heavy crossbows. The crossbows are aimed to fire down the hallway at anyone who disturbs the trip wire.

Trigger. A creature that walks through the trip wire triggers the trap.

Effect. The trap makes two attacks against the triggering creature. Each attack has a +8 attack bonus and deals 5 (1d10) piercing damage on a hit. This attack can't gain advantage or disadvantage.

Countermeasures. A successful DC 15 Wisdom (Perception) check reveals the trip wire. A successful DC 15 Dexterity check using thieves' tools disables the trip wire, and a check with a total of 5 or lower triggers the trap.

FALLING PORTCULLIS

Simple trap (level 1–4, moderate threat)

Some folk who build dungeons, such as mad wizards in search of new victims, have no intention of allowing their visitors to make an easy escape. A falling portcullis trap can be especially devious if it causes a portcullis to drop some distance away from the pressure plate that activates the trap. Although the trap is deep in the dungeon, the portcullis closes off the dungeon entrance, which is hundreds of feet away, meaning that adventurers don't know they are trapped until they decide to head for the exit.

Trigger. A creature that steps on the pressure plate triggers the trap.

Effect. An iron portcullis drops from the ceiling, blocking an exit or a passageway.

Countermeasures. A successful DC 20 Wisdom (Perception) check reveals the pressure plate. A successful DC 20 Dexterity check using thieves' tools disables it, and a check with a total of 5 or lower triggers the trap.

FIERY BLAST

Simple trap (level 5–10, dangerous threat)

The temple of Pyremius, a god of fire, is threatened by thieves who seek to steal the fire opals displayed there by the priests in tribute to their god. A mosaic on the floor of the entryway to the inner sanctum delivers a fiery rebuke to intruders.

Trigger. Anyone who steps on the mosaic causes fire to erupt from it. Those who openly wear holy symbols of Pyremius don't trigger this trap.

Effect. A 15-foot cube of fire erupts, covering the pressure plate and the area around it. Each creature in the area must make a DC 15 Dexterity saving throw, taking 24 (7d6) fire damage on a failed save, or half as much damage on a successful one.

Countermeasures. A successful DC 15 Wisdom (Perception) check reveals the presence of ash and faint burn marks in the area affected by this trap. A successful DC 15 Intelligence (Religion) check enables a creature to destroy the trap by defacing a key rune on the perimeter of the mosaic that is within reach; failing this check causes the trap to activate. A successful *dispel magic* (DC 15) cast on the runes destroys the trap.

NET TRAP

Simple trap (level 1–4, dangerous threat)

Goblins, with their propensity to enslave their enemies, prefer traps that leave intruders intact so the victims can be put to work in the mines or elsewhere.

Pit traps are hilarious!
Because when one of you walking
things steps on one, you fall down!
And you get hurt! That's the best part.

Trigger. A trip wire strung across a hallway is rigged to a large net. If the trip wire is broken, the net falls on intruders. An iron bell is also rigged to the trip wire. It rings when the trap activates, alerting nearby guards.

Effect. A net covering a 10-foot-by-10-foot area centered on the trip wire falls to the floor as a bell rings. Any creature fully within this area must succeed on a DC 15 Dexterity saving throw or be restrained. A creature can use its action to make a DC 10 Strength check to try to free itself or another creature in the net. Dealing 5 slashing damage to the net (AC 10, 20 hp) also frees a creature without harming the creature.

Countermeasures. A successful DC 15 Wisdom (Perception) check reveals the trip wire and the net. A successful DC 15 Dexterity check using thieves' tools disables the trip wire without causing the net to drop or the bell to ring; failing the check causes the trap to activate.

Pit Trap

Simple trap (level 1–4, moderate threat)

The simplest of pit traps consists of a 10-foot-deep hole in the floor, concealed by tattered canvas that's covered with leaves and dirt to look like solid ground. This type of trap is useful for blocking off the entrance to a monster lair, and usually has narrow ledges along its sides to allow for movement around it.

Trigger. Anyone who steps on the canvas might fall into the pit.

Effect. The triggering creature must make a DC 10 Dexterity saving throw. On a successful save, the creature catches itself on the pit's edge or instinctively steps back. On a failed save, the creature falls into the pit and takes 3 (1d6) bludgeoning damage from the fall.

Countermeasures. A successful DC 10 Wisdom (Perception) check reveals the presence of the canvas and the 1-foot-wide ledge around the edges of the pit where it is safe to travel.

Poison Needle

Simple trap (level 1–4, deadly threat)

A tiny, poisoned needle hidden in a lock is a good way to discourage thieves from plundering a hoard. Such a trap is usually put in a chest or in the door to a treasure chamber.

Trigger. Anyone attempting to pick or open the lock triggers the trap.

Effect. The triggering creature must make a DC 20 Constitution saving throw. On a failed save, the creature takes 14 (4d6) poison damage and is poisoned for 10 minutes. While poisoned in this way, the creature is paralyzed. On a successful save, the creature takes half as much damage and isn't poisoned.

Countermeasures. A successful DC 20 Wisdom (Perception) check reveals the needle, but only if a character inspects the lock. A successful DC 20 Dexterity check using thieves' tools disables the needle, and a check with a total of 10 or lower triggers the trap.

Scything Blade

Simple trap (level 5–10, dangerous threat)

This trap uses moving blades that sweep down through a chamber, threatening anyone nearby. Typically, a scything blade trap is activated by manipulating a lever or some other simple device. Kobolds especially like this kind of trap, since it can take down bigger creatures.

Trigger. When the lever is pulled, the trap activates.

Effect. Each Medium or larger creature in a 5-foot-wide, 20-foot-long area must make a DC 15 Dexterity saving throw, taking 14 (4d6) slashing damage on a failed save, or half as much damage on a successful one.

Countermeasures. The lever isn't hidden. A successful DC 15 Wisdom (Perception) check involving the surfaces in the trap's area of effect reveals scrape marks and bloodstains on the walls and floor. A successful DC 15 Dexterity check using thieves' tools disables the lever.

Sleep of Ages

Simple trap (level 11–16, deadly threat)

When a sleep of ages trap activates, a pressure plate unleashes a spell that threatens to send intruders into a deep slumber. The dungeon's guardians can then more easily dispose of the sleepers.

Trigger. Stepping on the pressure plate triggers this trap.

Effect. When activated, this trap casts a *sleep* spell centered on the pressure plate, using a 9th-level spell slot.

Countermeasures. A successful DC 20 Wisdom (Perception) check reveals the pressure plate. A successful DC 20 Intelligence (Arcana) check made within 5 feet of the pressure plate disables the trap, and a check with a total of 10 or lower triggers it. A successful *dispel magic* (DC 19) cast on the pressure plate destroys the trap.

Designing Simple Traps

You can create your own simple traps by using the following guidelines. You can also adapt the example traps for different levels and severity of threat by modifying their DCs and damage values as shown below.

Purpose

Before diving into the details of your trap, think about its reason for being. Why would someone build such a trap? What is its purpose? Consider the trap's creator (in the adventure), the creator's purpose, and the location the trap protects. Traps have context in the world—they aren't created for no reason—and that context drives the trap's nature and effects.

Described below are a few of the general purposes a trap might have. Use them to inspire the creation of your own traps.

Alarm. An alarm trap is designed to alert an area's occupants of intruders. It might cause a bell or a gong to sound. This type of trap rarely involves a saving throw, because the alarm can't be avoided when the trap goes off.

Delay. Some traps are designed to slow down enemies, giving a dungeon's inhabitants time to mount a

defense or flee. The hidden pit is a classic example of this kind of trap. A 10-foot-deep pit usually deals little damage and is easy to escape, but it serves its purpose by impeding intruders. Other examples of delaying traps include collapsing walls, a portcullis that drops from the ceiling, and a locking mechanism that shuts and bars a door. If a delaying trap has moving parts that directly threaten characters when they operate, the characters are usually required to make Dexterity saving throws to avoid harm.

Restrain. A restraining trap tries to keep its victims in place, leaving them unable to move. Such traps are often employed in conjunction with regular guard patrols, so that victims are periodically extricated and taken away to be dealt with. But in an ancient dungeon, the guards might be long gone.

Restraining traps usually require a successful Strength saving throw to be avoided, but some don't allow saving throws. In addition to dealing damage, a restraining trap also renders a creature unable to move. Making a subsequent successful Strength check (using the trap's saving throw DC) or dealing damage against the trap can break it and free the captive. Examples include a bear trap, a cage that drops from a ceiling, and a device that flings a net.

Slay. Some traps are designed to eliminate intruders, plain and simple. Their effects include poisoned needles that spring out when a lock is tampered with, blasts of fire that fill a room, poison gas, and other lethal measures. Saving throws—usually Dexterity or Constitution—allow creatures to avoid or mitigate the trap's effects.

LEVEL AND LETHALITY

Before creating a trap's effects, think about its level and its lethality.

Traps are divided into four level ranges: 1–4, 5–10, 11–16, and 17–20. The level you choose for a trap gives you a starting point for determining its potency.

To further delineate the trap's strength, decide whether it is a moderate, dangerous, or deadly threat to characters in its level range. A moderate trap is unlikely to kill a character. A dangerous trap typically deals enough damage that a character hit by one is eager for healing. A deadly trap might reduce a creature to 0 hit points in one shot, and leaves most creatures hit by it in need of a short or long rest.

Consult the following tables when determining a trap's effects. The Trap Save DCs and Attack Bonuses table provides guidelines for a trap's saving throw DC, check DC, and attack bonus. The check DC is the default for any check used to interact with the trap.

The Damage Severity by Level table lists the typical damage a trap deals at certain character levels. The damage values given assume that the trap damages one creature. Use d6s for damage in place of d10s for traps that can affect more than one creature at a time.

The Spell Equivalent by Level table shows the spell slot level that is appropriate for a given character level and the severity of danger posed by the trap. A spell is a great foundation to use as the design of a trap, whether the trap duplicates the spell (a mirror that casts *charm person* on whoever looks into it) or uses its effects (an alchemical device that explodes like a *fireball*).

The Deadly entry for characters of 17th level or higher suggests combining a 9th-level and a 5th-level spell into one effect. In this case, pick two spells, or combine the effects of a spell cast using a 9th-level and a 5th-level slot. For instance, a *fireball* spell of this sort would deal 24d6 fire damage on a failed saving throw.

TRAP SAVE DCs AND ATTACK BONUSES

Trap Danger	Save/Check DC	Attack Bonus
Moderate	10	+5
Dangerous	15	+8
Deadly	20	+12

DAMAGE SEVERITY BY LEVEL

Character Level	Moderate	Dangerous	Deadly
1–4	5 (1d10)	11 (2d10)	22 (4d10)
5–10	11 (2d10)	22 (4d10)	55 (10d10)
11–16	22 (4d10)	55 (10d10)	99 (18d10)
17–20	55 (10d10)	99 (18d10)	132 (24d10)

SPELL EQUIVALENT BY LEVEL

Character Level	Moderate	Dangerous	Deadly
1–4	Cantrip	1st	2nd
5–10	1st	3rd	6th
11–16	3rd	6th	9th
17–20	6th	9th	9th + 5th

TRIGGERS

A trigger is the circumstance that needs to take place to activate the trap.

Decide what causes the trap to activate and determine how the characters can find the trigger. Here are some example triggers:

- A pressure plate that, when it is stepped on, activates the trap
- A trip wire that springs a trap when it is broken, usually when someone walks through it
- A doorknob that activates a trap when it is turned the wrong way
- A door or chest that triggers a trap when it is opened

A trigger usually needs to be hidden to be effective. Otherwise, avoiding the trap is usually easy.

A trigger requires a Wisdom (Perception) check if simply spotting it reveals its nature. The characters can foil a pit trap hidden by a leaf-covered net if they spot the pit through a gap in the leaves. A trip wire is foiled if it is spotted, as is a pressure plate.

Other traps require careful inspection and deduction to notice. A doorknob opens a door when turned to the left, but activates a trap when turned to the right. Such a subtle trap requires a successful Intelligence (Investigation) check to notice. The trigger is obvious. Understanding its nature is not.

The DC of the check, regardless of its type, depends on the skill and care taken to conceal the trap. Most traps can be detected with a successful DC 20 check, but a crudely made or hastily built trap has a DC of 15. Exceptionally devious traps might have a DC of 25.

You must then put some thought into what the characters learn with a successful check. In most cases, the check reveals the trap. In other cases, it uncovers clues, but foiling the trap still requires some deduction. The characters might succeed on the check but still trigger the trap if they don't understand what they have learned.

EFFECTS

Designing a trap's effects is a straightforward process. The tables for saving throw DCs, attack bonuses, damage, and the like give you a starting point for most simple traps that deal damage.

For traps with more complex effects, your best starting point is to use the Spell Equivalent by Level table to find the best match for your trap's intended effect. Spells are a good starting point because they are compact pieces of game design that deliver specific effects.

If you are using a spell as a starting point, check to see if you need to tweak its effects to fit the trap's nature. For instance, you can easily change the damage type a spell delivers or the saving throw it requires.

DISARMING A SIMPLE TRAP

Only one successful ability check is required to disarm a simple trap. Imagine how your trap operates, and then think about how the characters could overcome it. More than one kind of ability check might be possible. Some traps are so poorly concealed that they can be discovered or circumvented without active effort. For instance, a hidden pit trap is effectively disarmed as soon as the

characters notice it. After that, they can simply walk around it, or they can climb down one side, walk across the bottom of the pit, and climb up the other side.

Once you determine how a trap can be disarmed or avoided, decide the appropriate ability and skill combinations that characters can use. A Dexterity check using thieves' tools, a Strength (Athletics) check, and an Intelligence (Arcana) check are all commonly used for this purpose.

A Dexterity check using thieves' tools can apply to any trap that has a mechanical element. Thieves' tools can be used to disable a trip wire or a pressure plate, disassemble a poison needle mechanism, or clog a valve that leaks poisonous gas into a room.

A Strength check is often the method for thwarting traps that can be destroyed or prevented from operating through the use of brute force. A scything blade can be broken, a sliding block can be held in place, or a net can be torn apart.

A magic trap can be disabled by someone who can undermine the magic used to power it. Typically, a successful Intelligence (Arcana) check enables a character to figure out how a magic trap functions and how to negate its effect. For instance, the character could discover that a statue that belches a jet of magical flame can be disabled by shattering one of its glass eyes.

Once you know what kind of check is called for, you then determine what happens on a failed attempt to disable the trap. Depending on the kind of check involved and the nature of the trap, you might determine that any failed check has negative consequences—usually involving the triggering of the trap. At other times, you could assign a number that the check must exceed to prevent the trap from going off. If the total of the check is equal to or lower than that number, the trap activates.

PLACING A SIMPLE TRAP

Context and environment are critical when it comes to properly locating a trap. A swinging log trap that's meant to knock characters aside is a mere inconvenience on a typical forest path, where it can be easily circumvented. But it's a potentially deadly hazard on a narrow trail that hugs the side of a towering cliff face.

Choke points and narrow passages that lead to important places in a dungeon are good spots for traps, especially those that serve as alarms or restraints. The goal is to foil or delay intruders before they can reach a critical location, giving the dungeon's denizens a chance to mount a defense or a counterattack.

A treasure chest, a door leading to a vault, or any other obstacle or container that bars the way to a valuable treasure is the ideal location for a slaying trap. In such instances, the trap is the last line of defense against a thief or intruder.

Alarm traps, since they pose no direct physical threat, are appropriate for areas that are also used by a dungeon's denizens—assuming the residents know about the trap and how to avoid setting it off. Accidents can happen, but if a goblin stumbles inside its den and activates an alarm trap, there's no real harm done. The alarm sounds, the guards arrive, they punish the clumsy goblin, and they reset the trap.

COMPLEX TRAPS

A complex trap poses multiple dangers to adventurers. After a complex trap activates, it remains dangerous round after round until the characters avoid it or disable it. Some complex traps become more dangerous over time, as they accumulate power or gain speed.

Complex traps are also more difficult to disable than simple ones. A single check is not enough. Instead, a series of checks is required to slowly disengage the trap's components. The trap's effect degrades with each successful check until the characters finally deactivate it.

Most complex traps are designed so that they can be disarmed only by someone who is exposed to the trap's effect. For example, the mechanism that controls a hallway filled with scything blades is on the opposite end from the entrance, or a statue that bathes an area in necrotic energy can be disabled only by someone standing in the affected area.

DESCRIBING A COMPLEX TRAP

A complex trap has all the elements of a simple trap, plus special characteristics that make the trap a more dynamic threat.

Level and Threat. A complex trap uses the same level and severity designations that a simple trap does.

Trigger. Just like a simple trap, a complex trap has a trigger. Some complex traps have multiple triggers.

Initiative. A complex trap takes turns as a creature does, because it functions over a period of time. This part of a trap's description tells whether the trap is slow (acts on initiative count 10), fast (acts on initiative count 20), or very fast (acts on initiative count 20 and also initiative count 10). A trap always acts after creatures that have the same initiative count.

Active Elements. On a trap's turn, it produces specific effects that are detailed in this part of its description. The trap might have multiple active elements, a table you roll on to determine its effect at random, or options for you to choose from.

Dynamic Elements. A dynamic element is a threat that arises or evolves while the trap functions. Usually, changes involving dramatic elements take effect at the end of each of the trap's turns or in response to the characters' actions.

Constant Elements. A complex trap poses a threat even when it is not taking its turn. The constant elements describe how these parts of the trap function. Most make an attack or force a saving throw against any creature that ends its turn within a certain area.

Countermeasures. A trap can be defeated in a variety of ways. A trap's description details the checks or spells that can detect or disable it. It also specifies what happens, if anything, on a failed attempt to disable it.

Disabling a complex trap is like disarming a simple trap, except that a complex trap requires more checks. It typically takes three successful checks to disable one of a complex trap's elements. Many of these traps have multiple elements, requiring a lot of work to shut down every part of the trap. Usually, a successful check reduces a trap element's effectiveness even if it doesn't disable the trap.

RUNNING A COMPLEX TRAP

A complex trap functions in play much like a legendary monster. When it is activated, the trap's active elements act according to its initiative. On each of its initiative counts, after all creatures with that same initiative count have acted, the trap's features activate. Apply the effects detailed in the trap's description.

After resolving the effects of the trap's active elements, check its dynamic elements to see if anything changes about the trap. Many complex traps have effects that vary during an encounter. A magical aura might do more damage the longer it is active, or a swinging blade might change which area of a chamber it attacks.

The trap's constant elements allow it to have effects when it isn't the trap's turn. At the end of each creature's turn, look at the trap's constant elements to see if any of their effects are triggered.

EXPERIENCE FOR COMPLEX TRAPS

Overcoming a complex trap merits an experience point award, depending on the danger it poses. Judging whether a party has overcome a trap requires some amount of adjudication. As a rule of thumb, if the characters disable a complex trap or are exposed to its effects and survive, award them experience points for the effort according to the table below.

COMPLEX TRAP EXPERIENCE AWARDS

Trap Level	Experience Points
1–4	650
5–10	3,850
11–16	11,100
17–20	21,500

EXAMPLE COMPLEX TRAPS

The following complex traps can be used to challenge characters or to inspire your own creations.

PATH OF BLADES
Complex trap (level 1–4, dangerous threat)

Hidden within a buried pyramid that marks the location of the Lost City of Cynidicea is the tomb of King Alexander and Queen Zenobia. The entrance to their tomb is a long hallway riddled with traps, accessible only by cunningly hidden secret doors. The hallway is 20 feet wide and 160 feet long. It is mostly clear. After 80 feet, the floor is broken and cracked, becoming difficult terrain until the 130-foot mark.

Trigger. This trap activates as soon as a non-undead creature enters the hallway, and it remains active while any non-undead creature is within the hall.

Initiative. The trap acts on initiative count 20 and initiative count 10.

Active Elements. The Path of Blades includes a set of whirling blades along the first 80 feet of the trap, crushing pillars that slam down from the ceiling to the floor before rising back up to the ceiling in the next 50 feet, and a rune of fear in its final 30 feet.

Whirling Blades (Initiative 20). The blades attack each creature in the first 80 feet of the hallway, with a +5 bonus to the attack roll and dealing 11 (2d10) slashing damage on a hit.

Crushing Pillars (Initiative 10). Each creature in the 50-foot-long area beyond the first 80 feet of the hallway must make a DC 15 Dexterity saving throw. On a failed save, a creature takes 11 (2d10) bludgeoning damage and is knocked prone. On a successful save, the creature takes half as much damage and isn't knocked prone.

Rune of Fear (Initiative 10). Each creature in the 30-foot-long area beyond the Crushing Pillars must make a DC 15 Wisdom saving throw. On a failed saving throw, the creature becomes frightened by the rune, and it must immediately use its reaction to move its speed in the direction of the pillars. The frightened creature can't move closer to the far end of the hallway until it uses its action to make a DC 15 Wisdom saving throw, which ends the frightened condition on itself on a success.

Dynamic Elements. The blades and the rune become more dangerous the longer the trap remains active.

Blades Accelerate. The blades move with increasing speed, slowing only when they hit a target. Each time the blades miss with an attack, their next attack becomes harder to avoid. After each miss, the blades' attack bonus increases by 2, and their damage increases by 3 (1d6). These benefits apply until the blades hit a target, after which the values return to normal.

Rune's Defense. Tampering with the Rune of Fear increases the trap's power. Each successful check on an attempt to disable the rune increases the damage of the blades and the crushing pillars by 5 (1d10) and increases the rune's saving throw DC by 1.

Constant Elements. The Whirling Blades and the Rune of Fear affect each creature that ends its turn in an area affected by these elements.

Whirling Blades. Any creature that ends its turn in the blades' area is targeted by an attack: +5 attack bonus; 5 (1d10) slashing damage on a hit.

Rune of Fear. Any creature that ends its turn within 30 feet of the far end of the corridor must make a saving throw against the Rune of Fear effect.

Countermeasures. Each of the trap's active elements can be thwarted by particular countermeasures.

Whirling Blades. Characters can smash the blades, damage their components, or discern how to avoid them. The blades are disabled if their attack bonus is reduced to −8. Ways to reduce it are described below.

Intelligence (Investigation), DC 15. As an action, a creature that can see the blades can attempt an Intelligence (Investigation) check. A successful check means that the character has learned how to anticipate the blades' movement, imposing disadvantage on the blades' attacks against the creature while it isn't incapacitated.

Attack. A creature in the area can ready an attack to strike at one of the blades as it goes by. The blade

gains advantage on its attack against the creature. The creature then attacks. Each blade has AC 15 and 15 hit points. Destroying a blade reduces the Whirling Blades attack bonus by 2.

Dexterity check using thieves' tools, DC 15. Creatures can use thieves' tools in the area attacked by the blades to foil their mechanism. A successful check reduces the Whirling Blades attack bonus by 2.

Crushing Pillars. The pillars are not susceptible to countermeasures.

Rune of Fear. The rune can be disabled with three successful DC 15 Intelligence (Arcana) checks. Each check requires an action. A creature must be at the end of the hallway to attempt the check, and only one creature can work on this task at once. Once a creature attempts a check for this purpose, no other character can do so until the end of that creature's next turn. Alternatively, the rune can be disabled with three successful castings of *dispel magic* (DC 13) targeting the rune.

SPHERE OF CRUSHING DOOM
Complex trap (level 5–10, deadly threat)

The court jester devised a deadly trap to foil anyone who sought to steal his magic fool's cap. The jester's tomb is located at the end of a 10-foot-wide, 150-foot-long hallway that descends sharply from north to south. The entrance to the tomb is a door on the eastern wall at the bottom of the slope, at the south end of the hall.

Trigger. This trap activates as soon as the door leading to the jester's coffin is opened. A magic portal opens at the northern end of the hallway and disgorges an enormous steel sphere, which hurtles down the slope. When it reaches the bottom of the slope, a second portal briefly appears and teleports the sphere back to the top of the slope to begin the process again.

Initiative. The trap acts on initiative count 10 (but see the dynamic element below).

Active Element. Although the trap is complex in nature, it has a single active element. That's all it needs.

Sphere of Crushing Doom (Initiative 10). The trap's active element is a sphere of steel that almost fills the 10-foot width of the hallway and rolls to the bottom of the slope on its turn. Each creature in the sphere's path must make a DC 20 Strength saving throw. On a failed save, a creature takes 22 (4d10) bludgeoning damage and is knocked prone. On a successful save, a creature takes half as much damage and isn't knocked prone. Objects that block the sphere, such as a conjured wall, take maximum damage from the impact.

Dynamic Element. The longer it rolls, the more lethal the sphere becomes.

Speed Kills. After its turn, the sphere gains speed, represented by its damage increasing by 11 (2d10). While its damage is 55 (10d10) or greater, it acts on initiative count 20 and 10.

Countermeasures. The trap can be neutralized either by stopping the sphere or preventing it from teleporting.

Stop the Sphere. Stopping the sphere is the easiest way to disrupt the trap. A *wall of force* can do so easily, as can any object placed in its path that has enough hit points to absorb damage from the sphere without being destroyed.

Disrupt the Portals. Either portal can be neutralized with three successful DC 20 Intelligence (Arcana) checks, but the process of analyzing a portal to disrupt it takes time. Faint runes in the ceiling and floor at both ends of the hallway are involved in the functioning of the portals. A creature must first use an action to examine a set of runes, then use a subsequent action to attempt to vandalize the runes. Each successful check reduces the sphere's damage by 11 (2d10), as the disrupted sphere loses speed moving through the failing portal.

Alternatively, a set of runes can be disabled with three successful castings of *dispel magic* (DC 19) targeting any of the runes in the set.

If the southern portal is destroyed, the sphere slams into the south wall and comes to a halt. It blocks the door to the tomb, but the characters can escape.

POISONED TEMPEST
Complex trap (level 11–16, deadly threat)

This fiendish trap was built to eliminate intruders who infiltrate a yuan-ti temple. The trap is a room, 60 feet on a side, with 5-foot-wide stone doors in the middle of each wall. In each corner of the room stands a 10-foot-tall statue of a great serpent, coiled and ready to strike. The eyes in each statue are rubies worth 200 gp apiece.

Trigger. This trap activates when a ruby is pried from one of the statues. Each statue's mouth slides open, revealing a 1-foot-wide pipe that runs down its throat.

Initiative. The trap acts on initiative count 20 and initiative count 10.

Active Elements. The trap fills the room with poison and other deadly effects.

Locked Doors (Initiative 20). The four doors to this room slam shut and are locked in place by magic. This effect activates only once, the first time the trap is triggered.

Poison Gas (Initiative 20). Poison gas floods the room. Each creature inside must make a DC 20 Constitution saving throw, taking 33 (6d10) poison damage on a failed save, or half as much damage on a successful one.

Tempest (Initiative 10). Air and gas boils from the trap. Roll a d6, and consult the following table.

TEMPEST EFFECTS

d6	Effect
1	Hallucinatory gas scrambles the mind and senses. All Intelligence and Wisdom checks made in the room have disadvantage until the Tempest element activates again.
2	Explosive gas fills the area. If anyone holds an open flame, it causes an explosion. All creatures in the area must make a DC 20 Dexterity saving throw, taking 22 (4d10) fire damage on a failed save, or half as much damage on a successful one. The flame is then extinguished.
3	Weakening gas fills the room. All Strength and Dexterity checks made in the room have disadvantage until the Tempest element activates again.
4	Buffeting winds force each creature in the room to succeed on a DC 20 Strength saving throw or be knocked prone.
5	Smoke fills the room. Visibility is reduced to 1 foot until the next time the Tempest element activates.
6	Poison floods the room, forcing creatures to make saving throws as for the Poison Gas element.

Dynamic Element. The longer the poison gas remains in the room, the more lethal it becomes.

Increased Potency. The damage from the Poison Gas element increases by 11 (2d10) each round after it activates, to a maximum of 55 (10d10).

Countermeasures. There are a few ways that the trap can be overcome.

Open the Doors. Opening the doors is the quickest way to circumvent the trap, but they are warded with magic. To open the doors, a character must first succeed on a DC 20 Wisdom (Perception) check to find the locking mechanism. A successful DC 20 Intelligence (Arcana) check is then required to disable the sphere of force that surrounds the lock (*dispel magic* is ineffective against it). Success on a DC 20 Dexterity check using thieves' tools picks the lock. Finally, a successful DC 20 Strength (Athletics) check is needed to push the door open. Each check requires an action.

Disable the Statues. A statue can be disabled by blocking the flow of gas from its mouth. Heavily damaging a statue is a bad idea, for doing so leaves the gas vents open. Reducing a statue to 0 hit points (AC 17; 20 hp; resistance to fire, piercing, and slashing damage; immune to poison and psychic damage) or making a successful DC 20 Strength check to break it cracks the statue and increases the Poison Gas damage by 5 (1d10). A successful DC 20 Dexterity check using thieves' tools, or a successful DC 15 Strength check made to block up the statue with a cloak or similar object, decreases the poison damage by 5 (1d10). Once a character succeeds on the check, someone must remain next to the statue to keep it blocked up. When all four statues are blocked in this manner, the trap deactivates.

DESIGNING COMPLEX TRAPS

Creating a complex trap takes more work than building a simple one, but with some practice, you can learn the process and make it move quickly.

Familiarize yourself with the advice on designing a simple trap before proceeding with the guidelines on complex traps.

PURPOSE

Complex traps are typically designed to protect an area by killing or disabling intruders. It is worth your time to consider who made the trap, the trap's purpose, and its desired result. Does the trap protect a treasure? Does it target only certain kinds of intruders?

LEVEL AND LETHALITY

Complex traps use the same level designations and lethality descriptors that simple traps do. Refer to that section for a discussion of how level and lethality help determine saving throw and check DCs, attack bonuses, and other numerical elements of a complex trap.

MAP

A complex trap has multiple parts, typically relies on the characters' positions to resolve some of its effects, and can bring several effects to bear in each round. The traps are called complex for a reason! To begin the design process, consider drawing a map of the area to be affected by the trap on graph paper, using a scale of 5 feet per square. This level of detail allows you to develop a clear idea of what the trap can do and how each of its parts interact. Your map is the starting point and context for the rest of the design process.

Don't limit yourself to one room. Look at the passages and rooms around the area of the trap and think about the role they can play. The trap might cause doors to lock and barriers to fall into place to prevent escape. It could cause darts to fire from the walls in one area, forcing characters to enter rooms where other devices trigger and threaten them.

Consider how terrain and furniture can add to the trap's danger. A chasm or a pit might create a buffer that allows a trap to send bolts of magic at the characters, while making it difficult or even impossible for them to reach the runes they must deface to foil that attack.

Think of your map like a script. Where do the characters want to go? What does the trap protect? How can the characters get there? What are their likely escape routes? Answering these questions tells you where the trap's various elements should be placed.

ACTIVE ELEMENTS

A complex trap's active elements work the same way as a simple trap's effects, except that a complex trap activates in every round. Otherwise, the guidelines for picking saving throw DCs, attack bonuses, and damage are the same. To make your trap logically consistent, make sure the elements you design can activate each round. For instance, ordinary crossbows rigged to fire at the characters would need a mechanism for reloading them between attacks.

In terms of lethality, it's better to have multiple dangerous effects in a trap than a single deadly one. For example, the Path of Blades trap uses two dangerous elements and one moderate element.

It's useful to create multiple active elements, with each affecting a different area. It's also a good idea to use a variety of effects. Some parts of the trap might deal damage, and others might immobilize characters or isolate them from the rest of the party. A bashing lever might knock characters into an area engulfed by jets of flame. Think about how the elements can work together.

CONSTANT ELEMENTS

In addition to the active steps a complex trap takes, it should also present a continual hazard. Often, the active and constant effects are the same thing. Imagine a hallway filled with whirling saw blades. On the trap's turn, the blades attack anyone in the hall. In addition, anyone who lingers in the hallway takes damage at the end of each of their turns, accounting for the constant threat that the blades pose.

A constant element should apply its effect to any creature that ends its turn in that element's area. If an active element presents a threat when it isn't the trap's turn, define the threat it poses as a constant element. As a rule of thumb, keep the saving throw DC or attack bonus the same as for the active element but reduce the damage by half.

Avoid filling the entire encounter area with constant elements. Part of the challenge of a complex trap lies in figuring out which areas are safe. A moment's respite can help add an element of pacing to an encounter with a complex trap and give the characters the feeling that they aren't in constant peril. For example, walls that slam together might need to reset between slams, making them harmless when it isn't their turn to act.

DYNAMIC ELEMENTS

Just as a battle is more interesting if the monsters change their tactics or unveil new abilities in later rounds, so too are complex traps more fun if their nature changes in some way. The whirling blades that protect a treasure chest do more damage each round as they speed up. The poison gas in a room grows thicker as more of it floods the chamber, dealing greater damage and affecting line of sight. The necrotic aura around an idol of Demogorgon produces random effects each

time its active element is triggered. As water floods a chamber, the characters must swim across areas they could walk through just a round or two earlier.

Since a complex trap remains active over the course of several rounds, it might be possible to predict its future behavior by examining how it functions. This information can give its targets a much better chance of thwarting it. To minimize this possibility, design your trap so that it presents multiple threats that can change each round. The changes can include how a trap targets creatures (different attacks or saving throws), the damage or effects it produces, the areas it covers, and so on. Some traps might have a random effect each round, while others follow a carefully programmed sequence of attacks.

Dynamic elements usually occur according to a schedule. For a room that floods, you can plan out how the rising water level affects the area each round. The water might be ankle deep at the end of the first round, knee deep the next, and so on. Not only does the water bring a risk of drowning, it also makes it harder to move across the area. On the other hand, the rising water level might allow characters to swim to the upper reaches of the chamber that they couldn't get to from the floor.

Dynamic elements can also come into play in reaction to the characters' actions. Disarming one element of the trap might make the others deadlier. Disabling a rune that triggers a fire-breathing statue might cause the statue to explode.

TRIGGERS

The advice on triggers given for simple traps also applies to complex traps, with one exception. Complex traps have multiple triggers, or are designed such that avoiding a trigger prevents intruders from reaching the area the trap guards. Other complex traps use magical triggers that activate on specific cues, such as when a door opens or someone enters an area without wearing the correct badge, amulet, or robe.

Look at your map and consider when you want the trap to spring into action. It's best to have a complex trap trigger after the characters have committed to exploring an area. A simple trap might activate when the characters open a door. A complex trap that triggers so early leaves the characters still outside the trapped room, in a place where they could decide to close the door and move on. A simple trap aims to keep intruders out. A complex trap wants to lure them in, so that when it activates, the intruders must deal with the trap before they can escape.

The trigger for a complex trap should be as foolproof as you can make it. A complex trap represents a serious expenditure of effort and magical power. No one builds such a trap and makes it easy to avoid. Wisdom (Perception) and Intelligence (Investigation) checks might be unable to spot a trigger, especially a magical one, but they can still give hints about the trap before it triggers. Bloodstains, ashes, gouges in the floor, and other clues of that sort can serve as evidence of the trap's presence.

INITIATIVE

A complex trap acts repeatedly, but unlike characters and monsters, traps don't roll for initiative. As mechanical or magical devices, their active elements operate in a periodic manner. When designing a complex trap, you need to decide when and how often its active elements produce their effects.

In a trap with multiple active elements that work in concert, those different elements would act on different initiative counts. For instance, on initiative count 20, blades sweep across a treasure vault, driving the characters back into the hallway. On initiative count 10, magic darts fire from statues in the hallway while a portcullis falls to confine the characters.

Initiative 10. If a trap's active element takes time to build up its effects, then it acts on initiative count 10. This option is good for a trap that functions alongside allied monsters or other guardians; the delay before it acts can give guards the chance to move out of its area or force characters into the area before the trap triggers.

Initiative 20. If an element is designed to surprise intruders and hit them before they can react, then it acts on initiative count 20. This option is generally best for a complex trap. Think of it as the default. Such a trap acts quickly enough to take advantage of most characters, with nimble characters like rogues, rangers, and monks having the best chance to move out of the area before the element activates.

Initiative 20 and 10. Some active elements are incredibly fast acting, laying waste to intruders in a few moments unless countered. They act on initiative count 20 and 10.

Defeating Complex Traps

A complex trap is never defeated with a single check. Instead, each successful check foils some part of it or degrades its performance. Each element of the trap must be overcome individually to defeat the trap as a whole.

As part of determining how your trap can be overcome, look at your map and consider where the characters must be located to attempt an action that can foil part of the trap. As a rule, the characters should need to be near or adjacent to an element to have a chance of affecting it. An element can be designed so that it protects itself. A fighter might be able to break a whirling blade, but moving close enough to attack it requires giving the blade a chance to strike.

What methods are effective against your trap? Obvious candidates are activities covered by the same sorts of checks used to defeat simple traps, but use your knowledge of the trap's design to identify other options. A valve that leaks poison gas into a room can be stopped up. A statue that emits a deadly aura can be pushed over and smashed. Attacks, spells, and special abilities can all play a role in undermining a trap.

Leave room for improvisation by the characters. Don't create a few predetermined solutions and wait for the players to figure out the right approach. If you understand the mechanism behind how a trap works, that makes it much easier for you to respond to the players' ideas. If a character wants to try something you haven't allowed for, pick an ability, assess the chance of success, and ask for a roll.

Shutting down one part of a complex trap usually requires multiple successes. As a default, it takes three successful checks or actions to disable an element. The first successful check might reduce the element's saving throw DC or attack bonus. The second successful check might halve the element's damage, and the final successful check shuts it down.

For elements that don't attack, allow each successful check to reduce that element's effectiveness by one-third. A lock's DC is decreased, or a gate opens wide enough to allow a Small character to squeeze through it. A mechanism pumping poison gas into the room becomes defective, causing the gas's damage to increase more slowly or not at all.

It takes time to disable a complex trap. Three characters can't make checks in rapid succession to disarm a complex trap in a matter of seconds. Each would get in another character's way and disrupt the effort. Once a character succeeds on a check, another character can't attempt the same check against the same trap element until the end of the successful character's next turn.

Not all of the characters' options need to be focused on stopping a trap from operating. Think of what characters can do to mitigate or avoid a trap's effects. Making the trap vulnerable to this sort of effort is a way to engage characters who might be ill-suited to confront the trap directly. A successful Intelligence (Religion) check might provide insight into the imagery displayed by a trap in a temple or shrine, giving other characters a clue about how and where to direct their efforts. A character could stand in front of a dart trap while holding a shield that the darts can target harmlessly, while other characters trigger that element as they work to disable it.

Downtime Revisited

It's possible for the characters to start a campaign at 1st level, dive into an epic story, and reach 10th level and beyond in a short amount of game time. Although that pace works fine for many campaigns, some DMs prefer a campaign story with pauses built into it—times when adventurers are not going on adventures. The downtime rules given in this section can be used as alternatives to the approach in the *Player's Handbook* and the *Dungeon Master's Guide*, or you can use the material here to inspire the creation of your own options.

By engaging the characters in downtime activities that take weeks or even months to complete, you can give your campaign a longer time line—one in which events in the world play out over years. Wars begin and end, tyrants come and go, and royal lines rise and fall over the course of the story that you and the characters tell.

Downtime rules also provide ways for characters to spend—or be relieved of—the monetary treasure they amass on their adventures.

The system presented here consists of two elements. First, it introduces the concept of rivals. Second, it details a number of downtime activities that characters can undertake.

Rivals

Rivals are NPCs who oppose the characters and make their presence felt whenever the characters are engaging in downtime. A rival might be a villain you have featured in past adventures or plan to use in the future. Rivals can also include good or neutral folk who are at odds with the characters, whether because they have opposing goals or they simply dislike one another. The cultist of Orcus whose plans the characters have foiled, the ambitious merchant prince who wants to rule the city with an iron fist, and the nosy high priest of Helm who is convinced the characters are up to no good are all examples of rivals.

A rival's agenda changes over time. Though the characters engage in downtime only between adventures, their rivals rarely rest, continuing to spin plots and work against the characters even when the characters are off doing something else.

Complex Traps and Legendary Monsters

A complex trap is like a legendary monster in some ways. It has several tricks it can use on its turn, and it remains a threat throughout the round, not just on its turn. The trap's active elements are like a legendary creature's normal actions, and its constant elements are equivalent to legendary actions—except they are tied to specific areas in the trapped room.

Although a legendary creature can move, improvise actions, and so forth, a trap is set to a specific script—an aspect that has the potential to make a complex trap stale and predictable. That's where dynamic elements come in. They keep the players on their toes and make dealing with a complex trap feel like a challenging, evolving situation.

CREATING A RIVAL

In essence, a rival is a somewhat specialized NPC. You can use chapter 4 of the *Dungeon Master's Guide* to build a new NPC for this purpose, or pick one from your current cast of supporting characters and embellish that NPC as described below.

It's possible for the characters to have two or three rivals at a time, each with a separate agenda. At least one should be a villain, but the others might be neutral or good; conflicts with those rivals might be social or political, rather than manifesting as direct attacks.

The best rivals have a connection with their adversaries on a personal level. Find links in the characters' backstories or the events of recent adventures that explain what sparked the rival's actions. The best trouble to put the characters in is trouble they created for themselves.

EXAMPLE RIVALS

d20	Rival
1	Tax collector who is convinced the characters are dodging fees
2	Politician who is concerned that the characters are causing more trouble than they solve
3	High priest who worries the characters are diminishing the temple's prestige
4	Wizard who blames the characters for some recent troubles
5	Rival adventuring party
6	Bard who loves a scandal enough to spark one
7	Childhood rival or member of a rival clan
8	Scorned sibling or parent
9	Merchant who blames the characters for any business woes
10	Newcomer out to make a mark on the world
11	Sibling or ally of defeated enemy
12	Official seeking to restore a tarnished reputation
13	Deadly foe disguised as a social rival
14	Fiend seeking to tempt the characters to evil
15	Spurned romantic interest
16	Political opportunist seeking a scapegoat
17	Traitorous noble looking to foment a revolution
18	Would-be tyrant who brooks no opposition
19	Exiled noble looking for revenge
20	Corrupt official worried that recent misdeeds will be revealed

To add the right amount of detail to a rival you want to create, give some thought to what that NPC is trying to accomplish and what resources and methods the rival can bring to bear against the characters.

Goals. An effective rival has a clear reason for interfering with the characters' lives. Think about what the rival wants, how and why the characters stand in the way, and how the conflict could be resolved. Ideally, a rival's goal directly involves the characters or something they care about.

Assets. Think about the resources the rival can marshal. Does the character have enough money to pay bribes or to hire a small gang of mercenaries? Does the rival hold sway over any guilds, temples, or other groups? Make a list of the rival's assets, and consider how they can be used.

Plans. The foundation of a rival's presence in the campaign is the actions the rival takes or the events that occur as a result of that character's goals. Each time you resolve one or more workweeks of downtime, pick one of the ways a rival's plans might be advanced and introduce it into play.

Think about how a rival might operate in order to bring specific plans to fruition, and jot down three or four kinds of **actions** the rival might undertake. Some of these might be versions of the downtime activities described later in this section, but these are more often efforts that are specific to the rival.

A rival's action might be a direct attack, such as an assassination attempt, that you play out during a session. Or it might be a background activity that you describe as altering the campaign in some way. For example, a rival who wants to increase the prestige of the temple of a war god might hold a festival with drink, food, and gladiatorial games. Even if the characters aren't directly involved, the event becomes the talk of the town.

Some elements of a rival's plans might involve **events** in the world that aren't under the rival's control. Whether such an event can be easily anticipated or not, the rival's plans might include contingencies for taking advantage of such happenings.

EXAMPLE RIVAL: MARINA RODEMUS

The Rodemus clan was a small but powerful family of traders in the city, but years ago, they pulled up stakes and left town overnight. Marina Rodemus, the youngest child, has now returned to restore her family's prestige.

In truth, the family fled because its members became afflicted by lycanthropy. They joined a clan of wererats and delved into smuggling in a distant city, out of fear that their secret would be impossible to keep in their former home. After fighting her way to the top ranks of the wererat clans, Marina—along with a small army of followers—has returned to claim her place among the elite of her home city. She vows that if she doesn't succeed, she'll leave the city in ruins.

Goals. Marina wants to become the most respected, most important merchant in town—someone to whom even the prince must yield.

Assets. Marina has a small fortune in gold; her abilities as a wererat, alchemist, and necromancer; a group of wererats dedicated to her; and a shield guardian that protects her.

Plans. Marina works to discredit and ruin other merchants. Her wererats spy on her opponents and sneak into warehouses, unleashing hordes of rats to spoil goods. Marina even victimizes a few of her own warehouses to avoid suspicion.

If Marina's plans fail, she has a terrible alternative. Her knowledge of alchemy has enabled her to create a plague that she will unleash on the city through her rats. If she can't rule, then no one will.

Marina's Plans

Element	Description
Event	Rats become a noticeable problem in the streets, with swarms sighted in rundown neighborhoods. Folk demand that action be taken.
Action	Caravan raids by goblinoids become more common, and folk talk of gathering a militia. Marina contributes generously to the effort.
Action	Warehouses are overrun with rats, ruining thousands of gold pieces worth of goods. Marina blames the city for a lax effort in pest control.
Action	If the characters interfere, Marina sends her assassins against them.
Event	A sudden storm creates minor flooding, washing dozens of dead, bloated, diseased rats from the sewers. Terror over the plague rips through town.
Action	Marina fans the flames of panic, spreading rumors that the characters or other rivals in town are responsible for the disease.

Cheldar's Plans

Element	Description
Event	The grand festival of Pholtus fills the streets with somber worshipers, who maintain a day-long torchlit vigil. They offer food, drink, and shelter to all in the temple of Pholtus.
Action	Cheldar, along with a small group of followers, appears in a tavern frequented by adventurers and seeks converts. A few NPC adventurers join his cause.
Action	In a public address in the town square, Cheldar rails against the forces of chaos, laying blame for recent troubles on adventurers who are meddling in things best left alone.
Event	The characters find that all adventurers in town receive an icy reception at best.
Action	Cheldar demands that the city levy enormous taxes on adventurers, claiming that they must pay their fair share to keep the city safe.

EXAMPLE RIVAL: HIGH PRIEST CHELDAR

The temple of Pholtus, god of the sun, seeks to bring as many folk as possible under its sway. Though it has been in town for only two years, the temple is already an influential force because of the determination and the brilliant oration of Cheldar, its high priest.

Goals. Cheldar wants to make the temple of Pholtus the most popular religion in town by bringing about peace and security for all. He believes keeping adventurers in check or driving them out of town is an important step in that plan.

Assets. The charismatic high priest has his oratory skill, divine spellcasting ability, and a few hundred common folk recently converted to the temple's cause.

Plans. Cheldar is stern but fundamentally a good person. He tries to win support by providing charity, promoting peace, and working to enforce law and order. He is skeptical of the characters, however, convinced that they are troublemakers who will undermine the peace. He wants only officials of the town or the temple to be involved in handling any crises that arise. He strongly believes in his goals, yet he might still be made into an ally by good-hearted characters.

DOWNTIME ACTIVITIES

Downtime activities are tasks that usually take a workweek (5 days) or longer to perform. These tasks can include buying or creating magic items, pulling off crimes, and working at a job. A character selects a downtime activity from among those available and pays the cost of that activity in time and money. You, as DM, then follow the rules for the activity to resolve it, informing the player of the results and any complications that ensue.

Consider handling downtime away from the game table. For example, you could have the players pick their downtime activities at the end of a session, and then communicate about them by email or text, until you next see them in person.

RESOLVING ACTIVITIES

The description of each activity tells you how to resolve it. Many activities require an ability check, so be sure to note the character's relevant ability modifiers. Follow the steps in the activity, and determine the results.

Most downtime activities require a workweek (5 days) to complete. Some activities require days, weeks (7 days), or months (30 days). A character must spend at least 8 hours of each day engaged in the downtime activity for that day to count toward the activity's completion.

The days of an activity don't need to be consecutive; you can spread them over a longer period of time than is required for the activity. But that period of time should be no more than twice as long as the required time; otherwise you should introduce extra complications (see below) and possibly double the activity's costs to represent the inefficiency of the character's progress.

COMPLICATIONS

The description of each activity includes a discussion of complications you can throw at the characters. The consequences of a complication might spawn entire adventures, introduce NPCs to vex the party, or give the characters headaches or advantages in any number of other ways.

When minions come back from a mission, sometimes I send them shopping.

Shopping is this thing where minions give away their stuff to other people, and other people give them different stuff.

It's so strange.

Each of these sections has a table that offers possible complications. You can roll to determine a complication randomly, pick one from the table, or devise one of your own, and then share it with the player.

EXAMPLE DOWNTIME ACTIVITIES

The following activities are suitable for any character who can afford to pursue them. As DM, you have the final say on which activities are available to the characters. The activities you allow might depend on the nature of the area where the characters are located. For example, you might disallow the creation of magic items or decide that the characters are in a town that is too isolated from major markets for them to buy such items.

BUYING A MAGIC ITEM

Purchasing a magic item requires time and money to seek out and contact people willing to sell items. Even then, there is no guarantee a seller will have the items a character desires.

Resources. Finding magic items to purchase requires at least one workweek of effort and 100 gp in expenses. Spending more time and money increases your chance of finding a high-quality item.

Resolution. A character seeking to buy a magic item makes a Charisma (Persuasion) check to determine the quality of the seller found. The character gains a +1 bonus on the check for every workweek beyond the first that is spent seeking a seller and a +1 bonus for every additional 100 gp spent on the search, up to a maximum bonus of +10. The monetary cost includes a wealthy lifestyle, for a buyer must impress potential business partners.

As shown on the Buying Magic Items table, the total of the check dictates which table in the *Dungeon Master's Guide* to roll on to determine which items are on the market. Or you can roll for items from any table associated with a lower total on the Buying Magic Items table. As a further option to reflect the availability of items in your campaign, you can apply a −10 penalty for low magic campaigns or a +10 bonus for high magic campaigns. Furthermore, you can double magic item costs in low magic campaigns.

Using the Magic Item Price table, you then assign prices to the available items, based on their rarity. Halve the price of any consumable item, such as a potion or a scroll, when using the table to determine an asking price.

You have final say in determining which items are for sale and their final price, no matter what the tables say.

If the characters seek a specific magic item, first decide if it's an item you want to allow in your game. If so, include the desired item among the items for sale on a check total of 10 or higher if the item is common, 15 or higher if it is uncommon, 20 or higher if it is rare, 25 or higher if it is very rare, and 30 or higher if it is legendary.

BUYING MAGIC ITEMS

Check Total	Items Acquired
1–5	Roll 1d6 times on Magic Item Table A.
6–10	Roll 1d4 times on Magic Item Table B.
11–15	Roll 1d4 times on Magic Item Table C.
16–20	Roll 1d4 times on Magic Item Table D.
21–25	Roll 1d4 times on Magic Item Table E.
26–30	Roll 1d4 times on Magic Item Table F.
31–35	Roll 1d4 times on Magic Item Table G.
36–40	Roll 1d4 times on Magic Item Table H.
41+	Roll 1d4 times on Magic Item Table I.

MAGIC ITEM PRICE

Rarity	Asking Price*
Common	(1d6 + 1) × 10 gp
Uncommon	1d6 × 100 gp
Rare	2d10 × 1,000 gp
Very rare	(1d4 + 1) × 10,000 gp
Legendary	2d6 × 25,000 gp

*Halved for a consumable item like a potion or scroll

Complications. The magic item trade is fraught with peril. The large sums of money involved and the power offered by magic items attract thieves, con artists, and other villains. If you want to make things more interesting for the characters, roll on the Magic Item Purchase Complications table or invent your own complication.

MAGIC ITEM PURCHASE COMPLICATIONS

d12	Complication
1	The item is a fake, planted by an enemy.*
2	The item is stolen by the party's enemies.*
3	The item is cursed by a god.
4	The item's original owner will kill to reclaim it; the party's enemies spread news of its sale.*
5	The item is at the center of a dark prophecy.
6	The seller is murdered before the sale.*
7	The seller is a devil looking to make a bargain.
8	The item is the key to freeing an evil entity.
9	A third party bids on the item, doubling its price.*
10	The item is an enslaved, intelligent entity.
11	The item is tied to a cult.
12	The party's enemies spread rumors that the item is an artifact of evil.*

*Might involve a rival

CAROUSING

Carousing is a default downtime activity for many characters. Between adventures, who doesn't want to relax with a few drinks and a group of friends at a tavern?

Resources. Carousing covers a workweek of fine food, strong drink, and socializing. A character can attempt to carouse among lower-, middle-, or upper-class folk. A character can carouse with the lower class for 10 gp to cover expenses, or 50 gp for the middle class.

Carousing with the upper class requires 250 gp for the workweek and access to the local nobility.

A character with the noble background can mingle with the upper class, but other characters can do so only if you judge that the character has made sufficient contacts. Alternatively, a character might use a disguise kit and the Deception skill to pass as a noble visiting from a distant city.

Resolution. After a workweek of carousing, a character stands to make contacts within the selected social class. The character makes a Charisma (Persuasion) check using the Carousing table.

CAROUSING

Check Total	Result
1–5	Character has made a hostile contact.
6–10	Character has made no new contacts.
11–15	Character has made an allied contact.
16–20	Character has made two allied contacts.
21+	Character has made three allied contacts.

Contacts are NPCs who now share a bond with the character. Each one either owes the character a favor or has some reason to bear a grudge. A hostile contact works against the character, placing obstacles but stopping short of committing a crime or a violent act. Allied contacts are friends who will render aid to the character, but not at the risk of their lives.

Lower-class contacts include criminals, laborers, mercenaries, the town guard, and any other folk who normally frequent the cheapest taverns in town.

Middle-class contacts include guild members, spellcasters, town officials, and other folk who frequent well-kept establishments.

Upper-class contacts are nobles and their personal servants. Carousing with such folk covers formal banquets, state dinners, and the like.

Once a contact has helped or hindered a character, the character needs to carouse again to get back into the NPC's good graces. A contact provides help once, not help for life. The contact remains friendly, which can influence roleplaying and how the characters interact with them, but doesn't come with a guarantee of help.

You can assign specific NPCs as contacts. You might decide that the barkeep at the Wretched Gorgon and a guard stationed at the western gate are the character's allied contacts. Assigning specific NPCs gives the players concrete options. It brings the campaign to life and seeds the area with NPCs that the characters care about. On the other hand, it can prove difficult to track and might render a contact useless if that character doesn't come into play.

Alternatively, you can allow the player to make an NPC into a contact on the spot, after carousing. When the characters are in the area in which they caroused, a player can expend an allied contact and designate an NPC they meet as a contact, assuming the NPC is of the correct social class based on how the character caroused. The player should provide a reasonable explanation for this relationship and work it into the game.

Using a mix of the two approaches is a good idea, since it gives you the added depth of specific contacts while giving players the freedom to ensure that the contacts they accumulate are useful.

The same process can apply to hostile contacts. You can give the characters a specific NPC they should avoid, or you might introduce one at an inopportune or dramatic moment.

At any time, a character can have a maximum number of unspecified allied contacts equal to 1 + the character's Charisma modifier (minimum of 1). Specific, named contacts don't count toward this limit—only ones that can be used at any time to declare an NPC as a contact.

Complications. Characters who carouse risk bar brawls, accumulating a cloud of nasty rumors, and building a bad reputation around town. As a rule of thumb, a character has a 10 percent chance of triggering a complication for each workweek of carousing.

LOWER-CLASS CAROUSING COMPLICATIONS

d8	Complication
1	A pickpocket lifts 1d10 × 5 gp from you.*
2	A bar brawl leaves you with a scar.*
3	You have fuzzy memories of doing something very, very illegal, but can't remember exactly what.
4	You are banned from a tavern after some obnoxious behavior.*
5	After a few drinks, you swore in the town square to pursue a dangerous quest.
6	Surprise! You're married.
7	Streaking naked through the streets seemed like a great idea at the time.
8	Everyone is calling you by some weird, embarrassing nickname, like Puddle Drinker or Bench Slayer, and no one will say why.*

*Might involve a rival

MIDDLE-CLASS CAROUSING COMPLICATIONS

d8	Complication
1	You accidentally insulted a guild master, and only a public apology will let you do business with the guild again.*
2	You swore to complete some quest on behalf of a temple or a guild.
3	A social gaffe has made you the talk of the town.*
4	A particularly obnoxious person has taken an intense romantic interest in you.*
5	You have made a foe out of a local spellcaster.*
6	You have been recruited to help run a local festival, play, or similar event.
7	You made a drunken toast that scandalized the locals.
8	You spent an additional 100 gp trying to impress people.

*Might involve a rival

UPPER-CLASS CAROUSING COMPLICATIONS

d8	Complication
1	A pushy noble family wants to marry off one of their scions to you.*
2	You tripped and fell during a dance, and people can't stop talking about it.
3	You have agreed to take on a noble's debts.
4	You have been challenged to a joust by a knight.*
5	You have made a foe out of a local noble.*
6	A boring noble insists you visit each day and listen to long, tedious theories of magic.
7	You have become the target of a variety of embarrassing rumors.*
8	You spent an additional 500 gp trying to impress people.

*Might involve a rival

CRAFTING AN ITEM

A character who has the time, the money, and the needed tools can use downtime to craft armor, weapons, clothing, or other kinds of nonmagical gear.

Resources and Resolution. In addition to the appropriate tools for the item to be crafted, a character needs raw materials worth half of the item's selling cost. To determine how many workweeks it takes to create an item, divide its gold piece cost by 50. A character can complete multiple items in a workweek if the items' combined cost is 50 gp or lower. Items that cost more than 50 gp can be completed over longer periods of time, as long as the work in progress is stored in a safe location.

Multiple characters can combine their efforts. Divide the time needed to create an item by the number of characters working on it. Use your judgment when determining how many characters can collaborate on an item. A particularly tiny item, like a ring, might allow only one or two workers, whereas a large, complex item might allow four or more workers.

A character needs to be proficient with the tools needed to craft an item and have access to the appropriate equipment. Everyone who collaborates needs to have the appropriate tool proficiency. You need to make any judgment calls regarding whether a character has the correct equipment. The following table provides some examples.

Proficiency	Items
Herbalism kit	Antitoxin, *potion of healing*
Leatherworker's tools	Leather armor, boots
Smith's tools	Armor, weapons
Weaver's tools	Cloaks, robes

If all the above requirements are met, the result of the process is an item of the desired sort. A character can sell an item crafted in this way at its listed price.

Crafting Magic Items. Creating a magic item requires more than just time, effort, and materials. It is a long-term process that involves one or more adventures to track down rare materials and the lore needed to create the item.

Potions of healing and *spell scrolls* are exceptions to the following rules. For more information, see "Brewing Potions of Healing" later in this section and the "Scribing a Spell Scroll" section, below.

To start with, a character needs a formula for a magic item in order to create it. The formula is like a recipe. It lists the materials needed and steps required to make the item.

An item invariably requires an exotic material to complete it. This material can range from the skin of a yeti to a vial of water taken from a whirlpool on the Elemental Plane of Water. Finding that material should take place as part of an adventure.

The Magic Item Ingredients table suggests the challenge rating of a creature that the characters need to face to acquire the materials for an item. Note that facing a creature does not necessarily mean that the characters must collect items from its corpse. Rather, the creature might guard a location or a resource that the characters need access to.

MAGIC ITEM INGREDIENTS

Item Rarity	CR Range
Common	1–3
Uncommon	4–8
Rare	9–12
Very rare	13–18
Legendary	19+

If appropriate, pick a monster or a location that is a thematic fit for the item to be crafted. For example, creating *mariner's armor* might require the essence of a water weird. Crafting a *staff of charming* might require the cooperation of a specific arcanaloth, who will help only if the characters complete a task for it. Making a *staff of power* might hinge on acquiring a piece of an ancient stone that was once touched by the god of magic—a stone now guarded by a suspicious androsphinx.

In addition to facing a specific creature, creating an item comes with a gold piece cost covering other materials, tools, and so on, based on the item's rarity. Those values, as well as the time a character needs to work in order to complete the item, are shown on the Magic Item Crafting Time and Cost table. Halve the listed price and creation time for any consumable items.

MAGIC ITEM CRAFTING TIME AND COST

Item Rarity	Workweeks*	Cost*
Common	1	50 gp
Uncommon	2	200 gp
Rare	10	2,000 gp
Very rare	25	20,000 gp
Legendary	50	100,000 gp

*Halved for a consumable item like a potion or scroll

To complete a magic item, a character also needs whatever tool proficiency is appropriate, as for crafting a nonmagical object, or proficiency in the Arcana skill.

If all the above requirements are met, the result of the process is a magic item of the desired sort.

Complications. Most of the complications involved in creating something, especially a magic item, are linked to the difficulty in finding rare ingredients or components needed to complete the work. The complications a character might face as byproducts of the creation process are most interesting when the characters are working on a magic item: there's a 10 percent chance for every five workweeks spent on crafting an item that a complication occurs. The Crafting Complications table provides examples of what might happen.

CRAFTING COMPLICATIONS

d6	Complication
1	Rumors swirl that what you're working on is unstable and a threat to the community.*
2	Your tools are stolen, forcing you to buy new ones.*
3	A local wizard shows keen interest in your work and insists on observing you.
4	A powerful noble offers a hefty price for your work and is not interested in hearing no for an answer.*
5	A dwarf clan accuses you of stealing its secret lore to fuel your work.*
6	A competitor spreads rumors that your work is shoddy and prone to failure.*

*Might involve a rival

Brewing Potions of Healing. *Potions of healing* fall into a special category for item crafting, separate from other magic items. A character who has proficiency with the herbalism kit can create these potions. The times and costs for doing so are summarized on the Potion of Healing Creation table.

POTION OF HEALING CREATION

Type	Time	Cost
Healing	1 day	25 gp
Greater healing	1 workweek	100 gp
Superior healing	3 workweeks	1,000 gp
Supreme healing	4 workweeks	10,000 gp

CRIME

Sometimes it pays to be bad. This activity gives a character the chance to make some extra cash, at the risk of arrest.

Resources. A character must spend one week and at least 25 gp gathering information on potential targets before committing the intended crime.

Resolution. The character must make a series of checks, with the DC for all the checks chosen by the character according to the amount of profit sought from the crime.

The chosen DC can be 10, 15, 20, or 25. Successful completion of the crime yields a number of gold pieces, as shown on the Loot Value table.

To attempt a crime, the character makes three checks: Dexterity (Stealth), Dexterity using thieves' tools, and the player's choice of Intelligence (Investigation), Wisdom (Perception), or Charisma (Deception).

If none of the checks are successful, the character is caught and jailed. The character must pay a fine equal to the profit the crime would have earned and must spend one week in jail for each 25 gp of the fine.

If only one check is successful, the heist fails but the character escapes.

If two checks are successful, the heist is a partial success, netting the character half the payout.

If all three checks are successful, the character earns the full value of the loot.

LOOT VALUE

DC	Value
10	50 gp, robbery of a struggling merchant
15	100 gp, robbery of a prosperous merchant
20	200 gp, robbery of a noble
25	1,000 gp, robbery of one of the richest figures in town

Complications. A life of crime is filled with complications. Roll on the Crime Complications table (or create a complication of your own) if the character succeeds on only one check. If the character's rival is involved in crime or law enforcement, a complication ensues if the character succeeds on only two checks.

CRIME COMPLICATIONS

d8	Complication
1	A bounty equal to your earnings is offered for information about your crime.*
2	An unknown person contacts you, threatening to reveal your crime if you don't render a service.*
3	Your victim is financially ruined by your crime.
4	Someone who knows of your crime has been arrested on an unrelated matter.*
5	Your loot is a single, easily identified item that you can't fence in this region.
6	You robbed someone who was under a local crime lord's protection, and who now wants revenge.
7	Your victim calls in a favor from a guard, doubling the efforts to solve the case.
8	Your victim asks one of your adventuring companions to solve the crime.

*Might involve a rival

GAMBLING

Games of chance are a way to make a fortune—and perhaps a better way to lose one.

Resources. This activity requires one workweek of effort plus a stake of at least 10 gp, to a maximum of 1,000 gp or more, as you see fit.

Resolution. The character must make a series of checks, with a DC determined at random based on the quality of the competition that the character runs into. Part of the risk of gambling is that one never knows who might end up sitting across the table.

The character makes three checks: Wisdom (Insight), Charisma (Deception), and Charisma (Intimidation). If the character has proficiency with an appropriate gaming set, that tool proficiency can replace the relevant skill in any of the checks. The DC for each of the checks is 5 + 2d10; generate a separate DC for each one. Consult the Gambling Results table to see how the character did.

GAMBLING RESULTS

Result	Value
0 successes	Lose all the money you bet, and accrue a debt equal to that amount.
1 success	Lose half the money you bet.
2 successes	Gain the amount you bet plus half again more.
3 successes	Gain double the amount you bet.

Complications. Gambling tends to attract unsavory individuals. The potential complications involved come from run-ins with the law and associations with various criminals tied to the activity. Every workweek spent gambling brings a 10 percent chance of a complication, examples of which are on the Gambling Complications table.

GAMBLING COMPLICATIONS

d6	Complication
1	You are accused of cheating. You decide whether you actually did cheat or were framed.*
2	The town guards raid the gambling hall and throw you in jail.*
3	A noble in town loses badly to you and loudly vows to get revenge.*
4	You won a sum from a low-ranking member of a thieves' guild, and the guild wants its money back.
5	A local crime boss insists you start frequenting the boss's gambling parlor and no others.
6	A high-stakes gambler comes to town and insists that you take part in a game.

*Might involve a rival

PIT FIGHTING

Pit fighting includes boxing, wrestling, and other nonlethal forms of combat in an organized setting with predetermined matches. If you want to introduce competitive fighting in a battle-to-the-death situation, the standard combat rules apply to that sort of activity.

Resources. Engaging in this activity requires one workweek of effort from a character.

Resolution. The character must make a series of checks, with a DC determined at random based on the quality of the opposition that the character runs into. A big part of the challenge in pit fighting lies in the unknown nature of a character's opponents.

The character makes three checks: Strength (Athletics), Dexterity (Acrobatics), and a special Constitution check that has a bonus equal to a roll of the character's largest Hit Die (this roll doesn't spend that die). If desired, the character can replace one of these skill checks with an attack roll using one of the character's weapons. The DC for each of the checks is 5 + 2d10; generate a separate DC for each one. Consult the Pit Fighting Results table to see how the character did.

PIT FIGHTING RESULTS

Result	Value
0 successes	Lose your bouts, earning nothing.
1 success	Win 50 gp.
2 successes	Win 100 gp.
3 successes	Win 200 gp.

Complications. Characters involved in pit fighting must deal with their opponents, the people who bet on matches, and the matches' promoters. Every workweek spent pit fighting brings a 10 percent chance of a complication, examples of which are on the Pit Fighting Complications table.

PIT FIGHTING COMPLICATIONS

d6	Complication
1	An opponent swears to take revenge on you.*
2	A crime boss approaches you and offers to pay you to intentionally lose a few matches.*
3	You defeat a popular local champion, drawing the crowd's ire.
4	You defeat a noble's servant, drawing the wrath of the noble's house.*
5	You are accused of cheating. Whether the allegation is true or not, your reputation is tarnished.*
6	You accidentally deliver a near-fatal wound to a foe.

*Might involve a rival

RELAXATION

Sometimes the best thing to do between adventures is relax. Whether a character wants a hard-earned vacation or needs to recover from injuries, relaxation is the ideal option for adventurers who need a break. This option is also ideal for players who don't want to make use of the downtime system.

Resources. Relaxation requires one week. A character needs to maintain at least a modest lifestyle while relaxing to gain the benefit of the activity.

Resolution. Characters who maintain at least a modest lifestyle while relaxing gain several benefits. While relaxing, a character gains advantage on saving throws to recover from long-acting diseases and poisons. In addition, at the end of the week, a character can end one effect that keeps the character from regaining hit points, or can restore one ability score that has been reduced to less than its normal value. This benefit cannot be used if the harmful effect was caused by a spell or some other magical effect with an ongoing duration.

Complications. Relaxation rarely comes with complications. If you want to make life complicated for the characters, introduce an action or an event connected to a rival.

RELIGIOUS SERVICE

Characters with a religious bent might want to spend downtime in service to a temple, either by attending rites or by proselytizing in the community. Someone who undertakes this activity has a chance of winning the favor of the temple's leaders.

Resources. Performing religious service requires access to, and often attendance at, a temple whose beliefs and ethos align with the character's. If such a place is available, the activity takes one workweek of time but involves no gold piece expenditure.

Resolution. At the end of the required time, the character chooses to make either an Intelligence (Religion) check or a Charisma (Persuasion) check. The total of the check determines the benefits of service, as shown on the Religious Service table.

workweek spent in religious service brings a 10 percent chance of a complication, examples of which are on the Religious Service Complications table.

RELIGIOUS SERVICE COMPLICATIONS

d6	Complication
1	You have offended a priest through your words or actions.*
2	Blasphemy is still blasphemy, even if you did it by accident.
3	A secret sect in the temple offers you membership.
4	Another temple tries to recruit you as a spy.*
5	The temple elders implore you to take up a holy quest.
6	You accidentally discover that an important person in the temple is a fiend worshiper.

*Might involve a rival

RESEARCH

Forewarned is forearmed. The research downtime activity allows a character to delve into lore concerning a monster, a location, a magic item, or some other particular topic.

Resources. Typically, a character needs access to a library or a sage to conduct research. Assuming such access is available, conducting research requires one workweek of effort and at least 50 gp spent on materials, bribes, gifts, and other expenses.

Resolution. The character declares the focus of the research—a specific person, place, or thing. After one workweek, the character makes an Intelligence check with a +1 bonus per 100 gp spent beyond the initial 100 gp, to a maximum of +6. In addition, a character who has access to a particularly well-stocked library or knowledgeable sages gains advantage on this check. Determine how much lore a character learns using the Research Outcomes table.

RESEARCH OUTCOMES

Check Total	Outcome
1–5	No effect.
6–10	You learn one piece of lore.
11–20	You learn two pieces of lore.
21+	You learn three pieces of lore.

Each piece of lore is the equivalent of one true statement about a person, place, or thing. Examples include knowledge of a creature's resistances, the password needed to enter a sealed dungeon level, the spells commonly prepared by an order of wizards, and so on.

As DM, you are the final arbiter concerning exactly what a character learns. For a monster or an NPC, you can reveal elements of statistics or personality. For a location, you can reveal secrets about it, such as a hidden entrance, the answer to a riddle, or the nature of a creature that guards the place.

Complications. The greatest risk in research is uncovering false information. Not all lore is accurate or

RELIGIOUS SERVICE

Check Total	Result
1–10	No effect. Your efforts fail to make a lasting impression.
11–20	You earn one favor.
21+	You earn two favors.

A favor, in broad terms, is a promise of future assistance from a representative of the temple. It can be expended to ask the temple for help in dealing with a specific problem, for general political or social support, or to reduce the cost of cleric spellcasting by 50 percent. A favor could also take the form of a deity's intervention, such as an omen, a vision, or a minor miracle provided at a key moment. This latter sort of favor is expended by the DM, who also determines its nature.

Favors earned need not be expended immediately, but only a certain number can be stored up. A character can have a maximum number of unused favors equal to 1 + the character's Charisma modifier (minimum of one unused favor).

Complications. Temples can be labyrinths of political and social scheming. Even the best-intentioned sect can fall prone to rivalries. A character who serves a temple risks becoming embroiled in such struggles. Every

truthful, and a rival with a scholarly bent might try to lead the character astray, especially if the object of the research is known to the rival. The rival might plant false information, bribe sages to give bad advice, or steal key tomes needed to find the truth.

In addition, a character might run into other complications during research. Every workweek spent in research brings a 10 percent chance of a complication, examples of which are on the Research Complications table.

RESEARCH COMPLICATIONS

d6	Complication
1	You accidentally damage a rare book.
2	You offend a sage, who demands an extravagant gift.*
3	If you had known that book was cursed, you never would have opened it.
4	A sage becomes obsessed with convincing you of a number of strange theories about reality.*
5	Your actions cause you to be banned from a library until you make reparations.*
6	You uncovered useful lore, but only by promising to complete a dangerous task in return.

*Might involve a rival

SCRIBING A SPELL SCROLL

With time and patience, a spellcaster can transfer a spell to a scroll, creating a *spell scroll*.

Resources. Scribing a *spell scroll* takes an amount of time and money related to the level of the spell the character wants to scribe, as shown in the Spell Scroll Costs table. In addition, the character must have proficiency in the Arcana skill and must provide any material components required for the casting of the spell. Moreover, the character must have the spell prepared, or it must be among the character's known spells, in order to scribe a scroll of that spell.

If the scribed spell is a cantrip, the version on the scroll works as if the caster were 1st level.

SPELL SCROLL COSTS

Spell Level	Time	Cost
Cantrip	1 day	15 gp
1st	1 day	25 gp
2nd	3 days	250 gp
3rd	1 workweek	500 gp
4th	2 workweeks	2,500 gp
5th	4 workweeks	5,000 gp
6th	8 workweeks	15,000 gp
7th	16 workweeks	25,000 gp
8th	32 workweeks	50,000 gp
9th	48 workweeks	250,000 gp

Complications. Crafting a *spell scroll* is a solitary task, unlikely to attract much attention. The complications that arise are more likely to involve the preparation needed for the activity. Every workweek spent scribing

brings a 10 percent chance of a complication, examples of which are on the Scribe a Scroll Complications table.

SCRIBE A SCROLL COMPLICATIONS

d6	Complication
1	You bought up the last of the rare ink used to craft scrolls, angering a wizard in town.
2	The priest of a temple of good accuses you of trafficking in dark magic.*
3	A wizard eager to collect one of your spells in a book presses you to sell the scroll.
4	Due to a strange error in creating the scroll, it is instead a random spell of the same level.
5	The rare parchment you bought for your scroll has a barely visible map on it.
6	A thief attempts to break into your workroom.*

*Might involve a rival

SELLING A MAGIC ITEM

Selling a magic item is by no means an easy task. Con artists and thieves are always looking out for an easy score, and there's no guarantee that a character will receive a good offer even if a legitimate buyer is found.

Resources. A character can find a buyer for one magic item by spending one workweek and 25 gp, which is used to spread word of the desired sale. A character must pick one item at a time to sell.

Resolution. A character who wants to sell an item must make a Charisma (Persuasion) check to determine what kind of offer comes in. The character can always opt not to sell, instead forfeiting the workweek of effort and trying again later. Use the Magic Item Base Prices and Magic Item Offer tables to determine the sale price.

MAGIC ITEM BASE PRICES

Rarity	Base Price*
Common	100 gp
Uncommon	400 gp
Rare	4,000 gp
Very rare	40,000 gp
Legendary	200,000 gp

*Halved for a consumable item like a potion or scroll

MAGIC ITEM OFFER

Check Total	Offer
1–10	50% of base price
11–20	100% of base price
21+	150% of base price

Complications. The main risk in selling a magic item lies in attracting thieves and anyone else who wants the item but doesn't want to pay for it. Other folk might try to undermine a deal in order to bolster their own business or seek to discredit the character as a legitimate seller. Every workweek spent trying to sell an item brings a 10 percent chance of a complication, examples of which are on the Magic Item Sale Complications table.

MAGIC ITEM SALE COMPLICATIONS

d6	Complication
1	Your enemy secretly arranges to buy the item to use it against you.*
2	A thieves' guild, alerted to the sale, attempts to steal your item.*
3	A foe circulates rumors that your item is a fake.*
4	A sorcerer claims your item as a birthright and demands you hand it over.
5	Your item's previous owner, or surviving allies of the owner, vow to retake the item by force.
6	The buyer is murdered before the sale is finalized.*

*Might involve a rival

TRAINING

Given enough free time and the services of an instructor, a character can learn a language or pick up proficiency with a tool.

Resources. Receiving training in a language or tool typically takes at least ten workweeks, but this time is reduced by a number of workweeks equal to the character's Intelligence modifier (an Intelligence penalty doesn't increase the time needed). Training costs 25 gp per workweek.

Complications. Complications that arise while training typically involve the teacher. Every ten workweeks spent in training brings a 10 percent chance of a complication, examples of which are on the Training Complications table.

TRAINING COMPLICATIONS

d6	Complication
1	Your instructor disappears, forcing you to spend one workweek finding a new one.*
2	Your teacher instructs you in rare, archaic methods, which draw comments from others.
3	Your teacher is a spy sent to learn your plans.*
4	Your teacher is a wanted criminal.
5	Your teacher is a cruel taskmaster.
6	Your teacher asks for help dealing with a threat.

*Might involve a rival

WORK

When all else fails, an adventurer can turn to an honest trade to earn a living. This activity represents a character's attempt to find temporary work, the quality and wages of which are difficult to predict.

Resources. Performing a job requires one workweek of effort.

Resolution. To determine how much money a character earns, the character makes an ability check: Strength (Athletics), Dexterity (Acrobatics), Intelligence using a set of tools, Charisma (Performance), or Charisma using a musical instrument. Consult the Wages table to see how much money is generated according to the total of the check.

WAGES

Check Total	Earnings
9 or lower	Poor lifestyle for the week
10–14	Modest lifestyle for the week
15–20	Comfortable lifestyle for the week
21+	Comfortable lifestyle for the week + 25 gp

Complications. Ordinary work is rarely filled with significant complications. Still, the Work Complications table can add some difficulties to a worker's life. Each workweek of activity brings a 10 percent chance that a character encounters a complication.

WORK COMPLICATIONS

d6	Complication
1	A difficult customer or a fight with a coworker reduces the wages you earn by one category.*
2	Your employer's financial difficulties result in your not being paid.*
3	A coworker with ties to an important family in town takes a dislike to you.*
4	Your employer is involved with a dark cult or a criminal enterprise.
5	A crime ring targets your business for extortion.*
6	You gain a reputation for laziness (unjustified or not, as you choose), giving you disadvantage on checks made for this downtime activity for the next six workweeks you devote to it.*

*Might involve a rival

Awarding Magic Items

Magic items are prized by D&D adventurers of all sorts and are often the main reward in an adventure. The rules for magic items are presented, along with the Treasure Hoard tables, in chapter 7 of the *Dungeon Master's Guide*. This section expands on those rules by offering you an alternative way of determining which magic items end up in the characters' possession and by adding a collection of common magic items to the game. The section ends with tables that group magic items according to rarity.

The system in the *Dungeon Master's Guide* is designed so that you can generate all treasure randomly, and the tables also govern the number of magic items the characters receive. In short, the tables do the work. But a DM who's designing or modifying an adventure might prefer to choose the magic items that come into play. If you're in that situation, you can use the rules in this section to personalize your treasure hoards while staying within the game's limits for how many items the characters should ultimately accumulate.

Distribution by Rarity

This alternative method of treasure determination focuses on choosing magic items based on their rarity, rather than by rolling on the tables in the *Dungeon Master's Guide*. This method uses two tables: Magic Items Awarded by Tier and Magic Items Awarded by Rarity.

By Tier. The Magic Items Awarded by Tier table shows the number of magic items a D&D party typically gains during a campaign, culminating in the group's having accumulated one hundred magic items by 20th level. The table shows how many of those items are meant to be handed out during each of the four tiers of play. The emphasis on characters receiving more items during the second tier (levels 5–10) than in other tiers is by design. The second tier is where much of the play occurs in a typical D&D campaign, and the items gained in that tier prepare the characters for higher-level adventures.

By Rarity. The Magic Items Awarded by Rarity table takes the numbers from the Magic Items Awarded by Tier table and breaks them down to show the number of items of each rarity the characters are expected to have when they reach the end of a tier.

Minor and Major Items. Both tables in this section make a distinction between minor magic items and major magic items. This distinction exists in the *Dungeon Master's Guide*, yet those terms aren't used there. In that book, the minor items are those listed on Magic Item Tables A through E, and the major items are on

Behind the Design: Magic Item Distribution

The *Dungeon Master's Guide* assumes a certain amount of treasure will be found over the course of a campaign. Over twenty levels of typical play, the game expects forty-five rolls on the Treasure Hoard tables, distributed as follows:

- Seven rolls on the Challenge 0–4 table
- Eighteen rolls on the Challenge 5–10 table
- Twelve rolls on the Challenge 11–16 table
- Eight rolls on the Challenge 17+ table

Because many of the table results call for more than one magic item, those forty-five rolls will result in the characters obtaining roughly one hundred items. The optional system described here yields the same number of items, distributed properly throughout the spectrum of rarity, while enabling you to control exactly which items the characters have a chance of acquiring.

Magic Item Tables F through I. As you can see from the Treasure Hoard tables in that book, major magic items are meant to be handed out much less frequently than minor items, even at higher levels of play.

Magic Items Awarded by Tier

Character Level	Minor Items	Major Items	All Items
1–4	9	2	11
5–10	28	6	34
11–16	24	6	30
17–20	19	6	25
Total	**80**	**20**	**100**

Choosing Items Level by Level

You decide when to place an item in an adventure that you're creating or modifying, usually because you think the story calls for a magic item, the characters need one, or the players would be especially pleased to get one.

When you want to select an item as treasure for an encounter, the Magic Items Awarded by Rarity table serves as your item budget. Here's how to use it:

1. Jot down a copy of the table in your notes, so that you can make adjustments to the numbers as you select items to be placed in an adventure.
2. Refer to the line in the Level/CR column that corresponds to one of the following values (your choice): the level of the player characters, the challenge rating of the magic item's owner, or the challenge rating of the group of creatures guarding the item. The entries in that row of the table indicate the total number of items that would be appropriate for the characters to receive by the end of the tier represented by that row.

Magic Items Awarded by Rarity

	Minor Magic Items					Major Magic Items			
Level/CR	Common	Uncommon	Rare	Very Rare	Legendary	Uncommon	Rare	Very Rare	Legendary
1–4	6	2	1	0	0	2	0	0	0
5–10	10	12	5	1	0	5	1	0	0
11–16	3	6	9	5	1	1	2	2	1
17+	0	0	4	9	6	0	1	2	3
Total	**19**	**20**	**19**	**15**	**7**	**8**	**4**	**4**	**4**

3. Choose a magic item of any rarity for which the entry in this row is not 0.
4. When the characters obtain an item, modify your notes to indicate which part of your budget this expenditure came from by subtracting 1 from the appropriate entry on the table.

In the future, if you choose an item of a rarity that's not available in the current tier but is still available in a lower tier, deduct the item from the lower tier. If all lower tiers also have no items available of a given rarity, deduct the item from a higher tier.

Choosing Items Piecemeal

If you prefer a more free-form method of choosing magic items, simply select each magic item you want to give out; then, when the characters acquire one, deduct it from the Magic Items Awarded by Rarity table in your notes. Whenever you do so, start with the lowest tier, and deduct the item from the first number you come across in the appropriate rarity column for the item, whether its minor or major. If that tier doesn't have a number greater than 0 for that rarity, go up a tier until you find one that does, and deduct the magic item from that number. Following this process, you will zero out each row of the table in order, going from the lowest levels to the highest.

Overstocking an Adventure

The magic item tables in this section are based on the number of items the characters are expected to receive, not the number of items that are available in an adventure. When creating or modifying an adventure, assume that the characters won't find all the items you place in it, unless most of the loot is in easy-to-find locations. Here's a good rule of thumb: an adventure can include a number of items that's 25 percent higher than the numbers in the tables (round up). For example, an adventure designed to take characters from 1st to 4th level might include fourteen items rather than eleven, in the expectation that three of those items won't be found.

Are Magic Items Necessary in a Campaign?

The D&D game is built on the assumption that magic items appear sporadically and that they are always a boon, unless an item bears a curse. Characters and monsters are built to face each other without the help of magic items, which means that having a magic item always makes a character more powerful or versatile than a generic character of the same level. As DM, you never have to worry about awarding magic items just so the characters can keep up with the campaign's threats. Magic items are truly prizes. Are they useful? Absolutely. Are they necessary? No.

Magic items can go from nice to necessary in the rare group that has no spellcasters, no monk, and no NPCs capable of casting *magic weapon*. Having no magic makes it extremely difficult for a party to overcome monsters that have resistances or immunity to nonmagical damage. In such a game, you'll want to be generous with magic weapons or else avoid using such monsters.

Common Magic Items

The *Dungeon Master's Guide* includes many magic items of every rarity. The one exception are common items; that book includes few of them. This section introduces more of them to the game. These items seldom increase a character's power, but they are likely to amuse players and provide fun roleplaying opportunities.

The magic items are presented in alphabetical order.

Armor of Gleaming
Armor (any medium or heavy), common

This armor never gets dirty.

Bead of Nourishment
Wondrous item, common

This spongy, flavorless, gelatinous bead dissolves on your tongue and provides as much nourishment as 1 day of rations.

Bead of Refreshment
Wondrous item, common

This spongy, flavorless, gelatinous bead dissolves in liquid, transforming up to a pint of the liquid into fresh, cold drinking water. The bead has no effect on magical liquids or harmful substances such as poison.

Boots of False Tracks
Wondrous item, common

Only humanoids can wear these boots. While wearing the boots, you can choose to have them leave tracks like those of another kind of humanoid of your size.

Candle of the Deep
Wondrous item, common

The flame of this candle is not extinguished when immersed in water. It gives off light and heat like a normal candle.

Cast-Off Armor
Armor (light, medium, or heavy), common

You can doff this armor as an action.

Charlatan's Die
Wondrous item, common (requires attunement)

Whenever you roll this six-sided die, you can control which number it rolls.

Cloak of Billowing
Wondrous item, common

While wearing this cloak, you can use a bonus action to make it billow dramatically.

Cloak of Many Fashions
Wondrous item, common

While wearing this cloak, you can use a bonus action to change the style, color, and apparent quality of the garment. The cloak's weight doesn't change. Regardless of its appearance, the cloak can't be anything but a cloak. Although it can duplicate the appearance of other magic cloaks, it doesn't gain their magical properties.

Clockwork Amulet
Wondrous item, common

This copper amulet contains tiny interlocking gears and is powered by magic from Mechanus, a plane of clockwork predictability. A creature that puts an ear to the amulet can hear faint ticking and whirring noises coming from within.

When you make an attack roll while wearing the amulet, you can forgo rolling the d20 to get a 10 on the die. Once used, this property can't be used again until the next dawn.

Clothes of Mending
Wondrous item, common

This elegant outfit of traveler's clothes magically mends itself to counteract daily wear and tear. Pieces of the outfit that are destroyed can't be repaired in this way.

Dark Shard Amulet
Wondrous item, common (requires attunement by a warlock)

This amulet is fashioned from a single shard of resilient extraplanar material originating from the realm of your warlock patron. While you are wearing it, you gain the following benefits:

- You can use the amulet as a spellcasting focus for your warlock spells.
- You can try to cast a cantrip that you don't know. The cantrip must be on the warlock spell list, and you must make a DC 10 Intelligence (Arcana) check. If the check succeeds, you cast the spell. If the check fails, so does the spell, and the action used to cast the spell is wasted. In either case, you can't use this property again until you finish a long rest.

Dread Helm
Wondrous item, common

This fearsome steel helm makes your eyes glow red while you wear it.

Ear Horn of Hearing
Wondrous item, common

While held up to your ear, this horn suppresses the effects of the deafened condition on you, allowing you to hear normally.

Enduring Spellbook
Wondrous item, common

This spellbook, along with anything written on its pages, can't be damaged by fire or immersion in water. In addition, the spellbook doesn't deteriorate with age.

Ersatz Eye
Wondrous item, common (requires attunement)

This artificial eye replaces a real one that was lost or removed. While the *ersatz eye* is embedded in your eye socket, it can't be removed by anyone other than you, and you can see through the tiny orb as though it were a normal eye.

Hat of Vermin
Wondrous item, common

This hat has 3 charges. While holding the hat, you can use an action to expend 1 of its charges and speak a command word that summons your choice of a **bat**, a **frog**, or a **rat** (see the *Player's Handbook* or the *Monster Manual* for statistics). The summoned creature magically appears in the hat and tries to get away from you as quickly as possible. The creature is neither friendly nor hostile, and it isn't under your control. It behaves as an ordinary creature of its kind and disappears after 1 hour or when it drops to 0 hit points. The hat regains all expended charges daily at dawn.

Hat of Wizardry
Wondrous item, common (requires attunement by a wizard)

This antiquated, cone-shaped hat is adorned with gold crescent moons and stars. While you are wearing it, you gain the following benefits:

- You can use the hat as a spellcasting focus for your wizard spells.
- You can try to cast a cantrip that you don't know. The cantrip must be on the wizard spell list, and you must make a DC 10 Intelligence (Arcana) check. If the check succeeds, you cast the spell. If the check fails, so does the spell, and the action used to cast the spell is wasted. In either case, you can't use this property again until you finish a long rest.

Heward's Handy Spice Pouch
Wondrous item, common

This belt pouch appears empty and has 10 charges. While holding the pouch, you can use an action to expend 1 of its charges, speak the name of any nonmagical food seasoning (such as salt, pepper, saffron, or cilantro), and remove a pinch of the desired seasoning from the pouch. A pinch is enough to season a single meal. The pouch regains 1d6 + 4 expended charges daily at dawn.

Horn of Silent Alarm
Wondrous item, common

This horn has 4 charges. When you use an action to blow it, one creature of your choice can hear the horn's blare, provided the creature is within 600 feet of the horn and not deafened. No other creature hears sound coming from the horn. The horn regains 1d4 expended charges daily at dawn.

Instrument of Illusions
Wondrous item, common (requires attunement)

While you are playing this musical instrument, you can create harmless, illusory visual effects within a 5-foot-radius sphere centered on the instrument. If you are a bard, the radius increases to 15 feet. Sample visual effects include luminous musical notes, a spectral dancer, butterflies, and gently falling snow. The magical effects have neither substance nor sound, and they are obviously illusory. The effects end when you stop playing.

Instrument of Scribing

Wondrous item, common (requires attunement)

This musical instrument has 3 charges. While you are playing it, you can use an action to expend 1 charge from the instrument and write a magical message on a nonmagical object or surface that you can see within 30 feet of you. The message can be up to six words long and is written in a language you know. If you are a bard, you can scribe an additional seven words and choose to make the message glow faintly, allowing it to be seen in nonmagical darkness. Casting *dispel magic* on the message erases it. Otherwise, the message fades away after 24 hours.

The instrument regains all expended charges daily at dawn.

Lock of Trickery

Wondrous item, common

This lock appears to be an ordinary lock (of the type described in chapter 5 of the *Player's Handbook*) and comes with a single key. The tumblers in this lock magically adjust to thwart burglars. Dexterity checks made to pick the lock have disadvantage.

Moon-Touched Sword

Weapon (any sword), common

In darkness, the unsheathed blade of this sword sheds moonlight, creating bright light in a 15-foot radius and dim light for an additional 15 feet.

Mystery Key

Wondrous item, common

A question mark is worked into the head of this key. The key has a 5 percent chance of unlocking any lock into which it's inserted. Once it unlocks something, the key disappears.

Orb of Direction

Wondrous item, common

While holding this orb, you can use an action to determine which way is north. This property functions only on the Material Plane.

Orb of Time

Wondrous item, common

While holding this orb, you can use an action to determine whether it is morning, afternoon, evening, or nighttime outside. This property functions only on the Material Plane.

Perfume of Bewitching

Wondrous item, common

This tiny vial contains magic perfume, enough for one use. You can use an action to apply the perfume to yourself, and its effect lasts 1 hour. For the duration, you have advantage on all Charisma checks directed at humanoids of challenge rating 1 or lower. Those subjected to the perfume's effect are not aware that they've been influenced by magic.

Pipe of Smoke Monsters

Wondrous item, common

While smoking this pipe, you can use an action to exhale a puff of smoke that takes the form of a single creature, such as a dragon, a flumph, or a froghemoth. The form must be small enough to fit in a 1-foot cube and loses its shape after a few seconds, becoming an ordinary puff of smoke.

Pole of Angling

Wondrous item, common

While holding this 10-foot pole, you can speak a command word and transform it into a fishing pole with a hook, a line, and a reel. Speaking the command word again changes the fishing pole back into a normal 10-foot pole.

Pole of Collapsing

Wondrous item, common

While holding this 10-foot pole, you can use an action to speak a command word and cause it to collapse into a 1-foot-long rod, for ease of storage. The pole's weight doesn't change. You can use an action to speak a different command word and cause the rod to revert to a pole; however, the rod will elongate only as far as the surrounding space allows.

Pot of Awakening

Wondrous item, common

If you plant an ordinary shrub in this 10-pound clay pot and let it grow for 30 days, the shrub magically transforms into an **awakened shrub** (see the *Monster Manual* for statistics) at the end of that time. When the shrub awakens, its roots break the pot, destroying it.

The awakened shrub is friendly toward you. Absent commands from you, it does nothing.

Rope of Mending

Wondrous item, common

You can cut this 50-foot coil of hempen rope into any number of smaller pieces, and then use an action to speak a command word and cause the pieces to knit back together. The pieces must be in contact with each other and not otherwise in use. A *rope of mending* is forever shortened if a section of it is lost or destroyed.

Ruby of the War Mage

Wondrous item, common (requires attunement by a spellcaster)

Etched with eldritch runes, this 1-inch-diameter ruby allows you to use a simple or martial weapon as a spellcasting focus for your spells. For this property to work, you must attach the ruby to the weapon by pressing the ruby against it for at least 10 minutes. Thereafter, the ruby can't be removed unless you detach it as an action or the weapon is destroyed. Not even an *antimagic field* causes it to fall off. The ruby does fall off the weapon if your attunement to the ruby ends.

SHIELD OF EXPRESSION

Armor (shield), common

The front of this shield is shaped in the likeness of a face. While bearing the shield, you can use a bonus action to alter the face's expression.

SMOLDERING ARMOR

Armor (any), common

Wisps of harmless, odorless smoke rise from this armor while it is worn.

STAFF OF ADORNMENT

Staff, common

If you place an object weighing no more than 1 pound (such as a shard of crystal, an egg, or a stone) above the tip of the staff while holding it, the object floats an inch from the staff's tip and remains there until it is removed or until the staff is no longer in your possession. The staff can have up to three such objects floating over its tip at any given time. While holding the staff, you can make one or more of the objects slowly spin or turn in place.

STAFF OF BIRDCALLS

Staff, common

This wooden staff is decorated with bird carvings. It has 10 charges. While holding it, you can use an action to expend 1 charge from the staff and cause it to create one of the following sounds out to a range of 60 feet: a finch's chirp, a raven's caw, a duck's quack, a chicken's cluck, a goose's honk, a loon's call, a turkey's gobble, a seagull's cry, an owl's hoot, or an eagle's shriek.

The staff regains 1d6 + 4 expended charges daily at dawn. If you expend the last charge, roll a d20. On a 1, the staff explodes in a harmless cloud of bird feathers and is lost forever.

STAFF OF FLOWERS

Staff, common

This wooden staff has 10 charges. While holding it, you can use an action to expend 1 charge from the staff and cause a flower to sprout from a patch of earth or soil within 5 feet of you, or from the staff itself. Unless you choose a specific kind of flower, the staff creates a mild-scented daisy. The flower is harmless and nonmagical, and it grows or withers as a normal flower would.

The staff regains 1d6 + 4 expended charges daily at dawn. If you expend the last charge, roll a d20. On a 1, the staff turns into flower petals and is lost forever.

TALKING DOLL

Wondrous item, common (requires attunement)

While this stuffed doll is within 5 feet of you, you can spend a short rest telling it to say up to six phrases, none of which can be more than six words long, and set a condition under which the doll speaks each phrase. You can also replace old phrases with new ones. Whatever the condition, it must occur within 5 feet of the doll to make it speak. For example, whenever someone picks up the doll, it might say, "I want a piece of candy." The doll's phrases are lost when your attunement to the doll ends.

UNBREAKABLE ARROWS

TANKARD OF SOBRIETY

Wondrous item, common

This tankard has a stern face sculpted into one side. You can drink ale, wine, or any other nonmagical alcoholic beverage poured into it without becoming inebriated. The tankard has no effect on magical liquids or harmful substances such as poison.

UNBREAKABLE ARROW

Weapon (arrow), common

This arrow can't be broken, except when it is within an *antimagic field*.

VETERAN'S CANE

Wondrous item, common

When you grasp this walking cane and use a bonus action to speak the command word, it transforms into an ordinary longsword and ceases to be magical.

WALLOPING AMMUNITION

Weapon (any ammunition), common

This ammunition packs a wallop. A creature hit by the ammunition must succeed on a DC 10 Strength saving throw or be knocked prone.

Wand of Conducting
Wand, common

This wand has 3 charges. While holding it, you can use an action to expend 1 of its charges and create orchestral music by waving it around. The music can be heard out to a range of 60 feet and ends when you stop waving the wand.

The wand regains all expended charges daily at dawn. If you expend the wand's last charge, roll a d20. On a 1, a sad tuba sound plays as the wand crumbles to dust and is destroyed.

Wand of Pyrotechnics
Wand, common

This wand has 7 charges. While holding it, you can use an action to expend 1 of its charges and create a harmless burst of multicolored light at a point you can see up to 60 feet away. The burst of light is accompanied by a crackling noise that can be heard up to 300 feet away. The light is as bright as a torch flame but lasts only a second.

The wand regains 1d6 + 1 expended charges daily at dawn. If you expend the wand's last charge, roll a d20. On a 1, the wand erupts in a harmless pyrotechnic display and is destroyed.

Wand of Scowls
Wand, common

This wand has 3 charges. While holding it, you can use an action to expend 1 of its charges and target a humanoid you can see within 30 feet of you. The target must succeed on a DC 10 Charisma saving throw or be forced to scowl for 1 minute.

The wand regains all expended charges daily at dawn. If you expend the wand's last charge, roll a d20. On a 1, the wand transforms into a *wand of smiles*.

Wand of Smiles
Wand, common

This wand has 3 charges. While holding it, you can use an action to expend 1 of its charges and target a humanoid you can see within 30 feet of you. The target must succeed on a DC 10 Charisma saving throw or be forced to smile for 1 minute.

The wand regains all expended charges daily at dawn. If you expend the wand's last charge, roll a d20. On a 1, the wand transforms into a *wand of scowls*.

CREATING ADDITIONAL COMMON ITEMS

The "Special Features" section in chapter 7 of the *Dungeon Master's Guide* is useful if you want to design other common magic items. For example, the What Minor Property Does It Have? table might inspire you to create a magic item that allows a character to speak and understand the Goblin language (based on the table's Language property), a magic item that glows in the presence of fiends (based on the Sentinel property), or a magic item that projects its user's voice over a great distance (based on the War Leader property).

MAGIC ITEM TABLES

The tables in this section classify the magic items from the *Dungeon Master's Guide* and the new items presented here into minor items and major items, then separate the items in each group according to rarity. Each table entry includes the item's type and an indication of whether the item requires attunement. Artifacts aren't included here; they are beyond even major items in power and importance.

MINOR ITEMS, COMMON

Item	Type	Attune?
Armor of gleaming	Armor	No
Bead of nourishment	Wondrous item	No
Bead of refreshment	Wondrous item	No
Boots of false tracks	Wondrous item	No
Candle of the deep	Wondrous item	No
Cast-off armor	Armor	No
Charlatan's die	Wondrous item	Yes
Cloak of billowing	Wondrous item	No
Cloak of many fashions	Wondrous item	No
Clockwork amulet	Wondrous item	No
Clothes of mending	Wondrous item	No
Dark shard amulet	Wondrous item	Yes (warlock)
Dread helm	Wondrous item	No
Ear horn of hearing	Wondrous item	No
Enduring spellbook	Wondrous item	No
Ersatz eye	Wondrous item	Yes
Hat of vermin	Wondrous item	No
Hat of wizardry	Wondrous item	Yes (wizard)
Heward's handy spice pouch	Wondrous item	No
Horn of silent alarm	Wondrous item	No
Instrument of illusions	Wondrous item	Yes
Instrument of scribing	Wondrous item	Yes
Lock of trickery	Wondrous item	No
Moon-touched sword	Weapon	No
Mystery key	Wondrous item	No
Orb of direction	Wondrous item	No
Orb of time	Wondrous item	No
Perfume of bewitching	Wondrous item	No
Pipe of smoke monsters	Wondrous item	No
Pole of angling	Wondrous item	No
Pole of collapsing	Wondrous item	No
Pot of awakening	Wondrous item	No
Potion of climbing	Potion	No
Potion of healing	Potion	No
Rope of mending	Wondrous item	No
Ruby of the war mage	Wondrous item	Yes (spellcaster)
Shield of expression	Armor	No
Smoldering armor	Armor	No
Spell scroll (cantrip)	Scroll	No
Spell scroll (1st level)	Scroll	No
Staff of adornment	Staff	No
Staff of birdcalls	Staff	No

Item	Type	Attune?
Staff of flowers	Staff	No
Talking doll	Wondrous item	Yes
Tankard of sobriety	Wondrous item	No
Unbreakable arrow	Weapon	No
Veteran's cane	Wondrous item	No
Walloping ammunition	Weapon	No
Wand of conducting	Wand	No
Wand of pyrotechnics	Wand	No
Wand of scowls	Wand	No
Wand of smiles	Wand	No

MINOR ITEMS, UNCOMMON

Item	Type	Attune?
Alchemy jug	Wondrous item	No
Ammunition, +1	Weapon	No
Bag of holding	Wondrous item	No
Cap of water breathing	Wondrous item	No
Cloak of the manta ray	Wondrous item	No
Decanter of endless water	Wondrous item	No
Driftglobe	Wondrous item	No
Dust of disappearance	Wondrous item	No
Dust of dryness	Wondrous item	No
Dust of sneezing and choking	Wondrous item	No
Elemental gem	Wondrous item	No
Eyes of minute seeing	Wondrous item	No
Goggles of night	Wondrous item	No
Helm of comprehending languages	Wondrous item	No
Immovable rod	Rod	No
Keoghtom's ointment	Wondrous item	No
Lantern of revealing	Wondrous item	No
Mariner's armor	Armor	No
Mithral armor	Armor	No
Oil of slipperiness	Potion	No
Periapt of health	Wondrous item	No
Philter of love	Potion	No
Potion of animal friendship	Potion	No
Potion of fire breath	Potion	No
Potion of greater healing	Potion	No
Potion of growth	Potion	No
Potion of hill giant strength	Potion	No
Potion of poison	Potion	No
Potion of resistance	Potion	No
Potion of water breathing	Potion	No
Ring of swimming	Ring	No
Robe of useful items	Wondrous item	No
Rope of climbing	Wondrous item	No
Saddle of the cavalier	Wondrous item	No
Sending stones	Wondrous item	No
Spell scroll (2nd level)	Scroll	No
Spell scroll (3rd level)	Scroll	No
Wand of magic detection	Wand	No
Wand of secrets	Wand	No

MINOR ITEMS, RARE

Item	Type	Attune?
Ammunition, +2	Weapon	No
Bag of beans	Wondrous item	No
Bead of force	Wondrous item	No
Chime of opening	Wondrous item	No
Elixir of health	Potion	No
Folding boat	Wondrous item	No
Heward's handy haversack	Wondrous item	No
Horseshoes of speed	Wondrous item	No
Necklace of fireballs	Wondrous item	No
Oil of etherealness	Potion	No
Portable hole	Wondrous item	No
Potion of clairvoyance	Potion	No
Potion of diminution	Potion	No
Potion of fire giant strength	Potion	No
Potion of frost giant strength	Potion	No
Potion of gaseous form	Potion	No
Potion of heroism	Potion	No
Potion of invulnerability	Potion	No
Potion of mind reading	Potion	No
Potion of stone giant strength	Potion	No
Potion of superior healing	Potion	No
Quaal's feather token	Wondrous item	No
Scroll of protection	Scroll	No
Spell scroll (4th level)	Scroll	No
Spell scroll (5th level)	Scroll	No

MINOR ITEMS, VERY RARE

Item	Type	Attune?
Ammunition, +3	Weapon	No
Arrow of slaying	Weapon	No
Bag of devouring	Wondrous item	No
Horseshoes of a zephyr	Wondrous item	No
Nolzur's marvelous pigments	Wondrous item	No
Oil of sharpness	Potion	No
Potion of cloud giant strength	Potion	No
Potion of flying	Potion	No
Potion of invisibility	Potion	No
Potion of longevity	Potion	No
Potion of speed	Potion	No
Potion of supreme healing	Potion	No
Potion of vitality	Potion	No
Spell scroll (6th level)	Scroll	No
Spell scroll (7th level)	Scroll	No
Spell scroll (8th level)	Scroll	No

Minor Items, Legendary

Item	Type	Attune?
Potion of storm giant strength	Potion	No
Sovereign glue	Wondrous item	No
Spell scroll (9th level)	Scroll	No
Universal solvent	Wondrous item	No

Major Items, Uncommon

Item	Type	Attune?
Adamantine armor	Armor	No
Amulet of proof against detection and location	Wondrous item	Yes
Bag of tricks	Wondrous item	No
Boots of elvenkind	Wondrous item	No
Boots of striding and springing	Wondrous item	Yes
Boots of the winterlands	Wondrous item	Yes
Bracers of archery	Wondrous item	Yes
Brooch of shielding	Wondrous item	Yes
Broom of flying	Wondrous item	No
Circlet of blasting	Wondrous item	No
Cloak of elvenkind	Wondrous item	Yes
Cloak of protection	Wondrous item	Yes
Deck of illusions	Wondrous item	No
Eversmoking bottle	Wondrous item	No
Eyes of charming	Wondrous item	Yes
Eyes of the eagle	Wondrous item	Yes
Figurine of wondrous power (silver raven)	Wondrous item	No
Gauntlets of ogre power	Wondrous item	Yes
Gem of brightness	Wondrous item	No
Gloves of missile snaring	Wondrous item	Yes
Gloves of swimming and climbing	Wondrous item	Yes
Gloves of thievery	Wondrous item	No
Hat of disguise	Wondrous item	Yes
Headband of intellect	Wondrous item	Yes
Helm of telepathy	Wondrous item	Yes
Instrument of the bards (Doss lute)	Wondrous item	Yes (bard)
Instrument of the bards (Fochlucan bandore)	Wondrous item	Yes (bard)
Instrument of the bards (Mac-Fuirmidh cittern)	Wondrous item	Yes (bard)
Javelin of lightning	Weapon	No
Medallion of thoughts	Wondrous item	Yes
Necklace of adaptation	Wondrous item	Yes
Pearl of power	Wondrous item	Yes (spellcaster)
Periapt of wound closure	Wondrous item	Yes
Pipes of haunting	Wondrous item	No

Item	Type	Attune?
Pipes of the sewers	Wondrous item	Yes
Quiver of Ehlonna	Wondrous item	No
Ring of jumping	Ring	Yes
Ring of mind shielding	Ring	Yes
Ring of warmth	Ring	Yes
Ring of water walking	Ring	No
Rod of the pact keeper, +1	Rod	Yes (warlock)
Sentinel shield	Armor	No
Shield, +1	Armor	No
Slippers of spider climbing	Wondrous item	Yes
Staff of the adder	Staff	Yes (cleric, druid, or warlock)
Staff of the python	Staff	Yes (cleric, druid, or warlock)
Stone of good luck (luckstone)	Wondrous item	Yes
Sword of vengeance	Weapon	Yes
Trident of fish command	Weapon	Yes
Wand of magic missiles	Wand	No
Wand of the war mage, +1	Wand	Yes (spellcaster)
Wand of web	Wand	Yes (spellcaster)
Weapon of warning	Weapon	Yes
Weapon, +1	Weapon	No
Wind fan	Wondrous item	No
Winged boots	Wondrous item	Yes

Major Items, Rare

Item	Type	Attune?
Amulet of health	Wondrous item	Yes
Armor of resistance	Armor	Yes
Armor of vulnerability	Armor	Yes
Armor, +1	Armor	No
Arrow-catching shield	Armor	Yes
Belt of dwarvenkind	Wondrous item	Yes
Belt of hill giant strength	Wondrous item	Yes
Berserker axe	Weapon	Yes
Boots of levitation	Wondrous item	Yes
Boots of speed	Wondrous item	Yes
Bowl of commanding water elementals	Wondrous item	No
Bracers of defense	Wondrous item	Yes
Brazier of commanding fire elementals	Wondrous item	No
Cape of the mountebank	Wondrous item	No
Censer of controlling air elementals	Wondrous item	No
Cloak of displacement	Wondrous item	Yes

Item	Type	Attune?
Cloak of the bat	Wondrous item	Yes
Cube of force	Wondrous item	Yes
Daern's instant fortress	Wondrous item	No
Dagger of venom	Weapon	No
Dimensional shackles	Wondrous item	No
Dragon slayer	Weapon	No
Elven chain	Armor	No
Figurine of wondrous power (bronze griffon)	Wondrous item	No
Figurine of wondrous power (ebony fly)	Wondrous item	No
Figurine of wondrous power (golden lions)	Wondrous item	No
Figurine of wondrous power (ivory goats)	Wondrous item	No
Figurine of wondrous power (marble elephant)	Wondrous item	No
Figurine of wondrous power (onyx dog)	Wondrous item	No
Figurine of wondrous power (serpentine owl)	Wondrous item	No
Flame tongue	Weapon	Yes
Gem of seeing	Wondrous item	Yes
Giant slayer	Weapon	No
Glamoured studded leather	Armor	No
Helm of teleportation	Wondrous item	Yes
Horn of blasting	Wondrous item	No
Horn of Valhalla (silver or brass)	Wondrous item	No
Instrument of the bards (Canaith mandolin)	Wondrous item	Yes (bard)
Instrument of the bards (Cli lyre)	Wondrous item	Yes (bard)
Ioun stone (awareness)	Wondrous item	Yes
Ioun stone (protection)	Wondrous item	Yes
Ioun stone (reserve)	Wondrous item	Yes
Ioun stone (sustenance)	Wondrous item	Yes
Iron bands of Bilarro	Wondrous item	No
Mace of disruption	Weapon	Yes
Mace of smiting	Weapon	No
Mace of terror	Weapon	Yes
Mantle of spell resistance	Wondrous item	Yes
Necklace of prayer beads	Wondrous item	Yes (cleric, druid, or paladin)
Periapt of proof against poison	Wondrous item	No

Item	Type	Attune?
Ring of animal influence	Ring	No
Ring of evasion	Ring	Yes
Ring of feather falling	Ring	Yes
Ring of free action	Ring	Yes
Ring of protection	Ring	Yes
Ring of resistance	Ring	Yes
Ring of spell storing	Ring	Yes
Ring of the ram	Ring	Yes
Ring of X-ray vision	Ring	Yes
Robe of eyes	Wondrous item	Yes
Rod of rulership	Rod	Yes
Rod of the pact keeper, +2	Rod	Yes (warlock)
Rope of entanglement	Wondrous item	No
Shield of missile attraction	Armor	Yes
Shield, +2	Armor	No
Staff of charming	Staff	Yes (bard, cleric, druid, sorcerer, warlock, or wizard)
Staff of healing	Staff	Yes (bard, cleric, or druid)
Staff of swarming insects	Staff	Yes (bard, cleric, druid, sorcerer, warlock, or wizard)
Staff of the woodlands	Staff	Yes (druid)
Staff of withering	Staff	Yes (cleric, druid, or warlock)
Stone of controlling earth elementals	Wondrous item	No
Sun blade	Weapon	Yes
Sword of life stealing	Weapon	Yes
Sword of wounding	Weapon	Yes
Tentacle rod	Rod	Yes
Vicious weapon	Weapon	No
Wand of binding	Wand	Yes (spellcaster)
Wand of enemy detection	Wand	Yes
Wand of fear	Wand	Yes
Wand of fireballs	Wand	Yes (spellcaster)
Wand of lightning bolts	Wand	Yes (spellcaster)
Wand of paralysis	Wand	Yes (spellcaster)
Wand of the war mage, +2	Wand	Yes (spellcaster)
Wand of wonder	Wand	Yes (spellcaster)
Weapon, +2	Weapon	No
Wings of flying	Wondrous item	Yes

Major Items, Very Rare

Item	Type	Attune?
Amulet of the planes	Wondrous item	Yes
Animated shield	Armor	Yes
Armor, +2	Armor	No
Belt of fire giant strength	Wondrous item	Yes
Belt of frost/stone giant strength	Wondrous item	Yes
Candle of invocation	Wondrous item	Yes
Carpet of flying	Wondrous item	No
Cloak of arachnida	Wondrous item	Yes
Crystal ball (very rare)	Wondrous item	Yes
Dancing sword	Weapon	Yes
Demon armor	Armor	Yes
Dragon scale mail	Armor	Yes
Dwarven plate	Armor	No
Dwarven thrower	Weapon	Yes (dwarf)
Efreeti bottle	Wondrous item	No
Figurine of wondrous power (obsidian steed)	Wondrous item	No
Frost brand	Weapon	Yes
Helm of brilliance	Wondrous item	Yes
Horn of Valhalla (bronze)	Wondrous item	No
Instrument of the bards (Anstruth harp)	Wondrous item	Yes (bard)
Ioun stone (absorption)	Wondrous item	Yes
Ioun stone (agility)	Wondrous item	Yes
Ioun stone (fortitude)	Wondrous item	Yes
Ioun stone (insight)	Wondrous item	Yes
Ioun stone (intellect)	Wondrous item	Yes
Ioun stone (leadership)	Wondrous item	Yes
Ioun stone (strength)	Wondrous item	Yes
Manual of bodily health	Wondrous item	No
Manual of gainful exercise	Wondrous item	No
Manual of golems	Wondrous item	No
Manual of quickness of action	Wondrous item	No
Mirror of life trapping	Wondrous item	No
Nine lives stealer	Weapon	Yes
Oathbow	Weapon	Yes
Ring of regeneration	Ring	Yes
Ring of shooting stars	Ring	Yes (outdoors at night)
Ring of telekinesis	Ring	Yes
Robe of scintillating colors	Wondrous item	Yes
Robe of stars	Wondrous item	Yes
Rod of absorption	Rod	Yes
Rod of alertness	Rod	Yes
Rod of security	Rod	No
Rod of the pact keeper, +3	Rod	Yes (warlock)
Scimitar of speed	Weapon	Yes

Recharging without a Dawn

Some magic items can be used a limited number of times but are recharged by the arrival of dawn. What if you're on a plane of existence that lacks anything resembling dawn? The DM should choose a time every 24 hours when such magic items recharge on that plane of existence.

Even on a world that experiences dawn each day, the DM is free to choose a different time—perhaps noon, sunset, or midnight—when certain magic items recharge.

Item	Type	Attune?
Shield, +3	Armor	No
Spellguard shield	Armor	Yes
Staff of fire	Staff	Yes (druid, sorcerer, warlock, or wizard)
Staff of frost	Staff	Yes (druid, sorcerer, warlock, or wizard)
Staff of power	Staff	Yes (sorcerer, warlock, or wizard)
Staff of striking	Staff	Yes
Staff of thunder and lightning	Staff	Yes
Sword of sharpness	Weapon	Yes
Tome of clear thought	Wondrous item	No
Tome of leadership and influence	Wondrous item	No
Tome of understanding	Wondrous item	No
Wand of polymorph	Wand	Yes (spellcaster)
Wand of the war mage, +3	Wand	Yes (spellcaster)
Weapon, +3	Weapon	No

MAJOR ITEMS, LEGENDARY

Item	Type	Attune?
Apparatus of Kwalish	Wondrous item	No
Armor of invulnerability	Armor	Yes
Armor, +3	Armor	No
Belt of cloud giant strength	Wondrous item	Yes
Belt of storm giant strength	Wondrous item	Yes
Cloak of invisibility	Wondrous item	Yes
Crystal ball (legendary)	Wondrous item	Yes
Cubic gate	Wondrous item	No
Deck of many things	Wondrous item	No
Defender	Weapon	Yes
Efreeti chain	Armor	Yes
Hammer of thunderbolts	Weapon	Yes (Giant's Bane)
Holy avenger	Weapon	Yes (paladin)
Horn of Valhalla (iron)	Wondrous item	No
Instrument of the bards (Ollamh harp)	Wondrous item	Yes (bard)
Ioun stone (greater absorption)	Wondrous item	Yes
Ioun stone (mastery)	Wondrous item	Yes
Ioun stone (regeneration)	Wondrous item	Yes
Iron flask	Wondrous item	No
Luck blade	Weapon	Yes

Item	Type	Attune?
Plate armor of etherealness	Armor	Yes
Ring of air elemental command	Ring	Yes
Ring of djinni summoning	Ring	Yes
Ring of earth elemental command	Ring	Yes
Ring of fire elemental command	Ring	Yes
Ring of invisibility	Ring	Yes
Ring of spell turning	Ring	Yes
Ring of three wishes	Ring	No
Ring of water elemental command	Ring	Yes
Robe of the archmagi	Wondrous item	Yes (sorcerer, warlock, or wizard)
Rod of lordly might	Rod	Yes
Rod of resurrection	Rod	Yes (cleric, druid, or paladin)
Scarab of protection	Wondrous item	Yes
Sphere of annihilation	Wondrous item	No
Staff of the magi	Staff	Yes (sorcerer, warlock, or wizard)
Sword of answering	Weapon	Yes (creature of same alignment as sword)
Talisman of pure good	Wondrous item	Yes (creature of good alignment)
Talisman of the sphere	Wondrous item	Yes
Talisman of ultimate evil	Wondrous item	Yes (creature of evil alignment)
Tome of the stilled tongue	Wondrous item	Yes (wizard)
Vorpal sword	Weapon	Yes
Well of many worlds	Wondrous item	No

Never rely on magic items. they're so fickle. First, they work and then they don't. On, off, on, off—in the blink of my eye!

CHAPTER 3
SPELLS

ANY OF THE CHARACTER CLASSES IN THE *Player's Handbook* harness magic in the form of spells. This chapter provides new spells for those classes, as well as for spellcasting monsters. The Dungeon Master decides which of these spells are available in a campaign and how they can be learned. For example, a DM might decide that some of the spells are freely available, that others are unobtainable, and that a handful can be found only after a special quest, perhaps discovered in a long-lost tome of magic. Wizard spells, in particular, can be introduced to a campaign in spellbooks found as treasure.

When a DM adds spells to a campaign, clerics, druids, and paladins require special consideration. When characters of those classes prepare their spells, they have access to the entire spell list for their class. Given that fact, the DM should be cautious about making all of these new spells available to a player who is overwhelmed when presented with many options. For such a player, consider adding only story-appropriate spells to the spell list of that player's character.

SPELL LISTS

The following spell lists show which spells can be cast by characters of each class. A spell's school of magic is noted in parentheses. If a spell can be cast as a ritual, the ritual tag also appears in the parentheses.

So why can't people who use magic do it all the time? I can disintegrate things whenever I want. Like now. And now. And now. And now ... Hey, where'd everybody go?

BARD SPELLS

CANTRIPS (0 LEVEL)
Thunderclap (evocation)

1ST LEVEL
Earth tremor (evocation)

2ND LEVEL
Pyrotechnics (transmutation)
Skywrite (transmutation, ritual)
Warding wind (evocation)

3RD LEVEL
Catnap (enchantment)
Enemies abound (enchantment)

4TH LEVEL
Charm monster (enchantment)

5TH LEVEL
Skill empowerment (transmutation)
Synaptic static (enchantment)

9TH LEVEL
Mass polymorph (transmutation)
Psychic scream (enchantment)

CLERIC SPELLS

CANTRIPS (0 LEVEL)
Toll the dead (necromancy)
Word of radiance (evocation)

1ST LEVEL
Ceremony (abjuration, ritual)

3RD LEVEL
Life transference (necromancy)

5TH LEVEL
Dawn (evocation)
Holy weapon (evocation)

7TH LEVEL
Temple of the gods (conjuration)

DRUID SPELLS

CANTRIPS (0 LEVEL)
Control flames (transmutation)
Create bonfire (conjuration)
Frostbite (evocation)
Gust (transmutation)
Infestation (conjuration)
Magic stone (transmutation)
Mold earth (transmutation)
Primal savagery (transmutation)
Shape water (transmutation)
Thunderclap (evocation)

1ST LEVEL
Absorb elements (abjuration)
Beast bond (divination)
Earth tremor (evocation)
Ice knife (conjuration)
Snare (abjuration)

2ND LEVEL
Dust devil (conjuration)
Earthbind (transmutation)
Healing spirit (conjuration)
Skywrite (transmutation, ritual)
Warding wind (evocation)

3rd Level

Erupting earth (transmutation)
Flame arrows (transmutation)
Tidal wave (conjuration)
Wall of water (evocation)

4th Level

Charm monster (enchantment)
Elemental bane (transmutation)
Guardian of nature (transmutation)
Watery sphere (conjuration)

5th Level

Control winds (transmutation)
Maelstrom (evocation)
Transmute rock (transmutation)
Wrath of nature (evocation)

6th Level

Bones of the earth (transmutation)
Druid grove (abjuration)
Investiture of flame (transmutation)
Investiture of ice (transmutation)
Investiture of stone (transmutation)
Investiture of wind (transmutation)
Primordial ward (abjuration)

7th Level

Whirlwind (evocation)

Paladin Spells

1st Level

Ceremony (abjuration, ritual)

4th Level

Find greater steed (conjuration)

5th Level

Holy weapon (evocation)

Ranger Spells

1st Level

Absorb elements (abjuration)
Beast bond (divination)
Snare (abjuration)
Zephyr strike (transmutation)

2nd Level

Healing spirit (conjuration)

3rd Level

Flame arrows (transmutation)

4th Level

Guardian of nature (transmutation)

5th Level

Steel wind strike (conjuration)
Wrath of nature (evocation)

Sorcerer Spells

Cantrips (0 Level)

Control flames (transmutation)
Create bonfire (conjuration)
Frostbite (evocation)
Gust (transmutation)
Infestation (conjuration)
Mold earth (transmutation)
Shape water (transmutation)
Thunderclap (evocation)

1st Level

Absorb elements (abjuration)
Catapult (transmutation)
Chaos bolt (evocation)
Earth tremor (evocation)
Ice knife (conjuration)

2nd Level

Aganazzar's scorcher (evocation)
Dragon's breath (transmutation)
Dust devil (conjuration)
Earthbind (transmutation)
Maximilian's earthen grasp
 (transmutation)
Mind spike (divination)
Pyrotechnics (transmutation)
Shadow blade (illusion)
Snilloc's snowball swarm (evocation)
Warding wind (evocation)

3rd Level

Catnap (enchantment)
Enemies abound (enchantment)
Erupting earth (transmutation)
Flame arrows (transmutation)
Melf's minute meteors (evocation)
Thunder step (conjuration)
Tidal wave (conjuration)
Wall of water (evocation)

4th Level

Charm monster (enchantment)
Sickening radiance (evocation)
Storm sphere (evocation)
Vitriolic sphere (evocation)
Watery sphere (conjuration)

5th Level

Control winds (transmutation)
Enervation (necromancy)
Far step (conjuration)
Immolation (evocation)
Skill empowerment (transmutation)
Synaptic static (enchantment)
Wall of light (evocation)

6th Level

Investiture of flame (transmutation)
Investiture of ice (transmutation)
Investiture of stone (transmutation)
Investiture of wind (transmutation)
Mental prison (illusion)
Scatter (conjuration)

7th Level

Crown of stars (evocation)
Power word pain (enchantment)
Whirlwind (evocation)

8th Level

Abi-Dalzim's horrid wilting (necromancy)

9th Level

Mass polymorph (transmutation)
Psychic scream (enchantment)

Warlock Spells

Cantrips (0 Level)

Create bonfire (conjuration)
Frostbite (evocation)
Infestation (conjuration)
Magic stone (transmutation)
Thunderclap (evocation)
Toll the dead (necromancy)

1st Level

Cause fear (necromancy)

2nd Level

Earthbind (transmutation)
Mind spike (divination)
Shadow blade (illusion)

3rd Level

Enemies abound (enchantment)
Thunder step (conjuration)
Summon lesser demons (conjuration)

4th Level

Charm monster (enchantment)
Elemental bane (transmutation)
Shadow of moil (necromancy)
Sickening radiance (evocation)
Summon greater demon (conjuration)

5th Level

Danse macabre (necromancy)
Enervation (necromancy)
Far step (conjuration)
Infernal calling (conjuration)
Negative energy flood (necromancy)
Synaptic static (enchantment)
Wall of light (evocation)

6th Level

Investiture of flame (transmutation)
Investiture of ice (transmutation)
Investiture of stone (transmutation)
Investiture of wind (transmutation)
Mental prison (illusion)
Scatter (conjuration)
Soul cage (necromancy)

7th Level

Crown of stars (evocation)
Power word pain (enchantment)

8th Level

Maddening darkness (evocation)

9th Level

Psychic scream (enchantment)

Wizard Spells

Cantrips (0 Level)

Control flames (transmutation)
Create bonfire (conjuration)
Frostbite (evocation)
Gust (transmutation)
Infestation (conjuration)
Mold earth (transmutation)
Shape water (transmutation)
Thunderclap (evocation)
Toll the dead (necromancy)

1st Level

Absorb elements (abjuration)
Catapult (transmutation)
Cause fear (necromancy)
Earth tremor (evocation)
Ice knife (conjuration)
Snare (abjuration)

2nd Level

Aganazzar's scorcher (evocation)
Dragon's breath (transmutation)
Dust devil (conjuration)
Earthbind (transmutation)
Maximilian's earthen grasp
  (transmutation)
Mind spike (divination)
Pyrotechnics (transmutation)
Shadow blade (illusion)
Skywrite (transmutation, ritual)
Snilloc's snowball swarm (evocation)
Warding wind (evocation)

3rd Level

Catnap (enchantment)
Enemies abound (enchantment)
Erupting earth (transmutation)
Flame arrows (transmutation)

Life transference (necromancy)
Melf's minute meteors (evocation)
Summon lesser demons (conjuration)
Thunder step (conjuration)
Tidal wave (conjuration)
Tiny servant (transmutation)
Wall of sand (evocation)
Wall of water (evocation)

4th Level

Charm monster (enchantment)
Elemental bane (transmutation)
Sickening radiance (evocation)
Storm sphere (evocation)
Summon greater demon (conjuration)
Vitriolic sphere (evocation)
Watery sphere (conjuration)

5th Level

Control winds (transmutation)
Danse macabre (necromancy)
Dawn (evocation)
Enervation (necromancy)
Far step (conjuration)
Immolation (evocation)
Infernal calling (conjuration)
Negative energy flood (necromancy)
Skill empowerment (transmutation)
Steel wind strike (conjuration)
Synaptic static (enchantment)

Transmute rock (transmutation)
Wall of light (evocation)

6th Level

Create homunculus (transmutation)
Investiture of flame (transmutation)
Investiture of ice (transmutation)
Investiture of stone (transmutation)
Investiture of wind (transmutation)
Mental prison (illusion)
Scatter (conjuration)
Soul cage (necromancy)
Tenser's transformation (transmutation)

7th Level

Crown of stars (evocation)
Power word pain (enchantment)
Whirlwind (evocation)

8th Level

Abi-Dalzim's horrid wilting (necromancy)
Illusory dragon (illusion)
Maddening darkness (evocation)
Mighty fortress (conjuration)

9th Level

Invulnerability (abjuration)
Mass polymorph (transmutation)
Psychic scream (enchantment)

Spell Descriptions

The spells are presented in alphabetical order.

Abi-Dalzim's Horrid Wilting
8th-level necromancy

Casting Time: 1 action
Range: 150 feet
Components: V, S, M (a bit of sponge)
Duration: Instantaneous

You draw the moisture from every creature in a 30-foot cube centered on a point you choose within range. Each creature in that area must make a Constitution saving throw. Constructs and undead aren't affected, and plants and water elementals make this saving throw with disadvantage. A creature takes 12d8 necrotic damage on a failed save, or half as much damage on a successful one.

Nonmagical plants in the area that aren't creatures, such as trees and shrubs, wither and die instantly.

Absorb Elements
1st-level abjuration

Casting Time: 1 reaction, which you take when you take acid, cold, fire, lightning, or thunder damage
Range: Self
Components: S
Duration: 1 round

The spell captures some of the incoming energy, lessening its effect on you and storing it for your next melee attack. You have resistance to the triggering damage type until the start of your next turn. Also, the first time you hit with a melee attack on your next turn, the target takes an extra 1d6 damage of the triggering type, and the spell ends.

At Higher Levels. When you cast this spell using a spell slot of 2nd level or higher, the extra damage increases by 1d6 for each slot level above 1st.

Aganazzar's Scorcher
2nd-level evocation

Casting Time: 1 action
Range: 30 feet
Components: V, S, M (a red dragon's scale)
Duration: Instantaneous

A line of roaring flame 30 feet long and 5 feet wide emanates from you in a direction you choose. Each creature in the line must make a Dexterity saving throw. A creature takes 3d8 fire damage on a failed save, or half as much damage on a successful one.

At Higher Levels. When you cast this spell using a spell slot of 3rd level or higher, the damage increases by 1d8 for each slot level above 2nd.

Beast Bond
1st-level divination

Casting Time: 1 action
Range: Touch
Components: V, S, M (a bit of fur wrapped in a cloth)
Duration: Concentration, up to 10 minutes

You establish a telepathic link with one beast you touch that is friendly to you or charmed by you. The spell fails if the beast's Intelligence score is 4 or higher. Until the spell ends, the link is active while you and the beast are within line of sight of each other. Through the link, the beast can understand your telepathic messages to it, and it can telepathically communicate simple emotions and concepts back to you. While the link is active, the beast gains advantage on attack rolls against any creature within 5 feet of you that you can see.

Bones of the Earth
6th-level transmutation

Casting Time: 1 action
Range: 120 feet
Components: V, S
Duration: Instantaneous

You cause up to six pillars of stone to burst from places on the ground that you can see within range. Each pillar is a cylinder that has a diameter of 5 feet and a height of up to 30 feet. The ground where a pillar appears must be wide enough for its diameter, and you can target the ground under a creature if that creature is Medium or smaller. Each pillar has AC 5 and 30 hit points. When reduced to 0 hit points, a pillar crumbles into rubble, which creates an area of difficult terrain with a 10-foot radius that lasts until the rubble is cleared. Each 5-foot-diameter portion of the area requires at least 1 minute to clear by hand.

If a pillar is created under a creature, that creature must succeed on a Dexterity saving throw or be lifted by the pillar. A creature can choose to fail the save.

If a pillar is prevented from reaching its full height because of a ceiling or other obstacle, a creature on the pillar takes 6d6 bludgeoning damage and is restrained, pinched between the pillar and the obstacle. The restrained creature can use an action to make a Strength or Dexterity check (the creature's choice) against the spell's save DC. On a success, the creature is no longer restrained and must either move off the pillar or fall off it.

At Higher Levels. When you cast this spell using a spell slot of 7th level or higher, you can create two additional pillars for each slot level above 6th.

Catapult
1st-level transmutation

Casting Time: 1 action
Range: 60 feet
Components: S
Duration: Instantaneous

Choose one object weighing 1 to 5 pounds within range that isn't being worn or carried. The object flies in a straight line up to 90 feet in a direction you choose before falling to the ground, stopping early if it impacts against a solid surface. If the object would strike a creature, that creature must make a Dexterity saving throw. On a failed save, the object strikes the target and stops moving. When the object strikes something, the object and what it strikes each take 3d8 bludgeoning damage.

At Higher Levels. When you cast this spell using a spell slot of 2nd level or higher, the maximum weight of objects that you can target with this spell increases by 5 pounds, and the damage increases by 1d8, for each slot level above 1st.

Catnap

3rd-level enchantment

Casting Time: 1 action
Range: 30 feet
Components: S, M (a pinch of sand)
Duration: 10 minutes

You make a calming gesture, and up to three willing creatures of your choice that you can see within range fall unconscious for the spell's duration. The spell ends on a target early if it takes damage or someone uses an action to shake or slap it awake. If a target remains unconscious for the full duration, that target gains the benefit of a short rest, and it can't be affected by this spell again until it finishes a long rest.

At Higher Levels. When you cast this spell using a spell slot of 4th level or higher, you can target one additional willing creature for each slot level above 3rd.

Cause Fear

1st-level necromancy

Casting Time: 1 action
Range: 60 feet
Components: V
Duration: Concentration, up to 1 minute

You awaken the sense of mortality in one creature you can see within range. A construct or an undead is immune to this effect. The target must succeed on a Wisdom saving throw or become frightened of you until the spell ends. The frightened target can repeat the saving throw at the end of each of its turns, ending the effect on itself on a success.

At Higher Levels. When you cast this spell using a spell slot of 2nd level or higher, you can target one additional creature for each slot level above 1st. The creatures must be within 30 feet of each other when you target them.

Ceremony

1st-level abjuration (ritual)

Casting Time: 1 hour
Range: Touch
Components: V, S, M (25 gp worth of powdered silver, which the spell consumes)
Duration: Instantaneous

You perform a special religious ceremony that is infused with magic. When you cast the spell, choose one of the following rites, the target of which must be within 10 feet of you throughout the casting.

Atonement. You touch one willing creature whose alignment has changed, and you make a DC 20 Wisdom (Insight) check. On a successful check, you restore the target to its original alignment.

Bless Water. You touch one vial of water and cause it to become holy water.

Coming of Age. You touch one humanoid who is a young adult. For the next 24 hours, whenever the target makes an ability check, it can roll a d4 and add the number rolled to the ability check. A creature can benefit from this rite only once.

Dedication. You touch one humanoid who wishes to be dedicated to your god's service. For the next 24 hours, whenever the target makes a saving throw, it can roll a d4 and add the number rolled to the save. A creature can benefit from this rite only once.

Funeral Rite. You touch one corpse, and for the next 7 days, the target can't become undead by any means short of a *wish* spell.

Wedding. You touch adult humanoids willing to be bonded together in marriage. For the next 7 days, each target gains a +2 bonus to AC while they are within 30 feet of each other. A creature can benefit from this rite again only if widowed.

Chaos Bolt

1st-level evocation

Casting Time: 1 action
Range: 120 feet
Components: V, S
Duration: Instantaneous

You hurl an undulating, warbling mass of chaotic energy at one creature in range. Make a ranged spell attack against the target. On a hit, the target takes 2d8 + 1d6 damage. Choose one of the d8s. The number rolled on that die determines the attack's damage type, as shown below.

d8	Damage Type
1	Acid
2	Cold
3	Fire
4	Force
5	Lightning
6	Poison
7	Psychic
8	Thunder

If you roll the same number on both d8s, the chaotic energy leaps from the target to a different creature of your choice within 30 feet of it. Make a new attack roll against the new target, and make a new damage roll, which could cause the chaotic energy to leap again.

A creature can be targeted only once by each casting of this spell.

At Higher Levels. When you cast this spell using a spell slot of 2nd level or higher, each target takes 1d6 extra damage of the type rolled for each slot level above 1st.

Charm Monster

4th-level enchantment

Casting Time: 1 action
Range: 30 feet
Components: V, S
Duration: 1 hour

You attempt to charm a creature you can see within range. It must make a Wisdom saving throw, and it does so with advantage if you or your companions are fighting it. If it fails the saving throw, it is charmed by you until the spell ends or until you or your companions do anything harmful to it. The charmed creature is friendly to you. When the spell ends, the creature knows it was charmed by you.

At Higher Levels. When you cast this spell using a spell slot of 5th level or higher, you can target one additional creature for each slot level above 4th. The creatures must be within 30 feet of each other when you target them.

CONTROL FLAMES
Transmutation cantrip

Casting Time: 1 action
Range: 60 feet
Components: S
Duration: Instantaneous or 1 hour (see below)

You choose a nonmagical flame that you can see within range and that fits within a 5-foot cube. You affect it in one of the following ways:

- You instantaneously expand the flame 5 feet in one direction, provided that wood or other fuel is present in the new location.
- You instantaneously extinguish the flames within the cube.
- You double or halve the area of bright light and dim light cast by the flame, change its color, or both. The change lasts for 1 hour.
- You cause simple shapes—such as the vague form of a creature, an inanimate object, or a location—to appear within the flames and animate as you like. The shapes last for 1 hour.

If you cast this spell multiple times, you can have up to three non-instantaneous effects created by it active at a time, and you can dismiss such an effect as an action.

CONTROL WINDS
5th-level transmutation

Casting Time: 1 action
Range: 300 feet
Components: V, S
Duration: Concentration, up to 1 hour

You take control of the air in a 100-foot cube that you can see within range. Choose one of the following effects when you cast the spell. The effect lasts for the spell's duration, unless you use your action on a later turn to switch to a different effect. You can also use your action to temporarily halt the effect or to restart one you've halted.

Gusts. A wind picks up within the cube, continually blowing in a horizontal direction you designate. You choose the intensity of the wind: calm, moderate, or strong. If the wind is moderate or strong, ranged weapon attacks that enter or leave the cube or pass through it have disadvantage on their attack rolls. If the wind is strong, any creature moving against the wind must spend 1 extra foot of movement for each foot moved.

Downdraft. You cause a sustained blast of strong wind to blow downward from the top of the cube. Ranged weapon attacks that pass through the cube or that are made against targets within it have disadvantage on their attack rolls. A creature must make a Strength saving throw if it flies into the cube for the first time on a turn or starts its turn there flying. On a failed save, the creature is knocked prone.

Updraft. You cause a sustained updraft within the cube, rising upward from the cube's bottom side. Creatures that end a fall within the cube take only half damage from the fall. When a creature in the cube makes a vertical jump, the creature can jump up to 10 feet higher than normal.

CREATE BONFIRE
Conjuration cantrip

Casting Time: 1 action
Range: 60 feet
Components: V, S
Duration: Concentration, up to 1 minute

You create a bonfire on ground that you can see within range. Until the spell ends, the magic bonfire fills a 5-foot cube. Any creature in the bonfire's space when you cast the spell must succeed on a Dexterity saving throw or take 1d8 fire damage. A creature must also make the saving throw when it moves into the bonfire's space for the first time on a turn or ends its turn there.

The bonfire ignites flammable objects in its area that aren't being worn or carried.

The spell's damage increases by 1d8 when you reach 5th level (2d8), 11th level (3d8), and 17th level (4d8).

CREATE HOMUNCULUS
6th-level transmutation

Casting Time: 1 hour
Range: Touch
Components: V, S, M (clay, ash, and mandrake root, all of which the spell consumes, and a jewel-encrusted dagger worth at least 1,000 gp)
Duration: Instantaneous

While speaking an intricate incantation, you cut yourself with a jewel-encrusted dagger, taking 2d4 piercing damage that can't be reduced in any way. You then drip your blood on the spell's other components and touch them, transforming them into a special construct called a homunculus.

The statistics of the homunculus are in the *Monster Manual*. It is your faithful companion, and it dies if you die. Whenever you finish a long rest, you can spend up to half your Hit Dice if the homunculus is on the same plane of existence as you. When you do so, roll each die and add your Constitution modifier to it. Your hit point maximum is reduced by the total, and the homunculus's hit point maximum and current hit points are both increased by it. This process can reduce you to no lower than 1 hit point, and the change to your and the homunculus's hit points ends when you finish your next long rest. The reduction to your hit point maximum can't be removed by any means before then, except by the homunculus's death.

You can have only one homunculus at a time. If you cast this spell while your homunculus lives, the spell fails.

CROWN OF STARS
7th-level evocation

Casting Time: 1 action
Range: Self

DANSE MACABRE

Components: V, S
Duration: 1 hour

Seven star-like motes of light appear and orbit your head until the spell ends. You can use a bonus action to send one of the motes streaking toward one creature or object within 120 feet of you. When you do so, make a ranged spell attack. On a hit, the target takes 4d12 radiant damage. Whether you hit or miss, the mote is expended. The spell ends early if you expend the last mote.

If you have four or more motes remaining, they shed bright light in a 30-foot radius and dim light for an additional 30 feet. If you have one to three motes remaining, they shed dim light in a 30-foot radius.

At Higher Levels. When you cast this spell using a spell slot of 8th level or higher, the number of motes created increases by two for each slot level above 7th.

DANSE MACABRE
5th-level necromancy

Casting Time: 1 action
Range: 60 feet
Components: V, S
Duration: Concentration, up to 1 hour

Threads of dark power leap from your fingers to pierce up to five Small or Medium corpses you can see within range. Each corpse immediately stands up and becomes undead. You decide whether it is a zombie or a skeleton (the statistics for zombies and skeletons are in the *Mon-*

ster Manual), and it gains a bonus to its attack and damage rolls equal to your spellcasting ability modifier.

You can use a bonus action to mentally command the creatures you make with this spell, issuing the same command to all of them. To receive the command, a creature must be within 60 feet of you. You decide what action the creatures will take and where they will move during their next turn, or you can issue a general command, such as to guard a chamber or passageway against your foes. If you issue no commands, the creatures do nothing except defend themselves against hostile creatures. Once given an order, the creatures continue to follow it until their task is complete.

The creatures are under your control until the spell ends, after which they become inanimate once more.

At Higher Levels. When you cast this spell using a spell slot of 6th level or higher, you animate up to two additional corpses for each slot level above 5th.

DAWN
5th-level evocation

Casting Time: 1 action
Range: 60 feet
Components: V, S, M (a sunburst pendant worth at least 100 gp)
Duration: Concentration, up to 1 minute

The light of dawn shines down on a location you specify within range. Until the spell ends, a 30-foot-radius,

40-foot-high cylinder of bright light glimmers there. This light is sunlight.

When the cylinder appears, each creature in it must make a Constitution saving throw, taking 4d10 radiant damage on a failed save, or half as much damage on a successful one. A creature must also make this saving throw whenever it ends its turn in the cylinder.

If you're within 60 feet of the cylinder, you can move it up to 60 feet as a bonus action on your turn.

Dragon's Breath
2nd-level transmutation

Casting Time: 1 bonus action
Range: Touch
Components: V, S, M (a hot pepper)
Duration: Concentration, up to 1 minute

You touch one willing creature and imbue it with the power to spew magical energy from its mouth, provided it has one. Choose acid, cold, fire, lightning, or poison. Until the spell ends, the creature can use an action to exhale energy of the chosen type in a 15-foot cone. Each creature in that area must make a Dexterity saving throw, taking 3d6 damage of the chosen type on a failed save, or half as much damage on a successful one.

At Higher Levels. When you cast this spell using a spell slot of 3rd level or higher, the damage increases by 1d6 for each slot level above 2nd.

Druid Grove
6th-level abjuration

Casting Time: 10 minutes
Range: Touch
Components: V, S, M (mistletoe, which the spell consumes, that was harvested with a golden sickle under the light of a full moon)
Duration: 24 hours

You invoke the spirits of nature to protect an area outdoors or underground. The area can be as small as a 30-foot cube or as large as a 90-foot cube. Buildings and other structures are excluded from the affected area. If you cast this spell in the same area every day for a year, the spell lasts until dispelled.

The spell creates the following effects within the area. When you cast this spell, you can specify creatures as friends who are immune to the effects. You can also specify a password that, when spoken aloud, makes the speaker immune to these effects.

The entire warded area radiates magic. A *dispel magic* cast on the area, if successful, removes only one of the following effects, not the entire area. That spell's caster chooses which effect to end. Only when all its effects are gone is this spell dispelled.

Solid Fog. You can fill any number of 5-foot squares on the ground with thick fog, making them heavily obscured. The fog reaches 10 feet high. In addition, every foot of movement through the fog costs 2 extra feet. To a creature immune to this effect, the fog obscures nothing and looks like soft mist, with motes of green light floating in the air.

Grasping Undergrowth. You can fill any number of 5-foot squares on the ground that aren't filled with fog with grasping weeds and vines, as if they were affected by an *entangle* spell. To a creature immune to this effect, the weeds and vines feel soft and reshape themselves to serve as temporary seats or beds.

Grove Guardians. You can animate up to four trees in the area, causing them to uproot themselves from the ground. These trees have the same statistics as an awakened tree, which appears in the *Monster Manual*, except they can't speak, and their bark is covered with druidic symbols. If any creature not immune to this effect enters the warded area, the grove guardians fight until they have driven off or slain the intruders. The grove guardians also obey your spoken commands (no action required by you) that you issue while in the area. If you don't give them commands and no intruders are present, the grove guardians do nothing. The grove guardians can't leave the warded area. When the spell ends, the magic animating them disappears, and the trees take root again if possible.

Additional Spell Effect. You can place your choice of one of the following magical effects within the warded area:

- A constant *gust of wind* in two locations of your choice
- *Spike growth* in one location of your choice
- *Wind wall* in two locations of your choice

To a creature immune to this effect, the winds are a fragrant, gentle breeze, and the area of *spike growth* is harmless.

Dust Devil
2nd-level conjuration

Casting Time: 1 action
Range: 60 feet
Components: V, S, M (a pinch of dust)
Duration: Concentration, up to 1 minute

Choose an unoccupied 5-foot cube of air that you can see within range. An elemental force that resembles a dust devil appears in the cube and lasts for the spell's duration.

Any creature that ends its turn within 5 feet of the dust devil must make a Strength saving throw. On a failed save, the creature takes 1d8 bludgeoning damage and is pushed 10 feet away from the dust devil. On a successful save, the creature takes half as much damage and isn't pushed.

As a bonus action, you can move the dust devil up to 30 feet in any direction. If the dust devil moves over sand, dust, loose dirt, or light gravel, it sucks up the material and forms a 10-foot-radius cloud of debris around itself that lasts until the start of your next turn. The cloud heavily obscures its area.

At Higher Levels. When you cast this spell using a spell slot of 3rd level or higher, the damage increases by 1d8 for each slot level above 2nd.

Earthbind
2nd-level transmutation

Casting Time: 1 action
Range: 300 feet
Components: V
Duration: Concentration, up to 1 minute

Choose one creature you can see within range. Yellow strips of magical energy loop around the creature. The target must succeed on a Strength saving throw, or its flying speed (if any) is reduced to 0 feet for the spell's duration. An airborne creature affected by this spell safely descends at 60 feet per round until it reaches the ground or the spell ends.

Earth Tremor
1st-level evocation

Casting Time: 1 action
Range: 10 feet
Components: V, S
Duration: Instantaneous

You cause a tremor in the ground within range. Each creature other than you in that area must make a Dexterity saving throw. On a failed save, a creature takes 1d6 bludgeoning damage and is knocked prone. If the ground in that area is loose earth or stone, it becomes difficult terrain until cleared, with each 5-foot-diameter portion requiring at least 1 minute to clear by hand.

At Higher Levels. When you cast this spell using a spell slot of 2nd level or higher, the damage increases by 1d6 for each slot level above 1st.

Elemental Bane
4th-level transmutation

Casting Time: 1 action
Range: 90 feet
Components: V, S
Duration: Concentration, up to 1 minute

Choose one creature you can see within range, and choose one of the following damage types: acid, cold, fire, lightning, or thunder. The target must succeed on a Constitution saving throw or be affected by the spell for its duration. The first time each turn the affected target takes damage of the chosen type, the target takes an extra 2d6 damage of that type. Moreover, the target loses any resistance to that damage type until the spell ends.

At Higher Levels. When you cast this spell using a spell slot of 5th level or higher, you can target one additional creature for each slot level above 4th. The creatures must be within 30 feet of each other when you target them.

Enemies Abound
3rd-level enchantment

Casting Time: 1 action
Range: 120 feet
Components: V, S
Duration: Concentration, up to 1 minute

You reach into the mind of one creature you can see and force it to make an Intelligence saving throw. A creature automatically succeeds if it is immune to being frightened. On a failed save, the target loses the ability to distinguish friend from foe, regarding all creatures it can see as enemies until the spell ends. Each time the target takes damage, it can repeat the saving throw, ending the effect on itself on a success.

Whenever the affected creature chooses another creature as a target, it must choose the target at random from among the creatures it can see within range of the attack, spell, or other ability it's using. If an enemy provokes an opportunity attack from the affected creature, the creature must make that attack if it is able to.

Enervation
5th-level necromancy

Casting Time: 1 action
Range: 60 feet
Components: V, S
Duration: Concentration, up to 1 minute

A tendril of inky darkness reaches out from you, touching a creature you can see within range to drain life from it. The target must make a Dexterity saving throw. On a successful save, the target takes 2d8 necrotic damage, and the spell ends. On a failed save, the target takes 4d8 necrotic damage, and until the spell ends, you can use your action on each of your turns to automatically deal 4d8 necrotic damage to the target. The spell ends if you use your action to do anything else, if the target is ever outside the spell's range, or if the target has total cover from you.

Whenever the spell deals damage to a target, you regain hit points equal to half the amount of necrotic damage the target takes.

At Higher Levels. When you cast this spell using a spell slot of 6th level or higher, the damage increases by 1d8 for each slot level above 5th.

Erupting Earth
3rd-level transmutation

Casting Time: 1 action
Range: 120 feet
Components: V, S, M (a piece of obsidian)
Duration: Instantaneous

Choose a point you can see on the ground within range. A fountain of churned earth and stone erupts in a 20-foot cube centered on that point. Each creature in that area must make a Dexterity saving throw. A creature takes 3d12 bludgeoning damage on a failed save, or half as much damage on a successful one. Additionally, the ground in that area becomes difficult terrain until cleared. Each 5-foot-square portion of the area requires at least 1 minute to clear by hand.

At Higher Levels. When you cast this spell using a spell slot of 4th level or higher, the damage increases by 1d12 for each slot level above 3rd.

Far Step
5th-level conjuration

Casting Time: 1 bonus action
Range: Self
Components: V
Duration: Concentration, up to 1 minute

You teleport up to 60 feet to an unoccupied space you can see. On each of your turns before the spell ends, you can use a bonus action to teleport in this way again.

FIND GREATER STEED

FIND GREATER STEED
4th-level conjuration

Casting Time: 10 minutes
Range: 30 feet
Components: V, S
Duration: Instantaneous

You summon a spirit that assumes the form of a loyal, majestic mount. Appearing in an unoccupied space within range, the spirit takes on a form you choose: a griffon, a pegasus, a peryton, a dire wolf, a rhinoceros, or a saber-toothed tiger. The creature has the statistics provided in the *Monster Manual* for the chosen form, though it is a celestial, a fey, or a fiend (your choice) instead of its normal creature type. Additionally, if it has an Intelligence score of 5 or lower, its Intelligence becomes 6, and it gains the ability to understand one language of your choice that you speak.

You control the mount in combat. While the mount is within 1 mile of you, you can communicate with it telepathically. While mounted on it, you can make any spell you cast that targets only you also target the mount.

The mount disappears temporarily when it drops to 0 hit points or when you dismiss it as an action. Casting this spell again re-summons the bonded mount, with all its hit points restored and any conditions removed.

You can't have more than one mount bonded by this spell or *find steed* at the same time. As an action, you can release a mount from its bond, causing it to disappear permanently.

Whenever the mount disappears, it leaves behind any objects it was wearing or carrying.

FLAME ARROWS
3rd-level transmutation

Casting Time: 1 action
Range: Touch
Components: V, S
Duration: Concentration, up to 1 hour

You touch a quiver containing arrows or bolts. When a target is hit by a ranged weapon attack using a piece of ammunition drawn from the quiver, the target takes an extra 1d6 fire damage. The spell's magic ends on a piece of ammunition when it hits or misses, and the spell ends when twelve pieces of ammunition have been drawn from the quiver.

At Higher Levels. When you cast this spell using a spell slot of 4th level or higher, the number of pieces of ammunition you can affect with this spell increases by two for each slot level above 3rd.

FROSTBITE
Evocation cantrip

Casting Time: 1 action
Range: 60 feet
Components: V, S
Duration: Instantaneous

You cause numbing frost to form on one creature that you can see within range. The target must make a Constitution saving throw. On a failed save, the target takes 1d6 cold damage, and it has disadvantage on the next weapon attack roll it makes before the end of its next turn.

The spell's damage increases by 1d6 when you reach 5th level (2d6), 11th level (3d6), and 17th level (4d6).

GUARDIAN OF NATURE
4th-level transmutation

Casting Time: 1 bonus action
Range: Self
Components: V
Duration: Concentration, up to 1 minute

A nature spirit answers your call and transforms you into a powerful guardian. The transformation lasts until the spell ends. You choose one of the following forms to assume: Primal Beast or Great Tree.

Primal Beast. Bestial fur covers your body, your facial features become feral, and you gain the following benefits:

- Your walking speed increases by 10 feet.
- You gain darkvision with a range of 120 feet.
- You make Strength-based attack rolls with advantage.
- Your melee weapon attacks deal an extra 1d6 force damage on a hit.

Great Tree. Your skin appears barky, leaves sprout from your hair, and you gain the following benefits:

- You gain 10 temporary hit points.
- You make Constitution saving throws with advantage.
- You make Dexterity- and Wisdom-based attack rolls with advantage.
- While you are on the ground, the ground within 15 feet of you is difficult terrain for your enemies.

GUST
Transmutation cantrip

Casting Time: 1 action
Range: 30 feet
Components: V, S
Duration: Instantaneous

You seize the air and compel it to create one of the following effects at a point you can see within range:

- One Medium or smaller creature that you choose must succeed on a Strength saving throw or be pushed up to 5 feet away from you.
- You create a small blast of air capable of moving one object that is neither held nor carried and that weighs no more than 5 pounds. The object is pushed up to 10 feet away from you. It isn't pushed with enough force to cause damage.
- You create a harmless sensory effect using air, such as causing leaves to rustle, wind to slam shutters closed, or your clothing to ripple in a breeze.

HEALING SPIRIT
2nd-level conjuration

Casting Time: 1 bonus action
Range: 60 feet
Components: V, S
Duration: Concentration, up to 1 minute

You call forth a nature spirit to soothe the wounded. The intangible spirit appears in a space that is a 5-foot cube

you can see within range. The spirit looks like a transparent beast or fey (your choice).

Until the spell ends, whenever you or a creature you can see moves into the spirit's space for the first time on a turn or starts its turn there, you can cause the spirit to restore 1d6 hit points to that creature (no action required). The spirit can't heal constructs or undead.

As a bonus action on your turn, you can move the spirit up to 30 feet to a space you can see.

At Higher Levels. When you cast this spell using a spell slot of 3rd level or higher, the healing increases by 1d6 for each slot level above 2nd.

HOLY WEAPON
5th-level evocation

Casting Time: 1 bonus action
Range: Touch
Components: V, S
Duration: Concentration, up to 1 hour

You imbue a weapon you touch with holy power. Until the spell ends, the weapon emits bright light in a 30-foot radius and dim light for an additional 30 feet. In addition, weapon attacks made with it deal an extra 2d8 radiant damage on a hit. If the weapon isn't already a magic weapon, it becomes one for the duration.

As a bonus action on your turn, you can dismiss this spell and cause the weapon to emit a burst of radiance. Each creature of your choice that you can see within 30 feet of you must make a Constitution saving throw. On a failed save, a creature takes 4d8 radiant damage, and it is blinded for 1 minute. On a successful save, a creature takes half as much damage and isn't blinded. At the end of each of its turns, a blinded creature can make a Constitution saving throw, ending the effect on itself on a success.

ICE KNIFE
1st-level conjuration

Casting Time: 1 action
Range: 60 feet
Components: S, M (a drop of water or a piece of ice)
Duration: Instantaneous

You create a shard of ice and fling it at one creature within range. Make a ranged spell attack against the target. On a hit, the target takes 1d10 piercing damage. Hit or miss, the shard then explodes. The target and each creature within 5 feet of it must succeed on a Dexterity saving throw or take 2d6 cold damage.

At Higher Levels. When you cast this spell using a spell slot of 2nd level or higher, the cold damage increases by 1d6 for each slot level above 1st.

ILLUSORY DRAGON
8th-level illusion

Casting Time: 1 action
Range: 120 feet
Components: S
Duration: Concentration, up to 1 minute

By gathering threads of shadow material from the Shadowfell, you create a Huge shadowy dragon in an unoccupied space that you can see within range. The illusion lasts for the spell's duration and occupies its space, as if it were a creature.

When the illusion appears, any of your enemies that can see it must succeed on a Wisdom saving throw or become frightened of it for 1 minute. If a frightened creature ends its turn in a location where it doesn't have line of sight to the illusion, it can repeat the saving throw, ending the effect on itself on a success.

As a bonus action on your turn, you can move the illusion up to 60 feet. At any point during its movement, you can cause it to exhale a blast of energy in a 60-foot cone originating from its space. When you create the dragon, choose a damage type: acid, cold, fire, lightning, necrotic, or poison. Each creature in the cone must make an Intelligence saving throw, taking 7d6 damage of the chosen damage type on a failed save, or half as much damage on a successful one.

The illusion is tangible because of the shadow stuff used to create it, but attacks miss it automatically, it succeeds on all saving throws, and it is immune to all damage and conditions. A creature that uses an action to examine the dragon can determine that it is an illusion by succeeding on an Intelligence (Investigation) check against your spell save DC. If a creature discerns the illusion for what it is, the creature can see through it and has advantage on saving throws against its breath.

IMMOLATION
5th-level evocation

Casting Time: 1 action
Range: 90 feet
Components: V
Duration: Concentration, up to 1 minute

Flames wreathe one creature you can see within range. The target must make a Dexterity saving throw. It takes 8d6 fire damage on a failed save, or half as much damage on a successful one. On a failed save, the target also burns for the spell's duration. The burning target sheds bright light in a 30-foot radius and dim light for an additional 30 feet. At the end of each of its turns, the target repeats the saving throw. It takes 4d6 fire damage on a failed save, and the spell ends on a successful one. These magical flames can't be extinguished by nonmagical means.

If damage from this spell kills a target, the target is turned to ash.

INFERNAL CALLING
5th-level conjuration

Casting Time: 1 minute
Range: 90 feet
Components: V, S, M (a ruby worth at least 999 gp)
Duration: Concentration, up to 1 hour

Uttering a dark incantation, you summon a devil from the Nine Hells. You choose the devil's type, which must be one of challenge rating 6 or lower, such as a barbed

devil or a bearded devil. The devil appears in an unoccupied space that you can see within range. The devil disappears when it drops to 0 hit points or when the spell ends.

The devil is unfriendly toward you and your companions. Roll initiative for the devil, which has its own turns. It is under the Dungeon Master's control and acts according to its nature on each of its turns, which might result in its attacking you if it thinks it can prevail, or trying to tempt you to undertake an evil act in exchange for limited service. The DM has the creature's statistics.

On each of your turns, you can try to issue a verbal command to the devil (no action required by you). It obeys the command if the likely outcome is in accordance with its desires, especially if the result would draw you toward evil. Otherwise, you must make a Charisma (Deception, Intimidation, or Persuasion) check contested by its Wisdom (Insight) check. You make the check with advantage if you say the devil's true name. If your check fails, the devil becomes immune to your verbal commands for the duration of the spell, though it can still carry out your commands if it chooses. If your check succeeds, the devil carries out your command—such as "attack my enemies," "explore the room ahead," or "bear this message to the queen"—until it completes the activity, at which point it returns to you to report having done so.

If your concentration ends before the spell reaches its full duration, the devil doesn't disappear if it has become immune to your verbal commands. Instead, it acts in whatever manner it chooses for 3d6 minutes, and then it disappears.

If you possess an individual devil's talisman, you can summon that devil if it is of the appropriate challenge rating plus 1, and it obeys all your commands, with no Charisma checks required.

At Higher Levels. When you cast this spell using a spell slot of 6th level or higher, the challenge rating increases by 1 for each slot level above 5th.

INFESTATION
Conjuration cantrip

Casting Time: 1 action
Range: 30 feet
Components: V, S, M (a living flea)
Duration: Instantaneous

You cause a cloud of mites, fleas, and other parasites to appear momentarily on one creature you can see within range. The target must succeed on a Constitution saving throw, or it takes 1d6 poison damage and moves 5 feet in a random direction if it can move and its speed is at least 5 feet. Roll a d4 for the direction: 1, north; 2, south; 3, east; or 4, west. This movement doesn't provoke opportunity attacks, and if the direction rolled is blocked, the target doesn't move.

The spell's damage increases by 1d6 when you reach 5th level (2d6), 11th level (3d6), and 17th level (4d6).

INFERNAL CALLING

INVESTITURE OF FLAME
6th-level transmutation

Casting Time: 1 action
Range: Self
Components: V, S
Duration: Concentration, up to 10 minutes

Flames race across your body, shedding bright light in a 30-foot radius and dim light for an additional 30 feet for the spell's duration. The flames don't harm you. Until the spell ends, you gain the following benefits:

- You are immune to fire damage and have resistance to cold damage.
- Any creature that moves within 5 feet of you for the first time on a turn or ends its turn there takes 1d10 fire damage.
- You can use your action to create a line of fire 15 feet long and 5 feet wide extending from you in a direction you choose. Each creature in the line must make a Dexterity saving throw. A creature takes 4d8 fire damage on a failed save, or half as much damage on a successful one.

INVESTITURE OF ICE
6th-level transmutation

Casting Time: 1 action
Range: Self
Components: V, S
Duration: Concentration, up to 10 minutes

Until the spell ends, ice rimes your body, and you gain the following benefits:

- You are immune to cold damage and have resistance to fire damage.
- You can move across difficult terrain created by ice or snow without spending extra movement.
- The ground in a 10-foot radius around you is icy and is difficult terrain for creatures other than you. The radius moves with you.
- You can use your action to create a 15-foot cone of freezing wind extending from your outstretched hand in a direction you choose. Each creature in the cone must make a Constitution saving throw. A creature takes 4d6 cold damage on a failed save, or half as much damage on a successful one. A creature that fails its save against this effect has its speed halved until the start of your next turn.

INVESTITURE OF STONE
6th-level transmutation

Casting Time: 1 action
Range: Self
Components: V, S
Duration: Concentration, up to 10 minutes

Until the spell ends, bits of rock spread across your body, and you gain the following benefits:

- You have resistance to bludgeoning, piercing, and slashing damage from nonmagical attacks.

- You can use your action to create a small earthquake on the ground in a 15-foot radius centered on you. Other creatures on that ground must succeed on a Dexterity saving throw or be knocked prone.
- You can move across difficult terrain made of earth or stone without spending extra movement. You can move through solid earth or stone as if it was air and without destabilizing it, but you can't end your movement there. If you do so, you are ejected to the nearest unoccupied space, this spell ends, and you are stunned until the end of your next turn.

INVESTITURE OF WIND
6th-level transmutation

Casting Time: 1 action
Range: Self
Components: V, S
Duration: Concentration, up to 10 minutes

Until the spell ends, wind whirls around you, and you gain the following benefits:

- Ranged weapon attacks made against you have disadvantage on the attack roll.
- You gain a flying speed of 60 feet. If you are still flying when the spell ends, you fall, unless you can somehow prevent it.
- You can use your action to create a 15-foot cube of swirling wind centered on a point you can see within 60 feet of you. Each creature in that area must make a Constitution saving throw. A creature takes 2d10 bludgeoning damage on a failed save, or half as much damage on a successful one. If a Large or smaller creature fails the save, that creature is also pushed up to 10 feet away from the center of the cube.

INVULNERABILITY
9th-level abjuration

Casting Time: 1 action
Range: Self
Components: V, S, M (a small piece of adamantine worth at least 500 gp, which the spell consumes)
Duration: Concentration, up to 10 minutes

You are immune to all damage until the spell ends.

LIFE TRANSFERENCE
3rd-level necromancy

Casting Time: 1 action
Range: 30 feet
Components: V, S
Duration: Instantaneous

You sacrifice some of your health to mend another creature's injuries. You take 4d8 necrotic damage, and one creature of your choice that you can see within range regains a number of hit points equal to twice the necrotic damage you take.

At Higher Levels. When you cast this spell using a spell slot of 4th level or higher, the damage increases by 1d8 for each slot level above 3rd.

MADDENING DARKNESS
8th-level evocation

Casting Time: 1 action
Range: 150 feet
Components: V, M (a drop of pitch mixed with a drop of mercury)
Duration: Concentration, up to 10 minutes

Magical darkness spreads from a point you choose within range to fill a 60-foot-radius sphere until the spell ends. The darkness spreads around corners. A creature with darkvision can't see through this darkness. Nonmagical light, as well as light created by spells of 8th level or lower, can't illuminate the area.

Shrieks, gibbering, and mad laughter can be heard within the sphere. Whenever a creature starts its turn in the sphere, it must make a Wisdom saving throw, taking 8d8 psychic damage on a failed save, or half as much damage on a successful one.

MAELSTROM
5th-level evocation

Casting Time: 1 action
Range: 120 feet
Components: V, S, M (paper or leaf in the shape of a funnel)
Duration: Concentration, up to 1 minute

A swirling mass of 5-foot-deep water appears in a 30-foot radius centered on a point you can see within range. The point must be on the ground or in a body of water. Until the spell ends, that area is difficult terrain, and any creature that starts its turn there must succeed on a Strength saving throw or take 6d6 bludgeoning damage and be pulled 10 feet toward the center.

MAGIC STONE
Transmutation cantrip

Casting Time: 1 bonus action
Range: Touch
Components: V, S
Duration: 1 minute

You touch one to three pebbles and imbue them with magic. You or someone else can make a ranged spell attack with one of the pebbles by throwing it or hurling it with a sling. If thrown, a pebble has a range of 60 feet. If someone else attacks with a pebble, that attacker adds your spellcasting ability modifier, not the attacker's, to the attack roll. On a hit, the target takes bludgeoning damage equal to 1d6 + your spellcasting ability modifier. Whether the attack hits or misses, the spell then ends on the stone.

If you cast this spell again, the spell ends on any pebbles still affected by your previous casting.

MASS POLYMORPH
9th-level transmutation

Casting Time: 1 action
Range: 120 feet
Components: V, S, M (a caterpillar cocoon)
Duration: Concentration, up to 1 hour

You transform up to ten creatures of your choice that you can see within range. An unwilling target must succeed on a Wisdom saving throw to resist the transformation. An unwilling shapechanger automatically succeeds on the save.

Each target assumes a beast form of your choice, and you can choose the same form or different ones for each target. The new form can be any beast you have seen whose challenge rating is equal to or less than the target's (or half the target's level, if the target doesn't have a challenge rating). The target's game statistics, including mental ability scores, are replaced by the statistics of the chosen beast, but the target retains its hit points, alignment, and personality.

Each target gains a number of temporary hit points equal to the hit points of its new form. These temporary hit points can't be replaced by temporary hit points from another source. A target reverts to its normal form when it has no more temporary hit points or it dies. If the spell ends before then, the creature loses all its temporary hit points and reverts to its normal form.

The creature is limited in the actions it can perform by the nature of its new form. It can't speak, cast spells, or do anything else that requires hands or speech.

The target's gear melds into the new form. The target can't activate, use, wield, or otherwise benefit from any of its equipment.

MAXIMILIAN'S EARTHEN GRASP
2nd-level transmutation

Casting Time: 1 action
Range: 30 feet
Components: V, S, M (a miniature hand sculpted from clay)
Duration: Concentration, up to 1 minute

You choose a 5-foot-square unoccupied space on the ground that you can see within range. A Medium hand made from compacted soil rises there and reaches for one creature you can see within 5 feet of it. The target must make a Strength saving throw. On a failed save, the target takes 2d6 bludgeoning damage and is restrained for the spell's duration.

As an action, you can cause the hand to crush the restrained target, which must make a Strength saving throw. The target takes 2d6 bludgeoning damage on a failed save, or half as much damage on a successful one.

To break out, the restrained target can use its action to make a Strength check against your spell save DC. On a success, the target escapes and is no longer restrained by the hand.

As an action, you can cause the hand to reach for a different creature or to move to a different unoccupied space within range. The hand releases a restrained target if you do either.

MELF'S MINUTE METEORS
3rd-level evocation

Casting Time: 1 action
Range: Self
Components: V, S, M (niter, sulfur, and pine tar formed into a bead)
Duration: Concentration, up to 10 minutes

You create six tiny meteors in your space. They float in the air and orbit you for the spell's duration. When you cast the spell—and as a bonus action on each of your turns thereafter—you can expend one or two of the meteors, sending them streaking toward a point or points you choose within 120 feet of you. Once a meteor reaches its destination or impacts against a solid surface, the meteor explodes. Each creature within 5 feet of the point where the meteor explodes must make a Dexterity saving throw. A creature takes 2d6 fire damage on a failed save, or half as much damage on a successful one.

At Higher Levels. When you cast this spell using a spell slot of 4th level or higher, the number of meteors created increases by two for each slot level above 3rd.

MENTAL PRISON
6th-level illusion

Casting Time: 1 action
Range: 60 feet
Components: S
Duration: Concentration, up to 1 minute

You attempt to bind a creature within an illusory cell that only it perceives. One creature you can see within range must make an Intelligence saving throw. The target succeeds automatically if it is immune to being charmed. On a successful save, the target takes 5d10 psychic damage, and the spell ends. On a failed save, the target takes 5d10 psychic damage, and you make the area immediately around the target's space appear dangerous to it in some way. You might cause the target to perceive itself as being surrounded by fire, floating razors, or hideous maws filled with dripping teeth. Whatever form the illusion takes, the target can't see or hear anything beyond it and is restrained for the spell's duration. If the target is moved out of the illusion, makes a melee attack through it, or reaches any part of its body through it, the target takes 10d10 psychic damage, and the spell ends.

MIGHTY FORTRESS
8th-level conjuration

Casting Time: 1 minute
Range: 1 mile
Components: V, S, M (a diamond worth at least 500 gp, which the spell consumes)
Duration: Instantaneous

A fortress of stone erupts from a square area of ground of your choice that you can see within range. The area is 120 feet on each side, and it must not have any buildings or other structures on it. Any creatures in the area are harmlessly lifted up as the fortress rises.

The fortress has four turrets with square bases, each one 20 feet on a side and 30 feet tall, with one turret on each corner. The turrets are connected to each other by stone walls that are each 80 feet long, creating an en-

MIGHTY FORTRESS

closed area. Each wall is 1 foot thick and is composed of panels that are 10 feet wide and 20 feet tall. Each panel is contiguous with two other panels or one other panel and a turret. You can place up to four stone doors in the fortress's outer wall.

A small keep stands inside the enclosed area. The keep has a square base that is 50 feet on each side, and it has three floors with 10-foot-high ceilings. Each of the floors can be divided into as many rooms as you like, provided each room is at least 5 feet on each side. The floors of the keep are connected by stone staircases, its walls are 6 inches thick, and interior rooms can have stone doors or open archways as you choose. The keep is furnished and decorated however you like, and it contains sufficient food to serve a nine-course banquet for up to 100 people each day. Furnishings, food, and other objects created by this spell crumble to dust if removed from the fortress.

A staff of one hundred invisible servants obeys any command given to them by creatures you designate when you cast the spell. Each servant functions as if created by the *unseen servant* spell.

The walls, turrets, and keep are all made of stone that can be damaged. Each 10-foot-by-10-foot section of stone has AC 15 and 30 hit points per inch of thickness. It is immune to poison and psychic damage. Reducing a section of stone to 0 hit points destroys it and might cause connected sections to buckle and collapse at the DM's discretion.

After 7 days or when you cast this spell somewhere else, the fortress harmlessly crumbles and sinks back into the ground, leaving any creatures that were inside it safely on the ground.

Casting this spell on the same spot once every 7 days for a year makes the fortress permanent.

MIND SPIKE
2nd-level divination

Casting Time: 1 action
Range: 60 feet
Components: S
Duration: Concentration, up to 1 hour

You reach into the mind of one creature you can see within range. The target must make a Wisdom saving throw, taking 3d8 psychic damage on a failed save, or half as much damage on a successful one. On a failed save, you also always know the target's location until the spell ends, but only while the two of you are on the same plane of existence. While you have this knowledge, the target can't become hidden from you, and if it's invisible, it gains no benefit from that condition against you.

At Higher Levels. When you cast this spell using a spell slot of 3rd level or higher, the damage increases by 1d6 for each slot level above 2nd.

MOLD EARTH
Transmutation cantrip

Casting Time: 1 action
Range: 30 feet
Components: S
Duration: Instantaneous or 1 hour (see below)

You choose a portion of dirt or stone that you can see within range and that fits within a 5-foot cube. You manipulate it in one of the following ways:

- If you target an area of loose earth, you can instantaneously excavate it, move it along the ground, and deposit it up to 5 feet away. This movement doesn't involve enough force to cause damage.
- You cause shapes, colors, or both to appear on the dirt or stone, spelling out words, creating images, or shaping patterns. The changes last for 1 hour.
- If the dirt or stone you target is on the ground, you cause it to become difficult terrain. Alternatively, you can cause the ground to become normal terrain if it is already difficult terrain. This change lasts for 1 hour.

If you cast this spell multiple times, you can have no more than two of its non-instantaneous effects active at a time, and you can dismiss such an effect as an action.

NEGATIVE ENERGY FLOOD
5th-level necromancy

Casting Time: 1 action
Range: 60 feet
Components: V, M (a broken bone and a square of black silk)
Duration: Instantaneous

You send ribbons of negative energy at one creature you can see within range. Unless the target is undead, it must make a Constitution saving throw, taking 5d12 necrotic damage on a failed save, or half as much damage on a successful one. A target killed by this damage rises up as a zombie at the start of your next turn. The zombie pursues whatever creature it can see that is closest to it. Statistics for the zombie are in the *Monster Manual*.

If you target an undead with this spell, the target doesn't make a saving throw. Instead, roll 5d12. The target gains half the total as temporary hit points.

POWER WORD PAIN
7th-level enchantment

Casting Time: 1 action
Range: 60 feet
Components: V
Duration: Instantaneous

You speak a word of power that causes waves of intense pain to assail one creature you can see within range. If the target has 100 hit points or fewer, it is subject to crippling pain. Otherwise, the spell has no effect on it. A target is also unaffected if it is immune to being charmed.

While the target is affected by crippling pain, any speed it has can be no higher than 10 feet. The target also has disadvantage on attack rolls, ability checks, and saving throws, other than Constitution saving throws. Finally, if the target tries to cast a spell, it must first succeed on a Constitution saving throw, or the casting fails and the spell is wasted.

A target suffering this pain can make a Constitution saving throw at the end of each of its turns. On a successful save, the pain ends.

PRIMAL SAVAGERY
Transmutation cantrip

Casting Time: 1 action
Range: Self
Components: S
Duration: Instantaneous

You channel primal magic to cause your teeth or fingernails to sharpen, ready to deliver a corrosive attack. Make a melee spell attack against one creature within 5 feet of you. On a hit, the target takes 1d10 acid damage. After you make the attack, your teeth or fingernails return to normal.

The spell's damage increases by 1d10 when you reach 5th level (2d10), 11th level (3d10), and 17th level (4d10).

PRIMORDIAL WARD
6th-level abjuration

Casting Time: 1 action
Range: Self
Components: V, S
Duration: Concentration, up to 1 minute

You have resistance to acid, cold, fire, lightning, and thunder damage for the spell's duration.

When you take damage of one of those types, you can use your reaction to gain immunity to that type of damage, including against the triggering damage. If you do so, the resistances end, and you have the immunity until the end of your next turn, at which time the spell ends.

PSYCHIC SCREAM
9th-level enchantment

Casting Time: 1 action
Range: 90 feet
Components: S
Duration: Instantaneous

You unleash the power of your mind to blast the intellect of up to ten creatures of your choice that you can see within range. Creatures that have an Intelligence score of 2 or lower are unaffected.

Each target must make an Intelligence saving throw. On a failed save, a target takes 14d6 psychic damage and is stunned. On a successful save, a target takes half as much damage and isn't stunned. If a target is killed by this damage, its head explodes, assuming it has one.

A stunned target can make an Intelligence saving throw at the end of each of its turns. On a successful save, the stunning effect ends.

PYROTECHNICS
2nd-level transmutation

Casting Time: 1 action
Range: 60 feet
Components: V, S
Duration: Instantaneous

Choose an area of nonmagical flame that you can see and that fits within a 5-foot cube within range. You can extinguish the fire in that area, and you create either fireworks or smoke when you do so.

Fireworks. The target explodes with a dazzling display of colors. Each creature within 10 feet of the target

SHADOW BLADE

properties (range 20/60). In addition, when you use the sword to attack a target that is in dim light or darkness, you make the attack roll with advantage.

If you drop the weapon or throw it, it dissipates at the end of the turn. Thereafter, while the spell persists, you can use a bonus action to cause the sword to reappear in your hand.

At Higher Levels. When you cast this spell using a 3rd- or 4th-level spell slot, the damage increases to 3d8. When you cast it using a 5th- or 6th-level spell slot, the damage increases to 4d8. When you cast it using a spell slot of 7th level or higher, the damage increases to 5d8.

SHADOW OF MOIL
4th-level necromancy

Casting Time: 1 action
Range: Self
Components: V, S, M (an undead eyeball encased in a
  gem worth at least 150 gp)
Duration: Concentration, up to 1 minute

Flame-like shadows wreathe your body until the spell ends, causing you to become heavily obscured to others. The shadows turn dim light within 10 feet of you into darkness, and bright light in the same area to dim light.

Until the spell ends, you have resistance to radiant damage. In addition, whenever a creature within 10 feet of you hits you with an attack, the shadows lash out at that creature, dealing it 2d8 necrotic damage.

SHAPE WATER
Transmutation cantrip

Casting Time: 1 action
Range: 30 feet
Components: S
Duration: Instantaneous or 1 hour (see below)

You choose an area of water that you can see within range and that fits within a 5-foot cube. You manipulate it in one of the following ways:

- You instantaneously move or otherwise change the flow of the water as you direct, up to 5 feet in any direction. This movement doesn't have enough force to cause damage.
- You cause the water to form into simple shapes and animate at your direction. This change lasts for 1 hour.
- You change the water's color or opacity. The water must be changed in the same way throughout. This change lasts for 1 hour.
- You freeze the water, provided that there are no creatures in it. The water unfreezes in 1 hour.

If you cast this spell multiple times, you can have no more than two of its non-instantaneous effects active at a time, and you can dismiss such an effect as an action.

SICKENING RADIANCE
4th-level evocation

Casting Time: 1 action
Range: 120 feet
Components: V, S
Duration: Concentration, up to 10 minutes

must succeed on a Constitution saving throw or become blinded until the end of your next turn.

Smoke. Thick black smoke spreads out from the target in a 20-foot radius, moving around corners. The area of the smoke is heavily obscured. The smoke persists for 1 minute or until a strong wind disperses it.

SCATTER
6th-level conjuration

Casting Time: 1 action
Range: 30 feet
Components: V
Duration: Instantaneous

The air quivers around up to five creatures of your choice that you can see within range. An unwilling creature must succeed on a Wisdom saving throw to resist this spell. You teleport each affected target to an unoccupied space that you can see within 120 feet of you. That space must be on the ground or on a floor.

SHADOW BLADE
2nd-level illusion

Casting Time: 1 bonus action
Range: Self
Components: V, S
Duration: Concentration, up to 1 minute

You weave together threads of shadow to create a sword of solidified gloom in your hand. This magic sword lasts until the spell ends. It counts as a simple melee weapon with which you are proficient. It deals 2d8 psychic damage on a hit and has the finesse, light, and thrown

Dim, greenish light spreads within a 30-foot-radius sphere centered on a point you choose within range. The light spreads around corners, and it lasts until the spell ends.

When a creature moves into the spell's area for the first time on a turn or starts its turn there, that creature must succeed on a Constitution saving throw or take 4d10 radiant damage, and it suffers one level of exhaustion and emits a dim, greenish light in a 5-foot radius. This light makes it impossible for the creature to benefit from being invisible. The light and any levels of exhaustion caused by this spell go away when the spell ends.

SKILL EMPOWERMENT
5th-level transmutation

Casting Time: 1 action
Range: Touch
Components: V, S
Duration: Concentration, up to 1 hour

Your magic deepens a creature's understanding of its own talent. You touch one willing creature and give it expertise in one skill of your choice; until the spell ends, the creature doubles its proficiency bonus for ability checks it makes that use the chosen skill.

You must choose a skill in which the target is proficient and that isn't already benefiting from an effect, such as Expertise, that doubles its proficiency bonus.

SKYWRITE
2nd-level transmutation (ritual)

Casting Time: 1 action
Range: Sight
Components: V, S
Duration: Concentration, up to 1 hour

You cause up to ten words to form in a part of the sky you can see. The words appear to be made of cloud and remain in place for the spell's duration. The words dissipate when the spell ends. A strong wind can disperse the clouds and end the spell early.

SNARE
1st-level abjuration

Casting Time: 1 minute
Range: Touch
Components: S, M (25 feet of rope, which the spell consumes)
Duration: 8 hours

As you cast this spell, you use the rope to create a circle with a 5-foot radius on the ground or the floor. When you finish casting, the rope disappears and the circle becomes a magic trap.

This trap is nearly invisible, requiring a successful Intelligence (Investigation) check against your spell save DC to be discerned.

The trap triggers when a Small, Medium, or Large creature moves onto the ground or the floor in the spell's radius. That creature must succeed on a Dexterity saving throw or be magically hoisted into the air, leaving it hanging upside down 3 feet above the ground or the floor. The creature is restrained there until the spell ends.

A restrained creature can make a Dexterity saving throw at the end of each of its turns, ending the effect on itself on a success. Alternatively, the creature or someone else who can reach it can use an action to make an Intelligence (Arcana) check against your spell save DC. On a success, the restrained effect ends.

After the trap is triggered, the spell ends when no creature is restrained by it.

SNILLOC'S SNOWBALL SWARM
2nd-level evocation

Casting Time: 1 action
Range: 90 feet
Components: V, S, M (a piece of ice or a small white rock chip)
Duration: Instantaneous

A flurry of magic snowballs erupts from a point you choose within range. Each creature in a 5-foot-radius sphere centered on that point must make a Dexterity saving throw. A creature takes 3d6 cold damage on a failed save, or half as much damage on a successful one.

At Higher Levels. When you cast this spell using a spell slot of 3rd level or higher, the damage increases by 1d6 for each slot level above 2nd.

SOUL CAGE
6th-level necromancy

Casting Time: 1 reaction, which you take when a humanoid you can see within 60 feet of you dies
Range: 60 feet
Components: V, S, M (a tiny silver cage worth 100 gp)
Duration: 8 hours

This spell snatches the soul of a humanoid as it dies and traps it inside the tiny cage you use for the material component. A stolen soul remains inside the cage until the spell ends or until you destroy the cage, which ends the spell. While you have a soul inside the cage, you can exploit it in any of the ways described below. You can use a trapped soul up to six times. Once you exploit a soul for the sixth time, it is released, and the spell ends. While a soul is trapped, the dead humanoid it came from can't be revived.

Steal Life. You can use a bonus action to drain vigor from the soul and regain 2d8 hit points.

Query Soul. You ask the soul a question (no action required) and receive a brief telepathic answer, which you can understand regardless of the language used. The soul knows only what it knew in life, but it must answer you truthfully and to the best of its ability. The answer is no more than a sentence or two and might be cryptic.

Borrow Experience. You can use a bonus action to bolster yourself with the soul's life experience, making your next attack roll, ability check, or saving throw with advantage. If you don't use this benefit before the start of your next turn, it is lost.

Eyes of the Dead. You can use an action to name a place the humanoid saw in life, which creates an invisible sensor somewhere in that place if it is on the plane of existence you're currently on. The sensor remains for as long as you concentrate, up to 10 minutes (as if you were concentrating on a spell). You receive visual and

auditory information from the sensor as if you were in its space using your senses.

A creature that can see the sensor (such as one using *see invisibility* or truesight) sees a translucent image of the tormented humanoid whose soul you caged.

STEEL WIND STRIKE
5th-level conjuration

Casting Time: 1 action
Range: 30 feet
Components: S, M (a melee weapon worth at least 1 sp)
Duration: Instantaneous

You flourish the weapon used in the casting and then vanish to strike like the wind. Choose up to five creatures you can see within range. Make a melee spell attack against each target. On a hit, a target takes 6d10 force damage.

You can then teleport to an unoccupied space you can see within 5 feet of one of the targets you hit or missed.

STORM SPHERE
4th-level evocation

Casting Time: 1 action
Range: 150 feet
Components: V, S
Duration: Concentration, up to 1 minute

A 20-foot-radius sphere of whirling air springs into existence, centered on a point you choose within range.

The sphere remains for the spell's duration. Each creature in the sphere when it appears or that ends its turn there must succeed on a Strength saving throw or take 2d6 bludgeoning damage. The sphere's space is difficult terrain.

Until the spell ends, you can use a bonus action on each of your turns to cause a bolt of lightning to leap from the center of the sphere toward one creature you choose within 60 feet of the center. Make a ranged spell attack. You have advantage on the attack roll if the target is in the sphere. On a hit, the target takes 4d6 lightning damage.

Creatures within 30 feet of the sphere have disadvantage on Wisdom (Perception) checks made to listen.

At Higher Levels. When you cast this spell using a spell slot of 5th level or higher, the damage for each of its effects increases by 1d6 for each slot level above 4th.

SUMMON GREATER DEMON
4th-level conjuration

Casting Time: 1 action
Range: 60 feet
Components: V, S, M (a vial of blood from a humanoid killed within the past 24 hours)
Duration: Concentration, up to 1 hour

You utter foul words, summoning one demon from the chaos of the Abyss. You choose the demon's type, which must be one of challenge rating 5 or lower, such as a shadow demon or a barlgura. The demon appears in an unoccupied space you can see within range, and the demon disappears when it drops to 0 hit points or when the spell ends.

Roll initiative for the demon, which has its own turns. When you summon it and on each of your turns thereafter, you can issue a verbal command to it (requiring no action on your part), telling it what it must do on its next turn. If you issue no command, it spends its turn attacking any creature within reach that has attacked it.

At the end of each of the demon's turns, it makes a Charisma saving throw. The demon has disadvantage on this saving throw if you say its true name. On a failed save, the demon continues to obey you. On a successful save, your control of the demon ends for the rest of the duration, and the demon spends its turns pursuing and attacking the nearest non-demons to the best of its ability. If you stop concentrating on the spell before it reaches its full duration, an uncontrolled demon doesn't disappear for 1d6 rounds if it still has hit points.

As part of casting the spell, you can form a circle on the ground with the blood used as a material component. The circle is large enough to encompass your space. While the spell lasts, the summoned demon can't cross the circle or harm it, and it can't target anyone within it. Using the material component in this manner consumes it when the spell ends.

At Higher Levels. When you cast this spell using a spell slot of 5th level or higher, the challenge rating increases by 1 for each slot level above 4th.

SUMMON LESSER DEMONS
3rd-level conjuration

Casting Time: 1 action
Range: 60 feet
Components: V, S, M (a vial of blood from a humanoid killed within the past 24 hours)
Duration: Concentration, up to 1 hour

You utter foul words, summoning demons from the chaos of the Abyss. Roll on the following table to determine what appears.

d6	Demons Summoned
1–2	Two demons of challenge rating 1 or lower
3–4	Four demons of challenge rating 1/2 or lower
5–6	Eight demons of challenge rating 1/4 or lower

The DM chooses the demons, such as manes or dretches, and you choose the unoccupied spaces you can see within range where they appear. A summoned demon disappears when it drops to 0 hit points or when the spell ends.

The demons are hostile to all creatures, including you. Roll initiative for the summoned demons as a group, which has its own turns. The demons pursue and attack the nearest non-demons to the best of their ability.

As part of casting the spell, you can form a circle on the ground with the blood used as a material component. The circle is large enough to encompass your space. While the spell lasts, the summoned demons can't cross the circle or harm it, and they can't target

anyone within it. Using the material component in this manner consumes it when the spell ends.

At Higher Levels. When you cast this spell using a spell slot of 6th or 7th level, you summon twice as many demons. If you cast it using a spell slot of 8th or 9th level, you summon three times as many demons.

SYNAPTIC STATIC
5th-level enchantment

Casting Time: 1 action
Range: 120 feet
Components: V, S
Duration: Instantaneous

You choose a point within range and cause psychic energy to explode there. Each creature in a 20-foot-radius sphere centered on that point must make an Intelligence saving throw. A creature with an Intelligence score of 2 or lower can't be affected by this spell. A target takes 8d6 psychic damage on a failed save, or half as much damage on a successful one.

After a failed save, a target has muddled thoughts for 1 minute. During that time, it rolls a d6 and subtracts the number rolled from all its attack rolls and ability checks, as well as its Constitution saving throws to maintain concentration. The target can make an Intelligence saving throw at the end of each of its turns, ending the effect on itself on a success.

TEMPLE OF THE GODS
7th-level conjuration

Casting Time: 1 hour
Range: 120 feet
Components: V, S, M (a holy symbol worth at least 5 gp)
Duration: 24 hours

You cause a temple to shimmer into existence on ground you can see within range. The temple must fit within an unoccupied cube of space, up to 120 feet on each side. The temple remains until the spell ends. It is dedicated to whatever god, pantheon, or philosophy is represented by the holy symbol used in the casting.

You make all decisions about the temple's appearance. The interior is enclosed by a floor, walls, and a roof, with one door granting access to the interior and as many windows as you wish. Only you and any creatures you designate when you cast the spell can open or close the door.

The temple's interior is an open space with an idol or altar at one end. You decide whether the temple is illuminated and whether that illumination is bright light or dim light. The smell of burning incense fills the air within, and the temperature is mild.

The temple opposes types of creatures you choose when you cast this spell. Choose one or more of the following: celestials, elementals, fey, fiends, or undead. If a creature of the chosen type attempts to enter the temple, that creature must make a Charisma saving throw. On a failed save, it can't enter the temple for 24 hours. Even if the creature can enter the temple, the magic there hinders it; whenever it makes an attack roll, an ability check, or a saving throw inside the temple, it must roll a d4 and subtract the number rolled from the d20 roll.

In addition, the sensors created by divination spells can't appear inside the temple, and creatures within can't be targeted by divination spells.

Finally, whenever any creature in the temple regains hit points from a spell of 1st level or higher, the creature regains additional hit points equal to your Wisdom modifier (minimum 1 hit point).

The temple is made from opaque magical force that extends into the Ethereal Plane, thus blocking ethereal travel into the temple's interior. Nothing can physically pass through the temple's exterior. It can't be dispelled by *dispel magic*, and *antimagic field* has no effect on it. A *disintegrate* spell destroys the temple instantly.

Casting this spell on the same spot every day for a year makes this effect permanent.

TENSER'S TRANSFORMATION
6th-level transmutation

Casting Time: 1 action
Range: Self
Components: V, S, M (a few hairs from a bull)
Duration: Concentration, up to 10 minutes

You endow yourself with endurance and martial prowess fueled by magic. Until the spell ends, you can't cast spells, and you gain the following benefits:

- You gain 50 temporary hit points. If any of these remain when the spell ends, they are lost.
- You have advantage on attack rolls that you make with simple and martial weapons.
- When you hit a target with a weapon attack, that target takes an extra 2d12 force damage.
- You have proficiency with all armor, shields, simple weapons, and martial weapons.
- You have proficiency in Strength and Constitution saving throws.
- You can attack twice, instead of once, when you take the Attack action on your turn. You ignore this benefit if you already have a feature, like Extra Attack, that gives you extra attacks.

Immediately after the spell ends, you must succeed on a DC 15 Constitution saving throw or suffer one level of exhaustion.

THUNDERCLAP
Evocation cantrip

Casting Time: 1 action
Range: 5 feet
Components: S
Duration: Instantaneous

You create a burst of thunderous sound that can be heard up to 100 feet away. Each creature within range, other than you, must succeed on a Constitution saving throw or take 1d6 thunder damage.

The spell's damage increases by 1d6 when you reach 5th level (2d6), 11th level (3d6), and 17th level (4d6).

THUNDER STEP
3rd-level conjuration

Casting Time: 1 action
Range: 90 feet
Components: V
Duration: Instantaneous

You teleport yourself to an unoccupied space you can see within range. Immediately after you disappear, a thunderous boom sounds, and each creature within 10 feet of the space you left must make a Constitution saving throw, taking 3d10 thunder damage on a failed save, or half as much damage on a successful one. The thunder can be heard from up to 300 feet away.

You can bring along objects as long as their weight doesn't exceed what you can carry. You can also teleport one willing creature of your size or smaller who is carrying gear up to its carrying capacity. The creature must be within 5 feet of you when you cast this spell, and there must be an unoccupied space within 5 feet of your destination space for the creature to appear in; otherwise, the creature is left behind.

At Higher Levels. When you cast this spell using a spell slot of 4th level or higher, the damage increases by 1d10 for each slot level above 3rd.

TIDAL WAVE
3rd-level conjuration

Casting Time: 1 action
Range: 120 feet
Components: V, S, M (a drop of water)
Duration: Instantaneous

You conjure up a wave of water that crashes down on an area within range. The area can be up to 30 feet long, up to 10 feet wide, and up to 10 feet tall. Each creature in that area must make a Dexterity saving throw. On a failed save, a creature takes 4d8 bludgeoning damage and is knocked prone. On a successful save, a creature takes half as much damage and isn't knocked prone. The water then spreads out across the ground in all directions, extinguishing unprotected flames in its area and within 30 feet of it, and then it vanishes.

TINY SERVANT
3rd-level transmutation

Casting Time: 1 minute
Range: Touch
Components: V, S
Duration: 8 hours

You touch one Tiny, nonmagical object that isn't attached to another object or a surface and isn't being carried by another creature. The target animates and sprouts little arms and legs, becoming a creature under your control until the spell ends or the creature drops to 0 hit points. See the stat block for its statistics.

As a bonus action, you can mentally command the creature if it is within 120 feet of you. (If you control multiple creatures with this spell, you can command any or all of them at the same time, issuing the same com-

TINY SERVANT

Tiny construct, unaligned

Armor Class 15 (natural armor)
Hit Points 10 (4d4)
Speed 30 ft., climb 30 ft.

STR	DEX	CON	INT	WIS	CHA
4 (−3)	16 (+3)	10 (+0)	2 (−4)	10 (+0)	1 (−5)

Damage Immunities poison, psychic
Condition Immunities blinded, charmed, deafened, exhaustion, frightened, paralyzed, petrified, poisoned
Senses blindsight 60 ft. (blind beyond this radius), passive Perception 10
Languages —

ACTIONS

Slam. *Melee Weapon Attack:* +5 to hit, reach 5 ft., one target. *Hit:* 5 (1d4 + 3) bludgeoning damage.

mand to each one.) You decide what action the creature will take and where it will move during its next turn, or you can issue a simple, general command, such as to fetch a key, stand watch, or stack some books. If you issue no commands, the servant does nothing other than defend itself against hostile creatures. Once given an order, the servant continues to follow that order until its task is complete.

When the creature drops to 0 hit points, it reverts to its original form, and any remaining damage carries over to that form.

At Higher Levels. When you cast this spell using a spell slot of 4th level or higher, you can animate two additional objects for each slot level above 3rd.

TOLL THE DEAD
Necromancy cantrip

Casting Time: 1 action
Range: 60 feet
Components: V, S
Duration: Instantaneous

You point at one creature you can see within range, and the sound of a dolorous bell fills the air around it for a moment. The target must succeed on a Wisdom saving throw or take 1d8 necrotic damage. If the target is missing any of its hit points, it instead takes 1d12 necrotic damage.

The spell's damage increases by one die when you reach 5th level (2d8 or 2d12), 11th level (3d8 or 3d12), and 17th level (4d8 or 4d12).

TRANSMUTE ROCK
5th-level transmutation

Casting Time: 1 action
Range: 120 feet
Components: V, S, M (clay and water)
Duration: Until dispelled

You choose an area of stone or mud that you can see that fits within a 40-foot cube and is within range, and choose one of the following effects.

Transmute Rock to Mud. Nonmagical rock of any sort in the area becomes an equal volume of thick, flowing mud that remains for the spell's duration.

The ground in the spell's area becomes muddy enough that creatures can sink into it. Each foot that a creature moves through the mud costs 4 feet of movement, and any creature on the ground when you cast the spell must make a Strength saving throw. A creature must also make the saving throw when it moves into the area for the first time on a turn or ends its turn there. On a failed save, a creature sinks into the mud and is restrained, though it can use an action to end the restrained condition on itself by pulling itself free of the mud.

If you cast the spell on a ceiling, the mud falls. Any creature under the mud when it falls must make a Dexterity saving throw. A creature takes 4d8 bludgeoning damage on a failed save, or half as much damage on a successful one.

Transmute Mud to Rock. Nonmagical mud or quicksand in the area no more than 10 feet deep transforms into soft stone for the spell's duration. Any creature in the mud when it transforms must make a Dexterity saving throw. On a successful save, a creature is shunted safely to the surface in an unoccupied space. On a failed save, a creature becomes restrained by the rock. A restrained creature, or another creature within reach, can use an action to try to break the rock by succeeding on a DC 20 Strength check or by dealing damage to it. The rock has AC 15 and 25 hit points, and it is immune to poison and psychic damage.

VITRIOLIC SPHERE

4th-level evocation

Casting Time: 1 action
Range: 150 feet
Components: V, S, M (a drop of giant slug bile)
Duration: Instantaneous

You point at a location within range, and a glowing, 1-foot-diameter ball of emerald acid streaks there and explodes in a 20-foot-radius sphere. Each creature in that area must make a Dexterity saving throw. On a failed save, a creature takes 10d4 acid damage and another 5d4 acid damage at the end of its next turn. On a successful save, a creature takes half the initial damage and no damage at the end of its next turn.

At Higher Levels. When you cast this spell using a spell slot of 5th level or higher, the initial damage increases by 2d4 for each slot level above 4th.

WALL OF LIGHT

5th-level evocation

Casting Time: 1 action
Range: 120 feet
Components: V, S, M (a hand mirror)
Duration: Concentration, up to 10 minutes

A shimmering wall of bright light appears at a point you choose within range. The wall appears in any orientation you choose: horizontally, vertically, or diagonally. It can be free floating, or it can rest on a solid surface. The wall can be up to 60 feet long, 10 feet high, and 5 feet thick. The wall blocks line of sight, but creatures and objects can pass through it. It emits bright light out to 120 feet and dim light for an additional 120 feet.

When the wall appears, each creature in its area must make a Constitution saving throw. On a failed save, a creature takes 4d8 radiant damage, and it is blinded for 1 minute. On a successful save, it takes half as much damage and isn't blinded. A blinded creature can make a Constitution saving throw at the end of each of its turns, ending the effect on itself on a success.

A creature that ends its turn in the wall's area takes 4d8 radiant damage.

Until the spell ends, you can use an action to launch a beam of radiance from the wall at one creature you can see within 60 feet of it. Make a ranged spell attack. On a hit, the target takes 4d8 radiant damage. Whether you hit or miss, reduce the length of the wall by 10 feet. If the wall's length drops to 0 feet, the spell ends.

At Higher Levels. When you cast this spell using a spell slot of 6th level or higher, the damage increases by 1d8 for each slot level above 5th.

WALL OF SAND

3rd-level evocation

Casting Time: 1 action
Range: 90 feet
Components: V, S, M (a handful of sand)
Duration: Concentration, up to 10 minutes

You create a wall of swirling sand on the ground at a point you can see within range. You can make the wall up to 30 feet long, 10 feet high, and 10 feet thick, and it vanishes when the spell ends. It blocks line of sight but not movement. A creature is blinded while in the wall's space and must spend 3 feet of movement for every 1 foot it moves there.

WALL OF WATER

3rd-level evocation

Casting Time: 1 action
Range: 60 feet
Components: V, S, M (a drop of water)
Duration: Concentration, up to 10 minutes

You create a wall of water on the ground at a point you can see within range. You can make the wall up to 30 feet long, 10 feet high, and 1 foot thick, or you can make a ringed wall up to 20 feet in diameter, 20 feet high, and 1 foot thick. The wall vanishes when the spell ends. The wall's space is difficult terrain.

Any ranged weapon attack that enters the wall's space has disadvantage on the attack roll, and fire damage is halved if the fire effect passes through the wall to reach its target. Spells that deal cold damage that pass through the wall cause the area of the wall they pass through to freeze solid (at least a 5-foot-square section is frozen). Each 5-foot-square frozen section has AC 5 and 15 hit points. Reducing a frozen section to 0 hit points destroys it. When a section is destroyed, the wall's water doesn't fill it.

WARDING WIND

2nd-level evocation

Casting Time: 1 action
Range: Self
Components: V
Duration: Concentration, up to 10 minutes

A strong wind (20 miles per hour) blows around you in a 10-foot radius and moves with you, remaining centered on you. The wind lasts for the spell's duration.

The wind has the following effects:

- It deafens you and other creatures in its area.
- It extinguishes unprotected flames in its area that are torch-sized or smaller.
- It hedges out vapor, gas, and fog that can be dispersed by strong wind.
- The area is difficult terrain for creatures other than you.
- The attack rolls of ranged weapon attacks have disadvantage if the attacks pass in or out of the wind.

WATERY SPHERE

4th-level conjuration

Casting Time: 1 action
Range: 90 feet
Components: V, S, M (a droplet of water)
Duration: Concentration, up to 1 minute

You conjure up a sphere of water with a 5-foot radius at a point you can see within range. The sphere can hover but no more than 10 feet off the ground. The sphere remains for the spell's duration.

Any creature in the sphere's space must make a Strength saving throw. On a successful save, a creature is ejected from that space to the nearest unoccupied space of the creature's choice outside the sphere. A Huge or larger creature succeeds on the saving throw automatically, and a Large or smaller creature can choose to fail it. On a failed save, a creature is restrained by the sphere and is engulfed by the water. At the end of each of its turns, a restrained target can repeat the saving throw, ending the effect on itself on a success.

The sphere can restrain as many as four Medium or smaller creatures or one Large creature. If the sphere restrains a creature that causes it to exceed this capacity, a random creature that was already restrained by the sphere falls out of it and lands prone in a space within 5 feet of it.

As an action, you can move the sphere up to 30 feet in a straight line. If it moves over a pit, a cliff, or other drop-off, it safely descends until it is hovering 10 feet above the ground. Any creature restrained by the sphere moves with it. You can ram the sphere into creatures, forcing them to make the saving throw.

When the spell ends, the sphere falls to the ground and extinguishes all normal flames within 30 feet of it. Any creature restrained by the sphere is knocked prone in the space where it falls. The water then vanishes.

WHIRLWIND
7th-level evocation

Casting Time: 1 action
Range: 300 feet
Components: V, M (a piece of straw)
Duration: Concentration, up to 1 minute

A whirlwind howls down to a point that you can see on the ground within range. The whirlwind is a 10-foot-radius, 30-foot-high cylinder centered on that point. Until the spell ends, you can use your action to move the whirlwind up to 30 feet in any direction along the ground. The whirlwind sucks up any Medium or smaller objects that aren't secured to anything and that aren't worn or carried by anyone.

A creature must make a Dexterity saving throw the first time on a turn that it enters the whirlwind or that the whirlwind enters its space, including when the whirlwind first appears. A creature takes 10d6 bludgeoning damage on a failed save, or half as much damage on a successful one. In addition, a Large or smaller creature that fails the save must succeed on a Strength saving throw or become restrained in the whirlwind until the spell ends. When a creature starts its turn restrained by the whirlwind, the creature is pulled 5 feet higher inside it, unless the creature is at the top. A restrained creature moves with the whirlwind and falls when the spell ends, unless the creature has some means to stay aloft.

A restrained creature can use an action to make a Strength or Dexterity check against your spell save DC. If successful, the creature is no longer restrained by the whirlwind and is hurled 3d6 × 10 feet away from it in a random direction.

WORD OF RADIANCE
Evocation cantrip

Casting Time: 1 action
Range: 5 feet
Components: V, M (a holy symbol)
Duration: Instantaneous

You utter a divine word, and burning radiance erupts from you. Each creature of your choice that you can see within range must succeed on a Constitution saving throw or take 1d6 radiant damage.

The spell's damage increases by 1d6 when you reach 5th level (2d6), 11th level (3d6), and 17th level (4d6).

WRATH OF NATURE
5th-level evocation

Casting Time: 1 action
Range: 120 feet
Components: V, S
Duration: Concentration, up to 1 minute

You call out to the spirits of nature to rouse them against your enemies. Choose a point you can see within range. The spirits cause trees, rocks, and grasses in a 60-foot cube centered on that point to become animated until the spell ends.

Grasses and Undergrowth. Any area of ground in the cube that is covered by grass or undergrowth is difficult terrain for your enemies.

Trees. At the start of each of your turns, each of your enemies within 10 feet of any tree in the cube must succeed on a Dexterity saving throw or take 4d6 slashing damage from whipping branches.

Roots and Vines. At the end of each of your turns, one creature of your choice that is on the ground in the cube must succeed on a Strength saving throw or become restrained until the spell ends. A restrained creature can use an action to make a Strength (Athletics) check against your spell save DC, ending the effect on itself on a success.

Rocks. As a bonus action on your turn, you can cause a loose rock in the cube to launch at a creature you can see in the cube. Make a ranged spell attack against the target. On a hit, the target takes 3d8 nonmagical bludgeoning damage, and it must succeed on a Strength saving throw or fall prone.

ZEPHYR STRIKE
1st-level transmutation

Casting Time: 1 bonus action
Range: Self
Components: V
Duration: Concentration, up to 1 minute

You move like the wind. Until the spell ends, your movement doesn't provoke opportunity attacks.

Once before the spell ends, you can give yourself advantage on one weapon attack roll on your turn. That attack deals an extra 1d8 force damage on a hit. Whether you hit or miss, your walking speed increases by 30 feet until the end of that turn.

Appendix A: Shared Campaigns

Coordinating a regular schedule of D&D game sessions, to keep a campaign active and vibrant, can be a challenge. If the campaign's only Dungeon Master or enough players aren't available, the next session might have to be postponed, and repeated problems of this sort can endanger the continuation of the campaign.

In short: in a world filled with distractions, it can be hard to keep a campaign going. Enter the concept of the shared campaign.

In a shared campaign, more than one member of the group can take on the role of DM. A shared campaign is episodic rather than continuous, with each play session comprising a complete adventure.

The largest shared campaigns are administered by the D&D Adventurers League and overseen by Wizards of the Coast. You can also create your own shared campaign for a school D&D club, at a game store, a library, or anywhere else where D&D players and DMs gather.

A shared campaign establishes a framework that allows a player to take a character from one DM's game to another one within the shared campaign. It creates a situation where almost nothing can prevent a scheduled session from happening. The roster of potential players can be quite large, virtually ensuring that any session has at least the minimum number of characters needed to play. If everyone shows up to play at the same time, multiple DMs ensure that everyone can take part.

In order to be successful, a shared campaign needs a champion—someone who takes on the responsibility of organizing and maintaining the group. If you're interested in learning more about how to run a shared campaign and seeing how the Adventurers League handles certain issues, then the rest of this appendix is meant for you.

Designing Adventures

Designing adventures for a shared campaign involves a different set of considerations than designing for a standard group of players. Most important, the adventure must be timed to conclude when the session is scheduled to end. You also need to balance combat encounters for a range of levels, since a wide range of characters might be experiencing the adventure at the same time.

Adventure Duration

Every adventure in a shared campaign begins and ends in the same play session. (If a group of participants wants to take longer to finish and all are willing to do so, they can exceed the time limit.) A session or an event can't end with the adventure unfinished, since there's no way to guarantee that the same players and DM will be available for the next session.

Typically, adventures in a shared campaign are designed to take either 2 hours or 4 hours. In each hour of play, assume the characters can complete the following:

- Three or four simple combat encounters, or one or two complex ones
- Three or four scenes involving significant exploration or social interaction

Within these constraints, it can be difficult to create open-ended adventures. A time limit assumes a specific starting point and endpoint. A good way to get around this restriction is to create an adventure with multiple possible endings.

Location-based adventures also work well with this format. A dungeon presents a natural limit on character options, while still giving the players choices. The adventure could be a quest to defeat a creature or recover an item, but the path to achieving that goal can be different for each group.

For more narrative adventures, try to focus on simple but flexible encounters or events. For instance, an adventure requires the characters to protect a high priest of Tyr from assassins. Give the players a chance to plan out how they want to protect the temple, complete with authority over the guards. A few well-fleshed out NPCs, some of whom might be suspected of working with the temple's enemies, add a layer of tension. Consider leaving some details or plot points for the DM to decide. For example, the DM might have the option to pick which member of the temple guards is the traitor, ensuring that the scenario is different for each group.

CODE OF CONDUCT

Time and time again, the core rulebooks come back to the point that the most important goal of a D&D play session is for everyone involved to have fun. In keeping with that goal, it's a good idea for a shared campaign to have a code of conduct. Because people who don't normally play together might end up at the same table in a shared campaign, it can be helpful to establish some ground rules for behavior.

On the broadest level, everyone in a shared campaign is responsible for making sure that everyone else has an enjoyable time. If anyone feels offended, belittled, or bullied by the actions of another person, the entire purpose of getting together to play is defeated.

The basic code of conduct for a shared campaign might be modeled on a similar document that another organization or location uses. Beyond that, some special policies might need to be added to account for what might happen at the table when players and DMs interact. As a starting point, consider the following material, which is excerpted from the Adventurers League code of conduct.

During a play session, participants are expected to ...

- Follow the DM's lead and refrain from arguing with the DM or other players over rules.
- Let other players speak, and allow other players to get attention from the DM.
- Avoid excessive conversation that is not relevant to the adventure.
- Discourage others from using social media to bully, shame, or intimidate other participants.
- Make the DM or the campaign's administrators aware of disruptive or aggressive behavior so that appropriate action can be taken.

COMBAT ENCOUNTERS

Design your adventure for one of the four tiers, as set forth in chapter 1 of the *Player's Handbook*: tier 1 includes levels 1–4, tier 2 is levels 5–10, tier 3 is levels 11–16, and tier 4 includes levels 17–20. Within each tier, it's a good idea to use a specific level as a starting point. Assume a party of five 3rd-level characters for tier 1, five 8th-level characters for tier 2, five 13th-level characters for tier 3, and five 18th-level characters for tier 4. Use that assumption when creating combat encounters, whether you use the encounter-building rules in the *Dungeon Master's Guide* or are making an estimate.

For each battle, provide guidelines to help DMs adjust the difficulty up or down to match stronger or weaker parties. As a rule of thumb, account for a party two levels higher and for a party two levels lower, and don't worry about balancing the adventure for parties outside the adventure's tier.

REWARDS

Adventures in a shared campaign that uses variant rules for gaining levels and acquiring treasure (such as those described below) don't include experience point awards or specific amounts and kinds of treasure.

CHARACTER CREATION

A shared campaign's guidelines for character creation might include definition of which races and classes players can choose from, how players generate ability scores, and which alignments players can choose.

PLAYER'S HANDBOOK PLUS ONE

You should think about which products players can use to create a character. The Adventurers League specifies that a player can use the *Player's Handbook* and one other official D&D source, such as a book or a PDF, to create a character. This restriction ensures that players don't need to own a lot of books to make a character and makes it easier for DMs to know how all the characters in the campaign work. Since a DM in a shared campaign must deal with a broad range of characters, rather than the same characters each week, it can be difficult to track all the interactions and abilities possible through mixing options freely. We strongly recommend this rule for any shared campaign.

ABILITY SCORES

For generating ability scores, we recommend allowing players to choose between the standard array—15, 14, 13, 12, 10, 8—and the option presented in "Variant: Customizing Ability Scores" in chapter 1 of the *Player's Handbook*.

STARTING EQUIPMENT

For the sake of simplicity and efficiency, it's a good idea to require that beginning characters must take the starting equipment specified by a character's class and background.

VARIANT RULES

A shared campaign might use some variant rules to handle certain aspects of the game. The Adventurers League, for instance, has variant systems for gaining levels and acquiring treasure. These "house rules," presented below, serve as a sort of common language, ensuring that the rewards all characters receive are equivalent no matter what kind of adventure a character experienced.

CHARACTER ADVANCEMENT

In a shared campaign, characters gain levels not by accumulating experience points but by reaching experience checkpoints. This system rewards every character (and player) for taking part in a play session.

A character reaches 1 checkpoint for each hour an adventure is designed to last. Note that the award is based on the adventure's projected playing time, rather than the actual time spent at the table. The reward for completing an adventure designed for 2 hours of play is 2 checkpoints, even if a group spends more than 2 hours playing through it.

If a character completes an adventure designed for a tier higher than the character's current tier, the character is awarded 1 additional checkpoint. For example, if a 2nd-level character completes a 6th-level adventure designed to take 2 hours, the character reaches 3 checkpoints.

Playing time might seem like an odd way to measure experience awards, but the concept is in keeping with how a shared campaign is meant to work. A character played for 10 hours reaches the same number of checkpoints, whether the character went up against a dragon or spent all that time lurking in a pub. This approach ensures that a player's preferred style is neither penalized nor rewarded. Whether someone focuses on roleplaying and social interaction, defeating monsters in combat, or finding clever ways to avoid battles, this system gives credit where credit is due.

USING CHECKPOINTS

The number of checkpoints needed to gain the next level depends on a character's level:

- At levels 1–4, reaching 4 checkpoints is sufficient to advance to the next level.
- At level 5 or higher, reaching 8 checkpoints is needed to advance to the next level.

At the end of a play session, characters must level up if they have reached enough checkpoints to do so. The required number of checkpoints is expended, and any remaining checkpoints are applied toward the next opportunity for advancement.

INDIVIDUAL TREASURE

In a shared campaign, each character receives a fixed number of gold pieces upon gaining a new level. (This gain represents the treasure a character might find in a standard adventure.)

As an additional benefit, characters are not required to put out gold to maintain a lifestyle. Instead, each character begins with a modest lifestyle, which improves as the character attains higher levels.

These benefits are summarized on the Individual Treasure table. Ways for characters to spend their treasure are covered in the "Buying and Selling" section below.

INDIVIDUAL TREASURE

Level Gained	Lifestyle	Reward
2–4	Modest	75 gp
5–10	Comfortable	150 gp
11–16	Wealthy	550 gp
17–20	Aristocratic	5,500 gp

MAGIC ITEMS

Characters earn treasure points from adventures, then redeem those points in exchange for magic items. The list of available magic items is agreed to and compiled by the DMs running the campaign.

GAINING TREASURE POINTS

Each character earns treasure points based on an adventure's tier and its intended playing time:

- 1 treasure point is awarded for every 2 hours played in a tier 1 or tier 2 adventure.
- 1 treasure point is awarded for every 1 hour played in a tier 3 or tier 4 adventure.

As with the variant rules for gaining levels, this award is based on the adventure's projected playing time, rather than the actual time a group spent at the table.

If a character completes an adventure of a tier higher than that character's tier, the character receives 1 additional treasure point for that adventure.

CREATING AN ITEM LIST

The DMs of the shared campaign should work together to compile a list of magic items that players can purchase. The magic item tables in chapter 2 of this book and in chapter 7 of the *Dungeon Master's Guide* are the obvious starting point. Choosing which items to allow or ban is a matter of personal preference, just as it is for the DM in a standard campaign. Involving all the DMs helps to ensure that the list meets everyone's expectations. When in doubt, disallow an item; it's easier to add it to the available items at a later time than it would be to remove it from the game once it has been handed out.

Naturally, the list of available items is longer for adventures in the higher tiers, and the point cost of those higher-tier items likewise increases. The Magic Items by Tier table provides the details.

For instance, treasure points from a tier 1 adventure can be spent on items from tables A, B, C, and F. Any item on the first three tables costs 4 points, and an item from table F costs 8 points.

MAGIC ITEMS BY TIER

Magic Item Table	Available at Tiers	Point Cost
A	1–4	4
B	1–4	4
C	1–4	4
D	2–4	8
E	3–4	8
F	1–4	8
G	2–4	10
H	3–4	10
I	3–4	12

SPENDING TREASURE POINTS

Players must spend treasure points at the end of a play session, immediately after determining whether their characters have gained a level. The order of these steps is important, since a character might enter a new tier because of the level gain.

Players are entitled to choose any approved item from one of the magic item tables available in the current tier. Treasure points can be spread across multiple items.

Many items cost more treasure points than a character can earn in a 2- or 4-hour adventure. To buy such an item, a character can make a deposit, spending treasure points on the item until it's paid off, at which time the character gains the item.

BUYING AND SELLING

Characters can use their monetary treasure to purchase anything from the equipment lists in chapter 5 of the *Player's Handbook*. In addition, the Adventurers League allows characters to purchase potions and *spell scrolls*, as detailed below. A *spell scroll* can be purchased only by a character who is capable of casting the spell in question.

POTIONS FOR SALE

Potion of ...	Cost	Potion of ...	Cost
Healing	50 gp	Water breathing	100 gp
Climbing	75 gp	Superior healing	500 gp
Animal friendship	100 gp	Supreme healing	5,000 gp
Greater healing	100 gp	Invisibility	5,000 gp

SPELL SCROLLS FOR SALE

Spell Level	Cost	Spell Level	Cost
Cantrip	25 gp	3rd	300 gp
1st	75 gp	4th	500 gp
2nd	150 gp	5th	1,000 gp

SELLING ITEMS

In a shared campaign, characters are not entitled to sell items they find on adventures or equipment they purchase with their personal funds. Weapons, armor, and other gear used by enemies are considered too damaged to have any monetary value.

Appendix B: Character Names

Some players and DMs have a knack for coming up with character names on the fly, while others find that task more of a challenge. The tables in this appendix are designed to make life easier for both kinds of people, whether you're naming a player character, a nonplayer character, a monster, or even a place.

Each table contains names that are associated with a nonhuman character race in the *Player's Handbook* or a real-world ethnic or language group, with a focus on groups from antiquity and the Middle Ages. You can select from the possibilities here, or use dice to determine a name.

Even though names are associated with races in this appendix, a character might not have a name from their own race. For instance, a half-orc might have grown up among dwarves and have a dwarven name. Or, as DM, you might decide that dragonborn in your campaign have a culture reminiscent of ancient Rome and therefore use Roman names, rather than the dragonborn names suggested here.

Nonhuman Names

Dragonborn, Female

d100	Name
01–02	Akra
03–04	Aasathra
05–06	Antrara
07–08	Arava
09–10	Biri
11–12	Blendaeth
13–14	Burana
15–16	Chassath
17–18	Daar
19–20	Dentratha
21–22	Doudra
23–24	Driindar
25–26	Eggren
27–28	Farideh
29–30	Findex
31–32	Furrele
33–34	Gesrethe
35–36	Gilkass
37–38	Harann
39–40	Havilar
41–42	Hethress
43–44	Hillanot
45–46	Jaxi
47–48	Jezean
49–50	Jheri
51–52	Kadana
53–54	Kava
55–56	Korinn
57–58	Megren
59–60	Mijira
61–62	Mishann
63–64	Nala
65–66	Nuthra
67–68	Perra

Dragonborn, Female

d100	Name
69–70	Pogranix
71–72	Pyxrin
73–74	Quespa
75–76	Raiann
77–78	Rezena
79–80	Ruloth
81–82	Saphara
83–84	Savaran
85–86	Sora
87–88	Surina
89–90	Synthrin
91–92	Tatyan
93–94	Thava
95–96	Uadjit
97–98	Vezera
99–00	Zykroff

Dragonborn, Male

d100	Name
01–02	Adrex
03–04	Arjhan
05–06	Azzakh
07–08	Balasar
09–10	Baradad
11–12	Bharash
13–14	Bidreked
15–16	Dadalan
17–18	Dazzazn
19–20	Direcris
21–22	Donaar
23–24	Fax
25–26	Gargax
27–28	Ghesh
29–30	Gorbundus

Dragonborn, Male

d100	Name
31–32	Greethen
33–34	Heskan
35–36	Hirrathak
37–38	Ildrex
39–40	Kaladan
41–42	Kerkad
43–44	Kiirith
45–46	Kriv
47–48	Maagog
49–50	Medrash
51–52	Mehen
53–54	Mozikth
55–56	Mreksh
57–58	Mugrunden
59–60	Nadarr
61–62	Nithther
63–64	Norkruuth
65–66	Nykkan
67–68	Pandjed
69–70	Patrin
71–72	Pijjirik
73–74	Quarethon
75–76	Rathkran
77–78	Rhogar
79–80	Rivaan
81–82	Sethrekar
83–84	Shamash
85–86	Shedinn
87–88	Srorthen
89–90	Tarhun
91–92	Torinn
93–94	Trynnicus
95–96	Valorean
97–98	Vrondiss
99–00	Zedaar

Dragonborn, Clan

d100	Name
01–02	Akambherylliax
03–04	Argenthrixus
05–06	Baharoosh
07–08	Beryntolthropal
09–10	Bhenkumbyrznaax
11–12	Caavylteradyn
13–14	Chumbyxirinnish
15–16	Clethtinthiallor
17–18	Daardendrian
19–20	Delmirev
21–22	Dhyrktelonis
23–24	Ebynichtomonis
25–26	Esstyrlynn
27–28	Fharngnarthnost
29–30	Ghaallixirn
31–32	Grrrmmballhyst
33–34	Gygazzylyshrift
35–36	Hashphronyxadyn
37–38	Hshhsstoroth
39–40	Imbixtellrhyst
41–42	Jerynomonis
43–44	Jharthraxyn
45–46	Kerrhylon
47–48	Kimbatuul
49–50	Lhamboldennish
51–52	Linxakasendalor
53–54	Mohradyllion
55–56	Mystan
57–58	Nemmonis
59–60	Norixius
61–62	Ophinshtalajiir
63–64	Orexijandilin
65–66	Pfaphnyrennish
67–68	Phrahdrandon
69–70	Pyraxtallinost
71–72	Qyxpahrgh

DRAGONBORN, CLAN

d100	Name
73–74	Raghthroknaar
75–76	Shestendeliath
77–78	Skaarzborroosh
79–80	Sumnarghthrysh
81–82	Tiammanthyllish
83–84	Turnuroth
85–86	Umbyrphrael
87–88	Vangdondalor
89–90	Verthisathurgiesh
91–92	Wivvyrholdalphiax
93–94	Wystongjiir
95–96	Xephyrbahnor
97–98	Yarjerit
99–00	Zzzxaaxthroth

DWARF, FEMALE

d100	Name
01–02	Anbera
03–04	Artin
05–06	Audhild
07–08	Balifra
09–10	Barbena
11–12	Bardryn
13–14	Bolhild
15–16	Dagnal
17–18	Dariff
19–20	Delre
21–22	Diesa
23–24	Eldeth
25–26	Eridred
27–28	Falkrunn
29–30	Fallthra
31–32	Finellen
33–34	Gillydd
35–36	Gunnloda
37–38	Gurdis
39–40	Helgret
41–42	Helja
43–44	Hlin
45–46	Ilde
47–48	Jarana
49–50	Kathra
51–52	Kilia
53–54	Kristryd
55–56	Liftrasa
57–58	Marastyr
59–60	Mardred
61–62	Morana
63–64	Nalaed
65–66	Nora
67–68	Nurkara

DWARF, FEMALE

d100	Name
69–70	Oriff
71–72	Ovina
73–74	Riswynn
75–76	Sannl
77–78	Therlin
79–80	Thodris
81–82	Torbera
83–84	Tordrid
85–86	Torgga
87–88	Urshar
89–90	Valida
91–92	Vistra
93–94	Vonana
95–96	Werydd
97–98	Whurdred
99–00	Yurgunn

DWARF, MALE

d100	Name
01–02	Adrik
03–04	Alberich
05–06	Baern
07–08	Barendd
09–10	Beloril
11–12	Brottor
13–14	Dain
15–16	Dalgal
17–18	Darrak
19–20	Delg
21–22	Duergath
23–24	Dworic
25–26	Eberk
27–28	Einkil
29–30	Elaim
31–32	Erias
33–34	Fallond
35–36	Fargrim
37–38	Gardain
39–40	Gilthur
41–42	Gimgen
43–44	Gimurt
45–46	Harbek
47–48	Kildrak
49–50	Kilvar
51–52	Morgran
53–54	Morkral
55–56	Nalral
57–58	Nordak
59–60	Nuraval
61–62	Oloric
63–64	Olunt

DWARF, MALE

d100	Name
65–66	Orsik
67–68	Oskar
69–70	Rangrim
71–72	Reirak
73–74	Rurik
75–76	Taklinn
77–78	Thoradin
79–80	Thorin
81–82	Thradal
83–84	Tordek
85–86	Traubon
87–88	Travok
89–90	Ulfgar
91–92	Uraim
93–94	Veit
95–96	Vonbin
97–98	Vondal
99–00	Whurbin

DWARF, CLAN

d100	Name
01–02	Aranore
03–04	Balderk
05–06	Battlehammer
07–08	Bigtoe
09–10	Bloodkith
11–12	Bofdann
13–14	Brawnanvil
15–16	Brazzik
17–18	Broodfist
19–20	Burrowfound
21–22	Caebrek
23–24	Daerdahk
25–26	Dankil
27–28	Daraln
29–30	Deepdelver
31–32	Durthane
33–34	Eversharp
35–36	Fallack
37–38	Fireforge
39–40	Foamtankard
41–42	Frostbeard
43–44	Glanhig
45–46	Goblinbane
47–48	Goldfinder
49–50	Gorunn
51–52	Graybeard
53–54	Hammerstone
55–56	Helcral
57–58	Holderhek
59–60	Ironfist

DWARF, CLAN

d100	Name
61–62	Loderr
63–64	Lutgehr
65–66	Morigak
67–68	Orcfoe
69–70	Rakankrak
71–72	Ruby-Eye
73–74	Rumnaheim
75–76	Silveraxe
77–78	Silverstone
79–80	Steelfist
81–82	Stoutale
83–84	Strakeln
85–86	Strongheart
87–88	Thrahak
89–90	Torevir
91–92	Torunn
93–94	Trollbleeder
95–96	Trueanvil
97–98	Trueblood
99–00	Ungart

ELF, CHILD

d100	Name
01–02	Ael
03–04	Ang
05–06	Ara
07–08	Ari
09–10	Arn
11–12	Aym
13–14	Broe
15–16	Bryn
17–18	Cael
19–20	Cy
21–22	Dae
23–24	Del
25–26	Eli
27–28	Eryn
29–30	Faen
31–32	Fera
33–34	Gael
35–36	Gar
37–38	Innil
39–40	Jar
41–42	Kan
43–44	Koeth
45–46	Lael
47–48	Lue
49–50	Mai
51–52	Mara
53–54	Mella
55–56	Mya

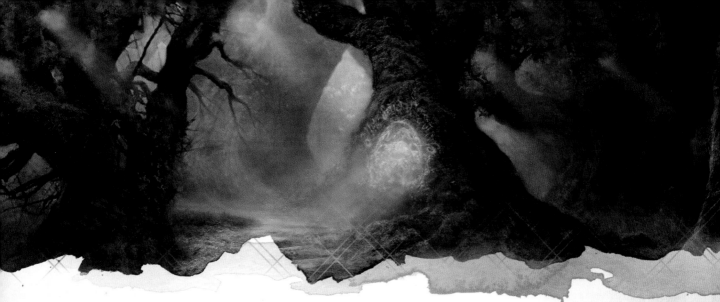

ELF, CHILD

d100	Name
57–58	Naeris
59–60	Naill
61–62	Nim
63–64	Phann
65–66	Py
67–68	Rael
69–70	Raer
71–72	Ren
73–74	Rinn
75–76	Rua
77–78	Sael
79–80	Sai
81–82	Sumi
83–84	Syllin
85–86	Ta
87–88	Thia
89–90	Tia
91–92	Traki
93–94	Vall
95–96	Von
97–98	Wil
99–00	Za

ELF, FEMALE ADULT

d100	Name
01–02	Adrie
03–04	Ahinar
05–06	Althaea
07–08	Anastrianna
09–10	Andraste
11–12	Antinua
13–14	Arara
15–16	Baelitae
17–18	Bethrynna
19–20	Birel

ELF, FEMALE ADULT

d100	Name
21–22	Caelynn
23–24	Chaedi
25–26	Claira
27–28	Dara
29–30	Drusilia
31–32	Elama
33–34	Enna
35–36	Faral
37–38	Felosial
39–40	Hatae
41–42	Ielenia
43–44	Ilanis
45–46	Irann
47–48	Jarsali
49–50	Jelenneth
51–52	Keyleth
53–54	Leshanna
55–56	Lia
57–58	Maiathah
59–60	Malquis
61–62	Meriele
63–64	Mialee
65–66	Myathethil
67–68	Naivara
69–70	Quelenna
71–72	Quillathe
73–74	Ridaro
75–76	Sariel
77–78	Shanairla
79–80	Shava
81–82	Silaqui
83–84	Sumnes
85–86	Theirastra
87–88	Thiala
89–90	Tiaathque
91–92	Traulam

ELF, FEMALE ADULT

d100	Name
93–94	Vadania
95–96	Valanthe
97–98	Valna
99–00	Xanaphia

ELF, MALE ADULT

d100	Name
01–02	Adran
03–04	Aelar
05–06	Aerdeth
07–08	Ahvain
09–10	Aramil
11–12	Arannis
13–14	Aust
15–16	Azaki
17–18	Beiro
19–20	Berrian
21–22	Caeldrim
23–24	Carric
25–26	Dayereth
27–28	Dreali
29–30	Efferil
31–32	Eiravel
33–34	Enialis
35–36	Erdan
37–38	Erevan
39–40	Fivin
41–42	Galinndan
43–44	Gennal
45–46	Hadarai
47–48	Halimath
49–50	Heian
51–52	Himo
53–54	Immeral
55–56	Ivellios

ELF, MALE ADULT

d100	Name
57–58	Korfel
59–60	Lamlis
61–62	Laucian
63–64	Lucan
65–66	Mindartis
67–68	Naal
69–70	Nutae
71–72	Paelias
73–74	Peren
75–76	Quarion
77–78	Riardon
79–80	Rolen
81–82	Soveliss
83–84	Suhnae
85–86	Thamior
87–88	Tharivol
89–90	Theren
91–92	Theriatis
93–94	Thervan
95–96	Uthemar
97–98	Vanuath
99–00	Varis

ELF, FAMILY

d100	Name
01–02	Aloro
03–04	Amakiir
05–06	Amastacia
07–08	Ariessus
09–10	Arnuanna
11–12	Berevan
13–14	Caerdonel
15–16	Caphaxath
17–18	Casilltenirra
19–20	Cithreth

ELF, FAMILY

d100	Name
21–22	Dalanthan
23–24	Eathalena
25–26	Erenaeth
27–28	Ethanasath
29–30	Fasharash
31–32	Firahel
33–34	Floshem
35–36	Galanodel
37–38	Goltorah
39–40	Hanali
41–42	Holimion
43–44	Horineth
45–46	Iathrana
47–48	Ilphelkiir
49–50	Iranapha
51–52	Koehlanna
53–54	Lathalas
55–56	Liadon
57–58	Meliamne
59–60	Mellerelel
61–62	Mystralath
63–64	Naïlo
65–66	Netyoive
67–68	Ofandrus
69–70	Ostoroth
71–72	Othronus
73–74	Qualanthri
75–76	Raethran
77–78	Rothenel
79–80	Selevarun
81–82	Siannodel
83–84	Suithrasas
85–86	Sylvaranth
87–88	Teinithra
89–90	Tiltathana
91–92	Wasanthi
93–94	Withrethin
95–96	Xiloscient
97–98	Xistsrith
99–00	Yaeldrin

GNOME, FEMALE

d100	Name
01–02	Abalaba
03–04	Bimpnottin
05–06	Breena
07–08	Buvvie
09–10	Callybon
11–12	Caramip
13–14	Carlin
15–16	Cumpen
17–18	Dalaba
19–20	Donella
21–22	Duvamil
23–24	Ella
25–26	Ellyjoybell
27–28	Ellywick
29–30	Enidda
31–32	Lilli
33–34	Loopmottin
35–36	Lorilla
37–38	Luthra
39–40	Mardnab
41–42	Meena
43–44	Menny
45–46	Mumpena
47–48	Nissa
49–50	Numba
51–52	Nyx
53–54	Oda
55–56	Oppah
57–58	Orla
59–60	Panana
61–62	Pyntle
63–64	Quilla
65–66	Ranala
67–68	Reddlepop
69–70	Roywyn
71–72	Salanop
73–74	Shamil
75–76	Siffress
77–78	Symma
79–80	Tana
81–82	Tenena
83–84	Tervaround
85–86	Tippletoe
87–88	Ulla
89–90	Unvera
91–92	Veloptima
93–94	Virra
95–96	Waywocket
97–98	Yebe
99–00	Zanna

GNOME, MALE

d100	Name
01–02	Alston
03–04	Alvyn
05–06	Anverth
07–08	Arumawann
09–10	Bilbron
11–12	Boddynock
13–14	Brocc
15–16	Burgell
17–18	Cockaby
19–20	Crampernap
21–22	Dabbledob
23–24	Delebean
25–26	Dimble
27–28	Eberdeb
29–30	Eldon
31–32	Erky
33–34	Fablen
35–36	Fibblestib
37–38	Fonkin
39–40	Frouse
41–42	Frug
43–44	Gerbo
45–46	Gimble
47–48	Glim
49–50	Igden
51–52	Jabble
53–54	Jebeddo
55–56	Kellen
57–58	Kipper
59–60	Namfoodle
61–62	Oppleby
63–64	Orryn
65–66	Paggen
67–68	Pallabar
69–70	Pog
71–72	Qualen
73–74	Ribbles
75–76	Rimple
77–78	Roondar
79–80	Sapply
81–82	Seebo
83–84	Senteq
85–86	Sindri
87–88	Umpen
89–90	Warryn
91–92	Wiggens
93–94	Wobbles
95–96	Wrenn
97–98	Zaffrab
99–00	Zook

GNOME, CLAN

d100	Name
01–02	Albaratie
03–04	Bafflestone
05–06	Beren
07–08	Boondiggles
09–10	Cobblelob
11–12	Daergel
13–14	Dunben
15–16	Fabblestabble
17–18	Fapplestamp
19–20	Fiddlefen
21–22	Folkor
23–24	Garrick
25–26	Gimlen
27–28	Glittergem
29–30	Gobblefirn
31–32	Gummen
33–34	Horcusporcus
35–36	Humplebumple
37–38	Ironhide
39–40	Leffery
41–42	Lingenhall
43–44	Loofollue
45–46	Maekkelferce
47–48	Miggledy
49–50	Munggen
51–52	Murnig
53–54	Musgraben
55–56	Nackle
57–58	Ningel
59–60	Nopenstallen
61–62	Nucklestamp
63–64	Offund
65–66	Oomtrowl
67–68	Pilwicken
69–70	Pingun
71–72	Quillsharpener
73–74	Raulnor
75–76	Reese
77–78	Rofferton
79–80	Scheppen
81–82	Shadowcloak
83–84	Silverthread
85–86	Sympony
87–88	Tarkelby
89–90	Timbers
91–92	Turen
93–94	Umbodoben
95–96	Waggletop
97–98	Welber
99–00	Wildwander

APPENDIX B | CHARACTER NAMES

HALFLING, FEMALE

d100	Name
01–02	Alain
03–04	Andry
05–06	Anne
07–08	Bella
09–10	Blossom
11–12	Bree
13–14	Callie
15–16	Chenna
17–18	Cora
19–20	Dee
21–22	Dell
23–24	Eida
25–26	Eran
27–28	Euphemia
29–30	Georgina
31–32	Gynnie
33–34	Harriet
35–36	Jasmine
37–38	Jillian
39–40	Jo
41–42	Kithri
43–44	Lavinia
45–46	Lidda
47–48	Maegan
49–50	Marigold
51–52	Merla
53–54	Myria
55–56	Nedda
57–58	Nikki
59–60	Nora
61–62	Olivia
63–64	Paela
65–66	Pearl
67–68	Pennie
69–70	Philomena
71–72	Portia
73–74	Robbie
75–76	Rose
77–78	Saral
79–80	Seraphina
81–82	Shaena
83–84	Stacee
85–86	Tawna
87–88	Thea
89–90	Trym
91–92	Tyna
93–94	Vani
95–96	Verna
97–98	Wella
99–00	Willow

HALFLING, MALE

d100	Name
01–02	Alton
03–04	Ander
05–06	Bernie
07–08	Bobbin
09–10	Cade
11–12	Callus
13–14	Corrin
15–16	Dannad
17–18	Danniel
19–20	Eddie
21–22	Egart
23–24	Eldon
25–26	Errich
27–28	Fildo
29–30	Finnan
31–32	Franklin
33–34	Garret
35–36	Garth
37–38	Gilbert
39–40	Gob
41–42	Harol
43–44	Igor
45–46	Jasper
47–48	Keith
49–50	Kevin
51–52	Lazam
53–54	Lerry
55–56	Lindal
57–58	Lyle
59–60	Merric
61–62	Mican
63–64	Milo
65–66	Morrin
67–68	Nebin
69–70	Nevil
71–72	Osborn
73–74	Ostran
75–76	Oswalt
77–78	Perrin
79–80	Poppy
81–82	Reed
83–84	Roscoe
85–86	Sam
87–88	Shardon
89–90	Tye
91–92	Ulmo
93–94	Wellby
95–96	Wendel
97–98	Wenner
99–00	Wes

HALFLING, FAMILY

d100	Name
01–02	Appleblossom
03–04	Bigheart
05–06	Brightmoon
07–08	Brushgather
09–10	Cherrycheeks
11–12	Copperkettle
13–14	Deephollow
15–16	Elderberry
17–18	Fastfoot
19–20	Fatrabbit
21–22	Glenfellow
23–24	Goldfound
25–26	Goodbarrel
27–28	Goodearth
29–30	Greenbottle
31–32	Greenleaf
33–34	High-hill
35–36	Hilltopple
37–38	Hogcollar
39–40	Honeypot
41–42	Jamjar
43–44	Kettlewhistle
45–46	Leagallow
47–48	Littlefoot
49–50	Nimblefingers
51–52	Porridgepot
53–54	Quickstep
55–56	Reedfellow
57–58	Shadowquick
59–60	Silvereyes
61–62	Smoothhands
63–64	Stonebridge
65–66	Stoutbridge
67–68	Stoutman
69–70	Strongbones
71–72	Sunmeadow
73–74	Swiftwhistle
75–76	Tallfellow
77–78	Tealeaf
79–80	Tenpenny
81–82	Thistletop
83–84	Thorngage
85–86	Tosscobble
87–88	Underbough
89–90	Underfoot
91–92	Warmwater
93–94	Whispermouse
95–96	Wildcloak
97–98	Wildheart
99–00	Wiseacre

HALF-ORC, FEMALE

d100	Name
01–02	Arha
03–04	Baggi
05–06	Bendoo
07–08	Bilga
09–10	Brakka
11–12	Creega
13–14	Drenna
15–16	Ekk
17–18	Emen
19–20	Engong
21–22	Fistula
23–24	Gaaki
25–26	Gorga
27–28	Grai
29–30	Greeba
31–32	Grigi
33–34	Gynk
35–36	Hrathy
37–38	Huru
39–40	Ilga
41–42	Kabbarg
43–44	Kansif
45–46	Lagazi
47–48	Lezre
49–50	Murgen
51–52	Murook
53–54	Myev
55–56	Nagrette
57–58	Neega
59–60	Nella
61–62	Nogu
63–64	Oolah
65–66	Ootah
67–68	Ovak
69–70	Ownka
71–72	Puyet
73–74	Reeza
75–76	Shautha
77–78	Silgre
79–80	Sutha
81–82	Tagga
83–84	Tawar
85–86	Tomph
87–88	Ubada
89–90	Vanchu
91–92	Vola
93–94	Volen
95–96	Vorka
97–98	Yevelda
99–00	Zagga

HALF-ORC, MALE

d100	Name
01–02	Argran
03–04	Braak
05–06	Brug
07–08	Cagak
09–10	Dench
11–12	Dorn
13–14	Dren
15–16	Druuk
17–18	Feng
19–20	Gell
21–22	Gnarsh
23–24	Grumbar
25–26	Gubrash
27–28	Hagren
29–30	Henk
31–32	Hogar
33–34	Holg
35–36	Imsh
37–38	Karash
39–40	Karg
41–42	Keth
43–44	Korag
45–46	Krusk
47–48	Lubash
49–50	Megged
51–52	Mhurren
53–54	Mord
55–56	Morg
57–58	Nil
59–60	Nybarg
61–62	Odorr
63–64	Ohr
65–66	Rendar
67–68	Resh
69–70	Ront
71–72	Rrath
73–74	Sark
75–76	Scrag
77–78	Sheggen
79–80	Shump
81–82	Tanglar
83–84	Tarak
85–86	Thar
87–88	Thokk
89–90	Trag
91–92	Ugarth
93–94	Varg
95–96	Vilberg
97–98	Yurk
99–00	Zed

TIEFLING, FEMALE

d100	Name
01–02	Akta
03–04	Anakis
05–06	Armara
07–08	Astaro
09–10	Aym
11–12	Azza
13–14	Beleth
15–16	Bryseis
17–18	Bune
19–20	Criella
21–22	Damaia
23–24	Decarabia
25–26	Ea
27–28	Gadreel
29–30	Gomory
31–32	Hecat
33–34	Ishte
35–36	Jezebeth
37–38	Kali
39–40	Kallista
41–42	Kasdeya
43–44	Lerissa
45–46	Lilith
47–48	Makaria
49–50	Manea
51–52	Markosian
53–54	Mastema
55–56	Naamah
57–58	Nemeia
59–60	Nija
61–62	Orianna
63–64	Osah
65–66	Phelaia
67–68	Prosperine
69–70	Purah
71–72	Pyra
73–74	Rieta
75–76	Ronobe
77–78	Ronwe
79–80	Seddit
81–82	Seere
83–84	Sekhmet
85–86	Semyaza
87–88	Shava
89–90	Shax
91–92	Sorath
93–94	Uzza
95–96	Vapula
97–98	Vepar
99–00	Verin

TIEFLING, MALE

d100	Name
01–02	Abad
03–04	Ahrim
05–06	Akmen
07–08	Amnon
09–10	Andram
11–12	Astar
13–14	Balam
15–16	Barakas
17–18	Bathin
19–20	Caim
21–22	Chem
23–24	Cimer
25–26	Cressel
27–28	Damakos
29–30	Ekemon
31–32	Euron
33–34	Fenriz
35–36	Forcas
37–38	Habor
39–40	Iados
41–42	Kairon
43–44	Leucis
45–46	Mamnen
47–48	Mantus
49–50	Marbas
51–52	Melech
53–54	Merihim
55–56	Modean
57–58	Mordai
59–60	Mormo
61–62	Morthos
63–64	Nicor
65–66	Nirgel
67–68	Oriax
69–70	Paymon
71–72	Pelaios
73–74	Purson
75–76	Qemuel
77–78	Raam
79–80	Rimmon
81–82	Sammal
83–84	Skamos
85–86	Tethren
87–88	Thamuz
89–90	Therai
91–92	Valafar
93–94	Vassago
95–96	Xappan
97–98	Zepar
99–00	Zephan

TIEFLING, VIRTUE

d100	Name
01–02	Ambition
03–04	Art
05–06	Carrion
07–08	Chant
09–10	Creed
11–12	Death
13–14	Debauchery
15–16	Despair
17–18	Doom
19–20	Doubt
21–22	Dread
23–24	Ecstasy
25–26	Ennui
27–28	Entropy
29–30	Excellence
31–32	Fear
33–34	Glory
35–36	Gluttony
37–38	Grief
39–40	Hate
41–42	Hope
43–44	Horror
45–46	Ideal
47–48	Ignominy
49–50	Laughter
51–52	Love
53–54	Lust
55–56	Mayhem
57–58	Mockery
59–60	Murder
61–62	Muse
63–64	Music
65–66	Mystery
67–68	Nowhere
69–70	Open
71–72	Pain
73–74	Passion
75–76	Poetry
77–78	Quest
79–80	Random
81–82	Reverence
83–84	Revulsion
85–86	Sorrow
87–88	Temerity
89–90	Torment
91–92	Tragedy
93–94	Vice
95–96	Virtue
97–98	Weary
99–00	Wit

Human Names

Arabic, Female

d100	Name
01–02	Aaliyah
03–04	Aida
05–06	Akilah
07–08	Alia
09–10	Amina
11–12	Atefeh
13–14	Chaima
15–16	Dalia
17–18	Ehsan
19–20	Elham
21–22	Farah
23–24	Fatemah
25–26	Gamila
27–28	Iesha
29–30	Inbar
31–32	Kamaria
33–34	Khadija
35–36	Layla
37–38	Lupe
39–40	Nabila
41–42	Nadine
43–44	Naima
45–46	Najila
47–48	Najwa
49–50	Nakia
51–52	Nashwa
53–54	Nawra
55–56	Nuha
57–58	Nura
59–60	Oma
61–62	Qadira
63–64	Qamar
65–66	Qistina
67–68	Rahima
69–70	Rihanna
71–72	Saadia
73–74	Sabah
75–76	Sada
77–78	Saffron
79–80	Sahar
81–82	Salma
83–84	Shatha
85–86	Tahira
87–88	Takisha
89–90	Thana
91–92	Yadira
93–94	Zahra
95–96	Zaida
97–98	Zaina
99–00	Zeinab

Arabic, Male

d100	Name
01–02	Abbad
03–04	Abdul
05–06	Achmed
07–08	Akeem
09–10	Alif
11–12	Amir
13–14	Asim
15–16	Bashir
17–18	Bassam
19–20	Fahim
21–22	Farid
23–24	Farouk
25–26	Fayez
27–28	Fayyaad
29–30	Fazil
31–32	Hakim
33–34	Halil
35–36	Hamid
37–38	Hazim
39–40	Heydar
41–42	Hussein
43–44	Jabari
45–46	Jafar
47–48	Jahid
49–50	Jamal
51–52	Kalim
53–54	Karim
55–56	Kazim
57–58	Khadim
59–60	Khalid
61–62	Mahmud
63–64	Mansour
65–66	Musharraf
67–68	Mustafa
69–70	Nadir
71–72	Nazim
73–74	Omar
75–76	Qadir
77–78	Qusay
79–80	Rafiq
81–82	Rakim
83–84	Rashad
85–86	Rauf
87–88	Saladin
89–90	Sami
91–92	Samir
93–94	Talib
95–96	Tamir
97–98	Tariq
99–00	Yazid

CELTIC, FEMALE

d100	Name
01–02	Aife
03–04	Aina
05–06	Alane
07–08	Ardena
09–10	Arienh
11–12	Beatha
13–14	Birgit
15–16	Briann
17–18	Caomh
19–20	Cara
21–22	Cinnia
23–24	Cordelia
25–26	Deheune
27–28	Divone
29–30	Donia
31–32	Doreena
33–34	Elsha
35–36	Enid
37–38	Ethne
39–40	Evelina
41–42	Fianna
43–44	Genevieve
45–46	Gilda
47–48	Gitta
49–50	Grania
51–52	Gwyndolin
53–54	Idelisa
55–56	Isolde
57–58	Keelin
59–60	Kennocha
61–62	Lavena
63–64	Lesley
65–66	Linnette
67–68	Lyonesse
69–70	Mabina
71–72	Marvina
73–74	Mavis
75–76	Mirna
77–78	Morgan
79–80	Muriel
81–82	Nareena
83–84	Oriana
85–86	Regan
87–88	Ronat
89–90	Rowena
91–92	Selma
93–94	Ula
95–96	Venetia
97–98	Wynne
99–00	Yseult

CELTIC, MALE

d100	Name
01–02	Airell
03–04	Airic
05–06	Alan
07–08	Anghus
09–10	Aodh
11–12	Bardon
13–14	Bearacb
15–16	Bevyn
17–18	Boden
19–20	Bran
21–22	Brasil
23–24	Bredon
25–26	Brian
27–28	Bricriu
29–30	Bryant
31–32	Cadman
33–34	Caradoc
35–36	Cedric
37–38	Conalt
39–40	Conchobar
41–42	Condon
43–44	Darcy
45–46	Devin
47–48	Dillion
49–50	Donaghy
51–52	Donall
53–54	Duer
55–56	Eghan
57–58	Ewyn
59–60	Ferghus
61–62	Galvyn
63–64	Gildas
65–66	Guy
67–68	Harvey
69–70	Iden
71–72	Irven
73–74	Karney
75–76	Kayne
77–78	Kelvyn
79–80	Kunsgnos
81–82	Leigh
83–84	Maccus
85–86	Moryn
87–88	Neale
89–90	Owyn
91–92	Pryderi
93–94	Reaghan
95–96	Taliesin
97–98	Tiernay
99–00	Turi

CHINESE, FEMALE

d100	Name
01–02	Ai
03–04	Anming
05–06	Baozhai
07–08	Bei
09–10	Caixia
11–12	Changchang
13–14	Chen
15–16	Chou
17–18	Chunhua
19–20	Daianna
21–22	Daiyu
23–24	Die
25–26	Ehuang
27–28	Fenfang
29–30	Ge
31–32	Hong
33–34	Huan
35–36	Huifang
37–38	Jia
39–40	Jiao
41–42	Jiaying
43–44	Jingfei
45–46	Jinjing
47–48	Lan
49–50	Li
51–52	Lihua
53–54	Lin
55–56	Ling
57–58	Liu
59–60	Meili
61–62	Ning
63–64	Qi
65–66	Qiao
67–68	Rong
69–70	Shu
71–72	Shuang
73–74	Song
75–76	Ting
77–78	Wen
79–80	Xia
81–82	Xiaodan
83–84	Xiaoli
85–86	Xingjuan
87–88	Xue
89–90	Ya
91–92	Yan
93–94	Ying
95–96	Yuan
97–98	Yue
99–00	Yun

CHINESE, MALE

d100	Name
01–02	Bingwen
03–04	Bo
05–06	Bolin
07–08	Chang
09–10	Chao
11–12	Chen
13–14	Cheng
15–16	Da
17–18	Dingxiang
19–20	Fang
21–22	Feng
23–24	Fu
25–26	Gang
27–28	Guang
29–30	Hai
31–32	Heng
33–34	Hong
35–36	Huan
37–38	Huang
39–40	Huiliang
41–42	Huizhong
43–44	Jian
45–46	Jiayi
47–48	Junjie
49–50	Kang
51–52	Lei
53–54	Liang
55–56	Ling
57–58	Liwei
59–60	Meilin
61–62	Niu
63–64	Peizhi
65–66	Peng
67–68	Ping
69–70	Qiang
71–72	Qiu
73–74	Quan
75–76	Renshu
77–78	Rong
79–80	Ru
81–82	Shan
83–84	Shen
85–86	Tengfei
87–88	Wei
89–90	Xiaobo
91–92	Xiaoli
93–94	Xin
95–96	Yang
97–98	Ying
99–00	Zhong

Egyptian, Female

d100	Name
01–02	A'at
03–04	Ahset
05–06	Amunet
07–08	Aneksi
09–10	Atet
11–12	Baketamon
13–14	Betrest
15–16	Bunefer
17–18	Dedyet
19–20	Hatshepsut
21–22	Hentie
23–24	Herit
25–26	Hetepheres
27–28	Intakaes
29–30	Ipwet
31–32	Itet
33–34	Joba
35–36	Kasmut
37–38	Kemanub
39–40	Khemut
41–42	Kiya
43–44	Maia
45–46	Menhet
47–48	Merit
49–50	Meritamen
51–52	Merneith
53–54	Merseger
55–56	Muyet
57–58	Nebet
59–60	Nebetah
61–62	Nedjemmut
63–64	Nefertiti
65–66	Neferu
67–68	Neithotep

Egyptian, Female

d100	Name
69–70	Nit
71–72	Nofret
73–74	Nubemiunu
75–76	Peseshet
77–78	Pypuy
79–80	Qalhata
81–82	Rai
83–84	Redji
85–86	Sadeh
87–88	Sadek
89–90	Sitamun
91–92	Sitre
93–94	Takhat
95–96	Tarset
97–98	Taweret
99–00	Werenro

Egyptian, Male

d100	Name
01–02	Ahmose
03–04	Akhom
05–06	Amasis
07–08	Amenemhet
09–10	Anen
11–12	Banefre
13–14	Bek
15–16	Djedefre
17–18	Djoser
19–20	Hekaib
21–22	Henenu
23–24	Horemheb
25–26	Horwedja
27–28	Huya
29–30	Ibebi
31–32	Idu

Egyptian, Male

d100	Name
33–34	Imhotep
35–36	Ineni
37–38	Ipuki
39–40	Irsu
41–42	Kagemni
43–44	Kawab
45–46	Kenamon
47–48	Kewap
49–50	Khaemwaset
51–52	Khafra
53–54	Khusebek
55–56	Masaharta
57–58	Meketre
59–60	Menkhaf
61–62	Merenre
63–64	Metjen
65–66	Nebamun
67–68	Nebetka
69–70	Nehi
71–72	Nekure
73–74	Nessumontu
75–76	Pakhom
77–78	Pawah
79–80	Pawero
81–82	Ramose
83–84	Rudjek
85–86	Sabaf
87–88	Sebek-khu
89–90	Sebni
91–92	Senusret
93–94	Shabaka
95–96	Somintu
97–98	Thaneni
99–00	Thethi

English, Female

d100	Name
01–02	Adelaide
03–04	Agatha
05–06	Agnes
07–08	Alice
09–10	Aline
11–12	Anne
13–14	Avelina
15–16	Avice
17–18	Beatrice
19–20	Cecily
21–22	Egelina
23–24	Eleanor
25–26	Elizabeth
27–28	Ella
29–30	Eloise
31–32	Elysande
33–34	Emeny
35–36	Emma
37–38	Emmeline
39–40	Ermina
41–42	Eva
43–44	Galiena
45–46	Geva
47–48	Giselle
49–50	Griselda
51–52	Hadwisa
53–54	Helen
55–56	Herleva
57–58	Hugolina
59–60	Ida
61–62	Isabella
63–64	Jacoba
65–66	Jane
67–68	Joan

English, Female

d100	Name
69–70	Juliana
71–72	Katherine
73–74	Margery
75–76	Mary
77–78	Matilda
79–80	Maynild
81–82	Millicent
83–84	Oriel
85–86	Rohesia
87–88	Rosalind
89–90	Rosamund
91–92	Sarah
93–94	Susannah
95–96	Sybil
97–98	Williamina
99–00	Yvonne

English, Male

d100	Name
01–02	Adam
03–04	Adelard
05–06	Aldous
07–08	Anselm
09–10	Arnold
11–12	Bernard
13–14	Bertram
15–16	Charles
17–18	Clerebold
19–20	Conrad
21–22	Diggory
23–24	Drogo
25–26	Everard
27–28	Frederick
29–30	Geoffrey
31–32	Gerald

English, Male

d100	Name
33–34	Gilbert
35–36	Godfrey
37–38	Gunter
39–40	Guy
41–42	Henry
43–44	Heward
45–46	Hubert
47–48	Hugh
49–50	Jocelyn
51–52	John
53–54	Lance
55–56	Manfred
57–58	Miles
59–60	Nicholas
61–62	Norman
63–64	Odo
65–66	Percival
67–68	Peter
69–70	Ralf
71–72	Randal
73–74	Raymond
75–76	Reynard
77–78	Richard
79–80	Robert
81–82	Roger
83–84	Roland
85–86	Rolf
87–88	Simon
89–90	Theobald
91–92	Theodoric
93–94	Thomas
95–96	Timm
97–98	William
99–00	Wymar

FRENCH, FEMALE

d100	Name
01–02	Aalis
03–04	Agatha
05–06	Agnez
07–08	Alberea
09–10	Alips
11–12	Amée
13–14	Amelot
15–16	Anne
17–18	Avelina
19–20	Blancha
21–22	Cateline
23–24	Cecilia
25–26	Claricia
27–28	Collette
29–30	Denisete
31–32	Dorian
33–34	Edelina
35–36	Emelina
37–38	Emmelot
39–40	Ermentrudis
41–42	Gibelina
43–44	Gila
45–46	Gillette
47–48	Guiburgis
49–50	Guillemette
51–52	Guoite
53–54	Hecelina
55–56	Heloysis
57–58	Helyoudis
59–60	Hodeardis
61–62	Isabellis
63–64	Jaquette
65–66	Jehan
67–68	Johanna
69–70	Juliote
71–72	Katerine
73–74	Luciana
75–76	Margot
77–78	Marguerite
79–80	Maria
81–82	Marie
83–84	Melisende
85–86	Odelina
87–88	Perrette
89–90	Petronilla
91–92	Sedilia
93–94	Stephana
95–96	Sybilla
97–98	Ysabeau
99–00	Ysabel

FRENCH, MALE

d100	Name
01–02	Ambroys
03–04	Ame
05–06	Andri
07–08	Andriet
09–10	Anthoine
11–12	Bernard
13–14	Charles
15–16	Charlot
17–18	Colin
19–20	Denis
21–22	Durant
23–24	Edouart
25–26	Eremon
27–28	Ernault
29–30	Ethor
31–32	Felix
33–34	Floquart
35–36	Galleren
37–38	Gaultier
39–40	Gilles
41–42	Guy
43–44	Henry
45–46	Hugo
47–48	Imbert
49–50	Jacques
51–52	Jacquot
53–54	Jean
55–56	Jehannin
57–58	Louis
59–60	Louys
61–62	Loys
63–64	Martin
65–66	Michel
67–68	Mille
69–70	Morelet
71–72	Nicolas
73–74	Nicolle
75–76	Oudart
77–78	Perrin
79–80	Phillippe
81–82	Pierre
83–84	Regnault
85–86	Richart
87–88	Robert
89–90	Robinet
91–92	Sauvage
93–94	Simon
95–96	Talbot
97–98	Tanguy
99–00	Vincent

GERMAN, FEMALE

d100	Name
01–02	Adelhayt
03–04	Affra
05–06	Agatha
07–08	Allet
09–10	Angnes
11–12	Anna
13–14	Apell
15–16	Applonia
17–18	Barbara
19–20	Brida
21–22	Brigita
23–24	Cecilia
25–26	Clara
27–28	Cristina
29–30	Dorothea
31–32	Duretta
33–34	Ella
35–36	Els
37–38	Elsbeth
39–40	Engel
41–42	Enlein
43–44	Enndlin
45–46	Eva
47–48	Fela
49–50	Fronicka
51–52	Genefe
53–54	Geras
55–56	Gerhauss
57–58	Gertrudt
59–60	Guttel
61–62	Helena
63–64	Irmel
65–66	Jonata
67–68	Katerina
69–70	Kuen
71–72	Kungund
73–74	Lucia
75–76	Madalena
77–78	Magdalen
79–80	Margret
81–82	Marlein
83–84	Martha
85–86	Otilia
87–88	Ottilg
89–90	Peternella
91–92	Reusin
93–94	Sibilla
95–96	Ursel
97–98	Vrsula
99–00	Walpurg

GERMAN, MALE

d100	Name
01–02	Albrecht
03–04	Allexander
05–06	Baltasar
07–08	Benedick
09–10	Berhart
11–12	Caspar
13–14	Clas
15–16	Cristin
17–18	Cristoff
19–20	Dieterich
21–22	Engelhart
23–24	Erhart
25–26	Felix
27–28	Frantz
29–30	Fritz
31–32	Gerhart
33–34	Gotleib
35–36	Hans
37–38	Hartmann
39–40	Heintz
41–42	Herman
43–44	Jacob
45–46	Jeremias
47–48	Jorg
49–50	Karll
51–52	Kilian
53–54	Linhart
55–56	Lorentz
57–58	Ludwig
59–60	Marx
61–62	Melchor
63–64	Mertin
65–66	Michel
67–68	Moritz
69–70	Osswald
71–72	Ott
73–74	Peter
75–76	Rudolff
77–78	Ruprecht
79–80	Sewastian
81–82	Sigmund
83–84	Steffan
85–86	Symon
87–88	Thoman
89–90	Ulrich
91–92	Vallentin
93–94	Wendel
95–96	Wilhelm
97–98	Wolff
99–00	Wolfgang

GREEK, FEMALE

d100	Name
01–02	Acantha
03–04	Aella
05–06	Alektos
07–08	Alkippe
09–10	Andromeda
11–12	Antigone
13–14	Ariadne
15–16	Astraea
17–18	Chloros
19–20	Chryseos
21–22	Daphne
23–24	Despoina
25–26	Dione
27–28	Eileithyia
29–30	Elektra
31–32	Euadne
33–34	Eudora
35–36	Eunomia
37–38	Hekabe
39–40	Helene
41–42	Hermoione
43–44	Hippolyte
45–46	Ianthe
47–48	Iokaste
49–50	Iole
51–52	Iphigenia
53–54	Ismene
55–56	Kalliope
57–58	Kallisto
59–60	Kalypso
61–62	Karme
63–64	Kassandra
65–66	Kassiopeia
67–68	Kirke
69–70	Kleio
71–72	Klotho
73–74	Klytië
75–76	Kynthia
77–78	Leto
79–80	Megaera
81–82	Melaina
83–84	Melpomene
85–86	Nausikaa
87–88	Nemesis
89–90	Niobe
91–92	Ourania
93–94	Phaenna
95–96	Polymnia
97–98	Semele
99–00	Theia

GREEK, MALE

d100	Name
01–02	Adonis
03–04	Adrastos
05–06	Aeson
07–08	Aias
09–10	Aineias
11–12	Aiolos
13–14	Alekto
15–16	Alkeides
17–18	Argos
19–20	Brontes
21–22	Damazo
23–24	Dardanos
25–26	Deimos
27–28	Diomedes
29–30	Endymion
31–32	Epimetheus
33–34	Erebos
35–36	Euandros
37–38	Ganymedes
39–40	Glaukos
41–42	Hektor
43–44	Heros
45–46	Hippolytos
47–48	Iacchus
49–50	Iason
51–52	Kadmos
53–54	Kastor
55–56	Kephalos
57–58	Kepheus
59–60	Koios
61–62	Kreios
63–64	Laios
65–66	Leandros
67–68	Linos
69–70	Lykos
71–72	Melanthios
73–74	Menelaus
75–76	Mentor
77–78	Neoptolemus
79–80	Okeanos
81–82	Orestes
83–84	Pallas
85–86	Patroklos
87–88	Philandros
89–90	Phoibos
91–92	Phrixus
93–94	Priamos
95–96	Pyrrhos
97–98	Xanthos
99–00	Zephyros

INDIAN, FEMALE

d100	Name
01–02	Abha
03–04	Aishwarya
05–06	Amala
07–08	Ananda
09–10	Ankita
11–12	Archana
13–14	Avani
15–16	Chandana
17–18	Chandrakanta
19–20	Chetan
21–22	Darshana
23–24	Devi
25–26	Dipti
27–28	Esha
29–30	Gauro
31–32	Gita
33–34	Indira
35–36	Indu
37–38	Jaya
39–40	Kala
41–42	Kalpana
43–44	Kamala
45–46	Kanta
47–48	Kashi
49–50	Kishori
51–52	Lalita
53–54	Lina
55–56	Madhur
57–58	Manju
59–60	Meera
61–62	Mohana
63–64	Mukta
65–66	Nisha
67–68	Nitya
69–70	Padma
71–72	Pratima
73–74	Priya
75–76	Rani
77–78	Sarala
79–80	Shakti
81–82	Shanta
83–84	Shobha
85–86	Sima
87–88	Sonal
89–90	Sumana
91–92	Sunita
93–94	Tara
95–96	Valli
97–98	Vijaya
99–00	Vimala

INDIAN, MALE

d100	Name
01–02	Abhay
03–04	Ahsan
05–06	Ajay
07–08	Ajit
09–10	Akhil
11–12	Amar
13–14	Amit
15–16	Ananta
17–18	Aseem
19–20	Ashok
21–22	Bahadur
23–24	Basu
25–26	Chand
27–28	Chandra
29–30	Damodar
31–32	Darhsan
33–34	Devdan
35–36	Dinesh
37–38	Dipak
39–40	Gopal
41–42	Govind
43–44	Harendra
45–46	Harsha
47–48	Ila
49–50	Isha
51–52	Johar
53–54	Kalyan
55–56	Kiran
57–58	Kumar
59–60	Lakshmana
61–62	Mahavir
63–64	Narayan
65–66	Naveen
67–68	Nirav
69–70	Prabhakar
71–72	Prasanna
73–74	Raghu
75–76	Rajanikant
77–78	Rakesh
79–80	Ranjeet
81–82	Rishi
83–84	Sanjay
85–86	Sekar
87–88	Shandar
89–90	Sumantra
91–92	Vijay
93–94	Vikram
95–96	Vimal
97–98	Vishal
99–00	Yash

Japanese, Female

d100	Name
01–02	Aika
03–04	Akemi
05–06	Akiko
07–08	Amaya
09–10	Asami
11–12	Ayumi
13–14	Bunko
15–16	Chieko
17–18	Chika
19–20	Chiyo
21–22	Cho
23–24	Eiko
25–26	Emiko
27–28	Eri
29–30	Etsuko
31–32	Gina
33–34	Hana
35–36	Haruki
37–38	Hideko
39–40	Hikari
41–42	Hiroko
43–44	Hisoka
45–46	Hishi
47–48	Hotaru
49–50	Izumi
51–52	Kameyo
53–54	Kasumi
55–56	Kimiko
57–58	Kotone
59–60	Kyoko
61–62	Maiko
63–64	Masako
65–66	Mi
67–68	Minori
69–70	Mizuki
71–72	Naoki
73–74	Natsuko
75–76	Noriko
77–78	Rei
79–80	Ren
81–82	Saki
83–84	Shigeko
85–86	Shinju
87–88	Sumiko
89–90	Toshiko
91–92	Tsukiko
93–94	Ume
95–96	Usagi
97–98	Yasuko
99–00	Yuriko

Japanese, Male

d100	Name
01–02	Akio
03–04	Atsushi
05–06	Daichi
07–08	Daiki
09–10	Daisuke
11–12	Eiji
13–14	Fumio
15–16	Hajime
17–18	Haru
19–20	Hideaki
21–22	Hideo
23–24	Hikaru
25–26	Hiro
27–28	Hiroki
29–30	Hisao
31–32	Hitoshi
33–34	Isamu
35–36	Isao
37–38	Jun
39–40	Katashi
41–42	Katsu
43–44	Kei
45–46	Ken
47–48	Kenshin
49–50	Kenta
51–52	Kioshi

Japanese, Male

d100	Name
53–54	Makoto
55–56	Mamoru
57–58	Masato
59–60	Masumi
61–62	Noboru
63–64	Norio
65–66	Osamu
67–68	Ryota
69–70	Sadao
71–72	Satoshi
73–74	Shigeo
75–76	Shin
77–78	Sora
79–80	Tadao
81–82	Takehiko
83–84	Takeo
85–86	Takeshi
87–88	Takumi
89–90	Tamotsu
91–92	Tatsuo
93–94	Toru
95–96	Toshio
97–98	Yasuo
99–00	Yukio

Mesoamerican, Female

d100	Name
01–02	Ahuiliztli
03–04	Atl
05–06	Centehua
07–08	Chalchiuitl
09–10	Chipahua
11–12	Cihuaton
13–14	Citlali
15–16	Citlalmina
17–18	Coszcatl
19–20	Cozamalotl
21–22	Cuicatl
23–24	Eleuia
25–26	Eloxochitl
27–28	Eztli
29–30	Ichtaca
31–32	Icnoyotl
33–34	Ihuicatl
35–36	Ilhuitl
37–38	Itotia
39–40	Iuitl
41–42	Ixcatzin
43–44	Izel
45–46	Malinalxochitl
47–48	Mecatl
49–50	Meztli
51–52	Miyaoaxochitl
53–54	Mizquixaual
55–56	Moyolehuani
57–58	Nahuatl
59–60	Necahual
61–62	Nenetl
63–64	Nochtli
65–66	Noxochicoztli
67–68	Ohtli

Mesoamerican, Female

d100	Name
69–70	Papan
71–72	Patli
73–74	Quetzalxochitl
75–76	Sacnite
77–78	Teicui
79–80	Tepin
81–82	Teuicui
83–84	Teyacapan
85–86	Tlaco
87–88	Tlacoehua
89–90	Tlacotl
91–92	Tlalli
93–94	Tlanextli
95–96	Xihuitl
97–98	Xiuhcoatl
99–00	Xiuhtonal

Mesoamerican, Male

d100	Name
01–02	Achcauhtli
03–04	Amoxtli
05–06	Chicahua
07–08	Chimalli
09–10	Cipactli
11–12	Coaxoch
13–14	Coyotl
15–16	Cualli
17–18	Cuauhtémoc
19–20	Cuetlachtilo
21–22	Cuetzpalli
23–24	Cuixtli
25–26	Ehecatl
27–28	Etalpalli
29–30	Huemac
31–32	Huitzilihuitl

Mesoamerican, Male

d100	Name
33–34	Iccauhtli
35–36	Ilhicamina
37–38	Itztli
39–40	Ixtli
41–42	Mahuizoh
43–44	Manauia
45–46	Matlal
47–48	Matlalihuitl
49–50	Mazatl
51–52	Mictlantecuhtli
53–54	Milintica
55–56	Momoztli
57–58	Namacuix
59–60	Necalli
61–62	Necuametl
63–64	Nezahualcoyotl
65–66	Nexahualpilli
67–68	Nochehuatl
69–70	Nopaltzin
71–72	Ollin
73–74	Quauhtli
75–76	Tenoch
77–78	Teoxihuitl
79–80	Tepiltzin
81–82	Tezcacoatl
83–84	Tlacaelel
85–86	Tlacelel
87–88	Tlaloc
89–90	Tlanextic
91–92	Tlazohtlaloni
93–94	Tlazopillo
95–96	Uetzcayotl
97–98	Xipilli
99–00	Yaotl

NIGER–CONGO, FEMALE

d100	Name
01–02	Abebi
03–04	Abena
05–06	Abimbola
07–08	Akoko
09–10	Akachi
11–12	Alaba
13–14	Anuli
15–16	Ayo
17–18	Bolanle
19–20	Bosede
21–22	Chiamaka
23–24	Chidi
25–26	Chidimma
27–28	Chinyere
29–30	Chioma
31–32	Dada
33–34	Ebele
35–36	Efemena
37–38	Ejiro
39–40	Ekundayo
41–42	Enitan
43–44	Funanya
45–46	Ifunanya
47–48	Ige
49–50	Ime
51–52	Kunto
53–54	Lesedi
55–56	Lumusi
57–58	Mojisola
59–60	Monifa
61–62	Nakato
63–64	Ndidi
65–66	Ngozi
67–68	Nkiruka
69–70	Nneka
71–72	Ogechi
73–74	Olamide
75–76	Oluchi
77–78	Omolara
79–80	Onyeka
81–82	Simisola
83–84	Temitope
85–86	Thema
87–88	Titlayo
89–90	Udo
91–92	Uduak
93–94	Ufuoma
95–96	Yaa
97–98	Yejide
99–00	Yewande

NIGER–CONGO, MALE

d100	Name
01–02	Abebe
03–04	Abel
05–06	Abidemi
07–08	Abrafo
09–10	Adisa
11–12	Amadi
13–14	Amara
15–16	Anyim
17–18	Azubuike
19–20	Bapoto
21–22	Baraka
23–24	Bohlale
25–26	Bongani
27–28	Bujune
29–30	Buziba
31–32	Chakide
33–34	Chibuzo
35–36	Chika
37–38	Chimola
39–40	Chiratidzo
41–42	Dabulamanzi
43–44	Dumisa
45–46	Dwanh
47–48	Emeka
49–50	Folami
51–52	Gatura
53–54	Gebhuza
55–56	Gero
57–58	Isoba
59–60	Kagiso
61–62	Kamau
63–64	Katlego
65–66	Masego
67–68	Matata
69–70	Nthanda
71–72	Ogechi
73–74	Olwenyo
75–76	Osumare
77–78	Paki
79–80	Qinisela
81–82	Quanda
83–84	Samanya
85–86	Shanika
87–88	Sibonakaliso
89–90	Tapiwa
91–92	Thabo
93–94	Themba
95–96	Uzoma
97–98	Zuberi
99–00	Zuŕi

NORSE, FEMALE

d100	Name
01–02	Alfhild
03–04	Arnbjorg
05–06	Ase
07–08	Aslog
09–10	Astrid
11–12	Auda
13–14	Audhid
15–16	Bergljot
17–18	Birghild
19–20	Bodil
21–22	Brenna
23–24	Brynhild
25–26	Dagmar
27–28	Eerika
29–30	Eira
31–32	Gudrun
33–34	Gunborg
35–36	Gunhild
37–38	Gunvor
39–40	Helga
41–42	Hertha
43–44	Hilde
45–46	Hillevi
47–48	Ingrid
49–50	Iona
51–52	Jorunn
53–54	Kari
55–56	Kenna
57–58	Magnhild
59–60	Nanna
61–62	Olga
63–64	Ragna
65–66	Ragnhild
67–68	Ranveig
69–70	Runa
71–72	Saga
73–74	Sigfrid
75–76	Signe
77–78	Sigrid
79–80	Sigrunn
81–82	Solveg
83–84	Svanhild
85–86	Thora
87–88	Torborg
89–90	Torunn
91–92	Tove
93–94	Unn
95–96	Vigdis
97–98	Ylva
99–00	Yngvild

NORSE, MALE

d100	Name
01–02	Agni
03–04	Alaric
05–06	Anvindr
07–08	Arvid
09–10	Asger
11–12	Asmund
13–14	Bjarte
15–16	Bjorg
17–18	Bjorn
19–20	Brandr
21–22	Brandt
23–24	Brynjar
25–26	Calder
27–28	Colborn
29–30	Cuyler
31–32	Egil
33–34	Einar
35–36	Eric
37–38	Erland
39–40	Fiske
41–42	Folkvar
43–44	Fritjof
45–46	Frode
47–48	Geir
49–50	Halvar
51–52	Hemming
53–54	Hjalmar
55–56	Hjortr
57–58	Ingimarr
59–60	Ivar
61–62	Knud
63–64	Leif
65–66	Liufr
67–68	Manning
69–70	Oddr
71–72	Olin
73–74	Ormr
75–76	Ove
77–78	Rannulfr
79–80	Sigurd
81–82	Skari
83–84	Snorri
85–86	Sten
87–88	Stigandr
89–90	Stigr
91–92	Sven
93–94	Trygve
95–96	Ulf
97–98	Vali
99–00	Vidar

POLYNESIAN, FEMALE		POLYNESIAN, MALE		ROMAN, FEMALE		ROMAN, MALE	
d100	**Name**	**d100**	**Name**	**d100**	**Name**	**d100**	**Name**
01–02	Ahulani	01–02	Afa	01–02	Aelia	01–02	Aelius
03–04	Airini	03–04	Ahohako	03–04	Aemilia	03–04	Aetius
05–06	Alani	05–06	Aisake	05–06	Agrippina	05–06	Agrippa
07–08	Aluala	07–08	Aleki	07–08	Alba	07–08	Albanus
09–10	Anahera	09–10	Anewa	09–10	Antonia	09–10	Albus
11–12	Anuhea	11–12	Anitelu	11–12	Aquila	11–12	Antonius
13–14	Aolani	13–14	Aputi	13–14	Augusta	13–14	Appius
15–16	Elenoa	15–16	Ariki	15–16	Aurelia	15–16	Aquilinus
17–18	Emele	17–18	Butat	17–18	Balbina	17–18	Atilus
19–20	Fetia	19–20	Enele	19–20	Blandina	19–20	Augustus
21–22	Fiva	21–22	Fef	21–22	Caelia	21–22	Aurelius
23–24	Halona	23–24	Fuifui	23–24	Camilla	23–24	Avitus
25–26	Hi'ilei	25–26	Ha'aheo	25–26	Casia	25–26	Balbus
27–28	Hina	27–28	Hanohano	27–28	Claudia	27–28	Blandus
29–30	Hinatea	29–30	Haunui	29–30	Cloelia	29–30	Blasius
31–32	Huali	31–32	Hekili	31–32	Domitia	31–32	Brutus
33–34	Inia	33–34	Hiapo	33–34	Drusa	33–34	Caelius
35–36	Inina	35–36	Hikawera	35–36	Fabia	35–36	Caius
37–38	Iolani	37–38	Hanano	37–38	Fabricia	37–38	Casian
39–40	Isa	39–40	Ho'onani	39–40	Fausta	39–40	Cassius
41–42	Ka'ana'ana	41–42	Hoku	41–42	Flavia	41–42	Cato
43–44	Ka'ena	43–44	Hû'eu	43–44	Floriana	43–44	Celsus
45–46	Kaamia	45–46	Ina	45–46	Fulvia	45–46	Claudius
47–48	Kahula	47–48	Itu	47–48	Germana	47–48	Cloelius
49–50	Kailani	49–50	Ka'aukai	49–50	Glaucia	49–50	Cnaeus
51–52	Kamaile	51–52	Ka'eo	51–52	Gratiana	51–52	Crispus
53–54	Kamakani	53–54	Kaelani	53–54	Hadriana	53–54	Cyprianus
55–56	Kamea	55–56	Kahale	55–56	Hermina	55–56	Diocletianus
57–58	Latai	57–58	Kaiea	57–58	Horatia	57–58	Egnatius
59–60	Liona	59–60	Kaikoa	59–60	Hortensia	59–60	Ennius
61–62	Lokelani	61–62	Kana'I	61–62	Iovita	61–62	Fabricius
63–64	Marva	63–64	Koamalu	63–64	Iulia	63–64	Faustus
65–66	Mehana	65–66	Ka	65–66	Laelia	65–66	Gaius
67–68	Millawa	67–68	Laki	67–68	Laurentia	67–68	Germanus
69–70	Moana	69–70	Makai	69–70	Livia	69–70	Gnaeus
71–72	Ngana	71–72	Manu	71–72	Longina	71–72	Horatius
73–74	Nohea	73–74	Manuka	73–74	Lucilla	73–74	Iovianus
75–76	Pelika	75–76	Nui	75–76	Lucretia	75–76	Iulius
77–78	Sanoe	77–78	Pono	77–78	Marcella	77–78	Lucilius
79–80	Satina	79–80	Popoki	79–80	Marcia	79–80	Manius
81–82	Tahia	81–82	Ruru	81–82	Maxima	81–82	Marcus
83–84	Tasi	83–84	Tahu	83–84	Nona	83–84	Marius
85–86	Tiaho	85–86	Taurau	85–86	Octavia	85–86	Maximus
87–88	Tihani	87–88	Tuala	87–88	Paulina	87–88	Octavius
89–90	Toroa	89–90	Turoa	89–90	Petronia	89–90	Paulus
91–92	Ulanni	91–92	Tusitala	91–92	Porcia	91–92	Quintilian
93–94	Uluwehi	93–94	Uaine	93–94	Tacita	93–94	Regulus
95–96	Vaina	95–96	Waata	95–96	Tullia	95–96	Servius
97–98	Waiola	97–98	Waipuna	97–98	Verginia	97–98	Tacitus
99–00	Waitara	99–00	Zamar	99–00	Vita	99–00	Varius

SLAVIC, FEMALE

d100	Name
01–02	Agripina
03–04	Anastasiya
05–06	Bogdana
07–08	Boleslava
09–10	Bozhena
11–12	Danica
13–14	Darya
15–16	Desislava
17–18	Dragoslava
19–20	Dunja
21–22	Efrosinia
23–24	Ekaterina
25–26	Elena
27–28	Faina
29–30	Galina
31–32	Irina
33–34	Iskra
35–36	Jasna
37–38	Katarina
39–40	Katya
41–42	Kresimira
43–44	Lyudmila
45–46	Magda
47–48	Mariya
49–50	Militsa
51–52	Miloslava
53–54	Mira
55–56	Miroslava
57–58	Mokosh
59–60	Morana
61–62	Natasha
63–64	Nika
65–66	Olga
67–68	Rada
69–70	Radoslava
71–72	Raisa
73–74	Slavitsa
75–76	Sofiya
77–78	Stanislava
79–80	Svetlana
81–82	Tatyana
83–84	Tomislava
85–86	Veronika
87–88	Vesna
89–90	Vladimira
91–92	Yaroslava
93–94	Yelena
95–96	Zaria
97–98	Zarya
99–00	Zoria

SLAVIC, MALE

d100	Name
01–02	Aleksandru
03–04	Berislav
05–06	Blazh
07–08	Bogumir
09–10	Boguslav
11–12	Borislav
13–14	Bozhidar
15–16	Bratomil
17–18	Bratoslav
19–20	Bronislav
21–22	Chedomir
23–24	Chestibor
25–26	Chestirad
27–28	Chestislav
29–30	Desilav
31–32	Dmitrei
33–34	Dobromil
35–36	Dobroslav
37–38	Dragomir
39–40	Dragutin
41–42	Drazhan
43–44	Gostislav
45–46	Kazimir
47–48	Kyrilu
49–50	Lyubomir
51–52	Mechislav
53–54	Milivoj
55–56	Milosh
57–58	Mstislav
59–60	Nikola
61–62	Ninoslav
63–64	Premislav
65–66	Radomir
67–68	Radovan
69–70	Ratimir
71–72	Rostislav
73–74	Slavomir
75–76	Stanislav
77–78	Svetoslav
79–80	Tomislav
81–82	Vasili
83–84	Velimir
85–86	Vladimir
87–88	Vladislav
89–90	Vlastimir
91–92	Volodimeru
93–94	Vratislav
95–96	Yarognev
97–98	Yaromir
99–00	Zbignev

Spanish, Female

d100	Name
01–02	Abella
03–04	Adalina
05–06	Adora
07–08	Adriana
09–10	Ana
11–12	Antonia
13–14	Basilia
15–16	Beatriz
17–18	Bonita
19–20	Camila
21–22	Cande
23–24	Carmen
25–26	Catlina
27–28	Dolores
29–30	Dominga
31–32	Dorotea
33–34	Elena
35–36	Elicia
37–38	Esmerelda
39–40	Felipina
41–42	Francisca
43–44	Gabriela
45–46	Imelda
47–48	Ines
49–50	Isabel
51–52	Juana
53–54	Leocadia
55–56	Leonor
57–58	Leta
59–60	Lucinda
61–62	Maresol
63–64	Maria
65–66	Maricela
67–68	Matilde

Spanish, Female

d100	Name
69–70	Melania
71–72	Monica
73–74	Neva
75–76	Nilda
77–78	Petrona
79–80	Rafaela
81–82	Ramira
83–84	Rosario
85–86	Sofia
87–88	Suelo
89–90	Teresa
91–92	Tomasa
93–94	Valentia
95–96	Veronica
97–98	Ynes
99–00	Ysabel

Spanish, Male

d100	Name
01–02	Alexandre
03–04	Alfonso
05–06	Alonso
07–08	Anthon
09–10	Arcos
11–12	Arnaut
13–14	Arturo
15–16	Bartoleme
17–18	Benito
19–20	Bernat
21–22	Blasco
23–24	Carlos
25–26	Damian
27–28	Diego
29–30	Domingo
31–32	Enrique

Spanish, Male

d100	Name
33–34	Escobar
35–36	Ettor
37–38	Fernando
39–40	Franciso
41–42	Gabriel
43–44	Garcia
45–46	Gaspar
47–48	Gil
49–50	Gomes
51–52	Goncalo
53–54	Gostantin
55–56	Jayme
57–58	Joan
59–60	Jorge
61–62	Jose
63–64	Juan
65–66	Machin
67–68	Martin
69–70	Mateu
71–72	Miguel
73–74	Nicolas
75–76	Pascual
77–78	Pedro
79–80	Porico
81–82	Ramiro
83–84	Ramon
85–86	Rodrigo
87–88	Sabastian
89–90	Salvador
91–92	Simon
93–94	Tomas
95–96	Tristan
97–98	Valeriano
99–00	Ynigo